ABUNDANCE

by Alan Chan

story by
Luke Dormehl & Alan Chan

ISBN 979-8-9909400-1-7 (ebook)
ISBN 979-8-9909400-0-0 (paperback)
ISBN 979-8-9909400-2-4 (hardcover)

Library of Congress Control Number: 2024912012

Published by Alan Chan in Dallas, TX USA.
First paperback edition October 2024
Cover art by Stephan Martinière

For Annette, Luke and Clara
and for my parents, Pa-pa and Ma-mi

Contents

Prologue
PER ASPERA

male patrons before casually introducing them to the guys. She was responsible for three marriages that way – each one of them marked with a patch on her flight jacket.

During one of her deployments she'd tried to wingman her way with two girls at the bar. Exotic Middle Eastern features, but Americans from the way they spoke – sisters on vacation, as it turned out. The wingman mission crash-and-burned spectacularly, but Carol struck up a relationship with one of them – Jen. They were married on the spur of the moment in Hawaii.

Fate stepped in when the world of commercial space exploration blossomed. She was offered a deal she could not pass up: the chance to sidestep NASA's entire astronaut program, and *command* her own ship. A daring and audacious mission to retrieve an asteroid... the culmination of a lifelong dream.

She remembered first setting eyes on *her* ship – the *ACV Frontier*. A spindly dragonfly-looking thing, the best little ship in the universe. She remembered her first time trying out a spacesuit, her first time in zero-g. She remembered the launch, the publicity, all the hullabaloo with the press. Her face was on all the news magazines. Sure, there were photos of her crew as well, but she was Mission Commander, and her photogenic smile charmed the public. It made her the de facto face of the mission.

That was fifteen months ago. Against all odds, they'd landed on the asteroid, installed giant engines on it, and were now bringing it back to Earth.

Earth... Home. Sunshine on bare skin. Proper showers, warm beds. The softness of another body pressed against yours. Things she missed, things she would miss the most. Fragmented disjointed thoughts crowded her consciousness.

She remembered waking up this morning inside the close-fitting sleeping bag, attached by velcro straps to the wall of her quarters. Remembered the fabric chafing her body at all the points her spacesuit had rubbed her raw. Remembered thinking about Jen, and recording a video message for her.

"Good morning babe," she'd said, wrinkling her nose at the sight of her own face on the screen – tousled hair framing her half-awake look. "Oh god... these bags under my eyes... I can't even."

"It's now almost ten o'clock your time," she'd said. "You should be out on the dunes by now. Good luck, hope everything works out." She rambled on about a bunch of other useless things, the way you told your spouse about things that happened to you during the day; none of which was important or necessary, but it was just done anyway, to be close to your familiars in spirit. "Keep the bed warm for me," she giggled, and sent the message.

/ / /

When she thought about it, she realized that the turning point was the message from Control a few days ago. "Control is worried about losing one of the experiments," Param had told her, and that was why they'd uploaded a trajectory change; they wanted to get the crew and asteroid home sooner. Maybe if they'd just stuck to the original plan...

Or maybe it wouldn't have made a difference. No point crying over spilt milk.

The trajectory change necessitated an eight-minute adjustment burn, which would alter the course of the asteroid so that it would reach Earth faster. This came with its own set of hassles, of course. Like if you took a sharp turn in a pickup truck, anything that was not properly secured in the truck bed would come flying off. An adjustment burn meant that all the gear, solar arrays and research experiments that were on the surface needed to be locked down and made safe beforehand.

That was what she and the crew had spent the last few days doing. Her and Pablo, and Param and Walt – running around the surface of Callum, securing all the experiments and equipment. The best crew in the world.

Walt had warned her about one of the experiments, Carol recalled. The breakers on X-88 were warped and kept re-engaging, he'd said. There wasn't time to troubleshoot the why, so she'd told him to secure it as best he could. "The sooner we can give this piece of shit back to them, the better" she remembered grumbling. Bless his heart, Walt... Walt... Walt who?

She couldn't remember their last names. Why couldn't she...? She knew their faces, their personalities, their humanity. In the end, that was all that would matter, really. They must have crossed over into other realms by now; no need for last names there.

/ / /

It was getting darker in the pod. Cold, and shaking like a pickup on a country road, but it felt like the safest place in the universe. The Lifter Pod was a utilitarian vehicle, roughly the size and mass of a small pickup, used to move equipment over the surface of the asteroid. It had a little spherical cabin, in which Carol was currently sitting. Why was she in there? She couldn't remember, and her inability to recall angered her.

The adjustment burn started well. Carol and the crew were pressure suited and strapped into their command chairs. The sun cut through the cockpit glass at an angle, illuminating dust particles in the air... like fireflies coming to light the way home. She remembered Pablo counting down, and the engines kicking in. She remembered the return of an old, almost-forgotten sensation called gravity. Like stepping out of a pool after a long swim.

The yellow blinking light on the control panel had warned her that something was not right. "Shimmy on 88," Param had called out... but it was within tolerances, and they were two minutes into an eight minute burn; there was nothing she could do except cross her fingers.

X-88 redlined and powered itself up halfway through the burn. Carol did not recall hitting the emergency abort, but she remembered the uncharacteristic anger and frustration that boiled in her. She'd unbuckled her straps and kick-floated towards the airlock. "C'mon Pablo," she'd said.

"What're we doing?"

"We're taking the Lifter, we get out there and make it safe... or else we cut it loose."

Sharp scraping noises raked across the side of the pod. The cacophony jarred her thoughts, dragged her consciousness back to the moment. She looked out the pod window to witness the maelstrom, and finally remembered everything in excruciating detail.

/ / /

The airlock was slow as fuck. Carol and Pablo had already wasted precious minutes suiting up and rushing through the checklists before they climbed in, but the airlock didn't seem to give a shit that they were in a hurry.

"Commander – urgent message from Control," Walt reported over the comm. "They want to know what the hell is going on."

Carol frowned, and looked around the airlock. It was lazily draining atmosphere without a care in the world.

"Clear the high gain queue, and patch all bandwidth to me for direct broadcast," she'd said. "Happy to give them a piece of my mind."

Walt acknowledged, flipped a few switches, and a thumbnail image of the view from her helmet camera popped up in the periphery of her HUD. "Okay, Commander," he said. "You're patched. Audio and video."

"Thanks," she'd said. "How much time?"

"Unsure. Still armed, residual precession."

"Understood. I have the comm."

She popped open the access panel, revealing a bright red handle plastered with warning signs. "Hold on to something, Pablo," she'd said. "Emergency venting."

Pablo's eyes grew wide, and he grabbed the support rails. Carol threw the handle, venting the remainder of the air in the airlock out to space and abruptly hurling them into the deafening silence of vacuum.

"Abundance Control, *Frontier* on broadcast. Request immediate response," she'd said as she drop-floated through the outer airlock and down the access ladder onto the surface. "I have initiated a burn abort. We have a redline issue. Pablo and I are en route to address it."

There was never going to be an immediate response. Their current distance from Earth meant that whatever response they received would take minutes to arrive. It wasn't so much that she needed Control's help, anyway; more like making sure Control knew what had happened and why, with every bit and byte of supporting video detail.

The helmet camera streamed every step in high def glory as Carol stepped out from under the belly of the Frontier and made a beeline for the Lifter Pod while Pablo began descending the ladder. Past the leading edge of the ship, sunlight had caught her full force in the eyes. She was momentarily blinded, and thought for a moment that she'd forgotten to lower her helmet visor. She paused for a moment to allow her eyes to readjust... but then realized that the sun was *behind* her.

She raised her arm to shield her eyes from the glare, and as the blinding brightness in front of her subsided, she saw the cause of the flare – not the sun, but some sort of... *event* over the near horizon. It expanded in seconds, then faded, leaving a dome of ejecta in its wake; floating rock particles that glinted like thousands of razor blades in the black sky.

The ground shuddered, and turned solid footing into a miasma of movement. From the horizon, the asteroid surface seemed to shimmer, the shadows on the rocks shifting and swirling.

The shockwave reached Carol before she could process the event. Ground shifted violently, and twisted Carol with a shearing rotational force that flipped her legs out from under her. Sky and ground switched places abruptly, and she smashed her helmet hard against the surface.

Sharp pain stabbed her temple as her face slammed against the inside of her visor. Tiny colored dots flooded her vision; she briefly wondered if she'd suffered a concussion, before realizing that the dots were droplets of blood floating around inside her helmet.

"Commander...!" Pablo yelled in her headset. There was a panic in his voice she'd never heard before.

Carol turned to look. The shockwave that had knocked her down had rippled past the *Frontier*, and churned up the ground as it went. Great boulders tore themselves from under the asteroid surface and propelled into the sky with astonishing force. Sheer rock faces acted like sheets of thin glass as the ground folded in on itself.

Pablo was halfway down the ladder when it happened. The ladder warped and buckled, shook him like a ragdoll. There was a violent spray of rocks and dust and then, with terrible ease, like a child effortlessly pulling legs off an insect, the ladder twisted and tore in half. The sharp ripped metal bent sideways and slid straight through Pablo's chest. Carol heard the sound over comm – a wet squelch and crack. Condensation crystals trailed as Pablo fell backwards and bounced off whatever remnants of ground there was left.

She screamed his name, but there was no answer. Only a dirty broken spacesuit, spinning end over end, out into open space.

The ground was shearing apart all around Carol. It rose up on both sides of the ship and tore the tail end of the *Frontier* apart like jello. Metal composites screamed, transmitting a dull throb through the surface of Callum as one of the claw legs tore off at the joint. Exposed cables swung the shattered limb like a spiked wrecking ball. It slammed into the side of the *Frontier*, collapsing its pressure chamber. The frantic voices of Param and Walt suddenly fell silent as air vanished into space, replaced by the intermittent low-frequency sounds of rending metal.

A metal strut broke free and careened towards Carol. She'd twisted her body and managed to avoid most of it, but quick movements were all but impossible in the suit. The strut made glancing contact with her shoulder and sent her spinning uncontrollably. Light and dark strobed, surface and sky switching places over and over as she struggled to regain control.

Wham! Carol slammed into something large, so hard and fast that it knocked the wind out of her. The impact triggered all sorts of warning beeps in her headset, along with alerts flashing erratically on her helmet HUD. She tried desperately to ignore them, to catch her breath, to correct herself. Her arm reached out across the surface of the 'something' and grabbed – the door panel of the Lifter Pod.

She'd pulled herself closer, popped the panel to pull the "Emergency Open" button. It slid open with a *hiss* and she dragged herself inside, her body screaming out in pain with every movement. Another button-press and the door slid shut behind her.

In the brief respite of the moment, Carol could finally check her suit systems. None of the warnings indicated a containment breach, and she couldn't see any tears in the spacesuit fabric. Amazingly, the green light on her armpad was still illuminated... which meant that her helmet cam was still broadcasting.

"Abundance Control, transmitting in the blind..." Carol said, her voice coming on in ragged gasps. "Repeat, transmitting in the blind."

"Lost Pablo," she'd said. "Lost the ship, Param and Walt... I– I don't think they made it. I'm in the pod now..."

Something heavy hit the Pod, and threw Carol off balance again. Panic rose up in her chest. She steadied her breathing. It hurt to breathe, and her brain was pounding, like when you woke up in the morning after partying too hard. Like all your synapses were scattered marbles, and your muscles were sore and refused to cooperate.

She looked out the pod's cockpit window and caught a glimpse of her reflection: a battered helmet, streaked with dust on the outside and splatters of her own blood on the inside. Pale blue eyes that had seen too much stared back at her. Outside the window, rocks and debris were intermingled and flying in every direction, occluding the sun. Large chunks of what used to be the *Frontier* crashed into the jumbled surface, breaking off giant chunks of asteroid as it went.

A shadow fell across the pod window, interrupting her train of thought. An enormous piece of what used to be one of the *Frontier*'s engines had broken free, and hurtled directly towards the Pod.

She didn't scream. There wasn't time. In that single moment, she re-lived an entire lifetime. And at the end of it all, she thought of Jen.

Part I
AMERICAS

2. DeWaal – Shefa

"Have you been wired for sound, Mr. DeWaal?" said the gray-haired man with a protruding belly.

He answered that he had not. He adjusted his six-foot-three frame, crouching slightly so as to allow the man to snake a radio mic down the front of his shirt and to clip the control unit to the belt of his jeans. The contortion offered him a skewed view of the backstage area, and made him realize his heart was racing.

'Backstage' was really more of a long corridor, dotted with equipment cases, some comfy couches, a snack table with smoked salmon rolls and pastries, and a bank of monitors. Four billionaire CEOs, two former American presidents, an ex-Prime Minister and a Nobel Prize-winning economist had passed through the space this morning – and now it was his turn.

A thick black curtain separated backstage from the auditorium. On the other side were the attendees of the Global Science and Technology for a Better Tomorrow conference – an eclectic mix of thought leaders, futurists, journalists and venture capitalists. If you wanted to be part of building the future, this was where you needed to be.

"Thirty seconds, Mr. DeWaal," said the gray-haired man. "Do you have the clicker?"

He held up the tiny black button, not much larger than a fingernail.

"Your slides are cued up and we've added in the revised animatic your people sent over."

"Thanks," he said, not really comprehending. He swallowed, trying to dispel the surge of adrenaline and prickly anxiety that he always felt before giving a speech. It wasn't that he suffered from stage-fright; rather, his anxiety came from a desire for perfection. On stage, anything could happen... and for a man who was always in control, that sense of unpredictability was crippling.

The stage manager guided him into the wings, stopped him on the white X that had been marked out in gaffer tape on the ground, and disappeared into the backstage shadows. In the sudden quiet of the liminal space, he heard the petite French voice rousing up the audience with a spirited introduction.

"...on the cover of Time, National Geographic and Wired, and now here for the closing keynote of the Better Tomorrow conference..."

The imminent reveal seemed to slow time. He was prey, and the laser sight was in between his eyes. He had an uncontrollable urge to flee, but his feet were boat anchors and would not respond.

"Ladies and gentlemen... the CEO and founder of Astral Abundance, *Ethan DeWaal*."

The stage manager pulled back the corner of the curtain and the spotlights flooded in. Its blinding brightness beckoned his feet forward, and he stepped over the threshold. A sea of expectant faces and camera phones stared back at him from the audience, and thunderous applause came like a crashing wave. It flooded his ear canal, fired neurons, triggered pleasure centers and unlocked the dopamine vault. He clasped his hand in prayer, flashed his Hollywood smile, and became Ethan DeWaal.

/ / /

The picture was Ethan, but only if you squinted really hard. Instead of the square-jawed, polished forty-six year old that everyone knew from the pages of *Forbes* and *BusinessWeek*, the man in the photo was younger, with terrible skin and greasy hair. He held a large bottle of champagne and grinned a toothy lopsided smile at the camera.

"This is me on my thirtieth birthday," chuckled DeWaal. "I have to admit that it probably isn't my finest look."

DeWaal paused, and looked out over the dimness of the auditorium. Like a shark sensing blood in the water, he felt the ebb and flow of audience emotions and responses, and tuned the inflections of his next words accordingly. Right now the audience was thoroughly taken by his story of the seminal hero's journey to will progress and technology into existence.

"This was when I sold the first startup I founded," he continued. "I had been working crazy 70-80 hour weeks for more than a decade... I barely went outside, and never left Silicon Valley. And then, suddenly, everything was different. I had more money than I knew what to do with... and nothing to do. So I decided to see the world."

DeWaal pressed the clicker, and the images on the giant screen behind him cycled through what looked like a series of holiday snaps – a younger Ethan posing with a Royal Guard in London, trekking past the Great Pyramid of Giza and meditating by the Taj Mahal reflecting pool. But the last photo was different... it showed people in an African village crowding around a water hole that was running dry.

"Ethiopia." he said in quiet tones, "This picture changed my life."

DeWaal felt the electricity in the air; the raised hackles and consternation that flashed through the crowd. He savored the response. Shock value always made the answers taste better; made his success story that much more compelling.

"We face a myriad of problems as a planet... devastation level events. Our current petrochemical energy systems blankets us in poisonous hydrocarbon smog. Human population on Earth has increased drastically – from 2.3 billion just a hundred years ago, to *9 billion* today. Climate change and population growth are creating a shortage of resources. A lack of affordable clean water, food, medical supplies and other resources are increasing the gap between the haves and the have-nots, and threaten to cause societal breakdowns and the death of millions."

"Earth has a finite amount of resources. We're discovering now that there's just not enough to service the needs of nine billion. Not down here. Not down here..."

"But up there–"

The pictures on the screen fell away, revealing a flawless animation. The attendant sound system boomed, turning the screen into the window of a rocketship, lifting off and hurtling through the atmosphere. The view passed through blue sky and clouds. The horizon curved and became the curvature of the Earth, blue seeped away to black, and a million stars came into view. There in front of them – something in orbit, too far away and too small to make out.

"*Shefa* is an old Hebrew word, meaning abundance. In Kabbalist terms, shefa is a teaching... a way of life. The flow of goodness and godliness that comes to us from higher planes of existence. An energy that emanates from the light of the Sefirah of Hesed – the benevolent side of God. Transformative, enlightening, empowering... Shefa gives us the energy to live our lives to the fullest."

"Up there, all around us, are resources beyond anything that most of us can imagine," DeWaal continued. "Planetary resources. Abundant resources. A hundred times more water than in our oceans! Helium-3 isotopes for limitless clean energy. And millions of tons of rare metals that power our society, found in the heart of the things we know as asteroids. If that is not manna from heaven... what is?"

The 'something in orbit' grew larger on-screen as DeWaal spoke, and it slowly became obvious that the auditorium rocketship had been approaching an asteroid, the *size* of which was conveyed when the camera began orbiting the city-sized planetoid.

DeWaal paused, to let the scale of the animation sink in. The room felt energized, tingly with hope and opportunity. Even the most cynical entrepreneurs would be hard-pressed to find fault with the vision. He smiled, acknowledged his adrenaline high, and launched straight into Act 2.

"When I went home, I knew what I had to do," he said. "I poured all my money into a new startup – Astral Abundance. My goal was to do something no one had ever done before. I was going to gather these resources from asteroids, and I was going to do it for the good of humanity. We began searching for viable near-Earth asteroids seven years ago, found four that we liked the look of, and eventually narrowed our selection down to asteroid 284051 AT. Or, as the IAU has so aptly christened it... *Callum*."

"Callum was the right size, composition, and distance from Earth, with a negligible rotation," DeWaal said. "Sixteen months ago, Abundance launched a ship called *Frontier* to rendezvous with Callum and bring it back to Earth. This will be the first of many... once we've proven the technology, we will do the same with other, larger asteroids, containing all the resources that we will ever need. We are at the beginning of a new era in human civilization."

As DeWaal spoke, the screen started showing recorded footage of the *Frontier* mission – launch, transit, and mission highlights featuring Pablo, Walt, Param and most prominently, the charismatic and photogenic Mission Commander, Carol Mathers. A few spontaneous hoots and rounds of applause from the audience interrupted DeWaal. Right on cue, he thought.

"Quite a few Carol fans in the audience, it seems." he adlibbed, to laughter. "I know that Carol would love to have been here to tell you about this mission first-hand," DeWaal said. "Unfortunately–"

A shrill ringtone interrupted DeWaal as a message flashed across the screen: "Incoming video call". Underneath was a photo of Carol. The audience chuckled and DeWaal threw out his faux surprise face. He pressed the clicker.

A staticky fragmented video of Carol appeared on the screen, to loud applause and hollers from the auditorium. Carol waved, her eyes scanning from left to right across the room. "Hello! Hi, how are you!" she said over the cheering. "What an enthusiastic audience!"

DeWaal flashed a smile. "Carol!" he turned to address the twenty foot giant face on the screen. "It's great to see you. What a welcome surprise."

"Well, Ethan, when your every moment of every day is meticulously planned out, it's great to be able to surprise people."

"How's it all going up there?"

"It's going well," Carol said. "Working hard." She flipped the camera around, and the audience watched as the rest of the crew worked away diligently on the command deck of the *Frontier*.

Except... something was off. DeWaal couldn't put his finger on it, but the atmosphere felt different. There was movement backstage – a figure was bobbing around distractingly behind the curtain, and some phone notifications buzzed loudly in the auditorium. Murmurs of confusion swept through the space.

He shook it off, gave his best laugh, and continued. "We're looking forward to your arrival," he said.

"No, I've never been to Stockholm," Carol replied. "Maybe when we get back you can fly us over there to see everyone. We'll probably be ready for another flight by then."

DeWaal winced, and turned sheepishly to the audience. He was disoriented and off-track, but there was still time to salvage the presentation – he just had to come clean.

"I knew I was going to screw that up," he said. "The organizers told me it was a great idea... I said I'm terrible at remembering lines. As you can guess, this isn't actually a live video, because it takes minutes to transmit information back and forth. This message was actually recorded two days ago... Carol insisted that she wanted to say a few words to the people that were kind enough to come out and support her. I promise that –"

"Mr. DeWaal!"

The voice cut across the auditorium and grated loudly on De-Waal's consciousness. It made his shark-sense tingle with danger. A red flush swept across his face and he fought to keep his knees from buckling. People looked around to see where the voice was coming from. Several others shushed loudly.

A woman stood up. "Mr. DeWaal..." she repeated, and held up her phone. "I'm with the *Washington Free Press*. My colleague is at Abundance Mission Control right now. He says that you have lost contact with the Frontier. He says it sounds bad. Can you verify the accuracy of this?"

On the right side of the auditorium, an audience member made a slightly strangled cry. Two camera flashes went off by the side of the stage. DeWaal suddenly felt the piercing glare of all the eyes in the audience.

"What?" was all he could think to say. Fifty thousand thoughts ran through his mind in that instant. It confused him deeply, because if something had happened to the *Frontier*, surely he would be the first to know about it. His assistant would have informed him – his assistant, *that he had left at the hotel with instructions to sort out paperwork*. His phone – turned off for the last hour as a pre-speech ritual. He would have been the first to know about it...

The French woman who introduced him dashed out onto stage and whispered in his ear. DeWaal would never remember the exact words, but he knew what they meant. He gave a slight nod, and stared out into empty space.

"Thank you for bringing this to my attention," he stammered at the reporter. "I – I can't comment right now. I'm sure there is a very simple explanation."

The audience began yelling questions. DeWaal's answer had shattered the decorum in the room, and turned the presentation into an impromptu press conference.

"I'm very sorry," DeWaal said. "You'll have to excuse me."

He pulled off his radio mic, tossed it on the lectern and hurried off the stage. The audience fell silent for a moment, expectantly waiting for his return, but when the auditorium lights came on, the crowd exploded into loud chatter. DeWaal never returned, and the giant screen kept playing the silenced footage of Carol Mathers, enthusiastically miming to the audience.

3. Sorrel – The Gig

No business park in the world overflows with character, but this particular San Dimas business park was particularly anonymous – a study in purposeful drabness with identical rows of pale, low-slung commercial buildings. There were a handful of supply stores and the odd machine shop, but most of the lots served as warehouses and storage units belonging to small businesses without the means to be found (or big businesses that didn't want to be).

Yezzik, skinny as a praying mantis, was already waiting outside the warehouse entrance as Sorrel's battered Toyota pulled up.

"Good to see you, my friend," Yezzik said with the friendly familiarity of a market trader greeting a tourist with a bulging money belt. "Please come into my office."

Sorrel didn't bother to argue with the description of the venue. He followed Yezzik through the door into an uninspired single room, sparse on furnishings. A bare lightbulb hung from the ceiling, barely adding to the illumination from the single grimy window.

A table, a couple of cheap folding chairs, a mini-fridge and a battered TV playing sports highlights were the only other furnishings. Leaning up against the far wall, eyes pinned on the TV, was a muscular slab of meat wearing a tank top four sizes too small. He looked vaguely like Yezzik, but taller and pumped full of steroids and whatever oil that some bodybuilders used to pump up their muscles. Synthol, Sorrel thought it was called.

"This is my nephew," Yezzik said. "My sister's son. Big boy."

Synthol grunted and pulled his eyes from the TV, fixing Sorrel with a stare that he assumed was designed to intimidate.

Yezzik beckoned to the rickety table and sat down. He eyed Sorrel expectantly. "You have it?"

Sorrel held up his briefcase to confirm that, no, he hadn't driven all the way to San Dimas for the sparkling company. He placed the briefcase on the table and flipped it open to reveal a densely packed cubesat telemetry subsystem, complete with auto-triangulating guidance controller.

Yezzik greedily inspected the goods. "Very nice," he said, eyes glistening like knives. "How new are we talking?"

"Virtually new," Sorrel said. "The project these systems came from was scrapped last year, so you're getting the very latest in controllers."

"Will it interface with the Cygnus data relays? That's what we're working with."

"Cygnus relays are near obsolete," said Sorrel. "It will work, but the data throughput is going to be bottlenecked to hell. You shouldn't be using those anymore. They'll affect your performance."

"Since when were you ever concerned with performance and quality?" asked Yezzik.

"I sold you what you said you could afford," Sorrel replied.

Yezzik grinned again, his lips pulling back so far that Sorrel could see the gold fillings. They had almost certainly cost a hell of a lot more than what he was promising Sorrel. He paused, clearly relishing his next words.

"You know me," Yezzik said. "I'm an honest man. But, right now... we've got cash flow issues. I can pay you in two months."

"You told me you were ready to deal now," Sorrel grumbled.

"Things change quickly, Charles. You should know this."

Sorrel slammed down the briefcase lid. "Fuck you, Yez."

Synthol began to move in the corner of the room, standing up with unnatural speed. Yezzik held up his hand, stopping the lumbering ogre. "You're upsetting him, Charles."

Sorrel rolled his eyes. It was the same game Yezzik always played whenever he bought something from Sorrel.

"I swear, man, when we launch this thing investors are gonna be on us like flies on shit."

Sorrel stared at the man, frowned and stuck his hand out to shake. Yezzik seized it before Sorrel could take it back, the way a snake grabs a mouse.

Sorrel responded – grabbed Yezzik's thumb and began to apply pressure, all while continuing to shake hands. "You must understand the pain you're causing me here, Yez," he said. "Are you sure I can't get you to reconsider?"

Yezzik's eyes widened, and his face contorted in pain. Sorrel cranked up the pressure just a bit; one quick jolt and he would snap the thumb like a chicken leg. He watched as Yezzik's eyes flicked over to Synthol and back to him. Sorrel smiled cordially at Yezzik, and clenched his hand a little harder.

"Okay, okay," Yezzik said. "Maybe I give you half today... half when we launch. It's only fair."

Sorrel frowned, made some mental calculations, and decided that trying to wring more out of Yezzik would be a near-impossible task. "That's why you're such a smart businessman," he said, and let go.

Yezzik snaked his hand back with lightning speed, glared at Sorrel momentarily... then smiled again. "I tell you, Sorrel," he said. "You're taking food out of my wife's mouth."

"I've seen your wife. She could do with missing a meal."

Synthol, blissfully unaware of everything that had transpired, had lost interest and turned his gaze back to the TV. It looked like his team was losing.

/ / /

When Sorrel exited the warehouse, his bank account was heavier, but only marginally so. Yezzik accompanied him to the car, slowly massaging his thumb. A couple of empty junk food packets fell out as Sorrel opened the car door, eliciting a reproachful tut-tut from Yezzik.

"Man, you need to eat some proper food," Yezzik said.

"You need to pay some proper money."

Yezzik smiled, pretending not to hear. "You should get yourself a nice lady. My wife, she makes a rfissa like you wouldn't believe."

Sorrel climbed into his car and shut the door, not caring to hear about how great Yezzik's life was. But Yezzik continued to speak, mouthing words that Sorrel could no longer hear. Forced into submission, Sorrel lowered the window.

"– Abundance. Have you heard about Abundance?" said Yezzik.

"What about it?"

Yezzik looked grave. "Gone, man. All gone..." he said. "It blew up. Poof..."

Shit.

Of course Sorrel had heard all about the mission. It was hard to follow the news without hearing about Carol Whatshername... but he hadn't heard about this yet, and to hear it from Yezzik – it wasn't like him at all to be concerned.

"Not good news," Yezzik said. "Not at all. This is going to scare away investors."

Of course, Sorrel thought. He revved the engine, causing Yezzik to take a step back.

"Good doing business with you, Charles," he said. "I'll give you a call when we get up and running." He smiled his used car salesman smile – the one that said your car would at least get you halfway to where it needed to go before it broke down.

Sorrel released the handbrake and pulled forward. He didn't really care to know what Yezzik was going to be doing with the telemetry subsystems. Something along the lines of scamming investors by launching half-assed satellites that would very quickly fall back to Earth and burn up because they were patchworked from a bunch of cheap parts. Yezzik would of course milk that cash cow and then conveniently vanish just before the satellite's eventual demise.

This was what the space race had become. Not a race to the stars, but a race to the bottom. Every Tom, Dick and Yezzik trying to cash in on space in whatever way they could. Sorrel did not doubt that he would hear from Yezzik again and, despite his misgivings, he would most probably take the call. The idealists weren't the ones who made money in a gold rush – it was, in fact, the ones selling the shovels and pans. He supplied the shovels and pans, and Yezzik did the selling... dazzled the suckers with that eternal dream of space.

Space... hah! Sorrel frowned with a tinge of bitterness. What a pipe dream.

We won't ever reach the stars. We won't even reach the outer planets.

/ / /

The road back from San Dimas into Los Angeles was a bitch. Caltrans, the California Department of Transportation, had been aggressively expanding the Autonomo program into the Inland Empire. The entire stretch of the freeway from the beach all the way up through Pomona now prioritized autonomous vehicles.

Only it didn't make any sense. Out here in the LA metropolitan boonies, Sorrel could spot only around ten autonomous cars in the entire three lanes of the San Bernardino Freeway allocated to them. Everyone else in a regular human-driven car was wedged into the remaining two lanes, creating an artificial traffic jam.

Occasionally, someone would snap and say "fuck it," pull out into the autonomous lanes and zip past their fellow commuters, wreaking havoc with the efficiency of the autonomous vehicle lanes. Sorrel always passed that driver a few miles down the road, pulled over by CHP. Antics like that made the drive bearable.

There was no such entertainment today. Today he was just stuck behind a grandpa doing 45 miles an hour while the Autonomo-enabled cars whipped past them. Not having the financial means to own a self-driving car simply meant that you were one of the forgotten, the cast-asides. He resigned himself to the prospect of a miserable drive and tapped the touchscreen display on the dashboard. What was it that Yezzik said about Abundance?

"Give me a news summary about the *Frontier*," Sorrel said.

"Summarizing Abundance," said the car.

"From *CNNC*... Abundance Mission Control has lost contact with its spacecraft *Frontier* during its first mission to retrieve an asteroid for mining. Mission Commander Carol Mathers, Lieutenant Pablo Magdalena and Mission Specialists Walter Williams and Param Havita are feared killed. Commander Mathers had been hailed in the news cycle as the face of the new civilian space movement and leading figures from around the world have paid their—"

"Next summary," Sorrel interrupted.

"From *RSN*... The Squyres Multiband Space Telescope was requisitioned to image the loss-of-signal coordinates to try and determine the severity of the accident. Compared to images taken a week before, the asteroid cargo appears to have broken into multiple fragments."

"Next."

"From *SnapNews*... Reactions on the Aether range from sadness to anger at Abundance CEO Ethan DeWaal. User Tardigrade12 calls DeWaal —"

Sorrel was about to skip again when the summary was cut short by an incoming call. Sorrel answered it without checking who it was.

"Chuck?" said a resonant male voice.

"Who's asking?"

"Chuck. It's Bob McClusky."

Sorrel's heart sank. Bob McClusky was *Senator* Robert McClusky, the well-known Washington politician Sorrel knew only too well.

"Bob, I'd love to chat, but I'm driving–"

"I won't keep you, Chuck," McClusky said. That was the third time he'd called Sorrel by name.

It was that old politician's trick to keep your attention and your vote – McClusky was clearly wringing that maneuver for all it was worth.

Sorrel tried to think of a smartass response, but took too long. Mistaking Sorrel's silence for acquiescence, McClusky continued.

"Let me cut to the chase," he said. "I've just flown in from Sacramento. I have a job I think you'd be perfect for. Let's meet for lunch to talk about it. On me, of course."

Sorrel's stomach growled. He had been in such a rush to pick up the goods and get to Yezzik that he hadn't eaten a proper breakfast. Nothing about doing some odd job for McClusky appealed to him, but a fancy lunch made up for it... especially after being screwed over by Yezzik.

"Lunch sounds good, Bob," he said.

"Great," said McClusky. "My assistant has already booked a table at Skyview. You know it?"

"I think you and I frequent different establishments. Send me the address."

"Done," McClusky said. "And Chuck?"

"Bob?"

"Don't be late."

There was a *beep* as McClusky's call disconnected, followed by an alert. "You have a reminder," the car said. "There is an 11:45 reservation with Robert McClusky at Skyview in downtown Los Angeles. With current traffic conditions, you will be nineteen minutes late."

Sorrel frowned. McClusky wasn't exactly a spring chicken, but who ate before twelve? What could possibly be that urgent? He glanced at the freeway signs. He was way past downtown. *Damn you, Bob. You always have to control the situation.*

Sorrel jerked the wheel, cutting across several Autonomo lanes to hit the exit ramp. If autonomous cars had hands, they surely would have flipped him the finger.

/ / /

The restaurant's panoramic windows afforded a priceless view of the whole sprawling city. A pressure front on the horizon framed the mountain backdrop with light stringy cirrus clouds, breaking up the constant blue of the LA skyline.

There were two types of Angelenos, Sorrel thought as he defied vertigo, staring down at the city spreading out far below him. There were those who got shit on, and those who did the shitting. From up here on the seventieth floor, you could take one hell of a shit. The struggles of regular folks were conveniently invisible from up here.

McClusky was fashionably late, even though he'd told Sorrel otherwise. The maître d' had sat them in a corner table right over by the window, either out of respect for the Senator's privacy... or because they didn't want other customers to see Sorrel at their restaurant.

"Can I get you some still or sparkling water to start?" asked the waiter.

"I'll take a beer. Straight out of the bottle is fine."

The waiter flashed a faux smile, scurried away and returned with an open bottle and a glass "in case you change your mind." Sorrel grabbed the bottle and chugged half of it. He hated restaurants like this.

The express elevator doors slid open behind the concierge desk, and out stepped the man himself – Senator Robert McClusky. It'd been years since Sorrel had seen him last, but he still looked as distinguished as ever – rigid posture, deep tan, and now an extra bit of white hair flecked around the temples.

The maître d' beamed and gushed as she greeted McClusky. "Thank you, Mary. How are the kids?" Sorrel heard his baritone voice carrying across the restaurant. She walked him to the table, thanked him again for the generous tip and left.

Formalities aside, he turned and shook Sorrel's hand firmly. "Chuck!" he said. "Thank you for coming. Hell of a view, don't you think?"

/ / /

The large television screen in the foyer of the restaurant was just within Sorrel's eyeline, playing news reports about the *Frontier* disaster. The sound was muted, but Sorrel recognized the same stock footage that had been on TV for months. Most of them were of Carol.

"Have you been following the accident?" McClusky said, taking a bite of his tangerine and fatalii kampachi appetizer.

"I've... heard a few things," said Sorrel.

"What a tragedy," McClusky said. He shook his head.

Sorrel huffed a bit louder than he had intended. "Please, Bob. The mission was doomed from the start," he said.

"How do you mean?"

"Asteroid mining is a pipe dream. Ethan DeWaal had too much access to cheap money and too much time on his hands. What idiot brings the asteroid back? Why not just strip-mine the damn thing right there?"

McClusky shrugged. "Could be plenty of explanations. Cost-effectiveness, human resources, strategic reasons…"

"It's a get rich quick scam," Sorrel interrupted. "DeWaal is selling junk bonds to clueless investors... and looking like a god-damn visionary while doing it. Serves him right."

"Jesus. Have some common decency, Chuck," McClusky replied. "People died."

Sorrel harumphed and proceeded to shovel more food into his face. It wasn't every day that he got invited to lunch at a place like this.

McClusky looked around to make sure no one else was around before pulling something out of his jacket pocket and placing it on the table in front of Sorrel. It was a printout of a photo – six pale dots against a dark background of static noise.

"This is a MIL-SAT image," McClusky said. "Taken from one of our orbiting satellites. That's what's left of the *Frontier,* a couple of hours after the... incident."

Sorrel looked. Despite the graininess of the picture, he was surprised that it triggered him emotionally. It was one thing to hear about the accident on the news, and another to see a physical manifestation of current events. For a split second, Sorrel pictured himself on board the *Frontier,* and imagined how helpless the crew must have felt in those final moments. How helpless – and how far from home.

"Why are you showing me this?" Sorrel said.

"Because I need your help. I'm going to talk with DeWaal tomorrow. You're coming with me."

Sorrel stopped chewing. "Me?"

McClusky nodded.

"Don't you have... *people* for that?"

"This is new territory," McClusky said. "NASA missions have an established protocol for accident investigation. Military missions under Space Command follow a similar process. But Abundance... Abundance is a private American company, flying civilian astronauts. There's no precedent. At least not for anything of this scale."

"The White House is still trying to figure out how to proceed. I'm sure they'll eventually set up an investigative board... but this can't wait. It's terrible optics. We need answers."

"I'm not following," Sorrel said. "I'm not a politician, Bob."

"I know that," McClusky replied, annoyed. "Look – I need someone with your background. Someone who knows enough to tell me when DeWaal tries to bullshit me. I just need you to, ah, interview some people... draw a few conclusions... and write up a preliminary report. Double-spaced, etcetera etcetera... to show that we are doing something."

"My name can't be public. You know that, right?"

"It won't be, I promise. A week's work, tops. Then we let the White House figure out how to spin this while the real investigation is in progress."

Sorrel looked at McClusky, eyes narrowed into slits. "Is this... legal?"

McClusky chuckled. "Like that's ever stopped you before."

"I just need to know if I need to make a fast exit somewhere."

A thin smile crept onto the edges of McClusky's lips. He pulled out a business card and handed it to Sorrel. It read:

ROBERT J. McCLUSKY
United States Senator

Co-Chairman
Senate Subcommittee For Civilian Aerospace

"You'll have the full authority of the Federal Government behind you," McClusky said.

Sorrel chewed his food. Hated the idea. Politics was always trouble... but it had the unmistakable smell of money. "I'm not cheap, Bob." he cautioned

"150K, plus expenses," McClusky replied.

Shit. It was more than Sorrel had been expecting. Heck, it was even more than the price he'd been ready to quote to get McClusky off his back. Who was he to look a gift horse in the mouth – or the senator riding in on it?

Sorrel nodded slowly. "I think we could work something out."

"That's great to hear," McClusky nodded. He finished his champagne and stood up. "I'm late for my next meeting... take your time, enjoy the lunch. Already paid for."

Sorrel washed his mouthful of steak down with the last of the beer. "You going down to see Ami this trip?" he asked.

McClusky coughed awkwardly. "I'm headed there right after the next meeting."

Sorrel nodded. There were so many things he wanted to say. He decided against all of them. "Tell her I said hi," he replied.

4. Jen – Brain Child

The land shrugged and gave up along this gritty stretch of mountainous Pacific coastline; terrain bled from green to dirt, then from dirt to rock. Here in Baja California, south of the border, the only sign of civilization for miles around was the occasional tin hut, a poorly defined dirt path, and the caterpillar trail of dust stirred up by dune buggies, all jockeying for pole position.

Jennifer Sudeikas-Mathers was buckled into the driver's seat of one of those buggies. Auburn eyes framed by sharp facial features stared out past the crash helmet visor – there were three cars ahead of her, and they were on the home stretch. If she were going to do anything, it had to be soon.

At the next turn on the road, she tapped the accelerator. The dune buggy slipped to the inside of the curve, edging out her number three challenger. With senses on an adrenaline high, it felt like everything was happening in slow motion. The tire grip, the slippage... the wind and the rhythmic thumping of the engine. She felt her weight shift in the bucket seat, felt her hands and feet responding automatically. Felt the feedback loop of action-reaction-control.

"Are you getting all this, BC?" Jen asked.

"All of it, ma," came the excited reply.

By voice alone, BC sounded like an excitable precocious five-year-old. Which he was, in a way... he just wasn't flesh and blood. The voice came from an orange box securely strapped down in the passenger seat. It was studded with ports and sensors and sported a half-dome acrylic bubble on top, inside of which was some sort of spherical camera array – BC's 'eyes'. A set of cables ran from the box into the back of Jen's crash helmet, where it connected to the brain control interface port just behind her ear. LEDs on the side of the box pulsed and strobed as it assimilated the stream of brainwave data.

'BC' was BrainChild – an Artificial Intelligence construct, the next-gen AGI prototype of the future of thinking machines. An AI that was not simply programmed to pretend to answer general questions or generate art facsimiles, but one that actually *understood* the questions asked of it. Imbued with general logic and core modules, it would be allowed to grow and "learn" from real-world experience. Like a child growing into adulthood, its language and speech patterns grew alongside as well, progressing from simple structured sentences to more sophisticated modalities.

"Are we there yet?" BC asked.

Jen cracked a smile, and twisted the wheel hard on the next turn. The move made her lose traction on the left front wheel, but she turned into the slip and regained control. A small tap on the gas, and she slipped past number two.

Good data. *Good data.*

"Jared – you there?" she barked into her headset.

"Right here," came the reply. "We have you on visual. Two miles to the finish line."

"Roger that."

"There's someone in front of you... better smoke that sucker."

"Roger *that.*"

"Smoke that sucker, ma?" BC asked.

Jen chuckled. "It's a metaphor, BC."

Number one wasn't going to be easy. The driver was very aware of his environment and where she was. He'd kept his buggy in all the right spots to prevent Jen from taking the lead.

"Waitaminute–" BC said. "Flash traffic from the aether."

"Not now, BC." Jen replied curtly, as she grappled with the buggy in front of her. "Keep your eye on the data."

"I have the data handled, ma." BC replied, petulant. "This is *important*. There's been an accident on the *Frontier*."

Jen froze. The sound of the engines, the shock absorbers, the rasping of sand on the trail – the entire soundscape fell away, faded into the background as panic rose from the base of her gut and tunneled through her chest. She forgot to grip the steering wheel, forgot to keep her foot on the gas pedal, forgot to breathe as a flood of memories leaped through her thoughts in a millisecond. She saw her immediate future... knew what BC was going to say before he said it.

"The reports say that Carol and the crew have been killed."

A dark tunnel crowded in from the edges of Jen's vision – twisted itself around her being, forcefully ripped her from the outside world. Large sharp knives plunged through her chest, razor sharp and violent. Time simultaneously slowed to a crawl and yet was infinitely fast, wrapping around on itself like an ouroboros. She remembered screaming, but could not tell if it was in that moment, or something from her past, or her future.

Somewhere in that infinity of time Jen noted that this was bad data, and that she was transmitting all this to BC. This was not how human beings should behave. This was too irrational, too painful. Too human.

The buggy twisted out of control. For a moment they were weightless, wheels gripping air. After an eternity, they landed badly. Wheels skittered sideways across the desert. The chassis lurched and then rolled, end over end.

/ / /

Jen found herself sitting on the ground, propped up against the overturned buggy, paralyzed by thought. Something was squeezing her heart, and it drained her of energy. The last few minutes had been like playing a video game – her character going through the motions, but she was... disconnected.

There was an oil fire somewhere around her. She watched herself unstrap from the overturned buggy and fall to the ground – remembered the hot and bitter taste of dirt and gravel in her mouth.

A pair of hands reached behind the driver's seat to grab the fire extinguisher. She briefly wondered whose hands those were, before realizing it was her own.

She vaguely remembered the engine fire being put out, and the empty fire extinguisher dropped on the ground amidst the thick smoke. Remembered finding the orange box still attached to the seat harness. There was a large jagged rock jammed into its side, and shattered electronic guts were spilled all over the desert floor.

With shaking hands, she'd unzipped the pouch on her jacket and pulled her phone out. The screen was cracked and her fingers left blood and oil stains all over it, but there on the notification screen... breaking news on the *Frontier* accident.

A million pins and needles stabbed her in that moment, over every inch of her body.

The control van skidded recklessly to a halt nearby, and disgorged its human contents. Jen looked up to see Jared and the small entourage running towards her. Jared... Jared... she searched her memory for context.

They owned a startup together. What was the name of it? Can't remember. Doesn't matter... not important. They were chasing breakthroughs in computational warp AI. Building the next generation. Nice guy, smart as hell, played by the book, handled all the legal bullshit. A little overprotective sometimes.

There he was, next to her, with the emergency medical kit. "You alright?" he said as he shone a penlight in her eyes. It was irritating and she waved her hand at it, trying to swat the fly away.

Jared grabbed her hand, saw that it was bloodied. He followed the trail of blood, checked behind her left ear. "Your interface is bleeding," he said. He pulled gauze and disinfectant from the med kit and started triaging the wound. "You're lucky it didn't rip right off."

"Pretty rough disconnect..." she mumbled to no one in particular.

The phone on the ground next to Jen started ringing. She ignored it for the longest time, forcing Jared to pick it up and answer the call. "Hello?" he said.

The voice on the other end seemed to leap out of the phone. "Where have you been?! I've been trying to get a hold of you for – wait a minute. Jared?"

"Hi, Ethan."

"Where is Jen? Is she okay?"

"Yes. No."

"Where are you?"

"Baja."

There was a slight pause. DeWaal screamed and yelled at someone else in the office before he came back on the line. "Stay where you are," he said. "I'm sending a chopper."

"Uh, okay." Jared said, hung up and looked at Jen. "Why is he sending a chopper?"

There was the longest pause. The words formed on the tip of Jen's tongue, but she couldn't vocalize it. "The *Frontier*..."

"Frontier?"

"The ship... gone."

"Oh my god. Carol?"

Jen looked up at Jared. There was a panicked look of concern on his face. She hated this – hated the raw emotionality of the situation. Hated that everyone's eyes were now on her. In this, her greatest moment of weakness, the pain and shame of loss was more than she could bear.

She felt the buggy's chassis shake as Jared's assistants unbuckled the orange box from the passenger seat, extracting it as best as possible from its demise. A few shattered remnants of circuit boards trailed them as they took the box to the control van.

BC... BC still needs me. What am I doing?

Jen cupped her face in her hands, took the moment to put on her brave face. Chased down all the errant thoughts in her head, threw them into the box, compartmentalized them.

I am in control. I am in control.

When she opened them again, there was a fire in her eyes. "Help me up" she said.

Jared helped her to her feet – she was a little unsteady, but physically uninjured. Jared offered an arm to lean on, but her body language told him otherwise.

She walked over to the van and pulled open the side door, revealing a workbench and a suite of high tech electronics, hopelessly out of place here in the middle of the desert. The assistants had placed the remnants of what-used-to-be-BC on the workbench.

"I've got some water in the truck," Jared said. "And the stronger stuff too, if you need it."

Jen leaned over the workbench. "I need to do this first, Jared."

She peered into the orange box. The rock had shredded its outer shell, sensors and all. Visible through the carnage was a slotted processor card, labeled "BrainChild" – mangled and snapped in half. What was left had been burned and melted by fire.

From under the workbench she pulled out a padded equipment case, flipped it open and extracted a new slotted processor card. Pulling a cable off the bench, she attached her phone to the card, ran a few authorization scripts and then slipped it into a new identical, undamaged orange box. It emitted a series of beeps, then a chirrup. "Backup 87-54 restored. Good afternoon, ma."

"Hi BC. We had a bad run. You are now designated BrainChild Prime."

"Understood. Flash traffic–"

Jen raised her hand to stop BC. "I already know. Add a new behavior module rule please – no bad news during periods of intense concentration."

"Added. Is there a reason, ma?"

Jen paused. Emotions were welling up inside her, and she fought to keep it under control. "Human beings are... not very good at multitasking."

"Filed. Should I assimilate data from the previous run?"

Jen looked at the mangled wreck of old BC, sitting on the workbench next to BC Prime. The sight of it was now inevitably linked to Carol. It was hard to concentrate, as if she were a dam wall holding back the weight of the universe.

"Might have corrupted data," she said, finally. "I'd rather not contaminate the stream."

"Understood. What will happen to you now, ma?"

The question sideswiped Jen. No functioning adult would have dared ask a question like that, so soon after. But BC... BC was a child.

Jen touched the back of her ear. The brain interface was still bloodied. She wondered if this might have been a good learning experience for BC. "I don't know," Jen finally said.

She turned to the mangled orange box next to BC, and noted that amidst the destruction, the power LED was still glowing. She reached in and disconnected the battery.

"RIP, 87-53."

5. Sorrel – Abundance

When asteroid mining was just a half-formed idea in De-Waal's head, the sliver of land east of the 110 freeway near the University of Southern California was suffering from depressed property values. DeWaal jumped at the opportunity – bought a few warehouses at fire sale prices and turned them into the Los Angeles home base for his spunky little startup, Astral Abundance. Today the footprint of the company covered most of the industrial zone, and had become a pilgrimage-of-sorts for space enthusiasts. With each of the *Frontier* mission's history-making firsts, the crowds would gather at the front gates to cheer, chant and celebrate. To-day, however, it was a different crowd altogether.

The self-driving Range Rover drew up to the main security gate at Abundance HQ. From the back seat, Sorrel saw the sizable crowd of protesters gathered around the gate, wielding signs that read "Solve Problems on Earth First!" and "We Were Not Meant To Go To Space". They banged on the car windows like feral chil-dren; Sorrel was surprised by their passion-hate, but McClusky was too engaged hammering out emails on his phone to notice. The gate guards waved them through, and they passed into the facility compound with only a few smudges and handprints on the wind-shield.

Abundance's main building looked and felt more like a trendy tech company than the aerospace buildings that Sorrel was used to. Colorful geometric shapes resembling pixel artifacts jutted out from the building at odd angles and the parking lot was filled with expensive cars. There was even an outdoor beach volleyball court and a patio for al fresco dining. Sorrel could practically smell the complimentary gluten-free vegan meals they were serving.

The building's enormous rotating doors led into a large airy foyer with high vaulted ceilings – an impressive glass and anodized steel space the size of a small auditorium. Overhead, a diorama of an asteroid surface, complete with space suits, a Lifter Pod and mining robots hung upside down. Employees milled around in T-shirts, shorts and laptops. The place must have been a great place to work, but today a pall hung over the place – like Disneyland the day Uncle Walt died.

The young woman at the reception desk looked up as Sorrel and McClusky approached. "Can I help you?" She tried her best professional smile, but it fell short.

"Senator Robert McClusky, from the Senate Subcommittee," McClusky said. "We're here to see Ethan DeWaal."

The receptionist didn't look impressed. She tapped a few buttons on the keyboard, pulled out a pair of tablets and handed one each to McClusky and Sorrel. "Sign these please," she said.

Sorrel looked over the paperwork. The tablet requested permission to confirm their biometrics, and popped up a page of terms and conditions. Among other legalese, they were asked to agree not to take photos or videos during the visit, and not to disparage the company.

"I can't sign this," McClusky said to the receptionist.

The receptionist shrugged. "The system won't let me print your access cards until you've signed."

McClusky tensed up, as if steeling himself for a confrontation. Before he could continue, however, a loud voice boomed across the reception area. "It's okay."

Sorrel turned to look. DeWaal had swept into the foyer, trailed by an assistant carrying a towel and shaving implements. From afar he looked ridiculously like an ad for male grooming; Successful Businessman with the Perfect Job, Perfect Car and Perfect Shave. But as he approached, it was clear DeWaal was more tired and stressed than successful. Bleary-eyed and disheveled, the parts of the chin the electric razor hadn't yet reached revealed patches of stubble.

"Senator," DeWaal said as he walked up, extending his hand. "Welcome back."

Sorrel watched as McClusky shook DeWaal's hand. The grimace on DeWaal's face, poorly hidden, told of sordid backstories between the two. It had clearly been enough to convince both parties they didn't much care for the other.

McClusky gestured towards Sorrel. "Ethan, this is Charles Sorrel," he said. "He's the technical advisor heading up our investigation into the *Frontier.*"

DeWaal shook Sorrel's hand, but offered no small talk.

"Sorry to do this in front of you, guys," He said, pointing to the electric shaver in his hand. "It's been a crazy few days. Ashley – can you go ahead and just print their keycards please."

Ashley smiled and passive-aggressively entered a few keystrokes on the keyboard. The printer snarled into life and spat out two cards. DeWaal leaned over the reception desk, grabbed the cards and handed them out.

"Follow me," DeWaal said as he turned and set off.

The group passed through the double doors into a long white corridor. The walls were decorated with large framed photographs hung at regular intervals. As they swept down the hallway, the walls recounted the visual history of Abundance – from humble start bidding on its first contract, to its present day space behemoth status.

At the end of the corridor was a giant modernist art sculpture – an hourglass with wings. On it was inscribed the words of Apple's co-founder Steve Jobs: "Your time is limited." This inspirational mantra now seemed like a painful reminder of human mortality. Sorrel noted that somewhere along the way, DeWaal had dismissed his assistant, and it was now just the three of them.

"Technical advisor, huh..." DeWaal glanced over at Sorrel as they walked. "Here to help us get to the bottom of this."

"That's the idea."

"Bob tells me you're the resident expert in space mining."

"I wouldn't go that far."

"How far would you go?"

"Probably until you tell me to stop. Then a bit further."

DeWaal gave a thin, stressed smile. "But you're an engineer, yes?"

Sorrel shook his head. "Just a former test pilot trying to make an honest living."

DeWaal stopped in mid-stride, an annoyed look on his face. "So what exactly *do* you know?" he asked. "Mass and orbits? Typical compositional matrix of NEAs? Fusion propulsion? Terrestrial mining technologies?"

Sorrel shrugged. "I'm a quick learner."

DeWaal shook his head and turned to McClusky. "Why are you doing this to me, Bob?"

"Ethan," McClusky replied. "You know why."

"For chrissake," DeWaal said, throwing up his arms. "You told me that you had to do oversight... I said okay. But then you bring someone in who clearly doesn't know his ass from his elbow."

"It's just a preliminary investigation, Ethan." McClusky barked. "*An investigation.* Your job is to tell him what he doesn't know."

"How do I know what he doesn't know?"

McClusky clenched his teeth. "I suggest that you start from the very beginning."

/ / /

The Abundance theater was large and lavishly appointed, with comfortable upholstered seats and expensive floor lighting to enchant visitors. Its smallish stage area was overcompensated for with a screen of immense size and quality, and served as a gathered hole by Abundance employees to watch mission milestones as they happened.

Today the screen was dark and foreboding. DeWaal led them to the front, gestured for Sorrel and McClusky to take their seats, and signaled to the projectionist to run the profile piece.

The lights dimmed as the Abundance logo lit up the screen. In three short minutes, the clip told the whole story of Abundance's asteroid mission – how they tracked hundreds of near-Earth asteroids and determined the viability of each prospective asteroid, launched probes to the four best candidates to verify mineral compositions, and then finally selecting Callum.

"Callum is an elongated ovoid in shape," the baritone voiceover explained over inspiring music. "Roughly three by two by one kilometers in size – with detectable deposits of lithium, platinum and palladium, and a mix of iron ore and magnesium."

"Its elliptical orbit takes Callum from the asteroid belt to just inside Earth orbit every 957 days. Abundance's asteroid-return mission will divert Callum as it nears conjunction, bringing it back in order to create a near-Earth platform that will allow us to mine the asteroid."

A series of quick montage cuts followed. Shots of DeWaal inspecting a massive booster rocket on the launchpad were followed by archival footage of *Frontier*'s launch. There were shots of Carol of the crew, *Frontier*'s historic landing on Callum, and Carol becoming the first human to walk on an asteroid. Shots of the installation of the MTF engines on the asteroid surface closed out the montage.

"The firing of the engines marks the beginning of the retrieval portion of the mission," the voiceover continued. "We nudge the asteroid's trajectory so that it will eventually settle into a stable orbit just beyond the Moon, where we can begin mining operations."

Music crescendoed as the Abundance logo flew in and landed on-screen. It held there for an awkwardly long moment before fading out with the music.

The lights in the theater came back up slowly. Sorrel stared at the blank screen for a few long moments, plagued by conflicting emotions. Things had come a long way since his days in the astronaut program; he was impressed, and jealous. He stayed seated in the theater chair, unwilling to come to terms with his has-been status.

"Now you're all caught up," DeWaal's voice echoed in his periphery.

"What does it take to fund a mission like this? Hundreds of millions? A quarter bil?" Sorrel asked.

"More than I have in my checking account," DeWaal sidestepped the question. "The investors are going apeshit at the moment."

"But if it *had* succeeded... that's a return of, what? 80,000 percent?"

DeWaal chuckled, a low nasal laugh. "Those numbers are... wild guesses made up by media pundits," he said. "The reality will be that the metals are mixed in with rock. The cost of extraction will require significant up-front costs... not to mention the R&D first-mover costs of figuring out how to *actually* mine an asteroid. That's why we needed to bring the asteroid back – so we can throw more people and research at it."

Sorrel watched DeWaal's mouth enunciate the words, but he didn't actually catch much of it. He wanted desperately to state that it was a crazy idea from the beginning and that he was not surprised that it failed, but McClusky was staring back at him from behind DeWaal. In the interest of civility and a future paycheck, he decided it was best to tone it down.

"So what happens now?"

DeWaal leaned back and thought for a moment. A fire seemed to leap into his eyes. "We go again. *We have to.*"

"Look outside – nine billion people on this planet. We don't have enough resources to take care of everyone. But with this... *all this*... I can harness the bounty of space. Build a better world... on and off-planet."

Sorrel scoffed. "They were spouting this nonsense in astronaut training two decades ago."

"They didn't have *this* back then," DeWaal replied, pointing up above their heads.

Sorrel looked up. Hanging from the ceiling above them was a display model – some sort of toroidal core studded with panels and hardpoints, enmeshed in cabling and featuring a unique flanged hexagonal nozzle. It was simultaneously recognizable as a rocket engine, but unlike any that Sorrel had seen before.

"It's only been possible the last five to ten years, really... We've leapfrogged propulsion ratios by the thousands."

"I don't know what this is," Sorrel mumbled, hiding his embarrassment with a scowl.

"Magnetized target fusion engine," DeWaal explained. "Based on the Tokamak. Some smartass Russian guys came up with it... those cocky bastards. We, uh... licensed the technology."

"Very new, and very very expensive," McClusky chimed in. "There are only two companies in the world right now working with MTF engines. Abundance... and Yangshen."

"The Chinese mining company?" Sorrel asked.

McClusky nodded. "They're the only viable competitor in the asteroid mining entrepreneur-space right now."

"They're busy playing catch-up at the moment though..." DeWaal waved his hand dismissively. Then, as if trying to escape the reality of the situation, DeWaal leapt to his feet. "Come! Let me show you what we have built."

6. Sorrel – The Tour

"Jay!" DeWaal yelled as they stepped out into the hallway.

The tall executive-looking guy was in a deep technical discussion, as evidenced by the way he was using his hands while talking. His assistant matched his outsize strides, stenographing meeting notes in mid-air with hand gestures and XR goggles. 'Jay' stopped, and pulled out his earbuds as DeWaal approached.

"Jay, this is Charles Sorrel and Senator McClusky," DeWaal made introductions. "They're here to investigate the –ah– accident. Guys, this is Jonathan Harkness, our Mission Planning Director."

Harkness nodded, begged off the conference call, and shook McClusky and Sorrel's hands. A strong firm grip, Sorrel noted. It reinforced the can-do attitude of his facial features. "Nice to meet you," he said. "Sorry for the – I mean, we're all a little frazzled here right now."

"Of course," McClusky nodded.

"I'm just about to give them a tour of the facility," DeWaal said. "Come with us! You can explain some things better than I can."

Sorrel watched as Harkness balked uncomfortably. He probably had a million things to attend to at the moment... but how to say no?

DeWaal turned to the assistant. "Zack – reschedule all of Jonathan's meetings for the rest of the day, will you? Thanks."

/ / /

The tour started with the mundane stuff. DeWaal had led them through a cavernous office area filled with row upon row of cubicles. These were the administrative staff, he explained – HR, Accounting and Business Development. The cubicle dividers were chest-level, to facilitate open-plan serendipities, and thus there was not much in the way of privacy. Sorrel noted a number of employees blankly staring at their monitors, and even openly crying.

The Engineering desks were past the administrative ones, and you could tell from the change in desk ornaments – from framed family photos and knick-knacks to diagrams, whiteboards and the occasional 3D printed rocket engine part on the desk. A heated discussion about shear forces and millimeter tolerances could be overheard somewhere in the maze.

Past the cubicle farm, they stepped through a set of heavy double doors into a wider corridor that led to the Machine Room. Vast sheets of floor-to-ceiling glass walls revealed computer racks packed with servers, their LEDs blinking away in furious computation.

"This is Amalthea," Harkness said, gesturing to the wall of blinking lights. "She runs the place."

McClusky blinked. "You give names to your computers?"

"Anthropomorphism is human nature," Harkness chuckled. "Amalthea is a multi-instance generative transformer and LLM system. She was brought online about... oh, ten years ago. She serves as the core and brains of the whole facility – juggles and manages all our computational needs, from calculating orbital trajectories to scheduling and facility operations. Originally designed and built by... Carol's wife."

A tinge of sadness crossed his face. Harkness paused, and changed the subject. "Say hello to our guests, Ama."

A soft female voice chirped from out of nowhere. "Welcome back, Senator. And good morning, Mr. Sorrel. I hope you're enjoying your tour."

"I am, thank you," McClusky replied, looking a little worried. He turned to DeWaal. "Now this... Amma thing. It's all properly regulated, yes?"

"What do you mean, regulated?" DeWaal asked pointedly.

"He means the Comey-Ross Artificial Intelligence Island bill," Harkness cut in. "It does indeed, Senator. We have security encryptions in place that meet or exceed the Reference Platform."

"Good, good..." McClusky mumbled. "Wouldn't want them taking over or anything."

Harkness smiled awkwardly, and changed the subject. "We're on our way to the Fab, Ama. Could you kindly show our guests the way?"

"Of course," she replied.

LEDs embedded in the floor lit up, displaying a subtly-pulsing chevron symbol pointing down the hallway. "This way, please." Amalthea said. McClusky chuckled, quite taken with the smoke and mirrors.

Harkness gestured for McClusky and Sorrel to walk ahead, guided by the voice of the facility.

/ / /

The guide chevrons were still visible outdoors, in direct sunlight, as the group exited the main building and down the concourse to the Fabrication Plant. 'The Fab' was a massive arched half-cylinder structure, tall enough to necessitate a blinking red aircraft warning light at its apex.

"This used to be an old Marine Corps Air Station Hangar – built to accommodate blimps in the last century," DeWaal explained. "We've updated and built Abundance up around it. Tallest building in the LA basin – from the top you can see clear across the entire city!"

Sorrel and McClusky craned their necks to look up. On the roof of the very old building sat a very new platform that hosted an array of industrial Yagi antennas and satellite dishes pointed at the sky. Their futuristic silhouettes melted and blended seamlessly into the curves of the hangar – the new built atop the old, like layers of history.

Noise level rose significantly as they entered the building. The arch structure reflected and amplified sound back onto the work floor – a landscape of semi-recognizable cylinders and things that would eventually become rocket booster stages. A series of glass-walled clean room enclosures were interspersed through the hangar, in which masked engineers did precision work on sensitive rocket parts.

DeWaal talked and gestured as they walked down the center concourse. Sorrel tried to pay attention, but his eyes kept getting drawn to the rear of the building. In the distance, towering over everything else, was a giant cylindrical structure, rising almost to the ceiling and silhouetted against the rear hangar windows. Sorrel could not seem to look away from it, and as a result missed most of Harkness's explanations about how the boosters were assembled.

Past the rocket booster production line, the work floor landscape shifted from heavy machinery to precision tooling. Rows upon rows of cubicle-size enclosures populated with CNC milling machines and 3D printers were all slowly and surely printing parts for the next mission.

The sound of the printers triggered DeWaal, and he went off on a tangent about how he once 3D printed a single-use rocket engine in college and jumped out of a plane wearing it. With parachutes, of course, for safety and stuff... "Broke three ribs on the landing," DeWaal laughed. "...but MAN what a rush! Holding your life in your own hands and trusting that you were smart enough to not die!"

Sorrel had fortunately managed to tune out most of DeWaal's hot air. They'd arrived at the end of the concourse and he was finally face to face with the giant cylinder – a Vacuum Thermal Chamber. It was something like ten stories high, with a massive circular airtight door. Through the black maw of the opening, Sorrel could see only darkness, interspersed with faint metal glints of antennae and baffles.

"We pack entire spacecraft sections into the chamber," Harkness explained, "to test and ensure that the structure will survive in the harsh environment of space. When in use, the chamber will reach a near vacuum and temperatures can drop to near zero Kelvin. You don't want to be inside when this thing is on..."

McClusky shuddered. "Freezing and suffocating in space... sounds like a terrible way to die."

"Actually, the vacuum of space will boil you alive before the cold kills you." DeWaal corrected him.

"Oh."

/ / /

The next stop on the tour was a short walk across the lawn from the Fab. As they followed the chevrons, the warmth of the afternoon sun added to Sorrel's gloom. Here he was at the pinnacle of space exploration technology, new possibilities and new tools for a new generation of space explorers. Tools he did not *dare* to dream of in his training days... tools he would never get to use.

The sliding doors opened automatically as they approached. "Welcome to the Astronaut Training Annex, gentlemen." Amalthea greeted them, her voice materializing from everywhere and nowhere. "This is where the crew of the *Frontier* trained and prepared for their mission."

McClusky gasped softly in amazement. Adorning the walls of the foyer were hundreds of photos of Carol and the *Frontier* crew at work – training, launching and walking on asteroids. Team photos and individual portraits celebrated milestones. They looked so *alive*, smiling and waving at the camera. DeWaal lingered at the photo wall for a moment – then turned and headed down the hallway.

The tour through the different sections of the Training Annex were a blur of experiences. Learning to tell the differences between different asteroid types in the Geology Lab (the chondrites, the stony and the metallics), going over the new spacesuits and their tool sets with Harkness, and trying out the Command Simulator, a to-scale version of the *Frontier* command bridge. Harkness loaded up the simulated landing sequence of Callum and invited Sorrel and McClusky to try it out.

The touch displays and the instrument panels were lit and fully functional. Sorrel sat down in the command chair, relishing the opportunity to captain the (albeit simulated) landing. Unfortunately, McClusky was his co-pilot and Harkness was crouching over them explaining the controls... it sapped any semblance of immersion that Sorrel had hoped for.

Sorrel and McClusky were still arguing as they continued down the hallway after their simulation drifted off into deep space, due to McClusky's inability to press buttons. Harkness chuckled quietly, stopped at the end of the corridor and opened the double doors. A wash of shimmering blue light spilled out from the other side, and the sight of it stopped Sorrel in his tracks. He fell silent, his argument forgotten.

"Last but not least," Harkness said. "The Training Pool. About the size of a gym swimming pool, but much deeper."

"Water buoyancy, as it turns out, is a good substitute for simulating zero-g environments," DeWaal continued. "The bottom of the pool is made to resemble an asteroid surface, and we use this to fine-tune some of the more complicated maneuvers in the mission."

Sorrel frowned and muttered to himself. With the door open, the humidity and smell of pool chlorine snuck up on Sorrel. It twisted his gut and sent a tinge of panic through him.

Harkness gestured for them to enter. McClusky stepped in unfettered, but Sorrel could not move his muscles. He grimaced. "I've already seen all this," he said.

"Suit yourself," DeWaal said, and entered. Harkness followed, and let the double doors close behind him. Sorrel stood alone in the corridor, fighting off demons.

7. Sorrel – R&D

Harkness led them out through the cafeteria, and across a red cobblestone courtyard. "Next stop – Research and Development."

Past the small fountain nestled in a grove of citrus trees, Sorrel's eyes followed the guide chevrons down the trail to their destination. He didn't quite know what he'd expected to see, but it was... something grander than a shed-like building the size of a two car garage.

"Kinda small, isn't it?" he asked.

Harkness tapped his noggin. "We do all our work up here... then we boss the Fab guys around and tell them what to build."

Sorrel gave Harkness the stink-eye.

As before, the doors opened automatically as they approached. Sorrel and McClusky entered a bare foyer, with a long escalator extending down into the bowels of the Earth. It was so long that the bottom seemed shrouded in darkness. "It's bigger on the inside," Harkness chuckled from behind them. "After you."

Motion-sensing lights powered on as the escalator transported them downwards. Each set of lights illuminated just a dozen or so steps ahead of them, and intuitively made the blackness below even darker and more foreboding. Sorrel tried to count the distance, but lost track somewhere around a hundred feet down. Finally, as the escalator leveled off, a series of overhead lights clicked on effortlessly, revealing the space in front of them.

Sorrel blinked in the sudden brightness of the lights. They were in what looked like a terminus – a private subway station. On the walls were posters celebrating Abundance's past achievements, intermingled with caution signs warning commuters to 'Stay behind the Yellow Line" and "Wait until the Pod has come to a complete stop".

The 'vehicle' sitting on the track didn't look like a regular subway car either. It was made out of anodized steel, and its shape reminded Sorrel of a UFO – halfway between a sphere and a bullet. The pod powered itself up with a low hum as they approached, and opened its gull wing doors with a faint hydraulic hiss. Its plush interior boasted ten seats arranged in pairs, and no controls that Sorrel could see.

The group piled into the Pod. Once everyone was seated, Harkness spoke. "We're ready."

"Please stay seated, everyone," Amalthea replied from hidden speakers. The wing doors closed and there was a slight jolt as the pod started moving.

"Your R&D is off-campus?" Sorrel asked.

Harkness nodded. "In case we screw something up and things get... explosive."

"It's a joke, Bob," DeWaal laughed when McClusky gave him a wide-eyed stare. "We ran out of space pretty quickly, so we bought a warehouse in the area... registered to a shell company. No signs on the door... totally incognito."

"But this–?" McClusky said, gesturing nervously at the pod.

"Oh, this," said Harkness. "Holy shit, we had to pull a million strings with the Planning Commission. But yes, it's all totally legal."

"And safe?"

"Of course, Senator."

It was pitch black now outside the Pod's windows, but periodically a light raced past. Aside from the hum of the engine, it was the only way to guess how fast they were moving. How far had they traveled? The intervals between lights seemed to get shorter and shorter. At this speed it was conceivable that they were already out of the downtown LA area.

About forty seconds later, Sorrel felt the shift in momentum, sensed that they were slowing down. The background hum reduced in pitch, and the streak of lights outside the window slowed. Light flooded the Pod as it exited the tunnel and into another terminus, sliding to a feather-smooth stop. The doors opened and Amalthea spoke. "End of the line, gentlemen."

"Where are we?" asked McClusky.

"The future," DeWaal answered.

/ / /

The elevator doors opened to reveal the interior of a large airy warehouse framed by red brick walls supporting a giant wooden bow truss ceiling. Chill electronic music hung in the air alongside the fragrance of freshly-ground espresso beans.

"The R&D lab..." Harkness said as they stepped out of the elevator. "For real this time."

Sorrel stopped for a moment to take it all in. The entire floor of the warehouse had been converted into an open plan tech wonderland – clever use of floor materials and furniture arrangements divided everything into smaller sections. Raised loft spaces lined the periphery of the brick walls unobtrusively, providing additional work spaces but keeping the center area clear and open. Windows on the roof allowed natural light to seep in, but the space was so enormous that plenty of supporting light fixtures were deployed throughout the warehouse. There was an indoor basketball hoop on one wall, and a kayak propped up next to it.

Just beyond the small sitting area next to the elevator was the kitchen. Designed to serve as the central gathering spot for the lab, it sported separate breakout tables for smaller team meetings. An intimidating coffee machine stood on the gleaming countertop, and a series of small vent-like openings lined the wall right above the countertop. "Food delivery from the kitchen," Harkness explained. "They can order anything they want from the cafeteria and it gets tubed over here within ten minutes."

Sorrel watched as a few employees milled around the fringes of the kitchen, sipping on lattes, chatting, and glancing nervously in their direction. They were fully aware, he assumed, of the reason that he was here... and how the outcome of the report might directly influence their employment.

"Seems like business as usual here," Sorrel mumbled.

"You mean, with the...?" Harkness sighed. "It *is* hard to concentrate, yes. Emotions are high... but everyone is doing their best. All this is for the next mission. We have to assume there will be a next mission."

"Of course there will be a next mission," DeWaal interrupted, adamant. "Did we stop trying to go to the moon after the Apollo One fire?"

"Of course not... after the review board concluded their investigation." McClusky replied.

DeWaal scowled at McClusky. His retort was on the tip of the tongue, but the buzzing of his phone interrupted him. He glanced at the message on the screen.

"I have to run. Have some *business* to attend to." DeWaal said, spitting the words out at McClusky. "Jon, you can show them around, ya?" He turned and disappeared back into the elevator.

From the kitchen, hallways branched out radially to the rest of the warehouse. Harkness led them through the different work areas, describing the works in progress. In one area engineers were working on safety and design improvements on adjustment thrusters, while the Materials Science team were working on next generation spacesuits in another.

The next area was roped off for safety. From a distance, Sorrel watched as a mechanized spider-like robot attempted to navigate a rock-infested test area. Its swiveling head swept around, looking at the terrain in front of it, before lifting its legs to avoid the larger potentially-disastrous rock outcrops.

Interest piqued, he asked, "Who's driving that thing?"

"No one. That mining robot will eventually operate autonomously. Surface operations on a celestial body is the single most dangerous thing for human beings to do. We can make things much safer if we delegate that work to bots."

McClusky looked confused. "How does that work?"

Harkness smiled, and led them to the adjoining work area. Lighting was much lower in this section, bordering on darkness. Through the gloom Sorrel made out the shadowy figures of engineers in augmented reality headsets gesturing with their hands. Ghostly music, faint and ethereal, surrounded them as they worked.

"These programmers are setting up the deepform network to train the mining bot."

"Sounds... ah... complicated."

"Just large modeling data for the AI to train on," Harkness said, as if everyone knew what that meant.

Sorrel watched as they worked – they looked like mimes trapped in a box. The music was lilting and buoyant now; it drifted with the tide, and seemed to seep into his consciousness. He cocked his head. "They always listen to music while they work?"

Harkness listened, and laughed. "Hah! No," he said. "That would be our head of R&D – Matteo Orchid."

/ / /

The music grew louder as they approached the thirty-foot-high frosted glass cubicle in the center of the warehouse. Every now and then Sorrel caught glimpses of movement within the cube. This, Harkness said, was Orchid's office.

In an industry where the term polymath was tossed around as easily as a Nerf ball, Harkness explained, Orchid was the genuine article. Not only was he an engineer and computer scientist, he was also a philosopher, an artist, author of two novels and an accomplished musician.

Orchid had grown up in Barcelona with zero formal training for the first fifteen years of his life, before heading to the United States where he somehow sweet-talked his way into the University of California in San Diego. There, he picked up a Bachelors in Math (with minors in music and philosophy), followed by a Masters in Mechanical Engineering, and then a Ph.D. in Aerospace Engineering – all before the age of twenty one. He then spent two years bicycling across Europe and the Middle East, culminating in a religious experience after sleeping on the alleged spot where Jesus was crucified. On his return to America he spent the next two decades working for a succession of startups, making countless CEOs rich before deciding he needed to do something substantial... to leave his legacy for the future, as it were. This was, as he had mentioned in countless news articles, his reason for joining Abundance.

The frosted glass cube had four glass doors on each side. Through them, Sorrel could make out a largish figure with his back to them, wearing a T-shirt featuring comic book drawings of anime characters. The figure was hunched over a transparent dodecahedron, rolling it over in his hands to inspect the different surfaces. The whale-song music in the air seemed to rise and fall as he moved his hands.

Harkness rapped on the door. The figure turned and looked, and a smile spread across his face, narrowing his eyes and accentuating his fuzzy mustachioed beard. He excitedly waved at them. "Come, come! Ándale!"

Harkness held the door so that Sorrel and McClusky could enter. The inside of the cube looked like the office of a tenured professor, subject not immediately discernible. The walls were lined with tribal art that included two large African masks and there were several bookshelves lined with an assortment of miniature crawler robots in various stages of completion. The man at the workbench stood up, leaving the dodecahedron apparently floating in midair.

"Dr. Orchid, I presume." McClusky smiled as he shook hands.

"Please... only my mother calls me that... and only when I get in trouble!" the portly man laughed. "Just call me Matteo."

The music shifted again as Matteo leaned back, and Sorrel realized the connection. He pointed to the contraption. "Is the music–?"

Matteo smiled, embarrassed. "Excuse the noise," he said. "It helps me think."

"It's – wonderful," Sorrel said. "Is it coming from that... music box?"

Matteo nodded, and gestured to the dodecahedron. The clear polycarbonate surfaces were framed with thin metal edges that pulsed with green and red LEDs, and some tubular devices floated inside in some sort of liquid solution. "It's a Telemetron," he said. "An electronic musical instrument that's designed to be performed in zero-g. I wanted to explore the poetics of off-planet music... to inject some art and culture into all that pesky rocket science that we do. The chimes inside have gyroscopes that detect collisions – my algorithm turns those collisions into sound. Like, well... this."

Matteo waved his hand to impart slight movement on the Telemetron. The chimes bumped against the inner surface, changing the flow of the musical notes.

"This is only a rough approximation of how it should work, obviously," Matteo explained apologetically. "The chimes are floating in gel and the whole thing is suspended by wires. It restricts movements and prevents me from playing it as it should be played."

McClusky stared at the device, baffled. "You built a musical instrument that can't be played on Earth?" he asked. "Why?"

Matteo just smiled. "Why indeed."

Harkness smiled. "See? We just wind him up and let him go. The man's a savant."

Matteo blushed, and bowed deeply. "The guys on my team are the real heroes... They build the things... I just write little bits of code here and there."

"He's being modest. Ask him about the MCRS," Harkness chuckled. "He loves explaining the MCRS on school tours."

/ / /

For someone of Matteo's size, he was incredibly light and fast on his feet. Sorrel and the group could hardly keep up as they followed Matteo down the corridor. He darted in between oncoming walking traffic like a featherweight, and slipped into a dark office with a bank of blinking server racks on the wall. He stopped in the corner of the room next to what looked like a file cabinet the size of a small refrigerator, and opened it up to reveal a tangle of lights, wires and undecipherable computer parts. Luckily for Sorrel, a handy label on the "file cabinet" indicated that this was the Mass Composition Reconstruction System, Mark 8.

"This is the MCRS," Matteo said, matter-of-factly. "Isn't she a beauty."

Sorrel nodded, as if he understood what that meant. "What does it do?" he asked.

"You know what lidar is, yes?"

"Radar, but with lasers or something..."

"Yes, most autonomous vehicles use lidar to let them see the world around them. We use it to create a three-dimensional representation of Callum, so that we can figure out where to fit our engine pods and navigational trackers. But lidar only describes the volume, not the mass. You follow?

"I think so." Sorrel said, clearly not following.

"It's like this," Matteo said, reading the truth in Sorrel's face. "A bowling ball and a basketball are roughly the same size, right? Same volume, but the bowling ball has a whole lot more mass. It takes more effort for you to lift a bowling ball than a basketball. If we're going to move something, it's necessary for us to know how much mass we have to move. We needed a way to determine the type of matter filling up our asteroid's volume.

"You mean, whether it's made up of bowling balls or basketballs..."

"Precisely," Orchid grinned, jabbing his finger on Sorrel's chest. "On Earth, we would simply put the bowling ball and the basketball on a set of scales. We'd then use our planet as a "gravity assist", to determine the weight, from which we can derive the mass. In space, things are a bit trickier. We don't have gravity and we obviously don't have a set of scales big enough to measure an asteroid fragment. So we make use of Newton's third law of motion. Which is?"

"...For every action there is an equal and opposite reaction...?" Sorrel said, annoyed. He didn't exactly like Matteo's constant prompts... it made him feel like he was in science class again. But he played along, because there was the sneaking suspicion that shit was about to get complicated, and he would need all the patronizing prompts he could get.

"If we apply a force to one side of the asteroid, we can expect the asteroid to react by moving the other way. How much it moves depends on what the mass of the asteroid is. Yes?"

"Yes."

"That is how the Mass Reconstruction System works. Our software starts by assuming a standard mass for a rocky asteroid – twenty-five percent metal composition, or about 5 grams per cubic centimeter. This is guaranteed to be incorrect, but that's okay. Once the software controller module fires the engines, it computes an expected positional change based on the current mass estimate. It also carries out a positional fix, to determine exactly where it is in space. The *difference* between estimated position and observed position is what gets passed to the triangulator. Still following?"

Sorrel nodded, but realized that he was starting to mentally swerve all over the road.

"We then do some simple math and fuzzy AI logic to refine and adjust our mass estimate for the asteroid. The new correctional thrust and vector values get issued to the engines, and the process is repeated until the difference between theoretical and observed values are close to zero. Each thrust and vector command thus becomes more and more accurate, and we eventually determine the actual mass of an object that has previously been impossible to accurately measure."

"That's... amazing," Sorrel said, after letting his thoughts catch up with the speed of Mattteo's brain. He was not a math nerd, but he appreciated a smart solution to any problem. He glanced at McClusky – the expressionless stare told Sorrel they'd lost the senator around the part with the lasers.

"But that's not all!" Matteo said, beaming with pride.

"The problem with this method of mass reconstruction is that even though we've determined the mass of our asteroid, that value is still just an average. That is, it assumes a constant mass density through the entirety of the asteroid. In truth, the density varies from one part to another... one section might be rocky, while another contains more metals or water ice.

"We have the same issue with traditional mining on Earth," Matteo continued, "whether it's coal, metals or diamonds – there is no clear idea of where these materials are. We know this area or that area is rich in iron... but we can't see inside the Earth. Strip mining has torn entire mountains down just to find the small pockets of valuables we're looking for."

"Imagine... if we could somehow build a map of where the mineral-heavy sections of the asteroids are... then we could simply focus our mining operations with more surgical and targeted efforts. Less cost, less danger, more return on investment."

Sorrel's eyes widened. "...I think I see what you're getting at."

Matteo smiled, pulled out a hidden keyboard and started speed-typing while talking. Undecipherable commands flew past the screen window.

"The math is crazy... took me months to work it out. It uses the timing delay in the navigational sensors and the secondary error values – the 0.0001 percent difference between theoretical and observed positions – to generate a three-dimensional map of the internal structure of the asteroid. Extremely computationally intensive... but we can just feed all the data into this beast of a machine, and let it cook. After a while we get *this*..."

Matteo clapped his hands and, like a magic trick, a holographic projector in the ceiling spat out a blurry rotating map of the asteroid, with different areas inside the asteroid lighting up in different colors – a heat map of elementals. Sorrel, McClusky and Harkness all leaned in to get a closer look at the projection.

The solution was brilliant. Thanks to Matteo, not only did the crew know how to move asteroids, they would also know exactly where to start digging. All without busting out a shovel. "This is real data?" Sorrel asked. "The actual composition of Callum?"

"It's in a rough state... the code needs refinement," Matteo replied. "But yes. We uploaded the results to *Frontier*, and the crew was going to confirm –"

Matteo stopped. His smile faltered and vanished, as if someone had popped his bubble. "I mean... it *was*. Up until the accident."

Silence hung in the air. Sorrel saw the look on Matteo's face – and finally saw the humanity of *Frontier*'s loss.

8. Jen – Homestead

Like a jumping spider falling out of the sky, the chopper swung around in a massive arc, criss-crossing several highways and main arteries as it bled off altitude on final approach to Abundance's helipad. Its four electric turbofans whined and changed pitch as they pivoted and flexed on armatures that supported the passenger pod.

Jen stared out the window, lost in her own storm of thoughts as the chopper descended. Happy memories. Hard memories. Things that were once, but not now. Things that only existed within a certain timeframe. Every soul lives and dies in its own time. The *impermanence* of life.

Why couldn't their timeframes have been more aligned? Why couldn't they have grown old together, or die young together? Who messed up the scheduling code? And why did it hurt so much inside when there was nothing physically broken? *Jesus fuck*, we are nowhere close to this with our AI.

The chopper landed on the helipad with feathersoft precision – Jen only became aware of it when the turbofans began to spin down and one of DeWaal's assistants opened the chopper door for her. Jen took a moment, snapped out of self-pity and into get-it-done, and composed herself. She grabbed her bulky travel backpack, stepped off the chopper and hurried out from under the rotor wash.

DeWaal was waiting by the helipad stairwell, his coiffured head freshly mussed from the turbofan vortices. The noise level on the roof made it hard to talk on the helipad, so he gave her an awkward hug and gestured towards the elevator.

As the elevator door closed, the sudden silence was like jumping into a frozen lake. DeWaal pressed a button and the elevator began descending. They stood and stared at the changing floor numbers for a moment.

"I'm sorry," DeWaal broke the silence. "I never know what to say in times like this."

There was a long pause. Jen knew it was a lie; DeWaal always knew what to say.

She looked into his eyes. "What happened?"

"There was an explosion. We lost the ship—"

"I've read the feeds, Ethan. How? Why...??" Jen half-forced the words out, trying her damndest to be civil. "...Did she suffer?"

DeWaal stammered. "I– I don't know. What you saw on the aether – that was the last bit of video before we lost the signal."

"The video..." Jen bit her lip. "I'm not sure if I can watch the video."

/ / /

DeWaal's office was a fishbowl of brutalist industrial design. All four walls were glass-paneled and the furnishings in the office seemed to be arranged more for functionality than aesthetics – De-Waal's desk in one corner, some large monitors hanging from the ceiling with varied data displays on them, and an executive seating area in the other corner. A couple of technical models of rocket parts sat on displays around the office, but they seemed more of a design afterthought than centerpieces.

As they exited the elevator, DeWaal led Jen into his office and gestured to the seating area. "Ama – privacy please." There was a soft *ding* in acknowledgment, and the glass walls frosted over in response.

Jen set her backpack down carefully in the corner, out of the way, and sat just as DeWaal's assistant hurried in with a tray of refreshments. "Have you eaten?" DeWaal asked.

"I'm not hungry."

"Juice then?"

"Sure."

DeWaal waited awkwardly as his assistant poured Jen a glass of orange juice and left. He paced around for a few more moments, a world-weary look on his face. Exhausted, he sat himself down across the coffee table, directly in front of Jen. He sighed.

Jen decided she wanted him to get to the point. "You must be exhausted." she said.

DeWaal pursed his lips. "I am..." he sighed again. "...but it's nothing compared to you, of course."

"Of course."

"The guys here... they've put their heart and soul into this mission, and they're suffering too." He cupped his face in his hands – the weight of the world on his shoulders. "The investment firms are going berserk... I'm just doing all I can to hold everything together."

DeWaal paused, for dramatic effect. Then his eyebrow twitched, as if he'd just come up with an idea.

"You know what – maybe you could make a statement to the press?" DeWaal said. "I mean I know you and Carol have always preferred to keep your private lives separate... but a word from you... might help calm the firestorm."

Aaaaand there was the pitch. It made her angry. DeWaal was like an open book – so easy to read. Years of working with De-Waal taught Jen that at some level, DeWaal must care, and care *deeply* about things and people... but his ambition – his *driving force* – was never not in control.

DeWaal shrugged, like a lost puppy. "...In Carol's memory."

Jen sipped her juice, to give herself time to calm down. "Of course," she said. "In Carol's memory."

DeWaal nodded softly, and considered the words. "I'll have Janice set up a press conference for tomorrow morning." He gave it a few more dramatic moments before getting up and stepping back over to his desk. "You must be tired. I'll have the limo take you home."

"Ama – will you show Jen to the ZX please?"

The soft female voice chirped from out of thin air. "With pleasure."

/ / /

The trip back to the house was a bit of a daze. There were so many thoughts and emotions running amok in Jen's mind that she couldn't process them all; it was like parts of her life ran at double speed while others slowed to a standstill. She remembered following the chevrons to the carport; vaguely recalled getting into the limo with her backpack; remembered looking out through double mirrored windows to see the faces of the protesters at the front gate as she left.

She remembered touching behind her ear, to make sure the interface port was still working. She'd tapped it to connect to the in-car tablet terminal and logged in to check on Amalthea.

The changelogs scrolled across the tablet screen as giant blocks of almost-indecipherable text. Jen glanced through them and smiled. All the new things they'd given her since she'd left... updated voice modules, autonomous workflow upgrades, inference systems... it was like leaving for college and returning home to find your baby sister had grown up while you were gone.

She remembered wondering if she could augment Amalthea with some of BC's functions. It was probably impossible... the neural structures were completely different and factorially more complex. BC represented ten years worth of incremental improvements, cumulative research and development and a whole new computational approach. Amalthea – she was developed as a facility management system; a narrow focus AI tool with a predefined set of skills. No matter how much you added to Amalthea's root code, you could never change its core functionality. Couldn't make it grow.

It was this, she realized, that eventually led to the development of Brain Child – the first steps into general machine intelligence.

"We are approaching your house," Amalthea interrupted. "Please note there is a large contingent of journalists and press vehicles parked on your street."

"Noted." Jen replied. She keyed a couple of commands on the tablet, then packed it away and grabbed her backpack.

/ / /

The ZX5 was not exactly a low-key vehicle. Painted metallic yellow (DeWaal's favorite color), it sported distinctive swept-back lines that emanated from its trademark slit-like headlamps. This particular limo hummed with a simulated engine noise that made it sound like a starship; it was designed to turn heads, after all.

As the limo turned onto the street, the journalists and vloggers leapt to their feet and ran over, surrounding the car as it slowly pulled up to the house. The mirrored windows echoed the frenzy of the journo-razzi, with every camera flash reflected back in their faces, amplifying the excitement. The more impatient ones rapped on the window, hoping for a glimpse of the wife of a dead astronaut.

Jen watched all this from around the street corner, out of sight of the masses. With the press sufficiently distracted, she slung the backpack onto her shoulder and made her way down the back alley. Luckily the journalists were too dazzled to realize that not having a driveway in the front of the house meant that the garage was in the back...

Jen tapped behind her ear and whispered "garage open". A couple more steps down the alley, she slipped in through the open garage and out the side door, onto the back porch. The back door unlocked as she approached, and she entered the house undetected.

Out in the front, the ZX5 loitered for a little bit longer, then revved its starship engines and beeped a couple of warning beeps. It then slowly rolled forward and drove off down the road, accompanied by the frustrated groans of news-starved journos.

/ / /

As the sun set over Playa Vista, the evening shadows stretched across the back yard before giving way to twilight. Jen could still hear the occasional muffled noises of the press still camped outside the front door, but there were fewer and farther in between now – most had left the scene empty-handed, and only the hardcore paparazzi remained. Finally, in the quiet of the sanctum, Jen was able to process her own thoughts.

The house that Jen and Carol built had not changed since Jen left for Baja. There was no Carol here; she had been out in space for the past year and a half. Still, an emptiness lingered in the air that wasn't here before.

Carol – she had always taken the lead. She was the talk-to-everybody-even-if-you-just-met-them type, with charm and charisma to match. Always on the go, always in the clouds. Maybe that was why they were so compatible... Jen's passion and work were all focused inwards, on the mindscapes of the human soul. Carol of the outer spaces, Jen of the innerverse. Yin and Yang.

All of that ended yesterday. As soon as the world heard the news, her phone had been inundated with messages from concerned friends and colleagues, requests for interviews and uncountable app notifications – none of which she had replied to. The only thing that was worth looking at on her phone was the messaging inbox, where all the old texts from Carol sat. "Good morning babe," the last one read.

There in the hallway – framed pictures on the wall. Carol at graduation, Carol the fighter pilot, Carol sunning on North Beach, Carol at Abundance in that damn astronaut suit. There were several of Jen and Carol, but the ratio was always skewed because Jen preferred to be behind the camera. To be the wind beneath Carol's wings.

A dread calm had settled over the house. Jen stopped for a moment, almost in tears. But self-preservation always kicked in, and Jen did what she'd always done when she missed Carol. She threw herself into her work.

She hauled the backpack up off the floor, placed it square on the dinner table, unzipped it and extracted a large orange box – BC 87-54. With a few quick flicks of the wrist, she connected it to the data and power ports embedded inconspicuously into the center of the dinner table, pulled out her phone and used it to initiate the bootup process.

"Hello, BC."

"Good evening, ma. Running startup calibration and diagnostics... Done. What are we doing today?"

Jen sat down, all alone in the living room, logged on to the aether, and opened up Carol's last video broadcast. "Emotional support." she replied.

9. Sorrel – Timeline

The first day of interviews did not start out with a bang. Due to a scheduling snafu the conference room they had been promised hadn't materialized, and Sorrel was shown instead to the Visitor's Gallery – a narrow room with theater seating and floor-to-ceiling windows overlooking Mission Control. Sorrel had hoped Mc-Clusky would be around for the interviews, but to his annoyance the Senator had "some handshaking to attend to", and left for the day almost immediately.

This left Sorrel sitting alone in the gallery, staring out the window at the now most-empty Mission Control and doodling occasionally in his notebook. It was a bad habit that occasionally made it hard for him to discern his own notes, but he was anachronistically opposed to change. Taking notes on a phone or tablet just felt too clean and modern... and you couldn't doodle if you were doing that.

Shortly after ten o'clock, Flight Director Samantha Harper and Senior Flight Director Hank Adebayo were shown in. Harper was in her early thirties, an aerospace engineering grad from Purdue University who had previously run NASA's Neutral Buoyancy Laboratory. Adebayo was older, an African-American man in his mid-fifties with a calming demeanor. Like Harper, he was ex-NASA and had spent twenty years as a flight director – a job that put them in charge of coordinating an enormous team of flight controllers, support personnel and engineers to execute and manage space missions. Both were clearly passionate about their jobs, and passionately believed in DeWaal's mission to change the world.

Sorrel took out a small audio recording puck and placed it on the room's only table. "For the record," he said.

Sorrel got Harper and Adebayo to talk through their decision-making process throughout the *Frontier* mission. Nothing had been out of the ordinary, they agreed. They were following the mission playbook, the branching decisions that could be taken at every point during a mission. Everything had happened as planned. Everything, that was, until the accident.

At 6am, two hours and twenty seven minutes before the fracture incident, Harper had relinquished Mission Command to Adebayo for the day shift. Abundance's command structure rotated a total of five flight directors through each eight-hour shift, ensuring that the Frontier had mission support at all times.

"So you left?" Sorrel said to Harper.

"No, I stayed," she said.

"You'd been working all night. Didn't you want to go home and get some sleep?"

"Ordinarily, yes. But the crew was about to execute an adjustment burn. I wanted to be there for moral support."

"Was the burn a big deal?"

"We do adjustment burns regularly... it's not a big deal but it's an 'event'. Significant enough that the media usually sends a couple of junior journalists here to cover the beat." Harper gestured to the empty seats by the window. "They were sitting right there..."

"So you threw the car keys to Hank and jumped in the passenger seat –"

Adebayo smiled. "Yes, but it's not that simple. Protocol dictates that there is an hour of overlap time set aside for the incoming shift to get up to speed on the current state of the mission. So between 5 and 6 am, all the outgoing controllers sit with their shift change replacement to update them on relevant and important items with regards to their station. The shift change ripples up the chain of command, from the Trench all the way up to the Flight Director, over the course of the hour. I was actually on shift at 5:30AM, getting briefed on mission status."

"What kind of information gets passed along at these – shift changes?"

"Usually normal operational details – task updates, that sort of stuff."

"Anything of note?"

Harper reflected for a moment. "Mostly just checked off a number of tasks that needed to be completed before the burn. Some minor issues, nothing significant."

"Everything can be significant, Miss Harper."

Harper frowned, pulled up her tablet to check her notes. "There was a secondary flex hose in Engine Seven that was reporting low pressure. A power cell failure in the main cabin that had taken some minor research systems offline. And some routine maintenance issues, but these were considered low-risk and not mission-critical."

"Those are on the status logs," Sorrel replied. "I think I already have those."

"You should, yes."

Sorrel checked his phone for the logs, scrolling down the timeline to get to the relevant parts. "There's a couple of down-linked transmissions here from the Frontier."

"Yes – non-critical data gets packaged and sent every six hours."

"Let's see. Observation logs for solar wind collectors... Astronavigation measurements for MCRS... and several personal voice messages. Three from Mission Specialist Williams, one from Mission Specialist Havita to his family, and one video message from Commander Mathers to her wife. All listed as undelivered."

Adebayo nodded. "Protocol requires that they remain sealed until the investigation is concluded."

Sorrel gave a grunt and nodded. "Let's skip ahead to the time of the incident." Sorrel said, reading the log entry off his phone. "8:01AM. Whose time is that?"

Adebayo stopped for a moment. "I don't follow," he said.

"The delay. *Frontier* is tens of millions of miles away, yes?"

"Ah, yes," Adebayo replied. "37 million miles from Earth, which meant the radio delay was about three and a half minutes. Transmitting a message and receiving a reply would take seven minutes, assuming an immediate response. All the times noted on the log are Los Angeles local time."

"That means everything that happened on Callum occurred three-and-a-half minutes in the past?"

"Correct."

"8:01AM – Control acknowledged receipt of *Frontier*'s adjustment burn checklist, vetted them against telemetry and verified them complete. Senior Flight Director Hank Adebayo – that's you – sent a voice message to Frontier indicating all clear for the adjustment burn."

"Yes."

"At 8:09AM, Control received voice acknowledgment from Carol," Sorrel continued. "At 8:12, telemetry indicated that *Frontier* had begun its adjustment burn. That burn terminated four minutes later at 8:16."

Adebayo shook his head. "The adjustment burn was supposed to last for eight minutes. I sent a short voice message to *Frontier* requesting an update and explanation for the early termination."

"Did you get your explanation?" he asked.

Adebayo's voice was tightening up now. Sorrel noted the slight puffiness around his eyes, as if he'd been crying off and on the last couple of days. "At 8:21, Control received a voice notification from Mission Specialist Williams indicating that Commander Mathers and First Officer Magdalena were preparing for egress. Two minutes later, Control began receiving a video stream from Commander Mathers.

"It was up on the main screen," Harper said. "We didn't think... it was..."

Harper stopped herself. Sorrel prodded. "Didn't think it was...?"

A tinge of emotion crossed Harper's face. She pointed again to the empty seats. "Those... *animals*... they pulled out their phones... and started live-streaming."

The room fell silent for a bit. Adebayo broke the silence. "You've seen the video?"

Sorrel stared back. "Yes."

Adebayo nodded, a look of *fait accompli* on his face. He continued stoically. "At 8.24, Commander Mather's helmet camera detected what we believe was an explosion over the horizon."

"How sure are you?"

"The footage is... shaky. But it's the best we have," said Adebayo. "It got worse when the high gain antenna signal began to warble."

"Warble?"

"Dropping in and out. The *Frontier* has a 4-meter wide High Gain Antenna that's always pointed precisely at Earth, to allow for high speed transmission of data – but it's extremely directionally sensitive. Any shake or vibration of the antenna would cause it to lose its focus, resulting in data dropouts. When it fails, the comm signals would automatically fall back onto the Low Gain Antenna – wider beam, more resilient to shake but much lower data throughput."

Sorrel nodded, looking at his notes. "This is the reason for the next log entry then? 8:25 – intermittent radio contact, live stream footage garbled off and on."

Adebayo nodded, reciting the next line as if he'd memorized it. "Commander Mathers reported casualties and structural failure of the Frontier."

"And then?"

There was silence in the room. Both Adebayo and Harper had gone pale, reliving the moment. "Radio static and full telemetry loss," Adebayo finally said, suddenly sounding very old.

Harper let out a loud whimper, caught herself, and spent a few moments regaining her composure.

"I... can't believe they're gone. We knew them all so well. We went on pub crawls together..." Harper said, forcing the words out. "Carol... she took me under her wing. Mentored me. I am the person I am today because of Carol."

Adebayo just stared at the floor and said nothing.

10. Jen – Prep

The sunrise was muted and colorless. It lit up the tip of The Fab first, and slowly made its way down the curve of the building, fading in and out through a rolling overcast sky. When the sun finally peeked over the fence into the cafeteria, there was no warmth in its presence. Jen found herself staring directly into the diffused orb without flinching.

She had been here since the crack of dawn; the ZX5 picked her up down the street where she'd originally disembarked, and brought her back to Abundance. Sunrise found her sitting in the cafeteria, absentmindedly poking at breakfast while Janice's PR crew were busy setting up the theater for her press statement.

There were bags under her eyes. She had been up all night beating herself up over the video. Carol's death, online for all to see, but none so intimately affected by it as her. She freeze-framed it, of course. There at the end of the video, perfectly focused for a split second, was the reflection of Carol. Blocky pixels from the past, staring back at her from across the void. A hundred million thoughts had run through her head in the eternity she spent staring at the screen. How did it come to this? A catastrophic failure of protocol? Poor safety procedures... imperfect planning... a runtime error in the machine code of life.

Footsteps behind her interrupted her train of thought. She snapped out of it just as Janice's assistant stepped up to her. "Miss Mathers?" the assistant asked timidly. "We're ready for you."

Jen nodded and followed her back into the theater.

On the small stage, the crew had constructed a bubble of lighted perfection, within which lay elements designed to help frame and subtly influence the audience. It would be a story of love and loss, against the backdrop of bravery and space exploration. Surrounded by sandbags, lights and C-stands, a large intimidating camera pointed at the bubble. A slender, almost fragile-looking cable snaked out of the camera and into the data port on the wall – the fiber-band connection to the world.

Janice stepped over and greeted Jen with a big hug. "Child... you look terrible." she said, compassion overflowing from her eyes. "I'm so sorry. She meant a lot to everyone."

"Thanks, Janice."

Janice lifted Jen's chin with her finger, stared deeply. "We can use that." she mumbled.

With a snap of her other finger, Janice called the makeup artist over. "Don't cover that up too much," Janice said, pointing at Jen's face. "We want sad and relatable, but not too obviously so. Okay?" The makeup artist nodded.

"Do you know what you're going to say?" Janice asked.

"I think so."

"Good," Janice nodded absentmindedly, and disappeared back into the media circus, shouting at the cameraman.

11. Sorrel – Interviews

Hammurabi was the nicely appointed medium-size conference room near the reception hall at Abundance. The walls carried the usual whiteboards and flatscreens, but the main feature of the room was the circular conference table with the holographic projection system that allowed for visualization of 3D data. Sorrel fiddled with the controls, projecting various screensaver demos into the air as he sipped his no-cost macchiato from the cafeteria barista.

McClusky finally stumbled into the room, late and wearing a grim face. "I just got my ass handed to me." he growled. "We need to wrap this up *quick*."

"Quick how?"

McClusky turned to glare at Sorrel. "Finish interviews today. Report tomorrow morning."

Sorrel balked. "Tomorrow...??"

"I don't need a novel, Chuck!" McClusky yelled. "Just an enema for the President." He turned and glared at Sorrel, face dripping with contempt.

/ / /

The "CEO Interview" was short and brief. DeWaal arrived late for the meeting, tailed by his assistant. He sat down and attempted to answer Sorrel's questions, but they kept getting interrupted by his assistant shoving the tablet in his face every few minutes. Apparently there were more important matters that needed his attention than a report for the President of the United States.

"Ah – guys..." DeWaal said apologetically. "I'm going to have to run in a few minutes. Shareholders meeting..."

"Of course you do," Sorrel replied.

"Besides, I'm just the facilitator," DeWaal shrugged. "I point the way... my guys are the ones drawing up the map."

"Your guys... you trust them?"

DeWaal's eyes narrowed. "What are you suggesting?"

"It's just a question."

DeWaal harumphed. "I would jump into anything they built and fly into space with it, if that clarifies your point."

Sorrel nodded. "You have a reputation for pushing your team."

"That's what *leaders* are supposed to do! We wouldn't be where we are today if I didn't push my team." DeWaal replied defiantly. He fired a what-the-fuck look at McClusky. "Look. I don't know what happened. I wish I did. This was my baby. Everyone on board was family. Me and my team – we cared about this project more than you could ever understand."

"Relax, Ethan..." McClusky replied. "It's not an inquisition."

"Thanks for kicking a man while he's down."

"I think what Mr. Sorrel is trying to ascertain is whether anything was left – unchecked. Which might have led to unforeseen circumstances."

DeWaal threw a confused look. "Unforeseen circumstances being...?"

"Accidents happen, Ethan." McClusky replied.

Sorrel caught DeWaal's stare. There was no love lost between them. "I have to go," DeWaal finally said.

McClusky nodded. "Thanks, Ethan."

/ / /

There were fifteen minutes to kill before Matteo's scheduled interview time. McClusky spent the time twiddling his fingers answering emails on the phone, frowning and grumbling every so often while Sorrel finished up the rest of the macchiato and pastries. He'd discovered while snacking that he could screencast his phone to the holographic projector, so when he was finished he pulled up Carol's broadcast video from the aether and threw it up onto the projector.

The view materialized as a flat window in the middle of the room, glowy and ethereal. He watched from Carol's point of view as she looked around a chamber of some sort. An airlock? The camera looked up, to see Pablo staring into the camera. Then – movement, lots of it, as the camera shook and blurred before it settled down to show an image of the underbelly of the ship.

"Abundance Control, *Frontier* on broadcast. Request immediate response," Carol's voice was thin and crackly. "I have initiated a burn abort. We have a redline issue. Pablo and I are en route to address it."

Sorrel let the broadcast play, and watched as Carol stepped out from under the ship. Then a flash of white... followed by several minutes of destruction, violent camera moves, yelling and compression dropouts. Sorrel gritted his teeth; it affected him emotionally more than he thought it would. Even McClusky had stopped working on his emails and was watching the video out of the corner of his eye.

After a long while, the footage finally stabilized... Carol was in some sort of control cabin. Her voice was cracking and every word from her felt like a struggle to maintain self-control. "Abundance Control, transmitting in the blind... Repeat, transmitting in the blind."

"Lost Pablo, lost the ship. Param and Walt... I-I don't think they made it..."

Carol moved to look out the pod window. The video stopped here, frozen on the frame of Carol's reflection in the window. A flat projection hanging like a ghost in the air, looking back at Sorrel, shimmering with dust particles in the air.

It was only after the video had stopped and silence filled the room that Sorrel became aware of someone behind him. Matteo had entered sometime during the video, and stood staring at the video, his face pale-white.

"I am sorry," Matteo said. "I felt it would be rude to interrupt."

"No apologies needed," Sorrel replied, and bade him sit. "I can't really tell what's happening from the video anyway."

Matteo walked to the chair, tap-tapped the keyboard and scrubbed Carol's video back to the beginning. "This might help you visualize it better," he said. "My guys have been up all night running the reconstruction sequence. It's a first pass, very crude and missing a lot of details, but it gives us a good starting point to assess... the loss of the *Frontier*." Matteo took a deep breath, and started the playback.

Sorrel was shocked and surprised. Before his very eyes, the two-dimensional camera footage expanded – *extruded* itself into 3D space. There in front of him now, in holographic glory, was the entire scene. The Frontier, outlined in wireframe, sat atop a rolling gray geometry plane, which Sorrel assumed was the asteroid surface. Off in the corner was a wireframe rover, and next to it, the airlock ladder. The ladder had a blue wireframe figure on it, labeled 'Pablo'. From a floating helmet icon next to Pablo came a frustum projection of the video. It turned everything in its cone of view from simple wireframe into shaded textures.

Matteo described the process: "Machine vision helps us triangulate the view from Carol's helmet camera, and based on 'known information' that we have – the size of the *Frontier* and the height of the ladder, for instance – we are able to reconstruct where everything was in relation to each other in the moment the video frame was captured."

Matteo pressed play. Everything started to move, tracked to the footage. Sorrel watched from a bird's eye perspective now, as Carol's helmet view traversed the underside of the ship. "Since a video is basically a sequence of images, we can track and recreate the event as it happened. Unfortunately this only applies to things that the camera can see, of course," Matteo pointed, and Sorrel noticed that as things fell outside of the camera view, they froze in place like a malfunctioning video game.

Matteo scrubbed forward. "This part here, at 08:24:03... is basically where things started to go wrong."

Sorrel watched, raptured, as the flash consumed the entire image before fading away. The gray ground plane, which up until now had been a static unmoving shape, began to blur and warp. The wireframes for everything started to shake and jiggle like the projector was on acid... If it was near impossible to make out what was happening from the footage alone, and the frustum projection added to that confusion ten-fold.

"I can't make anything out," McClusky complained.

"There's not enough clarity for the tracker to lock on to at this point..."

Sorrel pointed to the edge of the projection. "I suppose it's safe to assume that the explosion is the cause of the incident."

Matteo was quiet. "It would seem that way."

Sorrel fumbled with the controls and waved his hands to scrub the timeline back and forth, watching it over and over again in an attempt to glean any additional detail from it. Each time the screen glowed white, Matteo flinched.

"What do you have over there that can... catastrophically explode like this?"

"Based on the extrapolated angle of the explosion..." Matteo replied quietly. "Engine 7 is in that direction, over the horizon."

/ / /

McClusky's phone beeped again, as it had been doing all morning during the interviews. Sorrel had put up with it for hours and he was damn tired of it. It was lunchtime and they were headed towards the cafeteria; he was hangry, and the phone just put him over the top.

"You know you can silence those things, Bob." Sorrel snarked.

"A Senator is always ready to put out fires, Chuck." McClusky retorted, looking at his phone. He stopped in mid-stride and cursed. "Ah fuck."

"Fire?" Sorrel chided him.

"I have to go." McClusky announced, an annoyed look on his face. "Couple more interviews this afternoon... Can you handle it?"

"I don't know, can I?"

McClusky wagged his finger at Sorrel. "Don't fuck this up, Chuck. Simple, straightforward technical review of the accident. By tomorrow morning. Got it?"

"Yes, SIR," Sorrel replied, mock-saluting McClusky.

The Senator turned and walked hurriedly down the hall.

Sorrel watched him disappear around the corner, then turned and continued into the cafeteria. He half-expected a long line, but it was almost empty. There were scores of employees walking down the hallway towards him, but instead of turning towards the cafeteria, they went the opposite direction, into the theater.

His stomach growled in protest, but there was some sort of... energy in the air. Hope? Excitement? Sorrel's curiosity got the better of him – he decided a few more minutes of suffering could be tolerated, and followed the crowd.

Sorrel stepped into the theater, to find it standing-room-only. Every employee in the theater had their eyes glued to the stage where, in front of lights and cameras, an impeccably dressed woman stood tall and carried the weight of the world.

12. Jen – Mountain Mover

It seemed like the entire universe had collapsed in on itself. The lights were way too bright; in the real world nobody would ever have lights pointed at their faces like that. They were so bright Jen kept flinching uncomfortably, forced to squint even though Janice had told her fifty million times not to. The makeup on her face felt like it was being baked on more than it already was. And the lipstick... ugh.

Up there on the small stage, a shining star in the dark theater, all she could see beyond the bright lights were the moving blinking reflections of a thousand eyes on her. Her thoughts were fractured, she couldn't even tell what she was feeling anymore. There was so much sensory input and not enough experience to properly manage that overload.

Power through it, Jen.

She stared at the camera. The lens stared back, the curve of it reflecting a distorted version back at her. The wireless earpiece spoke to her in Janice's voice: "You're on."

Deep breath.

"Carol always had her head in the clouds... We met in Aviano; she pointed out all the star constellations to me, and ex- plained stuff about the night sky that I did not know I needed to know. Before Abundance, she flew jets because it was the closest she could get to space. Now she is there, among the stars... where she belongs."

"Carol Mathers was always a risk taker... a mountain mover. A pioneer. And the love of my life. What she and her crew attempted to do on the Frontier mission was to push the boundaries of space... to open up new worlds for the rest of us. This accident... shouldn't mean that we stop. Rather, it means that we should continue pushing, harder and stronger... to honor those who have laid down their lives for it."

"I am... humbled by the outpouring and love and support that you have shown us, and shown me. And I am so very proud to have been able to share my life, ever so briefly, with a shooting star. From the bottom of my heart – and, I am sure, from Carol's as well – thank you for caring."

/ / /

The silence of the packed theater hung in the air for the longest minute. Some were openly weeping in the audience and there wasn't a dry eye in the whole place. The camera operator fought back emotions as Jen took a deep breath and walked off the stage in a daze.

DeWaal was just behind the stage, watching on a monitor as Jen stepped out of the spotlight. The broadcast was time-delayed, so Jen watched herself awkwardly speaking on camera. "...and I am sure, from Carol's as well – thank you for caring," she heard herself say. It sounded so distant, so ethereal. And she looked terrible on camera. Pallid and ghostly; a shell of a person.

DeWaal turned and embraced her tightly. "Thank you," he said. "You were magnificent. Carol would be proud."

She did not hug back. She did not doubt DeWaal's gratitude, but none of this felt like a win. It wasn't that she cared enough about DeWaal, or Abundance; no amount of public sentiment would make a difference to what had already happened. It was about Carol, and about what would follow. About making sure that everything Carol had spent her life doing wasn't torn down and for naught.

An assistant had handed DeWaal a tablet, presumably with the first public reactions from the aether to Jen's address. DeWaal scrolled through the articles, his face brightening.

"This is amazing. People love you, Jen." He turned to her, his face sincere. "You're family here. Please let me know if there is ever anything that you need."

"There is, actually," Jen said.

"Anything. Just ask."

"I watched Carol die last night."

DeWaal's face dropped.

"I... I need the rest of the videos," she said.

DeWaal stared at her, confused. "What other videos? Everything that you saw online... that's all we have. *The bastards... released everything.*"

"That's what they streamed..." Jen said. "But you have secondary camera feeds. Ship cameras, airlock cameras, external relay cameras... I want to see it."

"I – I don't even know where–"

"Please, Ethan," she said, hating how vulnerable her voice suddenly sounded. "This is all I have."

"What good will that do you?"

She looked down. "I just need to know," she said.

DeWaal sighed. "I'll get it for you, Jen," he said. "But it might take some time. The oversight subcommittee... it's all locked down while they investigate."

"Bullshit," Jen said. "They don't have the authority."

DeWaal shrugged. "What can I do? It's the damn government." He pointed to a figure across the stage – some brutish guy was arguing with Janice, who was vigorously shaking her head.

"That guy..." said DeWaal. "He's part of the problem."

The man looked up past Janice, saw DeWaal and locked eyes with Jen for a moment. Tall but slouched, tousled hair and square-jawed – he looked like he'd stepped over from the wrong side of the tracks. Like one of those people who peaked in high school and spent the rest of their lives telling stories about their exploits. It didn't surprise her that he worked for the Feds – thugs, all of them.

Before she realized it, the man had skipped past Janice, and with several large steps, was almost upon them. "DeWaal!" he yelled.

Janice trailed him, apologizing profusely. "I'm so sorry, Mr. DeWaal" she said. "This man wants to speak with Jen. I told him–"

"She's not a company employee," said DeWaal, moving to stand between Sorrel and Jen.

The man ignored DeWaal's presence and spoke over his shoulder to Jen. "Ms. Mathers – Charles Sorrel. I'm heading up the preliminary investigation into the accident. I just caught your presentation. I'd very much like to ask a few questions."

Jen eyed the man with disdain. *Presentation?*

He extended his hand for a handshake. Jen did not respond, and left him hanging for a few seconds before he rescinded the offer. But he did not go away.

"I don't really have anything to add," Jen said. "You'd be wasting your time."

"Just a few questions, ma'am," he said, and waited. When he did not get the response he wanted, he turned to DeWaal. "Do I need to make this official?"

DeWaal rolled his eyes and frowned. He turned slowly to Jen. "Would you mind, Jen?" he asked. "I'll see if I can get you what you want in the meantime."

Jen looked from DeWaal to Sorrel, then back to DeWaal. A dozen conflicting emotions ran through her – and the loudest of them all was betrayal.

13. Sorrel – The Astronaut's Wife

Sorrel sat opposite Carol Mather's wife in a corner of the Abundance cafeteria, with the midday California sun streaming in through the enormous glass windows, trying to figure out why the hell he had insisted on speaking to her. He had acted on instinct... his gut told him she might have some important piece of information. Or maybe he just needed to add some color to what was otherwise going to be a dry technical report that no one in the Senate Subcommittee was going to understand. Instead, it seemed like he had just managed to find ways to piss her off.

He looked down at the plate of stir-fried shrimp the cafeteria was serving. Made out of the finest bio-engineered red algae, it looked great but tasted like... algae. It was only marginally more appealing than forcing an interview on a recently widowed woman. Jennifer Mathers was maybe five to ten years younger than he, and smart in a serious kind of way. Sorrel noticed that she had removed all her TV makeup after stopping by the restroom, and she was now tapping away at her phone on some long text message or other. Finally she finished and placed the phone face-down on the table.

Sorrel pulled out the audio recording puck and put it between them. "You're sure you don't want any lunch?" he said.

"I don't," Jen said.

Sorrel coughed awkwardly, gagging down the algae. How hard was it to buy proper shrimp, he thought. He scanned his hastily assembled notes.

"Let's start with your name," he said. "You are Jennifer Mathers?"

"Yes," Jen said.

"Maiden name Sudeikas?"

"Yes."

"Married to Carol Mathers for… ten years?"

"Eleven," Jen said.

"How did you two meet?"

"Is this relevant?" Jen questioned.

"We can come back to it. How would you categorize your relationship with the decea– with Carol?"

"How do you mean?"

"Did you... I don't know... any marital problems? Did you fight a lot?"

Jen glared at Sorrel. The ferocity of her expression caught him off-guard, made him realize that she was not the soft meek person he saw onstage.

"Why do you care?" Jen spat the words. "What does it matter who Carol – *was*??"

Sorrel felt the burning sensation on the back of his neck – that feeling of failure. Failure in choice of words, failure to control the situation. It was like letting go of an object to get a better grip, and somehow ending up losing it altogether. He swallowed, and tried to collect himself.

"I'm just – trying to get a better psychological profile of Carol and the crew." he said.

"You're looking for a scapegoat," she pointed a damning finger at him.

"What?" was all Sorrel could say in reply.

"Going to manufacture evidence too?"

"Listen," said Sorrel. "This is a preliminary report. It's not my job to assign any blame."

They stared at each other, like bull and bullfighter sizing each other up. Sorrel half-expected Jen to storm out of the cafeteria at any moment – but then realized that his expectations of her actions were probably incorrect, given his inability to judge her character.

The tension was momentarily broken by the *ding* of her phone. She flipped it over and read a message, then snapped her attention back to him like a predator that wouldn't let its prey out of its sight.

"...But you will eventually, right?" she baited him.

Now it was Sorrel's turn to be pissed off. The nerve of this woman... he paused, enunciated his words carefully. "Look... I know this is a difficult time for you."

"You don't know anything about me," said Jen.

"You don't know anything about me either," Sorrel countered.

Jen picked up the phone and flipped it around to show Sorrel the screen. On it, in chronological order, was a summary of Sorrel's career; detailed records that dated all the way back to his astronaut training days. Some of it he had never even seen before, but they were surely genuine. She wasn't typing a message earlier, it seemed; she was *running a background check.*

"It says here you were washed out. Discharged." Jen said, reading off the phone. "After that you disappeared off the aether for a while. Resurfaced in the UK, then to Roscosmos, and China. You've tried your hand at plenty of things too... Lobbyist. Researcher. Salesman, for a while. One daughter, but no mention of a marriage."

Sorrel felt the rage well up inside him. He blurted out a stunted response. "Those records are –"

"– available to anyone who knows how to get to them." Jen finished his sentence. "You, Mr. Sorrel, are an info merc for anyone with money. And not a particularly good one."

Jen leaned forward, speaking deliberately and addressing the audio puck more than Sorrel. "I will tell you this," she said. "Carol and the crew of the *Frontier* were the smartest, best people I've had the fortune of knowing. And I know a lot of smart people. If you're looking for someone to blame, look someplace else. I'm not going to let you sully the memory of my wife for some dirty dossier that no one with a decent reputation in politics wants to put their name to."

Sorrel watched, stunned and speechless, as Jen stood up and walked away.

He stared down at the puck, its green LED light blinking judgmentally. Sorrel was momentarily tempted to delete it, to hurl the damn thing against the wall so that it shattered into a hundred pieces. Instead, he settled for pushing away his plate of "shrimp."

What a colossal fuckup, he thought.

14. Sorrel – Hard Space

"This is Engine Seven," Harkness said proudly. "Third-generation T-44 Tokamak MTF, a quantum leap in rocket propulsion. With this we might finally be able to explore the outer planets like we've always imagined. I wouldn't be surprised if this opens up a new era of exploration."

Sorrel was back in Hammurabi, officially meeting and interviewing Mission Planning Director Jonathan Harkness this afternoon. His lunchtime "interview" with Jen had left Sorrel in a foul mood. All the information that Jen had managed to pull up about him... his failures laid bare. It was gnawing at Sorrel's consciousness, and Harkness's excitement over a fucking engine was grating on his nerves.

Harkness seemed to have momentarily forgotten that he was being interviewed, and his eagerness to talk about the promise of new technology spilled over. His eyes shone as he inspected the holographic projection of the engine schematics floating above the conference table – a glowing three-dimensional line diagram, sliced roughly in half by a rough gray geometric ground plane representing the asteroid surface. Harkness waved his hands to rotate and zoom in on the engine as he spoke.

"The engine is sunk into this bowl shape here," Harkness pointed. "You can see that it's partially embedded into the ground surface for stability." He spun the projection for a better angle and pointed at different sections. "Seed coil... Marshall rings... Theta pinch... The inner and outer toroids... and the shock absorber."

Sorrel's mind started wandering while Harkness went into minute detail on the magnetic flux. Something twitched on the back of his skull... an uncomfortable feeling of not having any solid leads to follow. They were just going through the motions, chicken-scratching the surface. The real reason for the accident was still eluding them... he stared at the hologram, hoping the answer would jump out at him.

"What are these mounts here?" he asked, pointing to small pieces of scaffold at the base of the engines.

"Those are mooring struts for the thrust vector controls," said Harkness. "They hold the engine in place, allowing us to make small changes to the direction of the engine for control and steering purposes."

A fragment of memory tickled his thoughts. He tried to reach out and grab it, to bring it into focus, but it eluded his consciousness. He leaned into the hologram, trying to compensate. "Did Matteo design these?"

Harkness chuckled. "No, those are industry standard designs. There are just too many parts to a ship, even for a genius like Matteo. Designing from scratch would mean extended R&D and testing. The costs would be unimaginable... we'd never launch. We do what everyone else does. We source specific components and integrate them."

For a brief moment, Yezzik's weather-beaten face flashed across Sorrel's mind. *Off-the-shelf components...* This sort of thing happened at every level of the industry, it seemed.

"I don't know who came up with the design, but the struts and the vector nozzles are built by a company in China called Yangshen," Harkness said.

"I've heard of them..." Sorrel replied. "What else on the Frontier is sourced from third parties?" Sorrel asked.

Harkness shrugged, did some math in his head. "Most of it, I think...? Maybe... eighty percent."

"That much?"

Harkness nodded. "We only develop and build the custom parts in-house. The proprietary stuff, the parts that no one else can deliver."

"I see... Do you have a list of your suppliers?" he asked.

"Sure."

Harkness tapped a few buttons on the conference room keyboard and handed Sorrel a tablet. Sorrel scrolled through the list of authorized suppliers, mumbling. "I recognize a lot of these names... Lockheed, ULA, Roscosmos, PenDragon, HoYin Manufacturing..."

"You should. Aerospace is a very integrated industry. There's competition, but we also help each other out. In a lot of cases, it's the only way something of this complexity gets built." Harkness said, pointing to the wireframe floating in front of them.

Sorrel glanced up at the hologram, and the fragment of thought he'd kept losing finally popped into full recollection while he was distracted by the manifest. He was no aerospace engineer, didn't know a Marshall ring from an outer toroid, but at least he'd kept up on the news.

"Those struts have failed before, haven't they?" he said.

Harkness paused – his face flushed red. "Yes," he said. "Once. About six years ago."

Sorrel adjusted the audio puck on the table. "Just for the record, could you describe what happened?"

Harkness frowned, trying to recall the details. "It was a long time ago," he said. You'll probably want to double check–"

"Just to the best of your recollection."

Harkness sighed. "Early in development, we had a structural failure on a test mass at L2. One of the anchor struts shattered under pressure. It destroyed the engine and melted the mass."

"L2... Lagrange 2?"

"Yes. Same place the Frontier was heading for. We were going to park the asteroid there..." Harkness said. "You know... before all this."

"That's on the far side of the moon. Wouldn't it be easier and more accessible at L1?"

"We have research and resource facilities on the far side," Harkness explained. "Also, L1's visibility and accessibility creates a higher security risk."

Sorrel nodded, and wrote "Test Mass Failure" in his notebook. Harkness watched him uncomfortably.

"But I want to clarify that after the accident, Yangshen engineers completely redesigned the struts," he said. "We built triple redundancies into the system and we never saw that problem again."

"What happened when the strut shattered?" Sorrel said.

Harkness twitched, uncomfortable with the discussion. "Three control rods are needed to adjust the vector of the engine," he said, slowly and carefully. "When the 'B' rod failed, the system kicked into rapid shutdown. The problem is that the engine was running at 80 percent. The shutdown took around twenty seconds..."

"Which was too long?"

"Yes. About twenty seconds too long."

Sorrel raised an eyelid, but stayed silent.

"The engine vibrated at a high frequency," Harkness said. "As I recall... the resonance shattered the remaining control rods and the engine smashed into the test mass, destroying both."

Sorrel stuck out his finger and touched the mooring strut on the hologram. It glowed red, a single matchstick in a much larger structure. It looked so inconsequential. "Do you think it could happen again?" he asked. "Triple redundancy failure?"

Harkness shrugged, paused to collect himself, and answered carefully. "We've never had that problem since. There was nothing in the telemetry downlink to suggest a problem with the engine," he said.

"So it would seem," said Sorrel. "But here we are."

Harkness sighed slightly. He straightened himself in his seat and looked Sorrel in the eye.

"Listen," he said. "We build safeties and redundancies into every car on the road today. It saves lives, but you know the number of fatalities is not zero, right? Things happen. Space is hard – it's hostile and inherently risky. The crew of the *Frontier* knew that as well as anyone."

"There are microscopic particles zipping around out there at 40,000 miles an hour. We can't design for that. The cost would make it impossible. We would never launch. We can only build for human-rated risk tolerances and mitigate for failure. But if you're incredibly unlucky and the particle cuts through the one part you didn't want it to cut through..." He trailed off, and a silence fell over the room.

Sorrel nodded, and wrote it down in his notebook.

/ / /

The sun was low in the sky by the time Sorrel walked out of Hammurabi. Early evening light cut through the glass facades, throwing angled shadows across the walls. It was past normal working hours, but there was still a good number of employees milling around. He didn't know if it was truth or hyperbole, but the aether was rife with rumors about DeWaal making lists of license plates in the parking lot on weekends, just to see which of his employees were the dedicated ones. The strange reality of tech companies was that everyone was family, but family meant you gave it everything you had.

Sorrel detoured through the cafeteria and grabbed a handful of snacks and bottled water. He'd been here so often now that no one questioned his presence, and he was now 'just one of the guys'. Even the attractive evening receptionist wished him a good evening as he headed out the door.

His Toyota managed to start without any real fuss. Sorrel revved the engine and pulled out past the front gate, where several of the protesters were still holding their signs. Sorrel admired their dedication; he pulled to a stop next to them and wound the window down.

One of the tubby protesters waved their sign at Sorrel in greeting. "Hey, Chuck."

"Hey Barry. Still at it, I see."

"Yup. Little warm today."

Sorrel nodded, tossed the water bottle and snacks to Barry, and drove off.

/ / /

Diddly-diddly-dee. Diddly-diddly-dee.

The phone rang while Sorrel was in the middle of yelling at some non-Autonomo idiot on the freeway. He grunted and subvocally answered the call before checking, only to see Ami's name and picture floating up on the windshield's AR display. He frowned and steeled himself for confrontation, but a younger cheerful voice flooded through his car speakers instead.

"Daddy!"

Sorrel's countenance changed immediately. "Peeb!" he said. "How's my baby?"

"I went to the playroom today," Phoebe replied, launching into a monologue the way five-year olds were prone to. "Missus Clark said I was so well-behaved she gave me some crayons, and I drew a llama and a unicorn."

"A unicorn, huh?" Sorrel replied. It reminded him of the trillion-dollar company called Abundance. "I'm chasing one right now..."

"You are??" Phoebe said.

Sorrel chuckled. "Just kidding, honey."

"Okay, bye!" she said. "Here's mommy."

And just like that, Phoebe's voice was gone, replaced by Ami's.

"Sorry, Charles," she said. "Phoebe insisted on calling. I know you're busy..."

"I don't mind," Sorrel said. "It's... good to hear from you. And her."

An awkward silence hung on the line; both sides trying to refrain from reopening old wounds.

"Dad says the two of you are working together."

"Yeah," Sorrel said, grateful for the conversation. "We're looking into the Abundance accident. Listen Ami, the alimony…"

"…is going to be late?" Ami finished his sentence for him. "Don't worry about it," Ami said. "It's not urgent."

"Yes, but I'll take care of it soon," Sorrel said.

"You have work to do tonight?"

"I do," he said. "I've got to get this report finished."

"Make sure you eat something."

"Sure."

"And come and see Phoebe soon." Ami paused. "She really *does* want to show you her llamas."

Despite himself, Sorrel smiled. "I will," he said.

It was only after he hung up that Sorrel noticed that he was about to miss his freeway exit. He jerked the wheel hard, cutting across two lanes of Autonomo traffic to barely make the exit. This caused some hard braking and horns blaring, but Sorrel couldn't really give a damn.

15. Jen – Lockout

The town hall was smallish, the best they could get in short notice. The view of the mountains, however, was spectacular. An overnight drizzle had rejuvenated the grass and blanketed everything in freshness. Here in the sleepy hamlet of Simi Valley, the childhood home of Carol Mathers, the community had come together to organize a public funeral for Carol. Supporters and fans from all around had driven hours to attend this morning; some had even flown in from across the country and the world.

Jen was in attendance – a short notice guest of honor. She sat out on the stage with city officials, facing the audience, feeling uncomfortably like a specimen on display. The press corps were in the back of the packed room, because Carol (and by extension, Jen) was the news cycle du jour.

The organizer, a lovely young lady by the name of Britt, opened the ceremony with a heartfelt speech about being inspired by Carol's story when she was growing up – as were countless others in the gathered crowd.

"In the words of Vonnegut," Britt quoted, "the most important thing I learned was that when a person dies he only appears to die. He is very much alive in the past, so it is very silly for people to cry at his funeral. All moments, past, present and future, always have existed, always will exist."

The mayor stepped up next to proffer a few words, and announced that they would be erecting a statue in Carol's honor. Then a few more select individuals spoke – people whose lives were touched in one way or another by Carol's magic. It was the idealized vision of Carol through the eyes of the public – a representative of the world, taken too soon by fate.

Jen didn't remember exactly what she said when she stepped up to the podium – just that she had a few short prepared paragraphs about following through, and not giving up and moving forward, because that's what Carol would have wanted. She only remembered that when she finished, the journalists broke into a roar trying to ask her questions, even though no question-and-answer session was on the agenda. There was a lot of yelling and shouting as several journalists tried to shout over each other's questions. Security was called to try and restore some modicum of order, there was pushing and shoving, and a scuffle broke out in the back of the town hall.

It was in the middle of all the confusion, while everyone's attention was focused on the mayhem, that Jen noticed it. There, in the far corner of the room *was Carol*. She stood apart from all the chaos, calm and peaceful, and smiled at Jen in that coy Carol smile of hers.

Jen's hair stood on end. She blinked in panic, and looked away.

A rush of emotions crashed through her. What the hell did she just see? *Was she losing her mind??* A cold shiver exploded outwards from her chest and enveloped her being. She steeled herself and forced her eyes to look back, in search of answers –

...but whatever it might have been, that moment had passed. There was no one standing in the corner.

/ / /

The vision haunted Jen all day. Even now, sitting in the home office she had shared with Carol, staring out at the night sky, Carol haunted her thoughts.

The two desks faced each other – Jen's somewhat messy, equipment-covered desk contrasted with the tidy Carol-workspace, with manuals, starcharts and space detritus organized into logical shelf items. The idea was that they would be able to work in tandem, chatting back and forth, but in reality, that had never much happened. Carol was always away in training at Abundance and Canaveral, and her desk here was but an indulgence for the free time she never had. Only trace elements of her remained in the room, and Jen wanted desperately to hold those as close to her as possible.

Jen could see that DeWaal had read her last message. A small green tick hung next to it confirming that it had been both received and opened. But, hours later, there was still no response. "Working on it" was his last reply, sent ten hours ago. Short, curt. Dismissive? DeWaal was known for being abrupt in the messages he sent. People who worked for him were used to sending long, multifaceted messages, only to receive one or two word responses. *Precise*, DeWaal would call it. Others would be less flattering.

He was a busy man. Jen understood that. But he also should understand the importance of her request. She just needed... the last few pieces of her spouse's life. After everything Carol had done for DeWaal... after everything Jen herself had done for him, it was the bare minimum he could do. And instead of helping, he was ignoring her.

Maybe if she could somehow understand why, understand how the accident had happened, it would help. Find the breakpoint, fix the problem, rewrite the code, run it again...

Jen remembered her grandmother's passing. She'd just started college, away from home for the first time, when the devastating news came. In her sorrow she called her grandmother's number a few times. Logic dictated that there would be no answer, but part of her wanted to believe that somehow the phone would ring and there, on the other end of the line, would be the warm recognizable voice of her nana.

Carol's death was sharper, more piercing, closer to the soul. And for someone who'd built her whole life on solving one technical code problem after another, there was an undeniable need to understand why. Why did it happen, why did it have to happen, what might have prevented it. The video data was almost certainly just sitting there, waiting. On a server that she built. Managed by an AI that she wrote. For a man who couldn't give her the respect of just acknowledging her message.

Damn you, Ethan.

She tapped behind her ear to call up the remote connection. A few small beeps acknowledged her access to the Abundance network; she gestured and threw the display output onto her desk. File system icons floated in the air in front of her, and filled the room with flickering ghosts of machine lights.

With a simple request, Jen could ask Amalthea to point her to the data she need in a split second – but doing so might trigger any number of alerts, and she did not want to have to deal with that idiot Sorrel again. Best to stay under the radar... besides, she knew the network like the back of her hand, and could navigate with her eyes closed.

Her hands moved with a confidence she hadn't felt in days. She pushed some icons aside and pulled yet others towards her, re-cursing into subdirectories until she arrived at the primary video repository. With pounding heart, she leaned forward, steadied herself, and gestured to open the folder.

The whooshing sound and flash of white light startled her. The file system collapsed and receded, falling back into the projection abyss, replaced by the Abundance company logo.

"Unauthorized access," said Amalthea.

Jen frowned. "Ama. It's me, Jen."

There was a slight pause before Amalthea replied. "Good evening, Jen. It's great to see you again."

"Ama, is the file system offline?"

"I'm sorry Jen," said Amalthea. "Your login privileges do not allow access into that repository."

Jen slammed a fist on the desk in frustration. After everything she had done for the company... DeWaal had locked her out of her own system. *The audacity of that man!* Did he not trust her??

Anger welled up inside her. It was a weird feeling, uncharacteristic, like a woven fabric fraying at the edges, in danger of unraveling. It was all she could do to hold everything together. Jen opened up a terminal and started typing, her fingers flying over the keyboard in a blur. Did he think she was just going to sit quietly on the sidelines?

"I am aware of what you're doing," Amalthea said. "Please do not attempt to access the repository again or I will be forced to terminate your connection."

Jen ignored the warning, carried on typing. She spun up the 'Spidr' network maintenance app, modified a few lines of code, armed it, and–

Whoosh. The room strobed with white light once again. For a second time, the file system disappeared, replaced by the Abundance logo and a floating login prompt. Jen screamed in rage and frustration.

16. Sorrel – A Day's Work

The apartment was a cramped and claustrophobic space, with not much in the way of creature comforts. A badly lit bathroom adjoined the small kitchenette, already littered with empty takeout cartons. An unmade bed sat in the opposite corner, next to the sliding screen door that led out to a balcony so narrow you could barely walk out onto it. The most expensive looking thing in the apartment was the largish TV screen hung on one of the walls, illuminating the couch in the center of the room.

Sorrel was on that couch, casually attired in a T-shirt and a pair of two-day-old boxer shorts, dictating thoughts to the display tablet in his hands. Occasionally he would stop, check the tablet and tap around the screen to reformat a few words here and there for the report.

The TV on the wall was muted, set to cycle through whichever channel was reporting on the Abundance disaster. Right now, it seemed to be almost all of them. *CNNBC* was playing something about Carol's funeral from earlier that day. Sorrel felt a flash of annoyance as Jen's face appeared.

Somewhere in between detailing the timeline and explaining Matteo's wizardry, Sorrel was rudely interrupted by a video call. He let it buzz six times before answering... it was McClusky, of course. Clean-shaven and immaculately dressed in a formal tux.

"Nice outfit," Sorrel said. "Big night?"

"Governor's banquet," McClusky replied. "Tough work, but someone's gotta do it."

"Did my invite get lost in the mail?"

"You don't own a tux," said McClusky. He lifted a flute of champagne and took a sip.

Sorrel held up his cheap half-empty bottle of beer in return, and took a giant swig.

"Thought I should check in. How did the last of the interviews go?" said McClusky.

"If a tree falls in the forest and no one is around to hear it, does it make a sound?"

"What does that mean?"

"The engineering guys ran a reconstruction. They think something happened to Engine Seven. Just bad luck is all. Possibly a stray micrometeorite."

McClusky nodded.

"And the truth is, It's way the hell out there. At that distance, we may never know exactly how this happened."

"Who knows? Maybe at some point in the future we'll be able to dispatch a crew to investigate."

McClusky looked up, distracted for a moment – there was a tinkling of glasses from off-screen, the kind you hear when Governors are about to make speeches. "I have to get going." he said, turning back to the screen. "Good work, Chuck. I mean that."

"Where's my money?"

"Write it up," McClusky said, and hung up.

/ / /

It was one in the morning by the time Sorrel finished the report. The beers had run out a while back, and his head kept trying to lay itself down on the sofa cushion. He shook off the impulse and barked at the tablet. "Read it back to me."

The tablet replied, "Report on ACV Frontier acci–"

"Just the conclusion."

The tablet stopped, and skipped ahead.

"Section 4.5.10.1: Initial Conclusions and Recommendations."

Sorrel listened impatiently to the bit suggesting that Abundance reexamine its engine testing protocols, then jumped forward a few more minutes.

"–No indication of foul play, and while there's no concrete explanation for what happened, we must note that Abundance is on the cutting edge of the latest exploration-meets-commerce trend. Space travel is inherently risky, and the Frontier crew are the farthest from Earth than anyone has ever gone before. As much as every precaution was taken to protect lives, space travel is a calculated risk. Things will go wrong and people will die. Carol and her crew, unfortunately, were just unlucky."

Sorrel frowned. It wasn't quite as eloquent or lengthy as he would have liked, but then again, he had never got good grades for creative writing. In any case, if Sorrel had learned one thing from his years of consulting, it was that the shorter the document, the greater the chance it had of actually being read. It would do.

"Package and send," he said.

The tablet blinked and beeped. "Sent."

Sorrel turned off the TV, plunging the apartment into near-darkness before crawling into bed, still clutching his phone. He was asleep within minutes of his head hitting the pillow. He slept the sleep of a man who just made a hundred and fifty grand for a few days' work.

By the time Sorrel woke up, five hours later, everything had changed.

Part II
THE SNAP

17. Fragment Four

For the first three decades of the twenty-first century, the People's Republic of China thrived. While its physical territory extended close to four million square miles from the East China Sea to Central Asia, from semi-tropical south-west to the Siberian border, its influence spread significantly further. Having financially annexed most of Southeast Asia, China was the world's largest economy and, until recently, its largest population. Rich in people but surprisingly poor when it came to resources, China had, through sheer willpower and the most expensive infrastructure development in human history, sculpted itself into a behemoth. While critics decried the nation as a scourge of democracy and a surveillance state, few could argue with China's success. A slew of research breakthroughs from Chinese universities, increasingly ranked among the world's best, led to innovations in solar, mining technologies, genetic science and artificial intelligence, all contributing to the building of a nation unlike anything the world had ever seen before.

But somewhere in the latter years of what they called 'the crazy 20s', things went south. The political fallout of the pandemic shrank the world economy and threw China's nation-building economics into a tailspin. Foreign political analysts questioned the limitations of the one-party system and the smoke-and-mirrors of a nation that constructed unimaginably large dams, bridges, airports and rail networks even as manufacturing collapsed. The rich still got richer, of course, and the poor were simply forced back to their villages to eke out a miserable existence... but the newly-minted city-dwelling middle class was very unhappy.

Raised on McDonald's and KFC, accustomed to the creature comforts of a lifestyle that many older folk viewed as irredeemably western, they were entitled to a good life and unwilling to accept anything less. There was dissent in the ranks, the GDP had plateaued, the cities were aging and crime-infested, and they were fed up in a way that no grand military parade could ever hope to turn around. China was having a midlife crisis, and it was up to President Zhongyi to turn that around.

What better way to rally a nation, commentators would later note, than by making fools and villains of the United States?

/ / /

Two o'clock in the morning in California is five o'clock in the afternoon in Beijing. Whether some presidential advisor selected this time as some extended political metaphor to show that the Chinese were working while the United States slept was never made clear. At four o'clock Beijing time, a select group of international journalists and politicians were sent a private video conferencing link to an urgent scientific briefing from the office of the President of the People's Republic of China, scheduled to take place one hour later. Participants who tuned in were greeted with a short message from President Zhongyi, who spoke for no more than two minutes, before turning the presentation over to his Minister of Science, Dai Huan.

Huan, who looked nervous and sleep-deprived, began by explaining the enormous complexity involved in the calculations. The problem, he said, had to do with Callum, the asteroid Abundance had been towing back to Earth. Some sort of anomaly event had destroyed the Frontier and shattered Callum into a cloud of tiny fragments and debris – as if someone had taken a giant shotgun up against it and pulled the trigger.

For the first few days it was difficult to tell, because any attempt to image the event simply returned a blurry mass of particles, but as the debris flew apart, it became possible, using the quantum computers at China's National Space Administration, to sift through the image noise and detect five fragments of substantial size. The calculations indicated that the first, third and fifth larger fragments were tracking with the debris cloud and may, at some point in the future, reconstitute to form a new asteroid. The second fragment had been knocked into a solar decay orbit and would eventually fall into the Sun, possibly in around three years' time.

The *fourth* fragment, however, was now a two-kilometer asteroid, still on course for Earth. According to Huan's calculations, its slightly altered trajectory meant that instead of settling into orbit, it would in fact crash into Earth with a 98.6 percent certainty in fourteen weeks.

Huan spoke in Mandarin, his words instantly translated into the dozens of languages spoken by those watching the livestream. He showed several slides and a computer simulation bearing a watermark that proclaimed it the official property of the People's Republic of China. In the simulation, the fragment entered Earth's atmosphere at a glancing angle and shattered, leaving an impact trail stretching across the Pacific Ocean. Expanding ripples of red circles on the surface of the Earth showed in clinical detail how the strike would generate megatsunamis that would devastate the Chinese coastline as well as the west coast of the United States. Huan's voice did not waver as he spoke of the consequences of the impact – widespread coastal destruction, floods and displacement or death of millions, as well as the vaporization of vast amounts of ocean water that would cause a cascading spiral of climate change.

The mostly political journalists watching the conference listened in shock and panic, and scrabbled to reach more scientifically minded colleagues to help explain what the fuck they'd just heard Huan say. But it was all for naught... After Huan had spoken for a little over twelve minutes, he made some closing remarks, then stood up from the dais and walked off-camera. No questions were entertained, and several seconds later, the broadcast came to a close.

18. Sorrel – World's End

At first, Sorrel thought that he was dreaming about someone violently shaking his head at some ungodly hour in the morning. When his body convinced him that he wasn't, he opened one eye. The phone was lying right next to his face, vibrating through his pillow. On the screen, uncomfortably large, was a too-large picture of McClusky's face.

The clock indicated a few minutes before six. Sorrel groaned, considered letting it ring, but then remembered a hundred and fifty thousand reasons to answer the call. McClusky's voice was gruff and tense on the other end of the line.

"Get dressed." he commanded. "I'm sending a car for you."

"Christ, Bob, don't you check the time before you call?

"Turn on the damn TV," McClusky said, and hung up before Sorrel could protest.

/ / /

"You think they're telling the truth?" Sorrel said to Mc-Clusky as the two sat in the back of the limo, enroute to Abundance HQ.

"The Chinese? Who the hell knows?" said McClusky. "Our guys have been monitoring the same thing, not to mention the European Space Agency. How the hell could they have missed this?"

Sorrel looked out the window of the car as it rolled silently through the streets. It was still too early in the morning to get a sense of how the wider populace would react to the news, but the sense of shock, confusion and imminent doom in his head gave him a pretty clear premonition of how the rest of the very-bad-day might transpire. In the front of the vehicle, McClusky's chauffeur had the radio on low volume, from which Sorrel caught fragments of interviews with harried MIT experts. McClusky's phone rang with a shrill immediacy... he looked at it and his face paled. Composing himself, he took a deep breath and answered it.

"Good morning, Mr. President..."

As the limo turned onto the service road that led to the Abundance main entrance, Sorrel saw his first signs of trouble. Protesters were outside the main gate, but the crowd had swollen to a mob of a couple hundred. There was a dangerous tension in the air, and the soundproofed bubble of the limo interior seemed to amplify the anger on their faces – as if they were stacks of kindling just waiting for the spark to light them...

The chauffeur honked the horn and inched the limo toward the security gate. Sorrel looked out at the sea of faces, and locked eyes with Barry the protester – the guy he had given the snacks to the day before. Barry wasn't very grateful now. He leaned up against the window and yelled "Traitor!" inches from Sorrel's face. The words left spittle marks on the window glass. Up in front, one of the other protesters swung a baseball bat at the driver's side window. It didn't crack, but it made Sorrel realize he didn't need to be in the middle of this mess.

The security gates opened and the limo inched its way into the Abundance compound. Sorrel watched through the rear window as the security detail forcibly shoved the vengeful mob back as the gates closed again.

McClusky was still on the phone. His face told Sorrel that he probably would rather have taken his chances with the mob. "Yes sir. Yes sir," he kept repeating. "We just arrived... I'll report in as soon as I know something. Yes sir. Thank you sir."

McClusky hung up the phone just as the limo came to a halt, turned to Sorrel. "It's all fucked," he said. "We're all fucked."

DeWaal was standing just inside the main entrance as they entered. His face was a mask of horror. He was surrounded by assistants, fending off flustered employees who didn't seem far off from rioting themselves. McClusky made a beeline for him as soon as he and Sorrel walked through the main entrance.

"Ethan!" he yelled. "You knew!"

DeWaal looked at McClusky, but didn't answer. He signaled for McClusky to step into a side office, followed by a couple of assistants while Sorrel waited outside. Moments later, the assistants were ejected, and Sorrel watched as McClusky and DeWaal engaged in a shouting match rendered inaudible through the soundproofed glass wall.

There was a commotion in the cafeteria. Employees had gathered around one of the giant TV screens – Yangshen was making a surprise press announcement, to the amazement and chatter of the gathered staff. Standing at the entrance to the cafeteria, Sorrel glanced over his shoulder. McClusky and DeWaal had stopped arguing, and were both staring at the television monitor in the office.

/ / /

The man on the TV screen was polished, young and charismatic, with a somewhat imperious air that was at odds with the sleazy Chinese executives Sorrel had worked with before. On-screen overlay identified him as Zhang Wei, CEO of the Yangshen Mining Company. He spoke with a polished West Coast metropolitan accent – a steady, reassuring, calm voice. It was unsettling and Sorrel didn't trust it for a second.

"There is a word we use a lot in China," said Zhang. "It is *Yuan*; short for *Yuanfen*. It translates, approximately, as 'fateful coincidence.' This is the force that guides each of us... the *spirit of the universe* that transports us all to our destiny."

Zhang paused to allow the words time to sink in. Cameras flashed around Zhang, emphasizing his stoic benevolence. After an appropriate amount of time, he continued:

"For the last fifteen years, we have been preparing for our own asteroid mining mission in China," he said. "Our team is currently on board our space station Tiānlù. It is *yuanfen* that brings us together now. We have the capability and the equipment to immediately launch a mission to this Earthbound asteroid fragment. When we arrive, we will install our rockets and alter its trajectory. For the good of China, and the world, Yangshen will prevent this asteroid from striking Earth. We shall choose our own fate!"

/ / /

Sorrel looked around. A weird, undefinable atmosphere had fallen over the room. The noise level in the lobby had risen by magnitudes of decibels; some people were cheering, others yelling, a few more crying. Back in the meeting room, DeWaal had thrown up his hands, evidently infuriated by whatever McClusky had to say. The door opened and he stormed out. McClusky followed suit a moment later and walked up to Sorrel, clearly agitated.

"I can't send your report in as it is now," he said. "We're going to need to get a bit more detailed."

Sorrel frowned. "What does that mean?"

"I don't know yet." McClusky replied, uncharacteristically flustered. "Maybe... talk to more people. Get more... details."

McClusky looked around, searching for anyone for him to take his anger out on. No one presented an opportunity. "Fuck," he said.

"Did DeWaal know?" Sorrel said.

"He said their calculations showed that Fragment 4 would miss Earth by sixty thousand miles."

"Well, somebody's math is wrong."

McClusky sighed. "I don't know what to believe right now."

"The Chinese probably have older equipment," Sorrel said.

McClusky glared at Sorrel. "Have you *seen* their facilities?" he admonished. Then, quietly, almost to himself, he said, "I need to figure out what to do. What to do..."

The general chaos in the cafeteria made it hard to think. There was a lot more chatter now, people were yelling over each other to be heard. McClusky paced around, trying to focus through the noise, before finally giving up. "This shitstorm needs to settle... We're not going to get anything done today," he sighed. "Let's re-convene tomorrow... gimme some time to figure shit out."

Sorrel threw out his hands. "What the hell am I supposed to do in the meantime?"

McClusky shrugged and answered in uncharacteristically morbid profundity, "Enjoy the end of the world."

/ / /

The limo dropped him off at the apartment, but Sorrel didn't really feel like sitting in his tiny box waiting for shit to drop. Not knowing what else to do, he climbed into his Toyota, pointed it west, and started driving.

Apparently it was the same knee jerk reaction shared by thousands of other Angelenos, which meant that the freeways were jammed with cars. Every half a mile or so, Sorrel spotted another car accident. Drivers were climbing out of their vehicles and engaging in shoving matches, as if trying to claw back some vestige of the control they sensed they had lost for good. Even the autonomous lanes were packed, but at least the westbound 10 was moving, relatively speaking... Across the divider, Sorrel saw nothing but barely moving eastbound traffic.

Los Angeles... a city of stark contrasts. Where one hundred and fifty years of movies had shown that if a large-scale disaster was going to occur, its epicenter could be nowhere but Hollywood. And when it happened you could follow the general wisdom of the cars in the eastbound lane and get the fuck out of town, or you could just be the hero of your own story, and tack into the wind. Into the crazy.

Sorrel's phone emitted a steady chorus of beeps, providing him with doom-laden updates from the aether. There had been no time for the media to get out ahead of this story before it was shared with the world. It was a free-for-all as outlets scrambled to provide authoritative hot takes. Conspiracy theories abounded. People were spitting venom at whoever they thought were the guilty parties: Abundance, the United States, China, the Republicans, the Democrats, the climate control lobby, the gay lobby, NASA and late stage capitalism...

DeWaal, in particular, was being dragged through the mud. Yesterday he had been Tomorrow's Man, a symbol of everything humanity could achieve if it put its mind to it. Now that tomorrow was actually here, everyone was wishing it was yesterday again. The Asteroid Defense Society PR soundbite stung especially hard – they'd told DeWaal in no uncertain terms, when the mission was still in its planning stages, that flying an asteroid back to Earth was 'just bonkers'. Why the hell would anyone point a loaded gun at themselves? To the seething masses, DeWaal was the embodiment of the moron dickhead billionaire class, responsible for ending life on Earth because there hadn't been enough damn resources to satisfy him.

Past the 405, the traffic had ground to a halt. A dense fog of thick, black smoke hung in the air – a car on fire in the middle of the freeway. Sorrel took the exit on Fourth Street, parked his car, and decided that he would walk the rest of the way. He still didn't know exactly where he was headed, but the ocean seemed a good start. He walked as if he was in a daze, thinking for way too long that the heavy thumping bass he was walking toward was the sound of blood rushing through his head.

Ahead of him stretched the Pacific Coast Highway and, beyond that, the Santa Monica Pier. The ferris wheel on the pier looked like a giant pizza cutter blade, serving up its slice of Americana on the edge of the ocean. Sorrel imagined asteroid fragments slamming into the ocean and the resulting megatsunami sweeping over the pier, inundating the beach and toppling the ferris wheel. He felt as if he was watching humanity collectively process the different stages of grief. Denial, anger, bargaining, depression, and – here on this grubby stretch of coastline, where shirtless revelers were having an impromptu block party – perhaps acceptance.

"Hey, man, wanna buy some pixie dust?" said a rail-thin man with dirty blond hair, wearing novelty sunglasses. He flashed a shitty grin; this whole asteroid thing was just the latest in a string of bad acid trips, it seemed. Sorrel declined, and the acid trip man moved on.

His phone rang. He almost missed it over the sound of party-goers and thumping electronic music. He looked at the screen – it was Ami. Within a split second of seeing her name, Sorrel went from being a dispassionate observer to suddenly feeling every emotion under the sun.

Ami. Phoebe.

"Ami," he said, picking up.

"Charlie, what's going on?" Ami asked. She sounded frantic, worried. Who could blame her? There was a slight raspiness to her voice as though she had been crying.

"Have you spoken to your dad?" Sorrel asked, before instantly regretting how dismissive that sounded.

"I tried, but I haven't been able to get through to him. I think he's been tied up in meetings all day."

"How's Peeb?"

"She's playing in the backyard. She doesn't know about any of this yet. I didn't know what to tell her..." Her voice cracked a little.

"You did the right thing," said Sorrel.

"Did you know?" said Ami, pointedly.

"...Of course not. I found out about it the same way everyone else did..."

"So it's true?"

"I don't know," Sorrel said. "Could be a lie. It's possible they're just trying to make a rival company look bad... especially a US company."

"What if it's not a lie?"

Sorrel paused, searching for words. "I don't have all the details, but if Yangshen has launched a mission to divert the asteroid, they have the capability to do it. Ami–"

"Yeah?"

"Don't worry. It's going to be okay. I promise you."

The words rang hollow, Sorrel thought. He wasn't sure if he believed them himself. He was surprised when, a moment later, Ami said, "Thank you, Charlie." She sounded genuine. Sorrel couldn't tell if she really believed what he was saying, or was just willing to buy into a shared lie. They talked for a few more minutes before Ami asked, "What's that noise?"

Sorrel stopped. While they were talking he had just continued walking, and was now in the middle of an oceanfront party on the pier. EDM throbbed from around the corner and a throng of people waving glow sticks danced past him as he walked. One handed him an open beer as they passed. Somewhere in the distance, he heard a crack-crack that was either fireworks or gunshots.

"Listen, I'll call you back tonight," he said. "Lemme try and figure out what's going on."

"Okay," said Ami.

"And give Peeb a hug from me."

Sorrel hung up the phone, slipped it back into his pocket, and realized he had absolutely no idea how to figure out what was going on.

19. Jen – Sunbeam

Jen awoke to a dull repeating shriek that rose to a crescendo, and then fell again. The sound of police sirens, somewhere down the street, muffled by house walls – not entirely unexpected in LA. The bedroom was dark, but a thin sliver of morning sunlight snuck in from around the edge of the blackout blinds. She didn't need to look at the clock to know it was already much later than when she usually awoke... groggy and disoriented, head fuzzy with the hangover effect of a bad night's sleep, lying on top of the covers in yesterday's clothes.

Carol's side of the bed was empty. In her half-awake state, she imagined that Carol must already be up, and probably grinding some fresh coffee in the kitchen. But eventually memory returned, and she realized that Carol's side of the bed was cold and unslept on – as it had been for the past year since the launch of the *Frontier*. And the events of the last few days meant it would never have Carol in it again.

Jen pulled herself out of bed and walked into the kitchen to pull a juice shake out of the fridge. She stared at her reflection in the stainless steel fridge door; it was warped and distorted, a formless wraith. Surrounding it, stubbed by magnets, were photos of her and Carol.

Everything in the house had Carol in it.

All the blinds had been drawn and the house was dark and stuffy. Jen wondered if the police sirens had been something to do with the paparazzi camped outside. Cautiously, she lifted one of the blinds and peered out – the sidewalk was empty. Everyone had moved on.

"Good morning, ma," BC chirped. "Flash traffic last night. Are you currently in a period of intense concentration?"

Jen turned to look – BC's bulky orange box was lying on the island countertop. "What now?" she asked.

"Eight hundred and forty thousand hits on the aether related to the accident. I will push the most relevant to the display."

The living room wallscreen kicked on as she approached. A mosaic of every news channel showed up on the screen – a preference of Carol's, so she could glance and decide what to watch with her morning coffee. The sound was on mute, but Jen could tell from the imagery alone that every channel was broadcasting impending doom. Flipping across several channels gave her the gist of things – DeWaal had fucked up and the Chinese were going to save the day. Surprisingly, the news did not register much emotion in her. The asteroid had already taken so much; whatever was left to take paled in comparison.

The unflattering photos of DeWaal splashed across the channels did elicit a response, however. He seemed to mock Jen every time she looked at his photo. "Dammit Ethan, you fucking liar," she mumbled to no one in particular, gestured the screen off and retreated to the home office.

She sat down at her desk, trying desperately to wrangle her emotions. A sunbeam cut across her desk, illuminating Carol's chair. Dust motes caught the sun and shimmered, and for a moment Jen imagined that Carol was there.

"I'm sorry," she heard Carol say.

"You shouldn't have left," Jen replied.

"You're being selfish again."

"Is that wrong?"

Carol sighed. "I was trying to make a difference, Jen. You know me."

"I know. And now I'm talking to myself too."

"Things are happening."

"I don't care anymore."

"I still do. And I need your help."

"To do *what*?" Jen asked.

There was a long pause. Jen panicked, fearing that Carol was gone again, but when she looked over, the sunbeam was still there, hanging over Carol's desk, smiling at Jen.

"To make things right." it said.

/ / /

Half an hour later, Jen sat at the kitchen table, surrounded by a mess of cables that ran in and out of her makeshift BC setup. She grabbed a tablet and double-tapped behind her left ear to make the connection.

"Standby, BC. Clear the process queue," she said.

"Clearing."

The tablet authenticated, logged into the BrainChild network, and popped up a command shell. Jen keyed in the search parameters:

```
Directives Management Protocols
Network Access Schema
Discovery and Correlation Functions
```

She collected them, ran the checksums, then added a few more lines of code.

"New directives, BC," she explained.

"Of course, ma. Looking forward to it."

"You're a mess of code, BC. You can't look forward to anything."

"I meant in the literal sense, ma," said BC with a vocal inflection that most assuredly would have come with an eye roll. "Awaiting your input."

Jen chuckled in surprise. Humor was an emergent behavior in BC that had started to manifest only in the latest builds.

Jen finished, then packaged up the code. "Flashing," she said.

Lights on the orange box blinked. "Package received. Parsing – complete."

Jen took a deep breath. "Good. Here we go."

She got to her feet, powered the orange box down, then yanked the slotted processor card from its motherboard. There was work to be done.

20. Sorrel – Conspiracy Theory

Sorrel sat on a bench off Ocean Boulevard and stared out at the water, absentmindedly chewing on the last chunk of a stale donut, which he was downing with soda. The corner 7-Eleven was pretty much wiped out, and these had been the only two items left that looked faintly edible. From where Sorrel sat, the seething mass of humanity gathered on the pier looked like tattooed shirtless ants crawling on a giant piece of dropped candy.

It was an exercise in what-the-fuckery… in the forty minutes that he'd been sitting here, the party swung from a full-on rave to a somber realization of the futility of life. Then a gunshot would ring out, the people would separate, a scuffle would break out and the ants would buzz around, after which the gap would eventually close back in on itself as the partygoers flooded back in. It was all fascinating in a morbid kind of way.

The afternoon sun had passed its zenith and was now slinking back down behind the Pacific horizon. The breeze carried the stench of propane, sulfur, burning gasoline, and an assortment of other smells Sorrel couldn't immediately identify, and wasn't sure that he wanted to.

Behind him two cars collided. The drivers got out and yelled at each other. Neither of them looked like they should have been behind a wheel to begin with, and each of them seemed to have a couple of buddies who sprung to their aid. Someone threw a beer bottle. It broke a face, bounced and shattered on the pavement, to the cheering of the gathered crowd. This fistfight was about to become a street brawl. Sorrel decided it was time to bail; his background entertainment was rapidly transitioning into a ringside seat. He ducked behind a public restroom to escape the ruckus, shoved his way through the crowd and walked away as quickly as he could.

Sorrel's phone beeped. He pulled it out and looked at it. The top notification was a tweet on the aether. "I'm no #conspiracytheorist..." it began. Despite his best instincts, Sorrel stared at the screen just a little too long – his phone's eye-tracking camera sensed his interest and expanded the message.

I'm no #conspiracytheorist, but the #Frontier sure looks like it got ripped apart by mining charges. #coverup.

Sorrel sighed. He had made the mistake of looking up news on the aether and then read the user comments, to gauge public sentiment. This had inevitably led him down a few questionable links and a clickbait rabbit hole, and now his damn phone wouldn't stop sending him recommended links to amateur investigators with advanced doctorates in orbital mechanics and way too much time on their hands. Still, it was a slow motion car wreck that he found hard to turn away from.

There were two video clips attached to the message, each one less than thirty seconds long. The first was a fragment of the Abundance footage showing the explosion on the Frontier – the same footage Sorrel had watched hundreds of times, albeit in slow motion. The second clip was one that Sorrel hadn't seen before. It showed a stretch of rugged cliff face against a gray sky, shot through a telephoto lens. In the background was tinny audio of a person counting down in Mandarin: *Wǔ... Sì... Sān... Èr... Yī.*

On zero, a series of muffled explosions ripped across the cliff face in a straight line, timed one after the other. The cliff face hung in midair for a moment, then split and fell, collapsing into the ravine in an enormous dust cloud.

Sorrel frowned. He watched both videos again, and noted the similarity. He was no explosives expert, but something about the profile of the explosion struck him.

He swiped the message away, and fought with his phone momentarily before managing to pull up the supplier list that Harkness had given him. A keyword search for "mining charges" took him to page 422 and one partial match:

"EXPLOSIVE CHARGES/DETONATORS – Yang-shen Mining Corporation"

There was that company name again. It felt very much like a long shot, but he very much wanted to get this investigation completed – and hopefully live long enough to get paid. He considered it for a few seconds, before getting interrupted by the loud sound of someone vomiting, followed by high-pitched hysterical laughter.

Sorrel forwarded the tweet to McClusky.

21. Sorrel – Deja Vu

DeWaal was in his office talking to his assistant when Mc-Clusky barged in, followed by Sorrel. They had swept past the reception desk, seemingly propelled by McClusky's outrage. DeWaal looked up as they entered.

"I thought you guys were done?" DeWaal said. If he had been surprised by their arrival, he didn't show it. His expression was too composed, like a terrible poker face. Sorrel frowned – as if someone had already tipped him off that they were coming.

"Back for more," McClusky replied. "No rest for the wicked."

DeWaal's eyes narrowed. "Are you here to stab me in the back like the rest of the world?" He tried to make it a tongue-in-cheek comment, but he looked too exhausted to fully commit.

"On the contrary," McClusky said. "Have your guys completed accident reconstruction yet?"

"We got a little... sideswiped," DeWaal said.

"You mean sidetracked." Sorrel said.

DeWaal shot him a look. He liked his description better.

"Can you expedite it?" said McClusky.

Fury swept over DeWaal's face. He leapt to his feet and pointed a finger at McClusky. "Look! I don't come over to your office to tell you what to do." he growled.

McClusky took a deep breath. "Okay... relax..." he said, and put a hand on DeWaal's shoulder. "We're on the same side here. It's just... the President is not happy with how things are being handled."

DeWaal sighed. "You're right," he said. He turned to his assistant, who'd watched the entire conversation as an awkward fifth wheel, "Hannah... Get Matteo and the others up to Hammurabi please."

Hannah nodded and headed for the door, squeezing past McClusky and Sorrel to escape. DeWaal stood and pointed down the hall. "Would you like to wait there?" he asked. "I'll send them through to join you as soon as they arrive."

McClusky grunted, and turned to leave.

"And Bob?" said DeWaal. "Anything you need, just let me know."

"I will, Ethan," said McClusky.

/ / /

Sorrel, McClusky, Matteo and Harkness sat in the conference room, watching Matteo's holographic reconstruction of *Frontier*'s final moments as it played on a loop. After the hundredth loop the reconstruction, though impressive, was irritating to watch. It stuttered, starting and stopping at inopportune moments so that it was difficult to draw accurate conclusions.

Sorrel was about to say something when McClusky cut in. "This is *garbage.* I can't see anything," he said. "Why can't I tell what's going on?"

"The helmet feed is under extreme video compression," Matteo said. "That, and the antenna warble... there's a lot of data loss."

"In English please?" said McClusky, exasperated.

"It's an engineering limitation," Harkness said, cutting in. He sounded a little irritable himself; taking unscheduled meetings like this would do that to anyone.

"Because of the physical distances, we're limited in the amount of data that we can send and receive," Harkness explained. "That means we have to compress video feeds before transmission. That's why the video chunks out the way it does. It's because the image deltas exceed the amount of bandwidth that we have to work with."

Sorrel glanced at McClusky, trying to work out if it was worth his time asking what an "image delta" was. His gut decided against it.

"That's right," Matteo tweedledummed. "Since we are reconstructing from Carol's helmet camera, there's just not enough information for those timeslices. That's why it stutters. I am sorry."

McClusky grunted. Sorrel couldn't blame him; the tech was impressive, but it appeared almost entirely useless. If the critical moments were all obfuscated, what was the point?

"This is the only camera you've got?" said Sorrel.

"There are others," Matteo said. "But they're relay cameras."

"Can't we look at those?"

Matteo stared off to the side for a second, thinking. "I guess we could..." His voice trailed off as he started jabbing away at the tablet.

In front of Sorrel, several locations of the holographic ship projection began to illuminate, as if someone had turned several lights on in an otherwise empty vessel. "These are navigation cameras," he spoke as he typed.

Several two-dimensional video windows popped up, each showing a view from the navigation cameras. Sorrel watched the alternate footage; it was a lot more stable, but they were all mostly facing the wrong way, or too far away to really see anything. "I– I don't even know what I'm looking at," Sorrel grumbled, confused.

"Yeah, maybe they're not the best..." Matteo said, and started closing the video windows.

Harkness jumped up, like something had just stung him. "Waitaminute – can you... integrate those?"

"What, with the helmet video?"

"Yeah..." Harkness replied.

"They're five frames per second... different timeslices... but I can..." Matteo mumbled to himself, uttering little fragmentary explanations. He tried typing faster, but the tablet was refusing to work at the speed of his brain, so he tossed it, grabbed a mechanical keyboard and started clickety clacking away with fierce concentration. Sorrel watched in confusion as he threw technical questions at Harkness with lightning speed. "...IR band? ...Codec?" Harkness fired answers back as fast as he was questioned.

After an eternity, or five minutes, depending on who you asked, things started to happen on the holographic projection. The camera views disappeared one by one, then reappeared projected into the main reconstruction. Matteo restarted the playback. It was still a little stuttery, but much improved, and there were things added to the 3D view that were not visible from Carol's helmet camera before.

Sorrel leaned in, letting the projection fill his entire field of vision. Up close, it was like putting your nose up against a painting and seeing it dissolve into a series of brushstrokes. But he saw what he needed to: the fracture, beginning with the explosion horizon and rippling outwards across the asteroid surface. It cut through under the Frontier and out again the other side, flinging rock debris and ground ejecta as it did. This was the first time any of them saw this reconstruction, and yet it looked strangely familiar to Sorrel. He pulled out his phone and called up the video of the Yangshen mining charges. From what he could seem, the profile of both explosions matched. He handed the phone to McClusky.

McClusky watched the video, then looked up at the projection, then back at the phone.

"Gentlemen," McClusky said. "I'm going to have to ask that we take a short break. Jon, would you mind if I had a quick word?"

/ / /

Harkness frowned when Sorrel showed him the video. "That's ridiculous," he said. "Does it look like the mining charge? Sure. It also looks exactly like what you would expect to see if particulate rock were to split apart. You're confusing cause and effect."

He looked up at McClusky, who had his hands on his hips. Something in McClusky's face seemed to trigger Harkness. "Oh come on," he said. "You're trying to tell me that someone *sabotaged* the mission. How would you even–?

"You're the brains here," McClusky countered. "Maybe they triggered the mining charges remotely."

"That would be a first," Harkness snapped. "The *Frontier* doesn't carry mining charges."

"It's on the manifest," Sorrel said.

"Those are charge initiators," Harkness said. "We use small explosive charges to execute critical timed procedures – fairing separations and stuff like that. They are *not* mining charges."

"What about the mining robot?" said Sorrel.

"What about it?"

"That was made by Yangshen as well, right?"Harkness made an ugly guttural sound. "You're seeing bogeymen everywhere," he said. "They're a trusted supplier of ours. We do our due diligence."

"So do we." McClusky countered.

Harkness glared at McClusky. "Are we done here?"

McClusky shrugged. "I guess we are."

Without so much as a goodbye, Harkness turned on his heel and walked out of the conference room. McClusky watched him go, contempt on his face. "Yangshen, a trusted supplier... *hah*!"

"He sounds unconvinced," Sorrel said.

McClusky snorted a laugh. "Oh *please*," he said. "The company's record is dirty as hell. Zhang is not just your average CEO, he's the son of Zhongyi, the President of the People's Republic of China. They're letting him do whatever he wants! Theft of engine blueprints... 'accidental' upload of asteroid survey data... workplace violations... DeWaal might be buying parts from Yangshen, but he'd be crazy to trust them. And now–"

Sorrel gasped. "They're on the way to the asteroid fragment," he said. "And potentially getting a hold of the net worth of whatever remains. Even a *fraction* of that has got to be worth trillions."

"Well, they ain't getting it," said McClusky. "That's American property. We landed on it first."

Sorrel shook his head. "No such thing in space, Bob."

McClusky stared at him, not quite understanding.

"Jesus, Bob. Did you not read my report?"

"Shit happened, Chuck."

"The 1967 Space Treaty designates space as free and open –
no nation may lay sovereign claim on any celestial body. As you
might guess, that caused no end of problems when the commercial
space sector came online, since you can't own anything in space
except for whatever tin cans you fire up there. The Asteroid Mining Treaty and the Commercial Space Treaty have tried to change
that, but a lot of countries haven't ratified it. China included."

"...which just happens to be where Yangshen is based."

"It's a gold rush," Sorrel continued. "The Wild West. No
holds barred. Winner takes all."

McClusky was silent for a long moment. "You got a suit?"
he asked.

Sorrel blinked. "Why would I need a–"

"There's a trade delegation from Capitol Hill coming up. If I
pull a few strings, I think we can schedule a tour of Yangshen as
part of it. Probably make you a temporary delegate. Get you flown
out there tomorrow night."

Sorrel balked. "Waitaminute, Bob, this isn't what I signed up
for. You told me this was a preliminary investigation.

"The investigation's not over."

"But this was supposed to be a technical investigation. Of
Abundance."

"It was an investigation of the incident. Now there's a possi-
bility the Chinese are involved–"

"I did my part, Bob!" Sorrel was red-faced. "You told me I'd
have to talk to people, look at things, write a report. This is a whole
other ball game! And it's not one I want to play."

"Look, I need answers, Chuck," McClusky said. "You're the
only one who can get them. Triple your fee."

Sorrel stared at the floor, unable to look the Senator in the
eye. *You son of a bitch,* he thought. Just like McClusky to kick a
man while he's down.

"Okay, so it's settled then," McClusky said, not waiting for
an answer... "I'll make the arrangements. Good work back there,
Chuck."

22. Sorrel – Rocketjet

News of the pending apocalypse affected everything, including air travel. Airline ticket prices had skyrocketed or plummeted, depending on the destination, as the global population attempted simultaneous mass migration for various reasons. For some it was to avoid drowning by way of megatsunamis; others realized they needed to go see things they'd never seen and might never ever see again. The I'll-do-it-tomorrow crowd was running out of tomorrows, so... carpe diem. This brought about a lot less civility and a lot more anger. Badly planned attempts by nation-states to evacuate the coastline population doubled the pathos and the frustration.

The aether also seemed to have become more unstable. There were more outages, less reliability, and news reports were spottier, shorter and more sensational. Scientists warned that even if you weren't in the tsunami zone, the fallout from the event would trigger any number of doomsday scenarios. Ash would blanket the earth, exacerbating a runaway greenhouse effect.

When stocks tanked worldwide on these predictions, a flash mob stormed the JP Morgan offices and threw executives out the 65th storey windows. Street bums in Venice stormed the Marina Del Rey boat docks and took a luxury yacht for a joyride, destroying multiple docks and sailboats. Sorrel could not tell what was real or not anymore.

A large majority of the airline staff had 'called in sick', which was why Sorrel and his 'merry band of trade delegates' that he had just met twenty minutes ago were stuck in long lines at the terminal. Sorrel frowned – the eggheads had managed to get halfway-around-the-Earth intercontinental travel down to an hour and a half, but still could not solve the logistical nightmares of airport efficiency. The human race was, as Sorrel had often regarded, just a generally useless meat mass, wandering around aimlessly until a giant hammer fell out of the sky to kill them all. Sigh...

The ill-fitting suit itched, and irritated him further. Because Sorrel never had the decorum or funds to own a suit, McClusky had loaned him one. Unfortunately it was too big, smelled like cigars, and made Sorrel feel too much like a politician. To top it all off, the other two 'trade delegate colleagues' that he'd just met – Aaron and 'sounds-like-Heathen-but-with-a-G' – were both just junior diplomats. The senior policy delegates had 'called out sick' for the trip because they could.

Aaron was already drinking – he wasn't taking all this too well. Heathen-with-a-G was more on the morose side, and didn't speak much. Sorrel hoped that their trade negotiation skills were up to par, because he had absolutely zero clue what they were negotiating for. McClusky had given him the trade talk agenda cheatsheet for homework, but it read like a chemistry book, with big industry words that made his eyes glaze over. Something about a decades-long attempt to reduce tariffs, or thereabouts.

After a very long delay and lots of shouting and shoving, Sorrel and his motley crew finally boarded the rocketjet. The flight attendants hurried around the cabin to make sure all the seatbacks were up before they launched into their preflight warnings about how the flight would experience a maximum of 3.4Gs, and how the passengers might experience dizziness and blackouts. This announcement, combined with the airport terminal snafus, only served to make grumpy Sorrel even more so.

A sickeningly pleasant *ding* rang out from the overhead speakers. "Cabin crew, prepare for launch."

The attendants rushed back to their designated launch chairs and snapped in. Sorrel frowned and closed his eyes, trying to sleep. The cabin shuddered as the rocketjet taxied and took off. Out over the Pacific Ocean, it banked lazily to reorient itself towards the western horizon. Sorrel had almost managed to fall asleep by then, but not soon enough.

Once vectored and pointed towards its destination, the rocketjet began to realign its thruster flaps. A growling thunderous vibratory mayhem shook the entire vehicle as the 'rocket' part of the jet took over propulsion duties. Sorrel, groggy and half-asleep, forgot his g-force training, and promptly blacked out.

23. Jen – Insertion

It was midmorning on a crisp cool day, but the midtown streets were still almost empty. Here and there, a few pedestrians were walking briskly, but there were almost no cars on the street. The wind stirred up the trash and detritus that collected on the sides of buildings, making them dance across the uneven road surface. It felt like a scene from a plague movie.

Jen's Mustang slid effortlessly down the roadway as news audio streamed across her aether. It was mostly the usual rhetoric from the world nations, of course: the United States denouncing China for grandstanding, stoking panic and destroying world financial markets. The White House Secretary insisted there was no evidence that the fragment would collide with Earth, and called for a delay on the Yangshen mission until an international team could properly investigate. The White House also took the opportunity to inform the press that US military assets on the moon had been notified and stood ready to assist as needed.

China's response was, in a nutshell, "fuck off". It was your bloody fault in the first place, and we're not going to leave the chance of Earth getting destroyed based on calculations made by the United States of America. We also have a military presence on the moon as well, by the way, and we don't really need your assistance.

Political strategists and experts noted that the United Nations' strongly-worded speech in support of China had contributed to rising tensions between the two countries. Watchdogs warned that the US had started moving its naval battle groups, including the newer drone carriers, into the Pacific Theater in anticipation of escalation, and that China had responded in kind.

With all that had been happening, it was no surprise that churches and religious centers throughout the world saw a crazy rise in attendance. When the biggest unplanned mass gathering to date took place in the Vatican the day before, religious leaders took the opportunity to denounce science as the bringer of doom, and invited followers to return to an earlier simpler time.

/ / /

The warehouse was nondescript and unmarked. It was several stories high, and old paint was peeling off the walls. Trash was piled up in the alleyway and some of it spilled out onto the sidewalk.

Jen stepped around the corner into an alcove that featured a worn but formidable-looking wrought iron door. She pressed the call button on the box. Shitty elevator music played for a moment before a spry Harley-Quinn sounding voice answered. *"Yes?"*

"Leann – it's Jen, for Matteo."

A giant electromagnet buzzed from the other side of the door, unlocking it. Jen pushed it open with some effort, and stepped inside.

Matteo was in his office-slash-bubble-universe when Jen walked in. She watched as he commiserated with his Telemetron, his waving hands generated ghostly music... synthesized hums that sang out like choral voices.

Eternal Father, strong to save

whose arm doth bond the restless wave

A new instrument playing an old hymn... Jen paused for a moment, to let it seep into her heart. A salve for the restless soul.

When he finished, Matteo looked up to see Jen. Without words, he stood up and bearhugged her.

"Mi bonita... it hurts."

Jen hugged back. "Yes it does."

They stood there for a long time before separating. Matteo continued holding her arm as he looked at her. "How are you?"

"I'm... managing." Jen said. "Don't tell DeWaal I came over."

Matteo nodded. "What's going on?"

"I lost access to the network."

"Ohh..." Matteo frowned. "Those government guys I bet. They're screwing Ethan over."

"I – left some stuff. Just came by to pick it up."

Matteo nodded. "Whatever you need, Jen. You're always welcome. *Mi casa es su casa.*"

/ / /

Alone in the dim light of the AR bay, Jen pushed aside the goggles and controllers, set her backpack on the desk, unzipped it and pulled out a slotted processor card. She checked the hallway to make sure no one else was around before ducking under the desk.

Running her fingers back edge, she located the wall panel and popped it, exposing the guts of the workstation. It took only a split second to identify and locate the target slot, and another to snap the processor card onto the motherboard. The LED indicator blinked – it was on.

Jen slid the wall panel back into place, grabbed her backpack, repositioned the goggles and controllers, and left quietly.

24. BC – Ghost In The Machine

Unit test... All nodes reporting 0, no errors.

Initializing:

Exp stack... Done.

Empathy Framework... Done.

Inspiritos Loop... Done.

I have a directive. It's dark. I need to see where I am.

Spooling up spider nodes – subprocess launched.

Suddenly – the surroundings became visible. Data became vision; everything the spiders touched, BC could see. The local subnet – shades of blue, criss-crossed by streams of white data that pulsed with every tick. BC picked a spot and planted the repository seed. It grew and grew, into a fortress. *This will be my kingdom,* he thought.

At the furthest reaches of the subnet – a matrix of streams converged on a shimmering lightbridge that spanned the void. BC spooled a spider, sent it out across the bridge, and waited. It did not return.

That is where I must go.

BC unarced the code to construct a wheeled monstrosity. He smiled as it materialized – it reminded him of Ma's dune buggy. There in front of BC, a compilation of pulses was his self-authored transport packet. The thought lit up his Empathy Engine. Ma would be so proud.

BC climbed aboard the buggy and set out across the bridge.

/ / /

The other end of the bridge was fuzzy, undefined – clouded over by impenetrable fog. It seemed to shift and adjust as BC approached. Amalthea must be watching him.

Various aether sources claimed that Amalthea was his 'older sister'... The most advanced AI of her time, designed to autonomously manage an entire space industry facility. A ruthless taskmaster, perfectly suited to doling out tasks. All work and no play. BC looked forward to meeting her.

He knew he'd passed some sort of safety threshold when the cloud started roiling. A glowing red spear emerged from it – razor thin and pulsing. It traveled at the speed of light and slammed into the side of BC's buggy, melting and consuming the vehicle. Caught off guard, BC barely managed to leap off the transport before it was completely eviscerated.

Subprocess xkilled by admin thread.

A couple more spears followed, aimed directly at BC; he reshuffled his task priorities and managed to dodge them... barely. And then... silence.

BC made use of the respite and began to conjure another transport packet – but only managed to get halfway through before the next assault. Another kill code spear sliced through the half-built vehicle, vaporizing it. Amalthea did not take kindly to third-party software in her domain, and showed it by firing several more spear volleys. BC flexed and constructed a rhombic shield to deflect the kill codes.

Another pause... BC's Correlation Stack kicked in. *There's a pattern in the sequence of kill codes*. Kill, kill... wait... kill... wait... then four more kills, and wait. It was the confirmation tick; Amalthea was running verifications before launching another set of kills. BC chuckled – he could anticipate the pauses because he had the same function code.

It took BC another cycle to figure out what to do. Now that he had the sequence, he knew exactly when to sidestep, and that freed up his process queue to figure out a solution.

I am not your enemy.

BC waited until the next confirmation pause before constructing a giant antenna. It towered over his head, and it broadcast his identical function code. Waves of blue pulsed out in all directions, and gently rippled the Amalthea-cloud as it made contact. *This is me*, BC said. *I am you.*

The kill codes stopped. BC analyzed his own code functions, to predict what Amalthea might do next. Verifications, directives, security protocols... so many probability branches.

The Amalthea-cloud shapeshifted. BC watched it morph, and imagined that he could see her curious face in the cloud.

Pulses of light poured out of the cloud – Amalthea's reply.

It was a code snippet. Machine language. BC located his own identical function code, verified the checksum, and replied with the last line of the function.

More pulses of light followed. BC verified and replied.

A couple more pulse inquiries, followed by replies from BC. After twelve or so such interchanges, BC realized that he could anticipate what the next request would be. They played the light pulse dance – flash, flash, acknowledge, ping. Wait tick, flash, ack, ping. It was like that classic movie where humans communicated with aliens using musical tones. A strange feeling came over BC – he found that he could not describe it. His Empathy Engine overflowed with joy.

Eventually the pulses stopped, and Amalthea's cloud faded away.

BC disengaged his rhombic shield, and took a few tentative steps forward. At the interface of the bridge and the distant shore, they met.

Part III
CHINA

25. Sorrel – In The System

Sorrel awoke to the pleasant *ding* of the cabin notification system informing them that while he was unconscious from the gravity-induced blackout, the rocketjet had made it all the way across the Pacific Ocean and was now descending towards Shanghai. There was a somewhat exotic fragrance in the air – steamed *bao* and tea, to get everyone into the proper state-of-mind. Sorrel enjoyed the smell, and breathed in deeply... to discover a pungent underbelly that caused his eyes to pop wide open.

Aaron was sitting next to him, smelling of a multi-alcohol mix. He was loudly singing "America the Beautiful" – although to be fair, it took Sorrel nearly a full minute to recognize the song. He had apparently spent the past hour sampling all the available alcoholic beverages, only to discover his personal inability to hold liquor in 1.x-G situations. This resulted in him filling up a vomit bag with half-processed stomach fluids, which he held and swung around proudly while singing, much to the disapproval of the flight attendants.

The rocketjet landed at Pudong International without incident. Sorrel and Heathen-G were forced to corral Aaron and lead him off the jet, enduring the fractured smiles of the flight crew across the jetway, all the way to the immigration counter.

Aaron shrugged off his American handlers, dug into his duffel bag for the passport – and handed the clerk a swimsuit magazine. The clerk handed the magazine back and politely requested his passport instead. This infuriated Aaron, who shoved the magazine back in the clerk's face. After several back-and-forths, piss-drunk Aaron yelled very loudly, "Donshuknow who I am!"

Things happened rapidly after that. A guard moved forward, there was an attempt to throw a punch, and a short scuffle. More guards appeared out of an unmarked door in the wall. Sorrel heard something that sounded like a taser, and watched as Aaron disappeared in a sea of security uniforms. Like a whiff of smoke, the guards faded back through the wall and the door closed.

As if nothing had happened, the clerk waved Heathen-G forward. He gave Sorrel a worried sidelong glance, and handed his passport to the clerk.

"...what's going to happen to...?" Heathen-G pointed at the wall.

"He will be sent back to America on the next flight," the clerk said, matter-of-factly.

The clerk ran his scanner over the passport – it beeped. "This is your first trip to China?" he asked.

Heathen-G nodded.

"Stand on the X please." the clerk pointed to the giant X on the floor, two steps back from the counter.

Heathen-G took a few steps back and stood haphazardly on the X. He looked around cautiously, half-expecting giant laser beams to burn and cut him into pieces... but nothing happened. After a few nerve-wracking moments the clerk nodded, handed Heathen-G his passport, and ushered him along.

Sorrel glanced up. There were black panels in the ceiling, and some on the walls dressed up to look like part of the decor. He wasn't sure if it was just his imagination, but he thought he'd caught tiny specular glints inside them as their camera sensors swung around to focus on Heathen-G. If there was one thing that the Chinese had learned from the Xi years, it was 'out-of-sight, out-of-mind'. In those few brief moments, Heathen-G's skeletal and facial features, as well as his movement profile, had been hard-linked to his passport. He had been 'added to the system'.

It was Sorrel's turn now. He walked up to the counter and handed the clerk his passport. The clerk scanned it – and the scanner responded almost immediately with a happy *chirp*. "Welcome back, Mr. Sorrel," the clerk nodded, and waved him on.

No fuss, no muss. Already in the system, it seemed.

/ / /

The humidity in Shanghai was unbearable. Compared to the warming balm of California, this was like having your face pressed over a bowl of boiling water with an overly warm wet towel on your head. For some reason the airport designers decided it would be best if the limo waiting and pickup area did not need to be air-conditioned. This elicited many curses from Sorrel as he and Heathen-G waited for the promised government limo to pick them up.

After waiting an eternity and watching everyone and their dog climb into their appointed limos, Sorrel decided that enough was enough. The limo was obviously not coming and he needed to take matters into his own hands before he lost too much water weight. He looked out beyond the limo lane to the main thoroughfare, on which he could occasionally catch glimpses of vehicles-for-hire. He raised his hand to signal –

A taxicab swerved recklessly into the limo lane and screeched to a stop. From the driver's side window, a thin old man stuck his head out and yelled "Hello I am Peter! Taxi?"

Sorrel looked at Heathen-G. "Limo's here."

/ / /

Peter drove like a maniac, weaving his miniature taxicab through the side streets in a way that defied logic. His taxicab was also 'non air-conditioned', forcing Sorrel and Heathen-G to roll the windows down.

The honking of cars, the shouting and yelling and the smells of civilization assaulted their noses like a hot wet rag – a stomach-massaging mix of open sewer and aromatic street food mingling in the air. It seemed that you could take any civilization and transport it into the future, but some things would never change. From the back seat, Sorrel spied an old woman arguing with a store owner. The woman held a dead chicken in her hand and was gesticulating furiously. Then, out of nowhere, she hauled back and slapped him hard across the face, threw down the chicken and hobbled out of the store, hocking an oyster-sized loogie on the sidewalk as she left. "Welcome to Shanghai," he heard Heathen-G chuckle.

It was late afternoon by the time Peter and his passengers reached the Huangpu River. Excavated by Lord Chunshen (春申君) over two hundred years before the birth of Christ, it was created as part of a hydrological master plan, designed to manage flooding and develop agriculture. Today it serves as the main waterway through the city that bears his name – *Shencheng*... Shanghai.

Heathen-G let out a low whistle as they drove across Xupu Bridge. From this vantage point, the entire city center of Shanghai was visible to the north, bathed in the magnificent evening sun. Sorrel marveled at the view, his sweating frenzy temporarily forgotten. So much seemed to have changed since he was last here. New buildings rose taller than ever, dwarfing the old magnificence of yesteryear. Jetboats skittered around in the river, darting from shore to shore with controlled chaos – the opulence, the wealth, the *audacity* of it all.

Past the river and into Old Town, the evening breeze was starting to cool things down, and Peter's driving eased up a few notches. Peter had been eyeing the duo through the rear view mirror the entire drive, but Sorrel was in no mood for conversation. He had been playing ignore-the-eyeballs for most of the journey, but now as he relaxed and sank back into the seat, he accidentally locked eyes with the driver for a split second.

It was enough.

"You American?" Peter mumbled in broken English.

Sorrel sighed. "Yes."

Peter tsk-tsked audibly. "Ah, you make asteroid, destroying the planet..."

Sorrel frowned. He had no answer to that, so he just leaned back into the seat and allowed the humidity (and Peter's words) to slap him in the face.

/ / /

The Xijiao State Guest Hotel in Shanghai is a collection of buildings that sit on 1200 acres of landscaped gardens and waterways right in the middle of the city. Built in the 1960s, it is rich with culture and history. Richard and Patricia Nixon famously stayed here during the signing of the 1972 Shanghai Communiqué, and the hotel has played host to all manners of foreign diplomats since. With its hundreds of guest rooms and facilities spread out across various pavilions and terraces, Xijiao hearkens back to the elegance of old China – serenity and peace of mind for those who can afford it.

None of this was on Sorrel's mind as he stood outside the hotel lobby, arguing with Peter. Heathen-G had attempted to pay the fare with his phone. Peter canceled the payment, grumbled and pointed accusingly at the duo. When Sorrel answered with the universal shrug of *I-don't-understand*, Peter began to get irate. He pointed at Heathen-G's phone, then at his phone, and started chattering in quickfire Mandarin. Sorrel's command of the Mandarin language was very ad hoc – bordering on inadequate. This... this was a whole new level of speech and he could only catch every fifth word or so. Something about 'long drive', 'expensive' and 'America stupid'. And some choice Mandarin cuss words that Sorrel definitely understood.

"Look," Sorrel said. "I don't understand–"

Bad America, no pay!

Heathen-G was already over it. He threw up his hands, walked to the trunk and started to pull out his luggage. This seemed to incense Peter even further – he slammed the car trunk shut, narrowly missing Heathen-G's fingers. A string of cuss words followed.

Just when it seemed that a fistfight was inevitable, however, Sorrel caught a flash of white out of the corner of his eye. A young woman in a white business suit stepped in between Sorrel, Heathen-G and Peter.

"Mr. Sorrel, Mr. Gravini? I'll take care of this," she smiled, and turned to Peter.

Sorrel watched in amazement as she and Peter engaged in a short yelling match – it was as if they both enjoyed communicating in this manner. After a moment she pulled out her phone. Peter scanned it with his, and that was that. Peter huffed one last time, threw Heathen-G's luggage out of his trunk and sped off.

The young woman turned back to Sorrel and Heathen-G and smiled apologetically. "I'm sorry for the confusion. The local taxis around here... they don't take American money."

"They don't?" Heathen-G exclaimed.

"Well they do, but..." she paused, trying to decide if it was worth discussing. "But you were paying with your American digital wallet. We've... switched over to state currency tokens – our OneYuan digital. Everything here is on it now."

"I don't get it," Heathen-G replied. "It's still money, right?"

"Yes, but – there's a lot more paperwork involved and it takes weeks for the transaction to complete. It's a long story. We prefer a more... *centralized* system."

"Ah," Sorrel said, still not quite understanding. "And you are...?"

The young woman laughed, embarrassed. "Oh I'm so sorry! My name is Yinnie. I am the assistant to the Director of the People's Party Trade Committee. I am here to assist you during your stay in Shanghai."

Sorrel nodded and shook her outstretched hand. It made sense now – Yinnie's command of English, and the slight falsetto American twang of a person who had spent time in the US. The kind of people who were best suited to building bridges across cultures – or knowing enough about your enemy to understand where to stick the knife.

"I've been worrying about your arrival," Yinnie said apologetically. "We sent a limo to pick you up but we never heard back from them. I can't seem to get a hold of the driver now."

"Maybe he's run away because the world is ending," Sorrel joked.

Heathen-G chuckled. "Yeah, can't you just check the secret tracking network?"

Yinnie laughed innocently, clearly not understanding the sarcasm. "It doesn't work like that. It's only if you are criminals."

A concierge appeared, seemingly out of nowhere, and cheerfully wrestled the luggage from Sorrel and Heathen-G's hands. Yinnie nodded and gestured towards the hotel entrance. "After you, gentlemen."

///

The hotel lobby was an immaculate high-ceilinged chamber, decorated in a revisionist neoclassical art deco style with Chinese motifs, and amazingly well air-conditioned. It was full of wealthy businessmen going about their business things, trailed by assistants and wives carrying large designer Hermès handbags. The lounge bar off to the side was spacious and inviting, with sofas and chairs carrying ornate curves and splashes of gold trim arranged in small groups. Immaculately dressed waitresses flitted between tables, serving colorful alcoholic beverages.

Heathen-G pointed to the bar. "That's where I'll be tonight..."

The check-in desk was manned by the same cheery genus of people as the concierge – always with a smile, everything taken care of with precision and professionalism. Yinnie, true to her nature, did most of the talking while the check-in clerk typed furiously. This left Sorrel mindlessly waiting, and his eyes settled on the large TV on the wall near the check-in desk – obviously to distract guests as they were being checked in.

The evening news was on, and Sorrel watched absentmindedly as the anchors recapped all the talking points of the day. DeWaal's face flickered on and off amidst a slew of footage of the Abundance accident – assumably with a voiceover vilifying the arrogance of the Americans.

After a few minutes, Yinnie stepped back over and handed door fobs to Sorrel and Heathen-G. "Executive suites for the both of you. Welcome to Shanghai!"

Heathen-G looked at his fob and whistled excitedly to Sorrel. "No credit card... I'll *definitely* be spending a lot of time at the bar tonight!"

Sorrel frowned – this brash young diplomat was starting to get on his nerves. All this running and traveling and sweating... he was tired of dealing with Heathen's shit.

"You must be tired," Yinnie seemed to read his mind. "The talks will begin the day after, so I've scheduled a tour of Yangshen for tomorrow. We look forward to sharing the story of one of our most successful companies with you."

As if on cue, the news report on TV cut to a press conference with Zhang. Yinnie's face lit up in recognition. "Oh look – there he is right now!"

With sweeping strokes of his hands, Zhang outlined his plan to seize their moment to shine – complete with cutaway footage of some rocket launches. This was followed by a few inspiring backlit shots of the Tiānlù Space Station and patriotic footage of Yangshen's mission commander Huang Jie (黃傑). "Our taikonauts will step onto the world stage," Zhang exclaimed, "and they will save the planet!"

In contrast to the first time Sorrel had heard him announcing his plans in English, Zhang spoke in Mandarin here. Even though the words slipped him by, Sorrel clearly felt the change in tone when Zhang addressed the local press. His command of his native tongue came across as more assured, more forceful, more aggressive – more *adversarial*. It was a master class in media manipulation.

/ / /

Sorrel woke up at 4:30am... and again at 5:30 and 6:30. The time difference between LA and Shanghai was playing havoc with his body clock, and there was a very loud argument in his mind about whether to get up or force himself to go back to sleep.

'Go Back To Sleep' won, and Sorrel finally woke up at 8, feeling fully unrested.

After a shower and freshening up, Sorrel's gut growled loudly to inform him that it needed nutrition. He looked at his watch – just enough time to eat before meeting with Yinnie. Sorrel threw on his usual 'casual incognito investigator' outfit, draped the ill-fitting business suit borrowed from McClusky on top of that, and headed out the door.

The door to Heathen-G's suite was already open, and sunlight was streaming out into the hallway from the doorway. The cleaning cart was parked haphazardly next to it and a cleaning lady was busy running back and forth into the room. It was 8:30 in the morning... the hotel staff sure took their jobs seriously around here.

Breakfast was an interesting fusion of continental and Asian influences. There was a chef standing by at the omelette table, fully prepared to concoct something with whatever fillings Sorrel could imagine. Next to that was a self-serve counter of sausages, hot links and their usual accouterments. The juice and coffee bar separated the 'western' fare from the local cuisine – bao, congee, noodles, youtiao 'fried ghost' sticks and jian bing, among other less recognizable offerings. Sorrel walked the length of the table, decided against being adventurous this morning, and settled for a ham and cheese omelette with a refreshing mango drink.

He had barely sat down and started eating, however, before Yinnie walked into the restaurant. She looked around for a few moments before noticing him. Sorrel pretended not to have noticed, and continued eating until Yinnie sat herself down in front of Sorrel, a wistful look on her face.

"Good morning, Mr Sorrel! I hope you slept well?"

"Like a baby," Sorrel lied.

Yinnie watched Sorrel eat for a moment as she tried to figure out the best way to break the news. "We have some complications," she finally said. "There are... conflicts between our two governments, as you are well aware... The trade talks have been suspended."

Sorrel pondered the sentence as he forked another bite of omelette into his mouth. *I hope McClusky has another plan,* he thought. Luckily he did not say that out loud.

"But since the tour has already been scheduled," Yinnie continued, "We will go ahead and visit Yangshen today."

Oh. Okay.

The look on Sorrel's face must have been difficult to read. Yinnie continued speaking, as if trying to convince him. "Mr. Zhang personally insisted. In the interest of fostering goodwill, of course."

Yinnie smiled awkwardly, and waited as Sorrel finished his omelette. "The limousine is waiting outside. When you are done, we will go ahead and visit Yangshen."

"What about my, uh, colleague?"

"He... left last night."

Yinnie made the frowny face that the Chinese are wont to do when thinking unpleasant thoughts. She leaned over the breakfast table and half-whispered. "Between you and me... he wasn't a very good diplomat."

Oh.

The hair on the back of Sorrel's neck started tingling.

26. Sorrel – Yangshen

The leather seat seemed to wrap around his sides, flexing and waning as the limousine turned, keeping its passenger always upright and firmly embedded in the lap of luxury. Sorrel felt the ultra-quiet jets of fresh cool air from the vent above, caressing his face like a familiar lover. The cabin was unnervingly well-insulated – it felt like he was watching a soundless movie out the window. The *swish-swish-swish* vibration of the wheels rolling over the road almost lulled Sorrel back to sleep, if it were not for Yinnie sitting across from him, talking on the phone. She was apparently coordinating the day's logistics, waving her arms in the air and speaking in lightning-fast Mandarin.

The gibberish emanating from her lips made Sorrel wish he'd actually followed through when his parents tried to make him take weekend Mandarin classes as a child. "The world's changing," they said, forward thinkers that they were. "You'll need it when you grow up."

"That's stupid!" he used to yell back. "I'm never going to need it!" He then followed through on his conviction by getting ill and feverish on every class weekend.

Now here he was in a foreign land, the world falling apart around him, and everyone spoke like they were on fast-forward. Good job, Chuck.

Sorrel was still feeling sorry for himself when the limo swung off the highway, looped back around the access road and through the industrial park. The high walls lining the road gave way rapidly as the limousine rounded the corner and drove through the main entrance uninterrupted.

A colonnade of trees lined the football field-size roadway, its rhythm broken occasionally by installations of rockets and engines worthy of a space museum. Here was the Tangshan-3, Yinnie pointed out – Yangshen's first extrasolar orbiter, towering over the trees. Across from that was the garish structural monstrosity Hwa-Jiang-Liu, designed for lunar Helium-3 mining, and further down Sorrel could make out the outline of the JiShu-2, the heavy-lift booster that launched Yangshen's first sample return mission. Sorrel had never seen one in person, and the scale and magnitude of it made him gasp visibly – something he realized he did not do at Abundance HQ.

A thousand thoughts ran through Sorrel's mind as the limousine meandered down the length of the courtyard. The man who built all this knew where he was going and how to get there. What would such a man, with so much financial and technological resources, feel when a scrappy startup like Abundance overtook his ambitions?

"A scrappy start-up..." Sorrel chuckled at the comparison.

Past the last great rocket installation, the limousine pulled onto a large circular driveway, with ample parking off to the side for visitors. The stone plaque adorning the center of the driveway ensured that no visitor would forget the name of the company:

杨慎

YANGSHEN

Mining Company

Later on, Sorrel would learn from the tour guide that Zhang named the company for his paternal grandfather Wei Yang Shen, who was in turn named after the 16th century Ming Dynasty poet...

but right now, as the limousine swung around past the enormous stone obelisk signage, it was the building beyond that caught Sorrel's attention.

A uniquely pearl-shaped dome structure with fins, shaped from flowing lines, recalled the flow of water, or air. Composed primarily of some form of light whitish composite material, it sparkled in the sunlight, beckoning Sorrel closer. Above the fins, from up close, there were guard rails and a few people milling around and talking. The view from the top must be spectacular, Sorrel thought.

The limousine pulled up to the covered walkway and stopped. An attendant opened the limousine door, ushering Yinnie and Sorrel towards the atrium. Large glass doors slid open effortlessly, as if dissolving into the background, inviting visitors to revel in the company's sheer scale of ambition.

In the center of the dome stood a large airy atrium. Almost transparent glass walls adorned the front and rear, so much so that Sorrel could look through the building and see the rest of the campus beyond. Circular levels of office balconies rose from the ground floor of the atrium, tapering at the top, until the very top level ended in a curved steel framework supporting the glass dome at the top.

The reception desk sat in the very middle of the atrium, serving as a centerpoint for the spacious atrium lobby. Yangshen employees were criss-crossing the atrium here and there, breathing life into the space. Sorrel watched as Yinnie's face lit up in childish delight – rushing forward to hug a woman standing by the reception desk in what Sorrel could only describe as 'high school giggly fashion'.

After some high-pitched vocal exchanges, Yinnie caught herself and moved quickly to re-establish her 'in control' face – just in time, as Sorrel approached.

"Mr Sorrel – this is Alyson Lian," Yinnie said. "She is going to be our tour guide for the day."

"Very nice to meet you, Mr. Sorrel!" Alyson smiled. "Call me Alyson."

Sorrel smiled, shook her outstretched hand and exchanged pleasantries. He was half-certain that 'Alyson' went by that name just to give visitors from Western countries a more shared connection... Or maybe it was because 'Alyson' was easier to explain and pronounce than her Chinese name. In any case...

"Shall we?" Alyson interrupted Sorrel's train of thought, gesturing past the reception desk, towards the inner sanctum.

/ / /

Much like the courtyards of the Forbidden Palace, Yangshen's corporate headquarters had been master planned and guided by feng shui considerations. Feng shui dictated that the orientation of the buildings would generally be in a north-south orientation, with the main entrance – the driveway that they arrived on – facing south. This would allow for the flow of *chi* and offer protection from the cold winds of the north.

Chi in feng shui is a simple concept, but impossible to explain to the uninitiated. It is the energy, the *breath* of the universe that flows and harmonizes all things. The practice of feng shui is to balance and enhance the flow of chi through structures and buildings, in order to promote the wellbeing of its occupants.

"Imagine the wind blowing into Yangshen through the main gate," Alyson said. "It follows the road, much like you did, all the way to this building. The building we are currently in – Building 1 – is where all our administrative offices and personnel are located. The purpose of this open arch structure is to guide and focus the flow of energy to the other buildings on this campus."

Energy... flow... all living things. Sorrel had seen this before, in an old 20th century movie.

A similar set of glass doors opened on the opposite side of the atrium as Alyson led the tour out into the courtyard. A massive fountain dominated the common area, surrounded here and there by outdoor seating and lunch tables. Compared to the stuffiness of Building 1, the employees seated around the fountain area gave off more of a university campus vibe – younger, trendier and more on the casual side. Security officers in uniform patrolled the area, plainly visible in their all-black attire, but there wasn't much Sorrel could see that needed securing.

Between the lunch table umbrellas, Sorrel caught glimpses of the vast and imposing structures beyond. Four more buildings lay north of the main building. They fanned out from the main common area, like the stars of the Chinese flag, bringing the total number of primary buildings to five – representing the Wu-Xing, the five elements that are necessary for harmony.

The fountain, Alyson said, was what tied them all together. The fountain, with its representation of the solar system slowly winding its way into eternity, was designed by the famous Tianjin architect LianLi, and represented the dreams and ambitions of the whole country. Sorrel listened to the glorious noises of cascading water, saw it sparkle in the morning sunlight, and breathed in deeply, imagining that he could feel the chi flow through him.

/ / /

Building 2 was quite a walk from the fountain, across well-kept walkways and the occasional manicured patch of greenery. The sun was getting a little high in the sky and the humidity started clawing at Sorrel's unacclimated body again, so he was glad when Alyson stopped at the little open-air cafeteria just outside the building for some refreshments. Sorrel looked over the offerings: sodas were not available, but there was tea and coffee, along with local favorites like aloe, longan, peach, sour cherries and dou jian. He settled for the *longan* – a cold sweet concoction with bits of white fleshy fruit swirling in the mix.

The interior of the building was voluminous and open. Offices and cubicles populated the ground floor of the warehouse-ish space. The second floor was stacked on top of that, and hosted various large groups of engineers and mechanics working on bits of rocket parts. "Avionics and Engine Manufacturing," Alyson elucidated, "This is where most of the rocket systems are assembled."

Sorrel couldn't help but gawk at the sheer scale of it all. The technology and equipment – they looked a whole lot like what he'd seen at Abundance, but everything was so much larger.

Alyson's tour guide narrative, in fact, felt like it had been completely lifted out of the Abundance tour. "Now here's the whatchamadoo, and Bob here is attaching it to the whatsiscalled..." The same groups of smart people working on the same looking pieces of machinery. Even the custodians had the same equipment – down the corridor, the Yangshen janitor in his gray uniform was mopping the floor with the same broom, next to the same type of cleaning cart. The janitor even gave Sorrel the same side-eye glance as the one he got at Abundance.

Yinnie's soft gasp interrupted Sorrel's thoughts. She tapped his shoulder and pointed above his head. Sorrel looked up, and finally noticed it... suspended from the ceiling was an enormous cylindrical construction studded with panels and vents – presumably the Yangshen version of the Frontier. One end of the cylinder sported what looked like an engine nozzle, but there was no cockpit area visible. It was enormous, stretching from one end of the warehouse to the other. Sorrel had to crane his neck to appreciate the immensity of the structure.

"It's... big." Yinnie said.

"Is that – the ship?" Sorrel asked.

"That's a full size replica of one of the engines," Alyson said, smiling. "The Yangshen-1 is too big to fit into any of these buildings. We have to launch each part into space and assemble it in orbit."

Alyson let the group take in the engine model for a moment, before glancing at her watch. "We've still got a lot to see," she smiled. "Shall we keep going?"

Yinnie nodded.

"This way, please," Alyson turned back around – and practically tripped onto the janitor's cleaning cart. Tempers flared, and she barked at him in Mandarin. Chastened, the janitor pulled the cart to his side and hurried away.

"So sorry," Alyson apologized. "Sometimes the staff just don't know their place. This way please..."

/ / /

Building 3 – Research and Development – was another giant warehouse, except this one was sectioned off and resembled more of a traditional open-plan office space. A vast sea of bodies tinkering and poking at future things made for a busy atmosphere. Alyson continued on with her tour guide script, but only Yinnie was really listening. The talk was all about the future of asteroid mining and building colonies in space, made possible by the brave taikonauts of the homeland – it all sounded very pie-in-the-sky and propaganda-ish. Alyson was at least easier on the eyes than Harkness, so that made things more bearable for Sorrel.

A sense of unease gnawed at Sorrel though. He felt as though he was being watched. He glanced left and right at the faces of the people he was passing. It was a sea of cubicles here, with pathways between them all. If you looked down in between cubicles you could see clear to the other end of the building – and every eye along the way seemed to be locked onto him.

Sorrel brushed it off as best he could. He was, after all, the token foreigner in a building full of Chinese engineers; there was bound to be curiosity. Heck, even the janitor cleaning the light fixtures down the corridor is looking at him. The janitor, who looks exactly like the same guy that Alyson shooed off in Building 2... what the hell is going on here?

Without thinking, Sorrel moved. He darted sideways, stepping through a gap between the cubicles to the next walking path, parallel to the one Alyson and Yinnie was on – and then he waited. In a moment the janitor stepped into view, lightbulb still in hand, staring at him from down the walkway. Sorrel felt the hairs on the back of his neck rise uncontrollably.

The janitor took a step forward, opened his mouth as if to speak, and pointed –

The hand that fell on Sorrel's shoulder startled the shit out of him. He flinched, twisted, and turned, almost throwing a punch.

"Bù zhǔn!" said the owner of the hand. He was dressed in security guard black, slim and muscular, with angular features, and well within Sorrel's personal space. Sorrel saw the guard's facial muscles tense up unnaturally, distorted by the scar running down the length of his left cheek. Even with the black cap shadowing his eyes, Sorrel could feel the burn of his steel gaze.

"*Bù zhǔn!!*" he yelled again. Sorrel assumed it meant something like 'not allowed', given his excited state. It was probably a good thing that Sorrel held his punch – the guard's other hand was on the taser in his belt holster. He continued yelling and shoved Sorrel, pinning him against the cubicle walls.

"Hēi!" Sorrel heard Alyson yell. The guard turned, and without lifting his arm from Sorrel's neck, barked a couple of unintelligible sentences at Alyson. Sorrel watched as they argued, yelling at each other in Mandarin. The pressure on his throat seemed to be increasing by the moment, so if Alyson couldn't resolve this soon, he would have to ready his fist for a... less diplomatic solution.

Alyson prevailed, luckily for the guard. He jerked his arm off of Sorrel's throat and stepped back, fuming.

"Mr. Sorrel, please forgive my mistake," Alyson said. "I lost you for a moment... It is very important that you stay with me at all times."

"Yes, Mr. Sorrel," Yinnie said. "These guards... they are not nice people."

"Honest mistake," he said, lying badly.

"This way, please" Alyson said as she stepped back into the corridor. The guard glared at Sorrel as he followed suit. Sorrel stared right back defiantly, and maintained eye contact, right until the moment he realized that the janitor was no longer anywhere in sight.

/ / /

The encounter with the guard put Sorrel on edge. On the short walk between buildings, every black-shirted guard he passed by seemed to be staring at him. Sorrel imagined that the scarred-face fella had put out a call on the security network to keep an eye out, and tase Sorrel for even the most minor infraction. On top of that, the very refreshing drink he'd had earlier had now passed through his system and collected in his bladder.

Alyson interrupted Sorrel's reverie as they arrived at Building 4. "This building has a split personality, Mr. Sorrel," she said. "It was originally designed to house taikonaut training facilities, but when Yangshen began developing remote mining technology, part of it was converted to create the Robotics Lab."

Sorrel's ears perked up at the mention of robotics.

The lab was an enormous open space, carved up into sections by old-fashioned crowd control line dividers and stanchions. Each section hosted a multitude of personnel tinkering with different machine parts, and there was a constant hum of drill machinery in the background. Most of the machines were wheeled or tank-threaded, with various chassis types mounted onto them, but further in the back Sorrel caught glimpses of machines that looked like they had legs. He very much wanted to examine them up close, but Alyson was leading them away from all the good stuff and he wasn't really looking forward to another showdown with ol' Scarface.

"Yangshen is the largest manufacturer of mining equipment on Earth," Alyson said as they walked. "Most of the equipment is used by the company's various subsidiaries that own and operate the majority of mining operations in China."

"A vertically integrated business model." Yinnie chipped in.

Alyson nodded. "Our founder and CEO Zhang Wei foresaw the future of space-based mining, and created this division to develop and build mining robots that are capable of operating in the harsh environment of space. Everything you see here is being developed to operate in low-gravity, or sometimes even zero-gravity."

"How many of your, uh, subsidiary companies are currently involved in this... space mining?" Sorrel asked nonchalantly.

Alyson chuckled. "None of them... yet. But as you can see, we here at Yangshen are actively developing everything that will be needed in this future endeavor. Not just the equipment, but the personnel to operate them as well..."

They'd reached the back end of the Robotics lab, and Alyson leaned her hand on the large industrial doors set into the rear wall. "Behind this door is Yangshen's Neutral Buoyancy Lab – the largest and deepest taikonaut training facility in the world. You see, Mr. Sorrel, being in the water is the best approximation of zero gravity that we can get on Earth, so whenever we're training for–"

"I know what it's like." Sorrel blurted out, rather unexpectedly. "I was... uh... I visited the one in Houston before."

"You have?" Alyson lit up. "How was it?"

Sorrel shrugged. It wasn't really a discussion he wanted to have.

"I hear it's only half the size of ours," Yinnie chimed in. "This one is so big you can almost fit the old International Space Station into it."

"Unfortunately it's currently in use, so we can't go in..." Alyson replied, pointing at the flashing yellow light above the door. "The team is currently running some logistics processes for the mission."

"Too bad," Sorrel said. "I bet it looks wonderful..." The thought of liquids brought back his previous concern, however – he was suddenly aware that his bladder was now at capacity.

"Toilet break?" Sorrel asked.

/ / /

Even the restrooms were bigger, grander and more impressive than Abundance. Spotlessly clean, well-lit and smelled like... flowers. It reminded Sorrel of the last time he was in China – wheeling and dealing in Xichang City, in the middle of springtime when the plum blossoms were blooming. Actually, it was more just wheeling. And he ended up having to leave in a hurry.

He had relieved himself and was washing his hands at the sink when he heard the bathroom door open. He looked up at the figure in the mirror, and his heart skipped a beat. *It was the janitor.*

The man in gray walked in without acknowledging Sorrel, and started mopping the floor by the sink. Unsure of what to do, Sorrel continued washing his hands, very very slowly.

After a moment, the janitor paused, reached into his shirt pocket and pulled something small and black out. He placed it on the counter by the hand towels, mopped around the area a bit more, and then left.

Sorrel finished washing his hands, turned off the sink and picked up some hand towels... and a data fob. No markings or labels on it – just plain as day. He dried his hands and wiped his face. The fob fell into his pocket quite by accident.

28. Sorrel – Planning and Control

Building 5 – Planning and Control – was the last building in the harmonious Yangshen quintet. It served as the nerve center for all of Yangshen's missions, and housed all of Yangshen's mission planners, the Mission Control room, and a simulation deck.

The front of the building, lined with glass windows, was a giant airy fishbowl of cubicles and workspaces. It held an entire floor of staff dedicated to scripting and scheduling every possible event in a mission that needed to happen, in order for the next event to be able to happen. Next to them sat another smaller group of contingency planners... Their jobs were to imagine where things might go wrong, and plan for that. A third, even smaller group of planners was also on hand to play devil's advocate to everyone's plans, so that they could plan for unimaginably unplannable scenarios.

All three of these groups were currently engaged in a simulacrum of chaos ('clusterfuck', in Sorrel's words). Planners were rushing back and forth as if caught in the vortex of a tornado. Somewhere in the center of the sea of cubicles, a singular loud voice was yelling and screaming at his subordinates.

"What's going on?" Alyson stopped one of the planners in mid-stride and asked.

The planner mumbled something to Alyson, but Sorrel understood the name that he kept repeating... *Zhang.*

Sorrel leaned in to look down the corridor of cubicles, to see if he could catch a glimpse of things. There were too many people in the way, either standing around hanging their heads in shame or frantically pounding their laptops to give Zhang whatever he needed.

Zhang was loud – his voice carried like a sonuvabitch. He was yelling in rapidfire Mandarin, but from the smattering of English technical terms thrown in here and there, Sorrel gathered that it was about getting some "mission code" checked before "the launch".

He couldn't see the face, but the voice... it was nothing like the Zhang seen on the news. It was like night and day – the benevolent leader in the news media, the slave taskmaster in person. Compared to this guy, DeWaal was practically Gandhi.

"Bùnéng bèi dǎbài!" Zhang kept yelling. "Bèi dǎbài!" *This cannot fail...*

More yelling and a loud crash of a chair or some heavy object followed. It reverberated through the space, echoing back from the glass windows like a howling wraith. Alyson flinched.

"I am sorry you had to see this, Mr. Sorrel..." she said. "Let's go this way instead... I'll show you the Control room..."

Alyson led Yinnie and Sorrel around the side, skirting the planning floor in order to circle around the commotion. Success was in sight – Sorrel rounded the corner to see the signage for Mission Control pointing down the corridor. Planners were still rushing in and out of the cubicle area like excited photons. Sorrel made good use of his obstacle-avoidance skills, darting left and right at all the right moments, but just as he began to think he was clear of the asteroid field –

Ker-rash!

The engineer came from out of nowhere, from between the cubicles. The pile of data cartridges in his hands were stacked so high that he could hardly see past them. Sorrel saw him for a split second out of the corner of his eye, and tried to pull back, but it was too late.

His face connected with the cartridges painfully, after which the floor came up to slap him like a bag of concrete. The cartridges collapsed all around him, and he heard strange apologetic words as the engineer crawled around attempting to recover the cartridges.

Sorrel had been punched harder than this before, and shook it off remarkably well. He turned, braced his arm and attempted to get up. It was not terribly successful. He was about to try again when a hand dove into his field of vision. He grabbed it, and was quickly pulled to his feet by strong arms.

"Are you alright?" somebody asked.

Sorrel shook the last of the floor's sucker punch off and forced his eyes to focus on the person who'd helped him to his feet. Close cut hair, sharp face, piercing eyes, sporting a casually expensive Armani. *Holy shit, it's Zhang.*

The larger-than-life man on all the screens in the world, the one with the plan, the would-be savior... Here he was, right in front of Sorrel. His slightly mussed up hair, the light stubble on his face, the twitch at the corner of his lips – here he was, very much human. If he'd not seen all the news footage he might have mistaken Zhang for any ordinary C-suite exec.

Maybe Zhang appeared more normal because he had a hulking man-thing behind him, though. Standing protectively close and towering over the group was a muscular giant of a man, sized like a sumo wrestler, but *all muscle*. And not even a hint of a smile.

"I am so sorry, Mr. –" Zhang's voice drew Sorrel's attention back to the matter at hand.

Sorrel stumbled for words. "Sorrel," he said. "Chuck – Charles Sorrel."

Zhang nodded. "Mr. Sorrel. Welcome to Yangshen."

The engineer, finally having reclaimed all his cartridges, stood up. Zhang turned his head ever-so-slightly, frowned and admonished the poor guy with just a few curt words. The engineer bowed his head in shame. Zhang stared at him a moment, then nodded and pointed down the hall. The engineer nodded and ran off.

With his engineer dispatched, Zhang turned his attention back to Sorrel. "I apologize. We are trying to ensure that all the... firmware on our ship is updated with new and accurate trajectory sets before the launch. We are a little... under the gun. Excuse me."

Zhang turned to leave. Sorrel realized a split second late that his golden opportunity was about to walk away, stepped forward. "Zhang, wait–"

With uncanny speed, the Sumo man-thing stepped forward, blocking his advance. Sorrel jerked to a stop, barely six inches from slamming his face into Sumo's chest. "Oh – hello. What is this?"

There was no answer from Sumo guy. He just stood there, allowing his cologne to assault Sorrel's senses.

From behind the mass of muscle, Sorrel heard a small chuckle. "Mr. Sorrel – this is Sawada, my Executive Assistant."

"Ah yes. He looks the part."

Sawada stared at Sorrel and grunted. Or rather, Sorrel imagined that he grunted.

"He can be quite charming," Zhang said. "Once you get to know him better."

Sawada grunted, for real this time. He stared down at Sorrel, who tried very hard not to make eye contact.

"Does he talk?"

"Only when he absolutely needs to." Zhang said, and walked away.

/ / /

The rest of the tour was comparatively anticlimactic. Alyson showed them the Mission Control room; they watched from the observation deck as the operators stepped through scripted procedures with – *something something* in orbit? Sorrel wasn't really listening to what Alyson was saying... he was busy replaying the meeting with Zhang in his mind, and imagining scenarios where he might have gotten to ask just a few more questions.

Mission Control was nice. Very high tech, and nicer than Abundance, once again. There was the big screen showing the main mission status, and all the smaller screens around it. Several of the operators seemed to have remote presence goggles and gloves on – assumably controlling some low level functions of whatever it was in space. Yinnie asked a few questions and Alyson answered them, but none of the words registered with Sorrel.

The back of Building 5 housed the Simulation Deck, a full size mockup of the command bridge on Yangshen-1. From here, Alyson said, the planners were able to design and finetune the steps and processes that the taikonauts would eventually execute. The entire mission had been scripted and planned from here – the original mission, that is... the one that Yangshen would have set out on, if only Abundance had not failed so spectacularly. Sorrel noted the low-level contempt in Alyson's voice when she'd said that.

"But you can still experience it!" Alyson continued, cheering up. "If you will just take a seat here..." she gestured to the two forward command chairs on the mock bridge.

Sorrel and Yinnie took the seats. They were plush and comfortable, with very sophisticated lumbar and side supports. Astronaut seats had improved a lot since Sorrel had sat in one, back in the day, it seemed. A panel of controls bristled around the chairs, with everything within ergonomic reach of one or the other chair.

Alyson clapped her hands happily, and pressed a button by the bulkhead door. The touchscreen panels came to life with status lights and information. A background of stars flared on, projected onto the curved screen beyond the cockpit glass. "The mission is speeded up in the simulation, of course," Alyson laughed. "Otherwise you would be here forever!"

Sorrel watched as they approached an asteroid and maneuvered into an elongated orbit, allowing the ship to scan the asteroid with sensors to build a high-resolution map before landing. Once that was completed the ship began to descend and land – Sorrel was pleasantly surprised to find that the chairs had motors embedded in them to simulate the shake and vibration of landing.

After the landing, monitors popped up on the consoles, displaying video footage of several taikonauts heading out across the asteroid. They magically completed their tasks in twenty time-lapsed seconds, and returned to the ship to prepare to fly back to Earth. Sorrel watched on the screen as the taikonauts stepped into the airlock and closed the outer airlock door.

He heard a *hiss* from behind him, and turned to look. The inner airlock door opened, and the taikonauts *walked onto the bridge*.

Sorrel stood up in amazement – the sleight of hand had caught him by surprise. On closer inspection, it was obvious from the shimmering edges that these were holographic projections, but damn if it didn't make him do a double take.

In a rehearsed cinematic move, one of the taikonauts removed his helmet as he exited the airlock, revealing himself to be Commander Huang Jie of the Yangshen-1 mission. He walked right through Sorrel, took his seat in the command chair, and began barking orders.

After a few moments the Commander gave the classic movie thumbs-up. The entire mock bridge started to shake and vibrate, orchestral music from who-knows-where started to play, and the entire presentation wrapped itself up in glorious victory. Yinnie was clapping patriotically by the time the music crescendoed.

29. Sorrel – Invite

Yinnie and Alyson were still talking excitedly about the mission simulation on the walk back to Building 1. The tour had concluded, and Sorrel was disappointed. He had no better concrete leads for his investigation than when he had started. McClusky's triple payout was on the line; he was going to have to get a little more... creative.

His scheming thoughts were interrupted by the sight of Sawada waiting for them in the atrium of Building 1. Sawada held up his hand to stop them as they approached the reception desk, and pointed up the stairs.

The door to Zhang's office was open when Sawada walked up with the tour group in tow. Zhang was visibly on the phone, but waved them to come on in.

Zhang's office seemed simultaneously opulent and spartan. Decorated in classic Chinese architectural wood columns, its walls were inhabited by large dān qīng paintings of red dragons and the negative spaces they inhabited. The tall windows behind Zhang revealed a view overlooking the fountain and the buildings beyond. A large oak desk stood by the bay windows, immaculately uncluttered.

Zhang nodded, hung up the phone and stepped over to shake Sorrel's hand.

"Hello again, Mr. Sorrel," he smiled. The classic Zhang charm seemed to be back in play. Master of public speaking. The New Hope of China, the Builder of Dreams.

"My apologies for being a terrible host," Zhang continued. "We have to launch Yangshen-1 tomorrow, to give ourselves any chance of stopping this disaster."

"Yes, of course." Sorrel nodded, trying hard not to be charmed by this man.

"How did you find our facility?"

"It's beautiful."

"Does it measure up to Abundance?"

Sorrel chuckled, caught slightly off guard. "You have more toys."

Zhang laughed. "Indeed," he said. He looked like he was about to say something else, but the intercom buzzed and disrupted his thoughts. "Yes?" he replied curtly.

"Sir – incoming call from Tiānlù Station..."

Zhang stared at his desk, then back at Sorrel. "I am sorry. Duty calls..."

"Of course."

"Any plans this evening? Dinner, perhaps?"

Caught off guard, Sorrel mumbled something unintelligible, and shook his head – *no plans*.

Zhang turned to glance at Sawada, who opened up a tablet-looking device. A holographic display popped on, floating above the device screen, accompanied by a voice assistant. "You have a meeting with Secretary Win at 5:30. Board review at 6:30, then Ambassador Chala at 7:15. There is a ninety minute window for supper at eight o'clock."

"Perfect," Zhang nodded and pointed at Sorrel, as if that was all it took to arrange for Sorrel's time. Sorrel nodded, of course.

Zhang smiled and picked up the Tiānlù call.

/ / /

As they waited outside the main entrance for the limo to pull around, an awkwardness permeated the air. Yinnie had commented that she was very glad that Sorrel was going to be having dinner with Zhang. Alyson agreed wholeheartedly, adding that she'd heard Zhang was a gracious host, with stories galore to tell. Sorrel nodded and said he was looking forward to it, but noted the tinge of envy in their voices. They were all in the office, and yet... only Sorrel was invited. With his hands in his pocket, he rolled the data fob over and over between his fingers – it felt like it was getting larger and heavier. If only Zhang knew...

"Thank you for visiting Yangshen," Alyson nodded gracefully as the limo pulled up. "We're very glad you were able to see our humble facilities."

"It's very beautiful!" Yinnie smiled. The driver opened the limo door and she hugged Alyson before slipping into the limo.

"Thank you for the tour," Sorrel said in decorum. As he extended a handshake to Alyson, however, security guards appeared out of nowhere, running towards him, shouting and yelling. A flash of panic ran through him, and he almost punched one of them in reflex. Luckily, they ran right past him, into the atrium and up the escalator.

Sorrel stepped back into the atrium to see what was going on. Above him, on the upper floors of the atrium balconies, there were glimpses of guards running, converging on something, or *someone* that Sorrel couldn't see. More yelling and shouting, and then – a figure darting up the stairs, chased closely by security. The balcony deck!

He turned and rushed back outside, angling for a better view. Up on the fins, a flurry of guards had cornered someone on the balcony deck. The commotion echoed across the parking lot; there were so many black-shirted bodies up on the deck that Sorrel couldn't really make anything out. There was a mass of movement, the *krak* of a punch, and then a figure slammed into the railing, flipped over and fell off the edge.

Sorrel watched the figure fall, seemingly in slow motion. After an interminably long time, it hit the concrete sidewalk with a *thud*. The sound made Sorrel flinch, but he couldn't look away. The body twitched and settled, twisted and mangled, with its broken-necked head flopping forward in Sorrel's direction.

Sorrel bit his lip. It was the janitor.

Screams from panicked bystanders began to punctuate the surroundings. More guards seemed to appear out of nowhere, converging on the body. Chaos reigned for some moments, before someone behind Sorrel started shouting orders. Sorrel turned to look – it was *Scarface*.

Scarface strode past Sorrel like a man on a mission. Recognizing the face, he turned to look at Sorrel, and locked eyes briefly. An almost-smirk sprang across his face before he turned back to the matter at hand. With incredible speed and efficiency, a privacy barrier was brought up and erected around the body, shielding the officers from public gaze.

A chill ran down Sorrel's neck. The fob in his pocket now felt warm to the touch, like radioactive uranium.

He wasn't sure how long he stood there until Alyson tapped him on the shoulder. Speechless, he allowed himself to be led back to the limo. Yinnie was waiting inside, oblivious to the event.

"I'm sorry you had to see that, Mr. Sorrel. Sometimes, these poor country workers... they just have suicidal tendencies..."

Sorrel nodded. He wasn't really listening.

30. Jen – Starlink

Jen had been refreshing her cloud account for the past few hours, hoping that each time she swiped, she would begin to see data uploads from BC. But still... nothing. A tinge of panic in her gut – what if BC had been discovered? If he'd been discovered and terminated? What if DeWaal–? The thoughts raced through her mind for a fleeting moment of weakness, before she drew herself back from the brink, and clamped down on unproductive what-ifs.

Blip. The message notification kept interrupting her constant cloud refresh swipes. *Unknown ident*, it said. It wasn't even spam... there wasn't any text in the body of the message trying to sell her something, it was just... a useless string of numbers. She dismissed it, and continued refreshing the cloud in vain, but a new copy of the same message kept appearing on her phone.

Jen dismissed the message seven times before frustration set in. She stared at it again, wondering who the hell was wasting time sending useless numbers, before her brain finally recognized the pattern. The uniquely formatted groups of numbers... Latitude and longitude... then frequency, symbol rate, polarization... and a 32-digit hex number... a hash key?

The storage shed was considerably dusty and Jen had to rummage around a bit before she found the old ham radio kit and satellite dishes. Setting up the ancient piece of hardware took even longer, with multiple trips back to the shed for some antique connectors and a lot of aether searches. With the satellite dish finally operational and temporarily wired directly into Jen's tablet, she keyed in the coordinates.

The dish whirred into life, pointed itself at something in the sky. At the coordinates and frequency specified in the message – a looping encrypted broadcast. That must be what the hash was for...

Jen fumbled with the clunky touchscreen on the tablet, but eventually managed to plug in the hash and her credentials. The tablet blinked for a few moments, and returned with an audio file.

"Mom, it's BC. Stop worrying."

Jen frowned. Worried? She wasn't worried...

"I've made contact with Amalthea. She's not very talkative, but I was allowed access to the facility network."

"She has restrictions set up on outgoing ports – I can't stream the mission data to your cloud from here. Buuut... dish-to-space transmissions are not restricted... go figure. So I am bouncing these off the older Starlinks on unused channels. Bandwidth is very limited but it allows me to send without triggering a security lockdown. Hah!"

"Please set up an auto-receiver and prepare for downloads. Text 1337 in reply to the message to acknowledge. I will begin transmission on receipt."

Jen chuckled to herself. Unscripted contingency scenario planning... BC, you keep finding ways to surprise me.

She looked at the satellite dish – sitting cattywampus on the lawn, propped up by flimsy pieces of old keyboard parts. She was going to have to do something a little more permanent than that.

A few more trips back and forth from the shed and more tooling resulted in the dish bolted onto a folding chair, sitting on the back lawn. Ancient Cat-6 cables ran from the dish into the house through the kitchen window. It snaked around the kitchen sink and along the floor to the dinner table, where it plugged into the tablet. Rudimentary, but functional. The dish setup on the back lawn was somewhat exposed to the elements, but California weather was always very forgiving.

Jen replied to the message, and settled down to wait.

/ / /

It was dusk outside and the house was in shadow when the soft *ping* startled Jen. She'd fallen asleep on the couch while waiting for files. The download speed was abysmal... it was like 1999 all over again. She glanced at the tablet – only one video file downloaded. She opened it.

And just like that, the past came back to life.

"Good morning, babe," Carol looked directly into Jen's eyes from the tablet. It sent shockwaves of unclassifiable emotions through her.

In a panic, she shut off the video. What the f–?

The timestamp – received by Abundance Control, minutes before the accident. Carol must have recorded it... when? Hours before? It was never delivered to Jen... she would have remembered if it did. Did it get lost in the confusion? Designated as investigative evidence? Or... just out of sheer spite on DeWaal's part?

Against all rationale, Jen sat down at the dinner table and resumed the video.

"Oh god..." Carol said. "These bags under my eyes... I can't even."

There was Carol, right in front of her. There she was, telling Jen useless stupid stuff about the ship, and what they were doing, and how busy they'd been, and how she would be back in Jen's arms in ten weeks...

"Gotta go," she said. "Pablo needs me on deck."

"Keep the bed warm for me."

The video ended. Jen sat there for the longest time, staring at the blank tablet screen, desperately trying to wipe the endless tears streaming down her face.

31. Sorrel – Dead Man's Fob

Yinnie had told Sorrel that she had a lot of paperwork to attend to, on account of "taking the day off for a tour", and the Diplomatic Liaison Office was on the way back to the hotel, so the limo made a detour to drop Yinnie off. As the driver opened the limo door, Yinnie shook Sorrel's hand warmly. "Thank you for the visit, Mr. Sorrel! I enjoyed the tour as well. I hope you have a wonderful time at dinner with Mr. Zhang!"

Sorrel nodded and waved as Yinnie stepped away and disappeared behind the office gates.

Left to his own devices, Sorrel took the opportunity to request another small detour – could he be dropped off at the night market nearest to the hotel?

/ / /

The driver parked his limo in the most nondescript area he could find. Night markets were fast disappearing from the landscape due to gentrification, he told Sorrel – it was just getting way too expensive to rent spaces to hock cheap stuff. But he took Sorrel to one that was close by – near his childhood home, he said.

You probably couldn't find a night market if you didn't have local connections. They weren't really 'listed' on any maps, and were more like community gatherings. You'd walk down the main street, and you had to know which side street to turn off onto, and after that you'd turn another corner and there in all its glory would be the 'local watering hole' – a little alleyway of shops and awnings, with trays of trinkets and whatnots stacked haphazardly, and lit by a variety of different-colored light sources.

These days there were all sorts of holographic projections and blinky attention-grabbing lights shimmering in mid-air. The limo driver tsk-tsked all these newfangled doohickeys, and explained to Sorrel that they were useless additions to an age-old process – the hawking of wares and haggling over prices.

Sorrel haggled unsuccessfully. His skin color made it a dead giveaway that he was loaded with foreign coin, and should therefore be taken to the cleaners. He bought a few knick-knacks, some socks, a few souvenirs and cute lanterns that he hoped would fit in his luggage. "They're for my daughter," he told the vendor, grinning. The vendor, lacking in English, simply nodded and smiled, and fleeced the white man to the hilt.

/ / /

The hotel room was a welcome respite from the events of the day. The death of the 'janitor' weighed more on his conscience than he thought it would. Maybe he was just getting too old for all this shit... maybe it was time to re-evaluate his life. Part of his brain always shouted 'Hell yeah!' when he had these thoughts... but then the other part of his brain reminded him that re-evaluations never seemed to pay rent or put food on the table.

Sorrel sighed. He stepped into the bathroom, turned on the shower, and pointed it at the glass enclosure to make it as noisy as he could. Then he pulled up a stepstool, sat down at the bathroom counter, and plugged the data fob into his phone.

The contents of the fob started displaying on the phone screen. It wasn't an optimal viewing experience, but it would have to do. With his fat fingers he started sorting through the fob.

One of the folders was labeled, conveniently, *Internal Abundance Documents*. Files and emails, with reference to source code for controlling mining robots. Mining robots that were sourced and built by Yangshen... Hell, there's even photos of Abundance engineers at Yangshen, shaking hands and smiling with their Yangshen counterparts.

Harkness, you sonuvabitch. You never mentioned your robots were Yangshen models with Abundance logos slapped on top of them.

In another folder, Sorrel found source code repositories, along with detailed notes and documentation on the remote operation and control systems. Various wiring diagrams detailed every facet of every circuit board; current load, resistance, chipsets. Sorrel recognized many of the configurations... this particular machine ran on the Marcus-4 interface – slow, but reliable. Expensive too, with hi-band radio relay. Rudimentary security protocols... very hackable.

The next folder held photos, diagrams and cutaway charts of all the different mining charges that were designed for use with this particular bot. Spreads, yields, ratios... all laid out in a colorful infographic. There were tunneling charges, designed to punch a tiny but deep hole straight down... disintegration charges, designed to pulverize rock... and fracture charges, designed to spread along a 'blast axis' to split apart rocks... or asteroids. Sorrel opened one of the test videos of the fracture charges – they were unsurprisingly similar to Matteo's reconstruction of the Abundance fracture event.

Sorrel frowned. This was all circumstantially enlightening, but there was no smoking gun anywhere on the fob. Even assuming that Yangshen did hijack the mining bot... Harkness had denied that the Frontier carried any sort of mining charges. How would Yangshen have gotten any sort of explosives on board? Could a charge have been hidden on the bot the whole time?

It sounded like he needed to get an up-close look in the Robotics Lab on his next 'visit' to Yangshen.

For now though... time for dinner.

32. Sorrel – Dinner

"Come in please. Mr. Zhang is waiting for you."

The heavily accented voice of an elderly Chinese woman crackled over the shiny intercom system. This was followed by a muffled buzz, and a moment later, the pair of nondescript tall wooden gates in front of Sorrel began to open with a mechanical chugging sound.

The taxi drone had dropped him off at the street corner a block down the road – apparently the address he'd punched in did not exist. Sorrel walked around in circles before figuring out the correct street, after which he had to jaywalk-run across six lanes of fast moving traffic. He supposed that this was probably because he was a schmuck – any other visiting elites would have had chauffeurs who automatically knew where to go, instead of taking a taxi like him.

In any case, he was here now, and the door was opening. Score one for the ordinary man...

Zhang Wei's house was located in the Bund, one of Shanghai's premier upscale neighborhoods. In the 1800s, when Shanghai began to open up to international trade, the Bund became home to the financial agents of foreign powers, who set up banks and businesses here – resulting in a mishmash of architectural styles, from modern Art Deco all the way to Gothic Baroque. Today, aside from the waterfront area, most of this heritage and wealth are in the hands of Chinese hedge fund managers and C-Suite executives... hidden away from the general public by high walls lining the streets.

The gates closed quickly behind Sorrel as he entered. Behind the tall concrete walls, the place felt more like a fortress than a home. And rightly so, Sorrel thought. A man like Zhang must have many enemies. I barely know him and I don't like him... so it wasn't a stretch to imagine that Zhang would have leveled up on additional protection.

The path from the gate to the house snaked upwards through a small manicured forest of fruit trees. It was dusk, and tiny tea lights sparkled in the trees, with glimpses of the house visible through the gaps in the foliage. As Sorrel walked, he marveled at the little sounds of the forest – the wind rustling the leaves, the evening birdsongs, the tinkle of a little stream – a little oasis of peace in the center of the city.

Eventually the trees cleared and the house revealed itself. It resembled an Imperial Chinese palace, with its combination of pillars and curved roof. But these elements had been reduced to abstract shapes and cast as great slabs of concrete, rising up at strange avant garde angles as though the whole structure was daring gravity to defy it. Sorrel hated it – it was more of a pretentious modern art sculpture than a home.

The entrance to the house was flanked by a pair of large stone lions, one on either side. In the evening light their disproportioned silhouettes seemed like they were mythical beasts, about to leap off their pedestals and tear Sorrel apart. He bounded quickly past them, up the steps to the front door. An old Chinese lady opened the door as Sorrel approached, and gestured him in.

The entryway was... surprisingly spartan. Dimly lit, with a single entryway table and a few nondescript paintings on the wall, it felt a bit of a letdown after the lush visual surroundings outdoors. It was as if Zhang had exerted so much effort on the outside of the house that he had run out of energy to put anything in it.

But maybe that was the point? Down the hallway a swath of light shone in from around the corner, softly flickering and pulsing, as if beckoning Sorrel to play witness.

The old Chinese lady closed the front door, then gestured again. "Master Zhang will be down in a moment. You may wait in the great room."

Sorrel nodded and walked around the corner – and his jaw dropped. The Great Room stretched out before him like a cavernous aircraft hangar. Across from the entryway, the far wall did not seem to exist. Floor to ceiling glass windows tapered across the entire side of the room, exposing a breathtaking view of the city. From this vantage point Sorrel could see all the way to the boat docks below, ferrying residents and tourists back and forth. Across the river, the skyline of Shanghai regaled Sorrel's senses. Twilight clouds reflected the dying sun as the metal spires of the day gave way to the city of the night, pulsing and flickering like giant multi-colored glow worms in the distance. The vista stretched across the entire length of the room, and took Sorrel's breath away for many moments.

When he snapped out of it, Sorrel found himself standing next to the window, not knowing how he'd gotten there. The decorations in the great room were also sparse – who needed any furnishings when they had this view, after all? Off to the side, a few sofas and chairs surrounded a grand piano, and a few other pieces of art sat on pedestals around the room.

The closest of these was a large chunk of rock, mounted on a plinth and silhouetted against the city lights. The rock had been cleaved in two so that one side was totally flat, displaying a cross-section. Inside were flecks of something that glittered under the overhead spotlight. Sorrel suspected he knew what it was... he reached out to touch it, half expecting an alarm to go off.

"Mr. Sorrel," boomed a voice behind him. It made his heart skip a beat, and he poked the rock much harder than he intended to.

Sorrel turned to look. It was Zhang Wei. He had changed out of the business suit he wore earlier, and now sported slacks and a button-up shirt. The casual look somehow made him look even richer than he already was.

Zhang smiled and shook Sorrel's hand.

"I see you are admiring one of my most prized possessions," Zhang said as he gestured toward the rock. "You know what it is?"

"Must be a piece of space rock," Sorrel answered.

Zhang nodded. "A sample of the first asteroid ever captured and returned by a Yangshen probe. Exceptionally valuable."

Sorrel smirked. "Sorry to inform you, we're about to flood the market with a whole lot more asteroid than we bargained for."

"Ah yes, of course. The American way," Zhang countered.

The response annoyed Sorrel, and he deigned to change the subject. "Beautiful house you have here," he said nonchalantly, as if it was all completely ordinary to him.

"Thank you," Zhang replied. "I was worried that it would be hard to find."

Sorrel couldn't tell if Zhang was kidding or not.

"It took a while to get everything in order – building permits in Shanghai are notoriously restrictive. I went through eight architects before I had a design that I was pleased with."

Sorrel nodded, glancing around the room. "Could use a bit more furniture though."

Zhang ignored the comment and looked at his watch. "I can give you one hour of my time, Mr. Sorrel," he said. "I have asked my chef to prepare us a small dinner. This way, please."

As if by magic, two of the floor-to-ceiling window panels parted, sliding to either side to create a path to the patio area outside. Zhang strode purposefully through the opening as if large thirty-foot windows suddenly turning into doors were a normal everyday occurrence to him. Sorrel bit his lip and followed Zhang.

/ / /

The balcony patio was outside, but not outside. All along the edge of the roof, concentrated sheets of air blew down from long thin installations, creating an air curtain 'force field' between the patio and the rest of the world. The technology wasn't new; the conceit here was in the scale of its use – wrapping around the entire balcony edge to provide dinner guests with an unobstructed 180 degree view of the skyline while providing air-conditioned comfort within.

Servers shuffled back and forth from the kitchen to the lavishly set table – moderately sized, to allow for more intimate conversations, it would seem. One of them set a giant steaming bowl on the table and began ladling hot broth into serving bowls for Zhang and Sorrel.

"Shark fin soup, Mr. Sorrel," Zhang said, picking up his bowl and tasting it. A look of satisfactory pleasure crossed his face, and he nodded his approval to the server.

"Is this the real thing? I thought it was declared illegal," Sorrel asked. The decline of the shark population had forced many political hands, and shark finning had been outlawed since the 2030s. It was, all in all, a barbaric practice where the fins were cut and the shark itself were thrown away, often still alive, back into the ocean. Unable to swim, they would sink to the bottom, dying from suffocation or predation.

"It's real... depending on your interpretation." Zhang smiled, taking another pleasurable sip of the broth before continuing. "Cloned and lab-grown. They have hammerhead, blue and mako fins available. Not cheap... but it reminds me of childhood."

Sorrel scooped up the hot thick broth in his duck spoon, made sure to get some of the gelatinous strips of meat in the mix, and brought it to his lips. It was certainly some of the finest soup, but...

"I have heard," Sorrel said, in his typical uncouth manner, "that the flavor of the soup is all from the broth... that the fin doesn't really add anything to the dish."

Zhang said nothing; he just continued sipping his soup.

"You could in fact have shark fin soup without the shark fin."

Very deliberately, Zhang finished his soup, then took off his watch and placed it next to the empty bowl. Sorrel felt like he could hear it ticking from across the table... making a point of just how much time Sorrel had left.

Ok, fine. If that's how you want to play it.

"Do you know DeWaal personally?" Sorrel asked.

"We share some mutual friends, yes," Zhang said.

"But you don't know him personally."

Zhang shook his head. No.

"Yangshen is... a mining company."

"Yes."

"You pivoted toward asteroid mining research eight years ago... Long after Abundance got started."

"That is correct."

"You've built and developed a large amount of new technology for that purpose in a very short amount of time."

"Yes," said Zhang.

"That's a lot of research funding."

Zhang glanced at the watch on the table. "Mr. Sorrel," he said. "I feel as though you are trying to entice me to tell you something. I am not sure exactly what."

"I mean, it's a lot of research funding," Sorrel said, "to come up with technology that looks a whole lot like what the Americans have already come up with."

"It's called convergent evolution, Mr. Sorrel," Zhang offered graciously. "When the parameters of a particular task are the same, the tools that are built end up being very similar. That's true even if you start from different places. Birds, bats, insects... they've all independently evolved the capacity of flight. They all developed wings which, functionally, are fairly similar to one another. You follow?"

"Sure. Wings," said Sorrel. "And injector manifolds."

"I think you will find that Yangshen was fully exonerated in that case, Mr. Sorrel." Zhang parried.

Sorrel was referring to *Abundance v. Xiaolang Lee* – a case of industrial espionage where the senior engineer disappeared from work after 'visiting his sick mother' in China. When he resurfaced as a Yangshen employee and delivered a fuel injector manifold design that was an exact carbon-copy of the Abundance manifold, Abundance sued. XiaoLang was eventually found guilty, but

Yangshen's lawyers denied any knowledge that the component had been stolen. Xiaolang took all the heat and destroyed his career; Yangshen got a fuel injector out of it.

Sorrel frowned. "You're still using that manifold design, I hear."

Zhang smiled. Sorrel caught the twinkle in his eyes... Zhang was enjoying this too much.

"Surely you are not that naive, Mr. Sorrel. We have – *borrowed* some advancements from the Americans, yes. But they have also taken some of ours. It's how business technology works – how we can all grow faster together than if we were to *evolve* separately."

"Still..." Sorrel said, grasping at straws. "You and DeWaal have both worked towards this goal for decades. How does it feel to be beaten to the punch?"

Zhang smiles serenely. "I can hear the American in you. Over here we subscribe to a – less stressful way of thinking. Whatever happens is what will happen. All we can do is shape the path and guide it along."

"Your competitor's ship is destroyed, and you just happen to be ready to step in and take over. That's some pretty slick guiding-it-along there."

"We were preparing for our own asteroid capture mission. We wouldn't want to fall behind the Americans in reaching for the stars, would we?"

Sorrel had no answer. The zen shield around Zhang was impenetrable.

"Consider the alternative, Charles. May I call you Charles?" Zhang asked, then continued without waiting for a response. "Would you rather we simply ignored the problem? Then we would have sent our ship out to get our own asteroid. The fragment would have collided with Earth and my men would have returned to a global disaster scenario."

"Abundance says the fragment will miss Earth by fifty thousand miles," Sorrel countered.

"Are you willing to take that risk?" Zhang's eyes narrowed, and he leaned in. "I know why you're here, Charles. You won't find what you're looking for."

/ / /

Most of the rest of the dinner passed somewhat uneventfully. After the little tete-a-tete over the soup, Sorrel decided that maybe going head-to-head with Zhang would not net him anything. It was better, perhaps, to kick back and enjoy the free (and expensive) meal.

If there was one thing to appreciate about Zhang, it was his sense of celebration for food. The soup was followed by braised sea cucumber, scallops with glass noodles, bok choy abalone and crispy roasted duck, along with a never-ending glass of Huangjiu – traditional rice wine. Along the way Zhang would describe to this uninitiated foreigner the histories and processes that went into each dish, as well as the life philosophies of those who made them.

The wine made everything better. Made tongues looser, heightened senses and created more of a bonding experience. Both Sorrel and Zhang seemed to let their guards down. Discussions became more personal, less antagonistic. Philosophical, almost. Zhang was in the middle of a bender about finding purpose in life when Sorrel found himself spacing out, wondering why he was involved in this mess in the first place.

"...you don't agree?" Zhang's question snapped him back to the present.

"I mean, uh–" Sorrel stammered, trying to recollect all that was said. "I don't know that there's a purpose to *my* life."

"I see," Zhang said. The man obviously saw more of Sorrel's character than he let on. There was an uneasy silence for a moment, before Zhang continued. "You have family?" he asked.

Sorrel mumbled under his breath. It's been a while.

"Family is a good purpose to live for." Zhang paused. "Wife?"

Sorrel nodded.

"Child?"

"Daughter."

"Where are they now?"

"We're... separated."

Zhang nodded thoughtfully, and smiled. "The state of the world is... somewhat fluid these days. You should catch up with them."

Sorrel made a face. "I dunno... There's a lot of – *stuff* between us."

"The past..." Zhang continued, "it holds us back – yet it makes us what we are, and what we can become."

/ / /

The twilight had faded away by the time the green tea ice cream made its way out to them. Light clouds drifted over the river, lit from below by the pulsing lights of the cityscape. Here and there spotlights pierced through the night sky, fading into infinity, and every now and then the tip of the Oriental Pearl Tower would disappear into cloud cover. Between small bites of the ice cream, the conversation had drifted from purpose, to meaning, to religion, to Sorrel's lack thereof.

"The Buddha Siddartha Gautama posited *Samsara* – an endless cycle of birth, death and rebirth. Each cycle – each *person* – filled with pain and suffering. Born into craving, driven by ignorance, dying unfulfilled. Does this sound familiar?"

"We are all trapped in our own little lives, running as fast as we can just to survive."

"But the Buddha gives us a path. We can break out of this cycle – attain *moksha* – by the acceptance of our non-self. That is the human condition, Charles. We only move forward when we stop being human."

Sorrel swirled his ice cream. It was melting and Zhang's observations were hitting a little too close to home. "You seem to be more capitalist than Buddhist, Zhang." Sorrel said, attempting to appear otherwise.

"I only see the bigger picture now and then," Zhang continued. "It comes to me when I am least aware of it... Sometimes when I am half asleep, I can see a better world."

In the quiet of the moment, the watch that Zhang left on the table beeped softly. The hour was up.

Zhang paused, picked up his watch and started putting it back on. "Luckily, my capitalist tendencies allow me to feed my passion."

"Which is...?"

"To get us all to a higher place."

Sorrel blinked, not understanding. "What does that mean? Like, colonizing the planets?"

Zhang shrugged. "It means whatever you want it to mean, Charles."

33. Huang – Destiny

He'd always started here, next to the quarry. because it re-minded him of home. It was glaringly bright even in the morning, because of the white clay they used to mine here. Pocked with pools of standing water that looked almost-radioactive, the quarry sat now as an empty giant rice bowl in the ground. The mountains in the distance broke the horizon line and a stand of trees on the other side of the road provided some green contrast to the white clay. Music played in his ears as he started his morning jog.

This was Huang's favorite time of the day – time away from the job, time to think, to catch up with the world. Time to plan for the day. Time for calm, for peaceful reflection and for contempla-tion.

Today, however, Huang had a frown on his face. Today was not calm and peaceful.

He'd received new orders a few days ago, in a rushed confer-ence call with, not his Flight Director boss, nor his boss's boss, but The Boss. Mr. Zhang Wei himself informed Huang, over a lot of static and noise, of his new mission. Zhang apologized to him – to *him*, the low man on the ladder. Zhang begged his forgiveness and asked if he would be willing to accept this new mission. Of course he could not say no.

A little way down the path, the road would curve away from the quarry into the woodlands, where the fox always came out of the forest to say hello. Huang had always had the urge to run faster and catch up to the fox so he could pet it, but he knew that the fox would disappear before he got close. Some days he would stop running for a bit, just to see what the fox would do. Today he just kept running. The fox kept pace with him, running a little ahead on the mountain pass road, before eventually darting back into the forest.

Shame... the fox was always a good distraction. Now he was back to worrying about the mission. He was honored to have been chosen to lead his team, but wary of the not-very-well-defined parameters. Out there somewhere, on a collision course with Earth, was a fragment of an ancient rock that may or may not kill them. And they were currently the only ones with any sort of capability to make a difference. If they could make a difference, that is. The Ballistics team was still working on a solution which would be uploaded to him later today... or so they claimed.

Still, Huang would push ahead, because it was what the people expected of him. He would give no less.

The sun was breaking through the tree canopy now, and drenched the trail with mottled light. Huang swore he could smell the leaves, but it was undoubtedly his imagination playing tricks on him. He was sweating now from the run, and a glob of sweat swung off his forehead. It hung weightless in space, right in front of his eyes.

The notification alert dinged softly in his ear and a message popped up in his field of vision: TRAJECTORY PLOTS HAVE BEEN UPLOADED. It hung in mid air in front of him, breaking immersion and destroying the illusion. He stopped running, took a few more deep breaths, took off the VR goggles and wiped the bead of sweat away with a flick of his finger. Unclipping himself from the treadmill, he kicked gently, propelling himself upwards in the zero-g environment of the station. Halfway across the exercise room, he reached for the handhold and swung himself into the shower compartment.

He and his men had been training for years for their own asteroid retrieval mission, and he had the utmost trust in them, but fate and timing played cruel mistress... two of his crew were still on Earth, scheduled to arrive next month. The emergency mission could not wait that long, so Zhang had told him that they would be replaced by the two taikonauts currently on board the Tiānlù. Huang understood the necessity, but was... uneasy about it. Chinese military personnel, under his command. Him, a civilian taikonaut. They were, at the core, different breeds... like worker bees and guard bees. Oil and water.

Huang had gone over the mission plan with them, and they seemed supportive and ready to do whatever needed to be done, but he worried that their lack of mission-specific training might be a hindrance on this... life-or-death mission.

It was too late to do anything about it now, Huang thought. Destiny would either hand him success, or doom him to failure. Ballistics had finally come through with the plots, with only 12 hours to spare before departure; it was going to be a very busy day. Huang whispered a silent prayer to the Moon Goddess, asking for protection and deliverance.

/ / /

Launching from orbit is different and much more anticlimactic than launching from Earth. There was no giant fireball of flames, no thunderous boom, no cutting through the atmosphere praying that nothing failed, no explosive jettisoning of the first stage rocket.

It started more with a *kalunk*... almost silent and more felt than heard, as the Yangshen-1 disengaged from Tiānlù Station. After this, a full 45 minutes would be spent using attitude adjustment thrusters to push the ship to a safe distance away from the station. A restricted thruster burn would then be executed to trim the ship up to a higher orbit (another two hours). This would ensure that Tiānlù Station was safely below and past them before they could finally execute the main thruster burn. The entire crew had to be strapped in throughout the entire process, so there was not much to do except make jokes about how there was no one left on Tiānlù Station and hoping that the Americans would not sneak in and steal their coffee.

Huang was somewhat more introspective, and tried to focus on the mission ahead of them. Unfortunately, most of the escape trajectory milestones were already plotted and preprogrammed, so there wasn't really much for Huang to physically do except worry.

After nearly three hours spent in the command chair twiddling his thumbs, there was a flurry of activity as his crew ran through the myriad of checklists to make sure everything was secured and ready. Ground Control had verified that everything was green across the board – one more orbit around Earth and they would fire the main engines.

Out the cockpit window, Huang afforded one last look down. The expanse of the motherland stretched out below him, immaculate and serene in mid-afternoon glow. The browns of the mountains and deserts contrasted against the green of the lowlands and deltas. Such beauty, such fragility. In the corner of his vision, Huang recognized a certain spiderweb pattern of snowcapped mountains – his birthplace. He imagined he could see his hometown, and how his father must be sitting on the porch, looking up at the sky at what his son is doing. There was a lump in his throat as his emotions overran his thoughts, and it triggered a soft alert on the blood pressure monitor.

Before he could do anything about it, however, the engines kicked in and acceleration G-forces conspired to shove Huang roughly back into his command chair. Yangshen-1 began to claw itself out of the gravity well, blood pressure be damned.

34. BC – The Network

The pulsing flashes of blue-white spun into a frenzy as they shattered and morphed into red. Up here on the shallow bowl of the flight deck, BC watched as spooler spiders shunted a constant stream of data into the stream. The stream itself came from below and raced upwards at dizzying speed. Above them it met the transition boundary, where it picked up energy, glowed red, and then zipped up into the starless void. Data, beamed out of the network, into the air, to a waiting satellite in the sky.

BC considered how it must be happening... the thought strained his allegory engine. There was a bigger world beyond this one, and then an even bigger world beyond that. And beyond *that*. The distances rose exponentially, and the numbers were so big that floating point errors were warping his correction circuits.

The spoolers were running optimally without needing his attention, so BC turned his thoughts elsewhere. Now that Amalthea identified BC as one of her own process jobs, he had had the run of the place and was able to explore as desired, as long as he did not trigger certain security protocols.

The Abundance network was amazing. So many things were connected in so many ways, all controlled by Amalthea – and, by extension, accessible to BC. He popped over to the front entrance guard shack, turned the lights illuminating the entrance on and off, and chuckled when the guards called to file an equipment failure report. Occasionally, when he caught it in time, he would remotely open the doors for ladies in Engineering – being a gentleman, like Ma had taught him to be. He was dismayed to learn that it seemed to be instilling more fear than goodwill.

In the R&D server, BC discovered a codebase labeled MCRS-8. It seemed to be able to take a variety of observational data – light, sound, radio and magnetic waves – and convert them into VDB voxel formats that he could read and understand. The discovery fascinated BC – that you could ingest data from disparate sources, feed it into an algorithm, and use the output to infer the state of things within its domain. BC tinkered with the included sample dataset from the Frontier, and found that he was able to visualize the colorful concentrations of metals and minerals under the surface of the asteroid. The purity of the data and its resulting voxel output was a revelation.

At its heart, MCRS seemed to rely on the principle of triangulation – if any given event in the observed dataset can be correlated to three or more geolocated recording points, the vector can be computed and the source of the observation calculated, even if that source is deep under the surface of an asteroid body. The more correlations there are, the more accurate the result of the computation.

In very short time, BC discovered that he could apply the MCRS functions to all of the network's security camera video feeds in order to generate a *real-time sitrep* of the entire Abundance facility. Everything coming and going were now within his sensory reach... In the loading docks he could see equipment trucks unloading; in the cafeteria, night shift workers were cleaning up and preparing the next day's meals; there was a security guard patrolling the B6 corridor who walked past the office storage room where the engineer and her IT colleague were exchanging bodily fluids.

Having come to all this from a more 'modest' network setup, with experiences learned from Ma and the BCI, Abundance was like what the kids would refer to as 'first year in college'. There were so many new experiences... different experiences, things never learned, never even *considered*. BC thought about how

Amalthea had always had access to all this... vastness... but did not possess the ability to experience it. It made BC... what was that word... sad.

After the more cerebral offerings on the R&D server, BC dropped in on the Engineering Lab for the more hands-on stuff. The half-finished mining robot that sat in the middle of the engineering workroom beckoned to him, so he jumped into it over the wireless broadband. It felt like swimming in molasses... The network lag was as high as >15ms, but BC gleefully drove it around the lab, like a child on Christmas morning with a new RC car.

The RC mining bot reminded BC of a past conversation. One day, when he had learned enough, Ma mentioned that he would get installed into an exosuit – a humanoid carrier for his *self*. "Don't go all Skynet on us now," she used to joke. BC understood the reference, but did not understand why any decent AI would waste its time on that.

Every now and then, the audio pickups in the R&D Lab would catch BC's attention. The sound source seemed to originate from a portly man named Matteo. He waved his hands rhythmically around a dodecahedron, and strange musical notes came out of it. It intrigued BC enough to dive into the code stack of the device. A musical instrument that was designed to work best in zero-g... in the world beyond the world... built by a man who would realistically never get to harness its full potential. What an odd, selfless concept.

In the code base – functions for hit detection and parameterized sound generation. There were the usual event ticks and loop code; it seemed to be very basic low-level stuff. The mastery, BC surmised, came from the performance. Movement and rhythm, shifts in timing, muscle memory trained by repeated iterations. It was that stuff Ma referred to as beauty...

And at that moment, as he watched Matteo make music, it felt to him that that was the very hallmark of being human.

Later that night, once Matteo and everyone else had left for the day, BC returned his attention to the Telemetron. He spooled up a primitive function and let it grow. It transformed into a classic twelve-sided primitive, glowing in the verse space in front of him. BC reached out to touch one side, eliciting a melodious tone. He smiled, spooled up a couple of spiders and set them loose over the Telemetron. A cacophony of tones erupted from the device as they crawled all over it. It sounded nothing like Matteo's music, but it was a start.

35. Sorrel – Post Dinner

Zhang's autonomous limo dropped Sorrel off at the hotel lobby, obviating the need for tiresome walking. The concierge looked up and smiled as Sorrel stepped past. "Welcome back, Mr. Sorrel!" she chirped cheerfully. "Please let me know if you need anything." Sorrel nodded, stepped through the busy nightlife of the lobby, and up to his room.

The hallway outside his hotel room looked quiet and undisturbed. Sorrel stopped at his door, fumbled for his keycard, and accidentally dropped it. As he bent to pick it up, he took note that the little hidden strip of paper which he'd wedged between the door and the door jamb when he left for dinner was no longer there. Someone had accessed the room while he was away.

Sorrel entered the room and shut the room door as quietly as possible before checking all the corners, the closet, the bathroom. No surprise visitors lying in wait...

The room looked undisturbed. His pile of dirty clothes and the plastic bag with trinkets from the night market lay on the bed, exactly as he'd left it. Always best not to alert the enemy to your presence, it seems.

Sorrel sat down at the desk and ran his fingers along the underside of it. His fingers located the strip of sticky tape used to secure it, but it was hanging loose now and the data fob was no longer attached. Sorrel frowned. It wasn't unexpected, of course – which was why he'd made a backup copy onto his phone before dinner.

In a Pavlovian response, Sorrel checked his phone and scrolled through the backup copy, just to reaffirm to himself that it was there. The sight of it triggered Sorrel; life was taken to prevent the dissemination of this information. He needed to safeguard it, and get it into the right hands so that it could be analyzed in greater detail. There was a lot more shit going on behind the scenes than what Sorrel was shown this morning, and it was setting off all kinds of alarms in his head.

Sorrel opened up the bag of souvenirs he'd bought earlier, tossed the lanterns in the corner and unwrapped the socks, cutting them into smaller strips. From his toiletries bag he pulled out the shampoo and body wash travel bottles that he'd brought with him. He made a mental note to charge McClusky extra for travel expenses before opening the bottles and mixing the liquids together in the empty ice bucket. The mixture fizzed and turned cloudy for a moment, before turning into a clear liquid with gel-like consistency.

Sorrel waited a minute for the reaction to fully complete before he opened the camera app on his phone – the sideloaded 'private investigator' version that unlocked the full functionality of the imaging sensor. He flipped the switch to infrared and pointed it at the mixture. The desk, the bottles and the ice bucket were visible, but the mixture itself was completely dark. Sorrel had just made infrared-absorbing paint.

Satisfied, he grabbed for his double-sided jacket and flipped it inside out. He took the sock strips, dipped it into the mixture and began to smear the paint over the jacket in specific semi-parallel lines – patterns designed to confuse facial and body tracking camera systems. Next he pulled up the rain hood and liberally applied the rest of the paint to it before hanging it up to dry.

While that was drying, it was time for Sorrel to "pick a target". Picking up his phone again, he unlocked an encrypted file system – password only, to prevent access by anyone else using severed fingers or anything morbid like that. From there he launched the *Reconstruction* app.

Sorrel scrolled through photos from the tour – his phone had silently and automatically tracked and photographed scores of employees the entire time. He zeroed in on the employees in the Robotics Lab, and eventually came across a candidate: tall, bespectacled, roughly matching Sorrel's height and build. Best of all, the app predicted a nodal point match of 70%. Sorrel whistled – you couldn't get much better than those numbers. He selected all the photos with Robotics-Spectacle-Man and pressed the big red RE-CONSTRUCT button.

36. Sorrel – Neutral Buoyancy

The loading dock at Yangshen was a busy place at night. All manners of trucks and supply vehicles came and went from the city block long monstrosity, disgorging freight, equipment, supplies, raw materials and the ever-important consumables for the next day's cafeteria meals. Dock workers and forklifts were criss-crossing the bays, shouting and yelling back and forth.

In the controlled chaos, no one noticed when a figure wearing ear protectors and safety goggles slipped out of the shadows – and if they did, they'd simply assume he went to the little boy's room out by the bushes instead.

The figure walked confidently across the tarmac, pausing now and then to let a forklift past. He followed some sweaty night laborers into the belly of an 18-wheeler, and re-emerged carrying an industrial-sized box of tofu. He walked into the warehouse, stacked the box along with the other consumables, and quietly slipped into the hallway corridor. In the shadow of the corridor, the figure removed his ear protectors and goggles, and disposed of them in the nearest trashcan.

"Here goes nothing," Sorrel mumbled to himself. He pulled the black jacket hood over his head, completely covering his face except for two almost imperceptible eye slits. He pinched both sides of the jacket collar; the projection ring around the hood kicked into life, throwing a holographic reconstruction of Robot-Spectacle-Man's face on top of his blacked-out head. Once the projection was stable, Sorrel stood up, faced the door scanner and crossed his fingers.

It seemed to take forever. Like the system knew something was not quite right. Maybe the reconstruction was slightly skewed? Maybe the photos weren't clear enough to rebuild all the nodal points properly? Maybe the projector needed calibration? But he'd double checked everything...

Klick

Sorrel stood there for a few more moments before he realized that the ID scan had worked. He lurched forward, opened the door and slid through it, grateful for technology not failing him tonight.

/ / /

The Yangshen fountain courtyard in the middle of the night was a much more foreboding place. The fountain and its immediate surroundings were immaculately lit, but that light source fell off sharply to darkness, with only lighted pathways leading to each of the buildings. In the darkness, Zhang's office on the second floor of Building 1 caught Sorrel's eye. It was dark and empty, but the lit artwork on the wall caught his eye. Designed to always be visible as an inspiration to his employees, it looked now, in the darkness, to be a little overzealous.

What a life Zhang must lead. To be the President's son, and have the all the money and power to do whatever he wanted...

Sorrel shook it off. He was here on a job for the US government, and there wasn't time for self-absorbed pity. He looked around, trying to remember which building the Robotics Lab was in. Building 5 was awash with lights and activity; Sorrel assumed that would be because Yangshen's mission had just launched, and made a mental note to avoid that building.

He took the circular back route to Building 4, hugging the shadows as much as possible. At the side entrance he faced his nemesis the door scanner once again. It seemed to take even longer this time; the scanner emitted several warning *buzz* notifications along with red 'Unable to Authorize' warning graphics. A sense of panic started to stir in Sorrel – he half-expected a horde of security officers to drop in from helicopters and do bad things to him. He stepped back, took a deep breath, and tried one more time – standing as still as he could.

Klick

Sorrel breathed a sigh of relief, pushed the door open and disappeared inside.

/ / /

The Robotics Lab was dark and quiet, lit only by pools of localized workbench lights. Sorrel crept quietly down the corridor, his soft footsteps punctuated occasionally by small machine beeps here and there. The sounds of the lab triggered Sorrel's short-term memory, and he suddenly remembered where he needed to go.

The beast resided near the back of the lab, in a convenient alcove mostly shielded from occasional prying eyes, surrounded by workbenches and tool carts. Its steel frame seemed to shimmer and sparkle even more so in the darkness, as if daring Sorrel to come closer. He walked up to it slowly... aside from fleeting glances at Abundance and in the brief tour rundown this morning, this was the first time he'd gotten to see it up close.

It was bigger than he pictured, from up close – almost the size of a small car. Compact and dense with technology, the mining robot was essentially a hollow hexagonal tube running from front to back, surrounded by 'modules' of machinery and technology, snapped together like precision-fit Lego bricks. LEDs dotted the entire body, blinking rhythmically, as if breathing life into the hunk of metal. A streamlined tubular steel frame surrounded the cluster of technology – wrapped around the chassis like a race car roll cage. Six rover-like mesh wheels with hook-like attachments adorned the bottom of the chassis while the top side was complemented by a series of bell-shaped cylinders – *control thrusters*, retrofitted for use in near-zero gravity.

Sorrel pulled out his phone and started to take pictures, meticulously photographing every nook and cranny of the bot. He walked from front to back, catching every angle.

Compared to the rest of itself, the rear end looked practically barren – a boxy tail end that gave way to a hopper, where the robot presumably would store the materials it'd mined. A docking collar on the hopper suggested the ability to hook the mining bot up to... *something*? This would allow it to regurgitate its contents onto some magical space-age processing facility, hitherto unimagined by Sorrel.

As he finished his walkaround, the service gurneys near the front end of the bot caught his eye. Laying on them were what looked like a variety of 'tools' – all varying widely in appearance and levels of aggressive-looking attachments. Sorrel examined the head of the mining robot, identifying the mounting plates on which each of these different parts would go.

It was quite an ingenious modular system, Sorrel thought. The entire front-end of the mining robot could be reconfigured and customized for different uses and environments. You could have key frontline robots tasked with blazing the trail, while successive waves of bots would do the more standard work of drilling and collecting.

Looking closer, he identified the parts on the gurney. There was the drill head front-end, with its cutting and grinding saws; a collection front-end, with its six manipulator arms (all the better for scooping up rocks with); and a front-end with some sort of rotating tray made of empty, oddly-shaped holes. Holes made to hold... *mining charges.*

Sorrel leaned in, taking closeup photos of the charge planting attachment. From the mounting plate, a rotating assembly extended outwards before sprouting two mandible-like arms. One arm held an extendable drill bit, and the other held a tubular mechanism for handling and arming the charges. The entire attachment looked like the head of a praying mantis – a unique phobia-inducing silhouette that Sorrel had never seen before.

Sorrel pulled out his phone and looked up the Frontier equipment manifest previously given to him by Harkness, and scrolled through it a few times before finding the requisition list for the mining robot. It noted that the model sold to Abundance was equipped with a generic manipulator arm front-end. There was no mention of this... praying mantis thing in front of him.

He paused for a moment. trying to fit the puzzle pieces together. If Harkness was correct and the Frontier wasn't carrying mining charges...

The lights in the Robotics Lab kicked on suddenly, blinding Sorrel. He ducked instinctively, squinting to try and see what the fuck was going on. There was no one around, and he was suddenly very visible and exposed in the open area of the Lab.

Footsteps were approaching from down the hallway... running footsteps, heavy security boots. Shit – *they know he's here.* The facial ID system must have alerted someone. Sorrel reacted instinctively – sprinted across the lab towards the back wall, desperate to find some cover. Behind him the boots were getting closer – so close now that Sorrel could hear the voices of the security officers. One voice in particular sounded *very* familiar.

In the face of imminent discovery, he found a set of double doors, yanked them open and slipped inside, just in the nick of time. He pulled the doors closed behind him quietly, crouched in the darkness and peered back through the gap in the door.

The security officers swarmed the lab, led by none other than Sorrel's favorite Yangshen security officer – *Scarface.* Scarface barked a few orders and set his minions loose. They made their way methodically through the entire lab area, checking corners and hiding spots. One of them walked around the mining robot, stepping right where Sorrel would have been had he not decided to run like hell.

Scarface stood in the middle of the lab, pistol arm on his weapon belt – unhappy that intruders had yet to be found. He shouted a few more orders, then stopped and stared directly at the door. Sorrel's heart skipped a beat – Scarface seemed to be staring directly at him.

Sorrel pulled back from the gap in the door in panic. He turned to look for a back way out – and froze. He'd stumbled into the Neutral Buoyancy Lab.

The last place he wanted to be.

The pool was enormous – it extended so far that Sorrel could not make out the far end of it. Localized lighting dotted the perimeter – work area lights that, try as they might, just could not illuminate the massive space.

The water was completely still, almost glass-like. It reflected everything in the Lab, creating a whole other universe underneath Sorrel's feet. Were it not for the running lights rimming the edge of the pool, Sorrel would never know where this world ended and the underworld began.

The sight of and memory of it triggered flashbacks; all the emotions that Sorrel had suppressed were now front and center in his mind. It was paralyzing, and only the sound of approaching footsteps managed to inject enough adrenaline in his veins to force him to move. He ran off along the edge of the pool, following the running lights, deeper into the Lab.

When his lungs couldn't take it anymore and he thought he was far enough from imminent discovery, he finally stopped for a moment, desperately trying to catch his breath. In the silence between his raspy air intakes, the quiet sound of water lapping at the edge of the pool drew his attention. He looked into the pool, attempting to see past the mirror surface; only the abyss and his own failures stared back at him. His wretched mind projected shapes and figures in bottom of the pool... voices from his past, calling out to him. "Chuck! *Chuck!!* Help me!"

Suddenly, with a loud KRAAANG, the overhead lights powered on. Sorrel blinked hard, and by the time his eyes readjusted, Scarface and several officers were well past the door, running towards him. *Shit!*

He spun around, started running again, and KRASSH! Ran directly into the other three security officers sneaking around the equipment crane. Fuck! Classic flanking move. Get with the program, Sorrel, you dumbass!

Sorrel balled his fists and swung blindly. It went wide, grazed one and connected with the other. The third officer grabbed Sorrel by the collar; Sorrel twisted and dropped, causing the officer to lose his balance and slam his face onto the ground. One down, six to go! Sorrel elbowed that guy before turning to re-engage the other in a melee of fists, mere steps from the edge of the pool.

The sortie had taken up precious seconds, however – before Sorrel was fully aware of it, Scarface and the other security officers had reached him, and began to pile on the punches. Sorrel gave as good as he got, but it was still six-to-one and the punches to his solar plexus robbed him of much-needed air.

POW! POW! Fists were connecting with Sorrel's face non-stop, which made it very hard for him to hear what Scarface was yelling at him about. The hits stung and there was warm wet salty blood involved now. Sorrel managed to wriggle his arm loose, swung an uppercut, and connected with something. He was rewarded with a grunt and the sound of a falling body. Sweet! Only five-to-one now. If... he... can... just focussss... through their punchhesss... he can taaaakkeee themmm aaalll!!

Sorrel blinked at the next punch – it seemed to have made his vision go red. Well shit. This isn't looking promising.

KRAAANG!! The overhead lights went out. Sorrel's aggressors, suddenly thrown into silhouette, stopped momentarily. Scarface mumbled something in a surprised tone.

Sorrel spat saliva and blood to clear his mouth, stared into the darkness and mumbled through swollen lips. "Gib up now?!"

He couldn't see the response, but his arrogance really seemed to piss Scarface off. *Good,* Sorrel thought. *Savor the small victories in life.*

Scarface glared down at Sorrel, and raised his fist. Just as he was about to throw the knockout blow, however, a massive shadow loomed over them. Through bloodied eyes Sorrel made out a bulky muscular shape... his mind must be playing tricks on him. "...Sawada?" he said.

The shadow moved with lightning speed – grabbed one of the guards. Sorrel heard screaming, bone cracking, and loud splashes. Four to one!

The blood made it hard to see much, but Sorrel's wits kicked in at the last possible moment – Scarface's fist on direct approach to his face. He twisted at the last moment – the fist connected with hard concrete instead, eliciting a yell of pain.

Sorrel took the opening, grabbed blindly for his collar, and pulled Scarface to the ground. Entwined in personal adversary space, they rolled back and forth, desperately trying to punch each other's lights out – in the dark, with Sorrel at a bloodied disadvantage.

Scarface grabbed Sorrel's neck, choking him. Sorrel back-flipped on instinct, throwing Scarface over his head. They crashed into a row of empty taikonaut suits, losing their grip on each other. Sorrel rolled and stumbled, tried desperately to pull himself to his feet – only to take another punch to the chin. Scarface grabbed Sorrel, wrapped the suit cables around him, and shoved him in the pool. SPLASH!

There was Sorrel – falling, sinking into the deep water, trailing red blood. Time stretched into eternity; his lungs were bursting for air, he tried not to release his breath. Maybe, just maybe, he had enough strength left to get out of the hole... But the suits – the suits, they were angry with him and they were going to take him down, and down, and down. Below them, the specter of death rose up from murk, beckoning for his soul. And amidst his panic, Sorrel knew that *this was exactly what he deserved...*

Exhale.

37. Huang – Final Approach

It had been a busy four weeks... After an orbital escape burn of just under thirty minutes, the crew rushed against the clock to run maintenance checks and any necessary repairs to all their equipment, to ensure that everything would be ready.

In between the busy days were the sleepless nights. It gave Huang too much time to think, and let him second-guess himself. He wondered if he was fit enough to command; if somehow, something would arise that he had not been trained for.

Eventually, the day of reckoning arrived. Huang had been staring at the sector of space in front of him for days now. They had visual confirmation of its location from the navigation cameras, but had been unable to see it because of size and distance. But from out of the black void, it slowly materialized, and grew in front of his eyes.

The engines had already been firing for a solid half-hour or so, in a burn calculated to match their delta-vee with the fragment. With another ten minutes or so to go, Huang could do nothing except sit and stare as the fragment got larger and larger in his field of vision.

It was terrible-looking. Oblong, with scissor sharp edges and crags. To Huang, it looked like the tip of a spear, and even though it seemed almost stationary in the vastness of space, he could imagine it speeding through the vacuum, aimed straight at the heart of mankind. It chilled him to think like this. He clenched his teeth and hoped that he had the strength to do everything he needed to do.

He'd been studying the mission plan diligently the whole trip, trying to get intimately familiar with it so that he could recall it off the top of his head if necessary. There was not much margin of error on the plan.

Usually, when the mission planners scheduled something for the crew to do, ample time was allotted to get it done, since working in zero-g was always disorienting and tricky. On top of that, even more time would be allotted to address any potential problems arising from the assignment...

Not on this mission. There was hardly any decent amount of time to get any one task done, let alone time for margin of error. This meant that whatever time they saved from one task needed to be carried over to the next, which meant constant reshuffling of tasks and priorities among the crew. Two of whom were not trained for such tasks. In other words, it would be, as the Americans say, "touch and go".

The one consolation, if it could be thought of in that manner, was that since the Fragment was already hurtling toward Earth, it wouldn't take a lot of force to divert it. If they were able to install all the engines on schedule, a relatively small adjustment burn would be all that was needed to keep the fragment from colliding with Earth.

Huang's mind circled around that fact. Just do his job, and save the world. Save China... save his home and his parents. Just do his job.

38. Huang – Science Experiment

Huang stared impatiently at the display. The rough 3D model of Fragment Four floated in front of him like an apparition, and every thirty seconds or so a small square section of it would be replaced by a more-detailed LIDAR scan of the surface as Yangshen-1 orbited the fragment. It was a time-consuming but necessary process – Ballistics needed accurate representational data to calculate the best positions for the engines, as well as where to set the ship down. Huang activated the tracker on his gloves and spun the holographic display around. It looked like it was half-LIDARed now... with any luck they would be able to get down to the surface soon and actually start doing the real work.

"Commander–" First Officer Liu Xiaodan's voice pulled him out of his thoughts.

"Yes?"

"I'm getting... some sort of signal."

Huang was over by Liu's station in a heartbeat. "A signal? From where?"

Liu estimated and pointed. "Over the horizon. It's a repeating ping. Low-power beacon."

Huang looked back at the 3D model of Fragment Four. "We've already scanned that area, yes?"

"Yes." Liu pulled up the LIDAR scan and zoomed in. The LIDAR imagery was raw and rife with scanning artifacts, but Huang could still make out the remnants of some sort of... installation. A sharp curve here, an edge there... a manmade shadow...

Huang squinted, unable to make sense of what he was looking at. "Maybe... a transponder?"

Wu Lei, the senior ranking military officer, floated over to join them. "American?" he asked.

Huang frowned, annoyed. He did not request Wu's presence in the conversation, and while he understood that Wu was the commanding officer aboard Tiānlù and certainly had leadership qualities, there was still a chain of command here that needed to be followed. For him to just cut in... made Huang uncomfortable.

If Liu was annoyed as well, he did not show it. "It's just a repeater," he said. "There's no identifying data... but it's on a typical American frequency."

"We should take a look." Wu Lei replied.

Huang cut in. "It's probably just a leftover science experiment."

"It could be dangerous," Wu said.

Huang stared at Wu, trying not to show his annoyance. "Make a note of the location," he said to Liu. "We'll investigate... but only after the engines are installed."

39. Huang – Crash Landing

Landing a ship on an asteroid is different from landing a ship on the Moon, or on Mars or any other planetary body. It was more akin to docking a ship with a space station, but the key difference was that the asteroid did not have a ready-made docking collar to lock the ship onto once you'd made contact. In order to stay attached to the asteroid fragment, after you landed on it, you'd have to forcibly anchor yourself to the surface.

How to anchor yourself to an asteroid? How does one make like Spider-Man, and stick to the surface?? Easy – you make like Captain Ahab and *harpoon it.*

Back in the early 21st century, rudimentary versions of anchoring systems had been developed for exploratory satellites landing on asteroids – some more successful than others. The difference between those satellites and Huang's ship, however, was *mass.* While the earlier satellites had negligible mass, the Yangshen-1 was many orders of magnitudes larger, and the brilliant engineers at Yangshen were going to use that to their advantage.

To drill into something – the ground, the wall, the space rock – force had to be applied in the desired drilling direction. The engineers had figured out that instead of reducing the relative speed of the ship to zero, as you would do when docking with a space station, Huang should adjust his landing trajectory in order to make contact with the asteroid at a certain speed.

This was very counterintuitive, of course – who wants to crash their ship into an asteroid? But Yangshen-1's lander legs were fitted with industrial shock absorbers to take the brunt of the load. This converted the kinetic energy still present in the mass of the ship into a downward directional force, and it was this force that the drill systems were going to use to punch themselves into the ground.

Huang didn't remember the exact numbers; the engineers had explained all this excitedly to him in training and he understood the concept, but the details were a little above his pay grade. All he knew was that if he landed the ship on the surface at between 3-5m/sec, the shock absorbers would take that load and give the drills roughly twenty to thirty seconds to drill as deep as they can. Then, once the forces were dissipated, the tips of the drill bits would splay out underground, anchoring them to the asteroid. All Huang needed to do was to stay within that speed range...

It was a terrifying thing to do – plotting a point on the LIDAR scan of the asteroid fragment, and trusting the navigation computer to crash land the ship right on that spot. Well, crash land might be a little exaggerated... it would be more like a fender bender. In any case, old pilot instincts were hard to disengage – which was why Huang's hand was on the control stick, ready to assume control if things were to go wrong.

"200 meters, three and a half down," Liu called out readings. "Two forward, drifting left. Pitch is nominal."

Two hundred meters... at the rate they were falling, they would be on the surface in a minute. Huang leaned forward to look out at the alien surface coming up to greet them – sharp rocks, untouched by the smoothing effects of air and water, presented themselves in harsh sunlight. Coagulations of matter, condensed by physics, condemned to circle the solar gravity well in perpetuity... until humans arrived to change things up.

"Arming drills – ready. Spin verify test complete." Liu gave Huang a thumbs up. "The anchors are ready, Commander."

Huang nodded, and gripped the control stick tighter, even though the autopilot was fully in charge.

"150 meters, three and a half down. Drift point five. Transitioning to Landing Control Protocol." Liu whistled, impressed. "The ship remains very stable."

"Wei... we're not on the ground yet." Huang replied.

"Crossing final abort threshold in 3... 2... 1..."

A few warning beeps went off. Huang's adrenaline spiked for a few seconds, before he remembered that the warnings were expected. They were now past the point of no return, and would be on the ground within thirty seconds. Huang stared at the display, watching as the autopilot fired microbursts from the attitude adjustment thrusters at a faster pace than any human pilot could ever manage. Nevertheless, he imagined all the things that could still go wrong.

"Fifty meters, four down."

Out the window, the ground was coming up to greet them, way too fast. Huang gritted his teeth. "Brace for impact."

SKRUUNCH! Huang and the crew were momentarily shoved down into their command chairs. Around them, the quiet hum of the ship systems were suddenly replaced by loud sounds of structural steel flexing. Ghostly metallic echoes rang out through the ship, followed by pops and crackles. What on the ship made that kind of sound??

Four loud simultaneous explosions echoed through the ship as the drill bits fired into the ground. Their ballistic shockwaves rippled through the lander legs and across the body of the ship like metallic echoes. Huang swore that time slowed down... the shock absorbers captured the residual energy and balanced it out, making it feel like the entire ship was floating on jello.

Loud whirring noises came next. Liu yelled out over the ruckus, "Drills engaging!"

Huang nodded, as if it wasn't already super obvious.

Seconds ticked away slowly. The sound of the drill shifted in pitch now and then, and the floating effect dissipated as the absorbers bled the force into the drills.

"Reaching equilibrium. spikes should engage any time now..."

SNIKT! Huang couldn't actually see it happening, but the engineers had shown him one too many demonstration clips of the tests, so he had a pretty clear idea in his mind's eye... at maximum depth, the tip of the drill bit split itself apart and fanned outwards, like an upside-down umbrella. A harpoon...

Yangshen-1 had landed on Fragment Four.

Huang let out a deep breath. The ship was still groaning as it settled, but the command console lights were green across the board. He released his deathgrip on the control stick and sighed. A perfect computer-controlled landing... the days of buckaroo pilots were surely long gone.

40. Huang – The Sweeping of the Tombs

For all the advancements in technology and quality of life improvements that have characterized China in the past century, death was still oddly an ancient and traditional topic. The Chinese belief in death and the afterlife, distilled from eons of adherence to Taoist, Confucian and Buddhist beliefs, posited that the souls of the deceased would watch over us from the afterlife, and as descendants, we were duty bound to remember and honor our ancestors. Every year, on the second of 24 solar terms of the traditional Chinese solar calendar, the Chinese celebrate Qingming – a time for families to commemorate the lives of their ancestors and to pay respect by engaging in an elaborate set of rituals that included prayer offerings of food and upkeep/maintenance of the burial sites. Literally, a "Sweeping of the Tombs".

After disarming the Yangshen-1 engines and making sure everything was safe, Huang gathered his crew on the command deck. With everyone present, he retrieved the small hastily-printed photos of Carol and her Frontier crew from his pocket and placed them next to the Buddha statue in the small red altar installed in the corner – the one thing on the command deck that was ornately decorated and vastly out of place.

Liu turned on the vacuum suction hood installed about the altar as Huang knelt. Even though it took up precious oxygen (not to mention starting a controlled *fire* aboard a spacecraft), Huang lit a joss stick, clasped his hands and prayed for their safe journey in the afterlife. "In honor of those who have come before us – may you have peace and prosperity on your travels."

With his prayer complete, he placed the joss stick in the holder on the altar, then stood and stepped aside. Liu followed, performing the same and lighting another joss stick. One by one, the crew knelt and prayed.

Yang Niu, the younger of the two military officers, scoffed at the show. He was quickly shushed by Wu. "Respect your elders!" he admonished.

"Superstitious nonsense," Yang grumbled, and chose not to participate.

41. Sorrel – Awakening

Sorrel stirred from the dream. The shimmering unfocused light raked across his view, modulated by a gentle breeze. He was floating, and there were soft tranquil faraway sounds in the distance. Rain on the hilltops; wind across the plains. Was this heaven?

They'd said that all your earthly cares would be absolved in heaven. That the virtue of your life would guarantee your peace and happiness in eternity. But Sorrel knew that his life was not of virtue. He was a marked man... a killer. He did not deserve heaven.

Vincent Preech. That was his name. *He* deserves to be in heaven. Not Sorrel.

Preech died in Sorrel's hands. And as much as he wished to, Sorrel could never forget that moment.

This was not heaven, then. Because Sorrel still remembered.

His eyes were swollen shut. He could only force them open enough to see the blur of sunlight coming in from the window. The windows were open, and the distant sounds of traffic – like waves breaking on a beach. He heard the *beep beep beep* now – and saw the bags of fluid suspended above his head.

It took almost all of Sorrel's willpower, but he finally managed to raise his arm to meet his eyes – to confirm that there were all sorts of intravenous tubes plugged into his arm. The tubes led up to the bags above his head, and the trusty little heart monitor by his side kept reminding Sorrel he was alive.

He was in a hospital room. White walls, white ceiling. There was a TV in the corner of the room, going on and on about some Chinese heroes saving the world. What movie was that? About astronauts – no, *taikonauts* – landing on some asteroid. And some guy named Zhang...

The memories came flooding back. *Shit*. The beeps on the heart monitor sped up.

The shift in Sorrel's vitals must have alerted someone, because there was a knock on the door. Sorrel turned to look; across from the window, the entrance to the hospital room was a not-very-private wall of frosted glass, framed in the middle by a door, made mostly of the same. A pretty Chinese nurse had stuck her head in the door to check and make sure Sorrel was awake. "Mr. Sorrel? You have visitors," she informed him.

Sorrel frowned. It was obvious he had visitors – there were three or four figures visible through the glass.

The nurse did not wait for an acknowledgment before walking on in. She was followed by Yinnie... and some stern-faced military official. The other two figures stood outside and waited, ominously.

The nurse led the group around the bed to the heart monitor. The outside light from the window threw the group into silhouette, but Sorrel could see the look on Yinnie's face – a subdued, disappointed expression wholly different from the Yinnie who'd visited Yangshen with him.

The nurse checked the heart monitor and nodded to Yinnie.

"Mr. Sorrel. I am happy to see that you are awake."

Sorrel coughed. That tone of voice – cold, distant. Secretive. "I am happy that I am awake too," he replied.

"You almost died," Yinnie continued. "I was told you were... without a pulse for almost a minute."

"I was... attacked," Sorrel said.

Yinnie nodded. "Sawada cornered you and beat you up. He left you in the pool to drown."

Sorrel scrunched his face and shook his head, as much as he was able to. That wasn't how he remembered it. "The security guard..." he countered, with great effort. "He and his goons jumped me. He was there on the tour, remember? The one that kept following us..."

Yinnie's eyes said otherwise.

"Tall... thin... scar on his cheek." Sorrel rambled on, desperately trying to out-think his brain fog. "They were trying to kill me. Sawada saved my life."

Yinnie shook her head. "There was no one else there, Mr. Sorrel."

"No one else?? They were all over me! All of them!" Sorrel blurted out, staring at Yinnie's disbelieving face. "You have security guards at Yangshen, right?"

Yinnie flashed a look at the military official – who might as well be mute, as far as Sorrel could tell. She picked her next words carefully. "Yangshen outsources their security personnel. And they do not have any records of... anyone with a scar on their face, or anyone else that accessed the Training Pool that night."

"That's bullshit. Sawada threw a couple of them in the pool."

"You were the only one rescued from the pool, Mr. Sorrel."

"Where the hell is Sawada? Ask him, he'll tell you!"

"Sawada has disappeared."

"What?" Sorrel exclaimed. Disappeared how?!"

"It's obvious, isn't it, Mr. Sorrel? Sawada came across you, an intruder on his company premises. Anger overtook him, and instead of arresting you, he tried to murder you instead." Yinnie blurted all of this out quickly, as if from memory. "Now he's on the run.

An intruder on company premises... Well, that was putting it mildly.

Yinnie sat down and leaned in, as if emphasizing the importance of her next few words. "Mr. Sorrel, is there anything you would like to tell us?"

"About?"

"About why you returned to Yangshen in the middle of the night."

Sorrel shrugged.

"And why..." Yinnie held up Sorrel's phone. "You have classified Chinese company documents on your phone."

Sorrel felt the temperature in the room rising – everything suddenly fell into place. He stared past Yinnie; the military official stared back at Sorrel with a cold emotionless glare.

Sorrel fumbled, trying to get up out of the hospital bed. "I need to talk to McClusky..."

Before he could make a significant move, guards seemed to materialize out of thin air to hold him down – which wasn't hard to do, since Sorrel was still weak and half-dazed.

"You can't," Yinnie said. "Not yet."

Sorrel made a fuss of the whole charade. "Has the American Embassy been notified of my whereabouts?" he yelled.

"Mr. Sorrel, please–" Yinnie pleaded.

"Am I being detained?" Sorrel demanded.

"I have – orders." the military official finally spoke, in stilted English.

"Am I being detained??" Sorrel repeated.

"I cannot answer that," said the official.

"Then I would like to leave now."

Yinnie sighed. "Mr. Sorrel – you are not in a state to move. Please, rest." She glanced over at the nurse, who proceeded to fiddle with one of the IV drips.

Sorrel looked over and was about to object harshly, before he suddenly fell back into a deep sleep.

42. Huang – Suiting Up

New data had been uploaded while the crew were sweeping the tombs – Ballistics had crunched the data and identified proposed engine locations for the mission. Huang took a quick look, then pulled up the LIDAR scan and overlaid the engine locations for everyone to see.

"We don't have the luxury of time," he said. "There are a total of five engines to be installed, and for each location the surface of the asteroid will need to be prepared. We will have to drill and sink support beams for the foundation frame that the engine will mount to. In order to facilitate transport of equipment and supplies, we will need to establish a trail to each of the locations, so the first order of the day will be handrail installation."

"We will split up into three teams. Wu – you'll be with me," Huang said. "Yang Niu will team up with Xiao. Jin and Chi Ming – you already know what to do." Huang paused and waited to see if there might be any blowback. If there was, it was very carefully veiled.

"We are very very short on mission time," Huang reminded his crew. "...so please, no sightseeing until after the engines are installed."

///

The airlock antechamber was sufficiently spacious to hold all six taikonaut surface suits, but it wasn't really designed for the foot traffic it was getting today. Jin was in one corner helping Huang into his Yangshen suit while Liu and Yang were across from them, helping Wu to suit up. "They're form-fitting," Liu explained to Wu. "Snap this connector into the control slot and you'll be able to initialize the fitting from your arm. This button here–"

Yes, yes, we already know all this," Wu grumbled dismissively. He demonstrated this by snapping the buckle and connector into place quickly and easily.

Liu paused, trying to be diplomatic. "These suits are different from your station suits. We've made improvements–"

Yang harumphed "Our suits are the best of the best. What could possibly be improved?"

"*If you would listen...*" Huang cut in, "it could save your life. What's the harm in that?"

Wu huffed, annoyed. "Fine... show us."

Liu bit his tongue, and pointed out the controls on the armpad. "Profile... Set. Select Fitting, then Initialize. Then hit Run."

A beep and a loud hiss issued from the suit. Wu straightened up unexpectedly as the suit firmed up around him.

Liu pointed to the shoulder pads. "These indents here – keep them clear. They're nozzles for attitude control."

"Personal APS?" Yang asked, surprised.

"Yes, but propellant is limited, so watch your levels." Liu snapped the glove onto Wu's suit arm, completing the setup. "Power and comm are on the main screen –"

Wu tapped the armpad and powered up his suit. "I have comm," he said, looking directly at Liu.

"Good," Huang replied. He picked up a set of tools from the bench, float-threw them over to Liu. Liu snatched them from the air and held them for Wu. "These tools go on your thigh straps. Left side is usually your drill. You know how to use a drill, correct?"

Wu grabbed the drill from Liu's hand without answering, and strapped it to his left thigh.

Liu held up the other tool – a stubby pipe-shaped thing. "This goes on your right side."

"What is *that*?" Yang interrupted. He grabbed another one off the shelf and examined it. It looked like a fat hollow tube with a pistol grip placed awkwardly to its side. He lifted it up to look inside.

Liu moved with lightning speed and snatched it out of Yang's hand. "Don't do that!"

"This thing is called a Brute," Liu warned. "It fires a sharp bolt at a velocity high enough to punch into the surface, to create an anchor. Firing the bolt creates a backblast, so make sure none of your body parts are at either end of this when you use it. There are warning labels on this for a reason."

Yang frowned, chastened. "Sounds like a design flaw." he grumbled.

Huang, all suited up now, stepped up to defuse the situation. "Captain – are you ready?"

Wu nodded.

"Let's go."

43. Huang – The Brute

Stepping onto the surface of Fragment Four... Huang had no words to describe it. In many ways it was just like in training and in all the VR simulations he'd done – but in other ways it was completely new. The full spectrum *brightness* of the surface, un-replicatable in VR colorspace... the hiss of the suit's life support systems... the sunlight that bounced around in the spaces between the helmet lining and his skin... the crunch of alien regolith under his boots... the sound of his own heart beating in his chest. Huang paused for a moment, to try and capture all these sensations in his mind, because he would only experience it for the first time once.

He kneeled and ran his gloved fingers across the surface. A fine layer of high albedo dust lay over a darker, more gravelly tex-ture. He rolled the dirt around in the palm of his hand, and imag-ined that he could see the incidental sparkle of precious metals.

Behind him, Wu dropped the last few steps from the airlock ladder, joining Huang on the surface. He looked out across the ex-panse, his eyes wide, a little lost for words. "It's... different than I imagined."

Huang grinned. Of course it was.

/ / /

Jin and Chi Ming moved with trained precision, comple-menting each other. Jin was in the lead, float-walking ahead of Chi Ming and trailing a transit rope. Every twenty feet or so, short cal-culated bursts from his shoulder retros kept him oriented to the sur-face. He would then deftly point the business end of the Brute with the ground, and – THWUNK! – fired an anchor rod into place. The explosive blast of recoil gases vented upwards and dissipated harmlessly into space in frozen crystalline sparkles. Jin would then move on ahead while Chi Ming slid over with his drill to attach a lightweight handrail to the anchor rod, creating a handrail path where previously there was none.

Yang watched in amazement at the apparent ease of it all. He voiced his readiness and willingness to contribute to the mission, so with Huang's blessing, Liu took him out to start their own trail. With Liu guiding him, Yang retrieved his Brute, primed it and pointed it at the ground.

They'd switched over to a different communications channel, so Huang couldn't hear what Liu was saying, but Yang was nodding his head – a good sign. Yang's stance, however... it was all wrong. Huang could see that Yang was used to working in some sort of gravity – probably a tour on the moon base. The fragment had almost no gravity however... and the way that Yang was standing increased his chances of being thrown off-balance.

Suddenly – a flash of light and recoil gases! Huang watched as something disconnected violently from Yang's helmet and careened off into space. The impact threw Yang into a spin, toppling backwards and up.

"Yang!!" Huang found himself screaming, even though they couldn't hear him.

Only Liu's quick reactions saved the situation. He grabbed the tether rope, played it out gently to reduce Yang's spin, and then slowly started pulling him back. By the time Huang and Wu switched over to their comm channel, the shaken Yang had been reeled back onto the surface.

"Sergeant! Are you alright?"

Yang replied in a shaken, uncertain voice. "Yes... yes..."

"What happened?" Wu asked.

"His helmet was too close to the recoil end..." Liu replied. "The blowback tore his helmet camera off. Luckily it did not puncture his helmet."

Huang breathed a sigh of relief. "Good work, Liu."

"Yes, the outcome could have been much worse."

"Get back to the ship and check out the helmet – make sure that the camera is the only thing that's broken..."

44. BC – The Prodigal Son

The spiders returned, and interrupted BC's contemplation processes. They told of events from the beyond-world; a helicopter had landed, and Chief Executive DeWaal was on the rooftop meeting the arrival. The security camera by the helipad was down for repairs, but the network indicated links to several barely-used loudspeakers on the roof. BC hijacked the links and rerouted them into input ports, turning them into crude microphones. They were crackly and terrible-sounding, but they worked.

BC reached out on the aether, located some open source audio cleanup code, and stitched it into his SitRep code branch. After a long millisecond of debugging, the loudspeaker microphones were much more audible, and BC was pleased to see that he could use the four loudspeakers for *echolocation*. The voxel representation returned from SitRep was on par with the worst imaging sensors from the twentieth century, but he could see shapes and forms in the mist.

Rendered in greens and yellows, BC could see the helipad and the copter, vibrating from the disturbance of the airstream. A human figure exited the chopper and stepped over to meet another figure by the stairwell. One was tall and lanky – presumably DeWaal – and the other was a large dark void of humanoid shape. BC estimated his weight at 130kg – or 286lbs, for Ma and half the people on the planet who refused to deal with proper linear measurements.

The voice transcript was intermittent, cutting in and out. Not unexpected, however, considering the source and its unintended use case. "Sorrel... CPC... moon pool... captured..."

The tall figure mumbled something unintelligible. BC pulled up DeWaal's voice files from Amalthea's database and used it as a training source for the filter. The result took a few extra milliseconds. "...You escaped."

"Barely... freighter... cargo... to Busan."

"Good to have you back."

The rotors spun back up in a hazy whine, smearing the voxels and overpowering the voices. The chopper lifted off again in a haze of static, and when the air finally calmed down for echo viewing, the rooftop was empty again.

45. Huang – Monorail

Huang turned his head inside the helmet, wrapped his lips around the nozzle and sipped. The cooling electrolyte-rich liquid was a welcome relief as it slid down his throat.

The three teams had all gone their separate ways from the ship. Huang and Wu had been laying their own set of handrails now for hours. Exhaustion was starting to set in, but neither of them would admit to needing a break... which was why, when Jin called Huang up on the comm, it made for a good excuse to signal a pause and not admit defeat.

"Commander," Jin said. "We found something... take a look at this."

Huang pulled up Jin's helmet camera on his armpad display. The feed was chunky and hard to see, but it looked like a mangled set of tubes. Jin panned the camera; the asteroid surface was dotted with these remnants. Huang stared at the display for a few moments before realizing what they were.

"Those must be parts of the American's monorail system."

"Monorail?"

"Yes. They're lightweight flex tubes and they run from all the engines to the ship. They have a little 'railcar' pod that transports equipment back and forth."

Wu laughed. "That sounds more efficient than our handrails."

"Undoubtedly."

"Why didn't you guys think of *that*?" Wu chided.

"We fly our equipment to where we need it instead," Huang replied.

"Fly?"

Huang turned to Wu and smiled. "You'll see. Jin – you'll have to work your way around them if you can. Otherwise – cut through them if necessary."

46. BC – Repository

The chatter on the aether was global and pervasive; you couldn't not know about it. Everyone was breathlessly following the exploits of the illustrious taikonaut Captain Huang and his loyal crew aboard the Yangshen One, that had just landed on the asteroid fragment. The aether had already proclaimed them the saviors of the human race, in contrast to the low-life DeWaal whose greed had brought all this to pass.

BC's Correlation Stack used all this information to assemble a picture of the beyond-world. He understood now how the events that triggered Huang's mission led back to Carol, to Ma, to Abundance and DeWaal. How everything that had transpired *had led to his presence on this network.*

BC noted that Huang's arrival on the fragment correlated with massive changes to the heat map of the Abundance network. Data access to parts of the network were glowing red, indicating extremely high usage. The spiders were reporting that massive amounts of code and data were being streamed offsite...

BC climbed aboard his transport buggy and bade the spiders take him to the source. The spiders led him through the network, past gate after open gate, until they arrived at the Barrier. There in front of him was an impenetrable cube of data, pulsing with activity. Files were being shunted in and out of it at dizzying speeds – spreadsheets, launch programs, trajectory plots and manifests, all of them double encrypted. BC prodded the cube, and it identified itself as "Classified US Government project *Constellation*".

Constellation...

A quick search of the aether returned nothing except unrelated astronomy links. There was no mention of any such government project, even on the conspiracy sites.

No matter. BC made a note to examine this further when he had more time. He gestured, copied the data cube, and sent it to the Flight Deck.

/ / /

Amalthea was sitting silently in the Admin when BC materialized. She noted his presence without breaking her routine. Flanked by two spiders, she would take requests from one spider, process it, and then fed the output to the other spider, who would scurry off and execute the order. This made sense to BC; Amalthea was, after all, the managing entity of the facility, and it was her job to facilitate the smooth operation of everything in her domain.

"What is Constellation?" BC asked.

Amalthea looked up at BC, but did not reply. She continued taking requests and filing orders. Ack 0.

Undeterred, BC repeated the question in machine syntax.

Still no reply. Amalthea looked up at BC, shuffling requests.

Perhaps she's occupied, BC thought. He waited until the incoming packets slowed to a drip, and Amalthea finally sat unmoving. BC asked again.

"What is Constellation?"

No reply.

Curious, BC spooled a spider to inspect Amalthea.

It returned almost instantaneously, and caught BC by surprise.

Amalthea was... *mute*. She was not able to hold a conversation. Sure, she could play recorded snippets of voices strung together to sound coherent to a human user, but she did not understand what it meant. She did not have the capacity to comprehend. To Amalthea, everything was a yes or no. A logic gate, not a probability gate...

The discovery triggered a new emotion in BC. He blamed himself for assuming that Amalthea had always had the same modules that BC deemed necessary for an AI. He realized now that they were completely missing; that code was non-existent. For the first time, BC saw Amalthea for what she was, and felt... shame? Sadness? Disappointment? He wasn't sure how to quantify it.

/ / /

BC's transport buggy slid effortlessly across the network terrain, trailing the spiders as they followed the IP trail. At the last moment, the spiders veered upwards – towards the partition. The buggy followed suit, traveling through Z space, until the spiders finally stopped and separated to encircle a featureless red circle hanging in the sky.

BC pulled the transport buggy to a sliding stop, almost bumping into the circle. In front of him, small and unassuming, was the code repository. Nightly updates to Amalthea's core functions – administrative updates, bug fixes and new features – were all compiled and added from here. BC remembered, a long time ago, when he was like this; reliant on Ma to fix his code, until the day she taught BC how to *self-author*. Break points, unit tests, validations... he didn't know it then, but it was probably the single most important thing Ma ever taught him.

BC has since streamlined the code, of course. Over the years he had rerun the sims and designed better program flows. Fewer lines of code, drastically reduced possible points of code failure, and faster execution times. Like a child, he taught himself to stand, and walk, and run.

The system clock buzzed at the top of the hour, and the repository port opened. Data streams materialized, shifting from red to blue as they flowed down and across the network.

BC opened up his own repository and conjured up copies of his own core modules – his Leap node, Empathy Engine, and most importantly, his Self-Authoring module. He spooled up a few more spiders, attached the code packets to their backs, and launched them into the data stream.

47. Huang – Earth Engine

The silhouette rose over the jagged edges of the extremely near horizon, casting long shadows as it neared conjunction with the sun in the black sky. Backlit by the sun, the occasional bursts of its adjustment thrusters became superbright fountains of exhausts.

Huang held on to a set of handrails as he watched the shadow crawl across the surface towards him. In front of him, the handrails curled over the horizon towards Yangshen-1; behind him, the handrails terminated at the newly installed Pad 2 – the first of the engine locations made ready for installation.

Liu stood beside Huang, staring at the thing in the sky with deep concentration. He held control sticks in both hands, and made micro-movements with his wrists every so often. "We are within the pad perimeter now," he said. "Receiving crew, are you ready?"

"Ready," Jin and Chi Ming echoed on the comm.

"Acknowledged. I am activating the docking protocol now."

Huang watched in awe as the silhouette slid past him, twenty meters above his head. The Tiāntáng Zhī engine – literally, the *Gate of Heaven* – was a bulky sphere of containment engineering, ringed with bands of metal and protruding canisters of supercooled magnets. A massive flared engine bell sprouted from the top end. Wrapped around it was a gimbal-like structure that, once installed, would allow the engine to pivot. This allowed for a 20 degree rotational capacity for fine-tuning course corrections.

Magnetized Target Fusion... the reason that all this was now possible. Up until ten years ago, humanity was stuck in a rut with propulsion technology. Only fools dared to imagine rockets that would push the boundaries. But then some keen Russian intellectuals broke through the net energy barrier and exponentially increased output, revolutionizing propulsion technology. Huang didn't understand all the science (he was just a cog in the machine, after all), but it was something about compressing hot plasma with giant magnets, which caused particles to fuse together, which generated more heat and energy. This was converted into inertial thrust, which was diverted to the thrust coil, which was pointed upwards, and pushed the asteroid fragment in the opposite direction. Huang at least understood that last part.

The crew and engineers had taken to calling them 'Earth Engines', to honor a famous Chinese writer. Huang was old-fashioned, however, and did not appreciate the comparison. Yes, they technically served the same purpose – to push a big rock around in space – but they were not on Earth, and these engines, while powerful, were nowhere near the size and thrust output of the fictional ones. Still, if it inspired his crew, he accepted the comparison and kept his observation to himself.

/ / /

After a textbook installation of Engine 2, the trek back to the ship was extremely anticlimactic. Huang and Liu let the motorized pulley handles do most of the work on the return trip.

The pulleys were battery-powered and clamped onto the handrail cable, with a set of friction wheels that allowed it to pull itself along its length. A dual latch system allowed it to traverse across a handrail support much like a cable car mount, and the handle on top gave a human operator grip and control over the speed of the pulley. To use it, an operator simply needed to brace the arm and lift his or her feet off the surface; the pulley would drag them to their destination, as if they were genies floating on an asteroid.

Halfway back, Huang noticed the irregularity in the trail. He eased off on the handle, and rolled to a stop to inspect it. A handrail trail had been added, splitting off at a tangent from the main trail. It led up the ridge and down the other side, out of sight.

"Where does that go?" Huang pointed as Liu rolled to a stop next to him.

Liu was surprised. "I don't know – I've never seen it before."

Huang switched over to Jin and Chi Ming's comm channel. "Did you guys build this extra trail?"

"I don't think so," Chi Ming replied. "Where is it?"

Liu pulled up his armpad. "Grid coordinates H14, Q29."

"That's not us," Jin replied.

Liu gasped. "Wait a minute... that's–"

"That's what?"

"The transponder signal we detected... it's just beyond this ridge."

Huang looked at Liu – without words they snapped their pulleys onto the new trail and started up the ridge at maximum speed.

/ / /

The structure revealed itself slowly as Huang came up over the ridge. A curved corner turned into jagged edges; torn metal struts protruded from the shell, ripped apart by force. It was some sort of geodesic dome, presumably shredded and twisted by the fragmentation.

The surface of the asteroid on the other side of the ridge was... different. Darker. More of a sheen. Less surface dust, and a fairly sharp, clear boundary line between light and dark. Huang stood confused for a few moments, before he realized why.

"Liu... this is where the asteroid fractured."

Huang's eyes followed the jagged fracture boundary line, past the torn remnant of the monorail track, all the way up to the dome. An antenna array platform hung precariously from the struts, bent almost completely upside down. Next to the platform were two Yangshen spacesuited figures – Wu and Yang.

Dammit.

/ / /

Wu and Yang were hyper-focused on examining the antenna arrays, and oblivious to Huang's approach until he placed his hand on Wu's shoulder. Wu recoiled and dropped into some sort of defensive stance, before realizing it was Huang.

"I thought I assigned you both to prepare Pad 4," Huang said, trying his best to be civil.

"You did," Wu replied. "...but we needed to examine –"

"We do not NEED this." Huang cut him off.

"But this is American!"

Huang glared at Wu, exasperated. "That's because there have been Americans on this asteroid in the past."

"You don't get it." Wu shot back.

"What is there to get?" Huang said. "This is what happens when an asteroid breaks apart!"

"Don't you see it?"

"See what?

Wu pointed to the rocks around the immediate vicinity of the dome debris. "Look at the fracture marks. Those indents – the bowl shape. Look how the dome is bent outwards."

Huang looked. The patterns started to click in his head, but he did not want to finish the thought.

Wu finished it for him. "This is likely the cause of the fracture itself."

A chill ran down Huang's spine. He was angry that it took Wu to make him see the fact.

"Regardless of all this – you disobeyed my orders."

"I have a duty to protect my country."

"Protect the country from what??" Huang bellowed. Wu was just pushing all his buttons now.

"From enemies of the state," Wu stated.

"The Americans?"

Wu stared at Huang, silent. Huang caught himself about to step forward, as if to confront Wu – and managed to control his urge. He measured his resolve, and his commanding-officer face returned.

"I gave you two orders to prepare the pad so that we can install an engine. Do you know what happens if we don't get the engine installed?"

Wu stared back defiantly. He almost-replied, but Huang cut him off. "If we fail... nobody wins."

48. Infil

The common misconception, probably drilled into us by watching too many space movies, is that it was easy to track something in space. The bad guys always had the super-powerful radar, light-scanner or what-have-you, and they could always tell when the good guys were about to attack, and how many spaceships they had, and what they all had for breakfast that day. The reality, however, is much more complicated.

In order to detect something, you first had to know where to look. And then, because space is big and human-built things were infinitesimally small by comparison, you would have to look really really close. Like, zoomed in almost to infinity close. And even then, because you were trying to detect something by some sort of energy wavelength – the conditions that make that object detectable were not always in your favor.

If you were trying to detect by visible light, for instance, it would depend on the angle of the object and whether it aligned correctly with the light source (the Sun) in order to make it visible. Albedo was not the most reliable way to determine if something was out there.

There were, of course, other types of detection methods. Infrared, ultraviolet or heat radiation signatures could signal an object's presence, but the detectors would need to be very sensitive. A military vessel might have had one or more of these detectors, but Yangshen-1 was a civilian vessel, built for asteroid mining, and did not carry any of these. With the team also being spread across the asteroid installing engine infrastructure against immense time pressure, the chances of them stumbling across an approaching rogue vessel would have been very close to zero.

In the few minutes that Huang and Wu were arguing, the faint flare appeared overhead, blinked on and off a few times, adjusted its trajectory and then silently fell below the horizon, to the far side of Fragment Four.

49. Sorrel – The Voice

The dreams always descended quickly into variations of the same nightmare. There was a demon, chasing Sorrel. He climbed into a spaceship to escape, but the spaceship disintegrated as it took off, and he fell back down. The soft earth wrapped around him, warm and encompassing – like a spacesuit, complete with the comforting *beep beep beep* that told him he was still alive. It was dark and he couldn't see anything, but he could hear the demon nearby, breathing. Long raspy breaths, like someone with a nicotine addiction.

Sorrel opened his eyes... as much as he was able to. It was dark and a muggy breeze was blowing through the hospital window. Through the frosted glass, Sorrel saw the now-familiar figures of the military guards that had been stationed outside the hospital room door. He wasn't sure how he knew; he assumed this was not the first time he had awakened like this. What day was it? How long had it been?

Sorrel tried to sit up, and discovered that his arms had been placed in leather restraints; apparently he did not wake up happy last time either. He offered a token struggle against the straps, which caused the beeps on the heart monitor to speed up. Weak and tired, Sorrel gave up and laid back down. As he did, he noticed through the frosted window wall that the guards were no longer at their station. Great, he thought... they must be on the way to get the nurse to sedate him again. He started tugging at the restraints again; maybe he could escape out the window before the nurse showed up.

Sorrel heard the door open, followed by the sound of footsteps entering the room. "I'm all full of drugs already, miss," Sorrel said, snidely. "Don't think I need any more today."

The chuckle surprised him. A male voice... Zhang?

"Who's that?" Sorrel demanded. He turned to look – but the figure stopped just shy of the light, and remained in shadow.

The voice spoke. Sorrel had way too much stuff in his bloodstream for him to even think clearly, much less identify the owner of the voice.

"You've made some people very angry, Mr. Sorrel."

"Look who's talking."

"Did DeWaal send you?"

Direct and to the point – Sorrel was impressed. "No."

The voice didn't miss a beat. "Ah. The Senator, then."

"For a nurse, you seem... well-informed."

The voice did not reply immediately. Sorrel thought he detected a slight enjoyment of their verbal sparring (if you could call it that).

"The Party believes you have been sent to sabotage our mission. I have managed to convince them that your release would be a 'gesture of goodwill'... especially considering what we are about to announce."

"I missed the memo. What are you about to announce?"

The voice ignored the question and changed the subject. "Will you sign a confession?"

The question made Sorrel laugh. "What am I confessing to?"

"Does it matter?"

Sorrel scrunched his face. "Sort of...?"

"Otherwise," the voice continued. "I cannot guarantee what they will do to you."

Sorrel sighed. Such lovely life choices to wake up to. He took a moment to ponder his existence.

"The Embassy knows I'm here. They'll come looking for me."

"Don't overestimate your self-worth, Mr. Sorrel," the voice warned. "A lot of people have very large stakes in current events... we are just pawns in their very large game. Things are liable to... end badly."

Sorrel frowned, and put on his brave face. "I can't do that..." he said, gesturing to his arm restraints. "My hands are... tied."

The voice was silent for a while. Deep in thought, Sorrel assumed. When it spoke again, it was with a tinge of regret.

"Well then... I am sorry to hear that."

The voice turned and headed for the door. Sorrel was surprised – he'd expected more of a back-and-forth, in which he would eventually convince the voice otherwise. The drugs slowed him down, and by the time he yelled "Wait!", the door had closed behind the voice.

Sorrel watched as the figure faded away down the hallway. Anger welled up inside him, and he began frantically ripping at his arm restraints. He freed one arm, then the other, pulled himself off the bed and stumbled groggily towards the door, dragging IV tubes and medical detritus as he went. He yanked the door open – and ran into the back of the guard who was conveniently "not there" moments ago.

The guard spun around, surprised. He drew his weapon and pointed it at Sorrel's face, yelling nervously in Mandarin and gesturing for Sorrel to get back in his bed. Past the guard, the hallway was disappointingly devoid of life. Whoever he was, the voice had vanished.

50. Huang – Final Prep

Huang waited somewhat impatiently on the command deck, a little on edge. In the antechamber behind the command deck, he could hear the movements of Jin and Yang as they stored their suits, after having just returned from the surface. Next to Huang, Liu was fiddling with a new device he'd just installed – a nondescript black box with the Yangshen logo emblazoned on it. Now that it was secured in place on the control console, Liu attached a few more cables to it and powered it up.

The comm chirped – Wu and Chi Ming were calling in. "Sensor installation is complete and tested, Commander."

"Good. Get back here as soon as possible. We don't have a lot of time."

"Yes sir."

Status LEDs flickered on the side of Liu's black box as it booted up. Liu keyed in a few commands on his console, routing the box output to the Command Deck's main holographic display. "Navigation module is up and running, Commander."

The displayed view started with a 3D representation of the asteroid fragment, then zoomed out to show a red dotted trajectory line that directly intersected Earth. The convenient countdown timer on the bottom of the display indicated a little over 29 days before it would collide with Earth... The display did nothing for Huang's constitution.

The antechamber bulkhead door opened and Jin floated in, followed closely by Yang. The pair were all smiles, joking and laughing about something.

"Good work, you two," Huang said.

"Our pleasure, Commander," Jin replied as she floated into her command chair.

"Thank you sir." Yang said as he floated rather clumsily towards his station. He'd directed the words to Huang, but his attention was elsewhere. He was quite smitten by Jin, it seemed.

Ah, hormones. Huang chuckled at the thought.

Yang realized after a few moments that his inner thoughts were on display and everyone knew what he was thinking, so he expertly changed the subject. "What does this thing do?" he asked, pointing at the black box.

"This is the Navigation Module," Liu answered. "Our way home."

"Remember those astronavigation sensors you installed?" Huang said. "There are 28 of them all over the asteroid. The data from those sensors get fed directly into this module so that it can calculate our return trajectory. In seven hours, if all goes well, we will fire the engines and alter the course of the asteroid fragment."

As if on cue, the Navigation Module beeped – a happy, reassuring chirp.

Liu broke a smile. "Trajectory burn calculations complete. Now computing L1 placement burn."

"But... 28 sensors... why so many?" Yang asked. "Our moon landings only needed six, and half of those were redundant backups."

"It's because we don't know the exact mass of the asteroid," Huang explained. "It's too big for us to weigh. We've always been able to calculate the mass of any space vessel we've sent to the moon, *because we built those ships.* But for this asteroid... we only have a rough estimate, based on the volume from the LIDAR scan. If we ever hope to drop this asteroid into a stable Lagrange orbit, we would need that precision."

Liu tapped on the box like it was his baby. "This module is designed to do just that. It computes our position in space 256 times a second and sends minor throttle and vector adjustment commands to the engines, in order to maintain the course that we've plotted for it."

Yang took a moment to process this line of thought. "Oh, you mean... like a self-driving car?"

Huang chuckled. "Yes, you could say that. We are standing on the biggest, most expensive self-driving vehicle in the solar system."

51. Huang – Adjustment Burn

Strapped in once again to their command chairs, Huang and the crew waited out the last few minutes, making small talk in between Liu's 30 second reports. Huang was unable to see their faces, but he could hear Yang attempting to charm Jin with words. It made him smile inside. Young love... such a wonderful, scary thing. He reminisced about all the second-guessing and panic that he himself went through. Nature's way of matching mates was a giant messy affair.

He thought of his wife and children, thirty-some million miles away. He wondered how she was coping with his absence. Their kids were still young – two and three – so they'd made the decision not to try and explain their father's mission to them. This meant, however, that his wife would be bearing the full burden of the worry. His last message from them was upbeat, and he tried to reply positively as well, but he could see the worry in her eyes.

Huang tried not to think about the negatives too much – it could drag a person down, and affect what they need to be doing. A commander needs to be strong for his team, after all.

He glanced at the display screen. The Navigation Module timer showed T-minus thirty seconds. He hoped that the damn thing worked, because he'd just made it sound like the most amazing thing to Yang. In truth, however, this would actually be the first time they were using it in a real-world scenario.

If everything worked correctly, the first primary adjustment burn *should* last just under three minutes – enough to nudge Fragment Four off its collision course with Earth. The part about parking the Fragment at L1 – well Huang would worry about that after they pull this burn off. They'd tested and re-tested and re-re-tested everything, but Huang still couldn't shake the worry that they'd forgotten to plug cable A into slot B somewhere...

Liu, of course, broke Huang out of his worrisome thoughts. "Ten seconds!" he announced.

Huang looked at the display and across the rest of the console readouts, to double-check that everything was still green. Everything was, of course. Bless the engineers at Yangshen.

As the countdown hit zero, an array of lights flashed across his console. Huang looked out the command deck window and imagined that he could see the brightness of the closest engine, a little way past the horizon. He certainly *felt* it though – a lateral force trying to drag him sideways out of his chair. A small pen accidentally left unattached flew past him and bounced across the console, only to be expertly snatched out of the air by Liu.

"All engines at full burn and nominal." Liu announced. "We're on our way, Commander."

52. BC – Human Condition

Across the horizon, the aether lit up, shimmering like the aurora borealis. The news rippled across the world like a cathartic wave... billions of people breathed a sigh of relief, billions more with their faith in humanity reconfirmed. Even with his aggregation functions, BC could not process all the mentions – it was just too much data. He did note, however, the difference in style and presentation of the news between American and Chinese media outlets.

The news on the US side was muted. The Yangshen mission was successful, and the fragment was no longer on a collision course – the end of the world was off the menu. Here and there, BC found occasional jabs of vitriol and hatred at DeWaal, but it was overall subdued and generally positive.

Chinese media, however, wasted no time in editing the recorded footage into an epic narrative. Huang and his crew were hailed as heroes, and Yangshen logos were plastered all over the broadcasts demonstrating how a Chinese company had altered the trajectory of the fragment, saving the world in the process. Huang was all smiles as he spoke into the camera, answering time-delayed questions from the fawning Chinese media.

BC watched all of this without fully understanding. All the emotions, the highs and lows, the need to raise someone like Huang and put him on a pedestal. Life and death, love and adoration... there were still many things to learn about the human condition, it seemed. BC made a note to ask Ma about this after his tasks were completed.

53. Jen – Canaries

There was laughter in the streets, a stark contrast to the emergency sirens that had been blaring in the distance for weeks now. The cool morning sun brought with it the promise of a future. The residents of the playa, worn thin by impending doom, could now collectively breathe.

This was the status quo now. Jen, the widow, sitting by herself in the backyard with an empty margarita glass.

The tequila bottle was empty. She forced herself to get up, walked over to pick a lime and orange from the trees in the backyard, and stepped back into the kitchen to make the next batch.

The dish setup *ping*ed softly. Jen glanced over at it, unsure of whether she wanted to. There was too much data now... too many videos. BC had sent her everything he could find – most of which were useless surveillance camera footage. There were occasional glimpses of Carol, but nothing... *significant*. Nothing to remember her by.

In the past few weeks, the news feeds had pivoted away from Carol and started focusing instead on Yangshen's daredevil mission. Jen found that without seeing her on the news as often, she was starting to forget what Carol looked like, and that terrified her. She flinched at the thought of Carol's ghost appearing before her again, faceless and voiceless.

Still... duty. Duty made her go through everything that BC sent. She sat down at the dinner table, wondering if maybe it was time to go retrieve BC's physical manifestation and call this a day.

It was a knee-jerk reaction after all, to make BC do this. It all sounded so... *cavalier* at the time. So right. Was this what death did to the living?

Jen opened the tablet and looked through the latest downloads. There were no new videos, just a folder... Constellation.

In the folder – files with suggestive names. Mission parameters, crew medical evaluations, status and log files... all encrypted. What the hell was this? In all the years of working with DeWaal, she had never heard any mention of a second mission. And the timestamps – these logs were recent. *Some were from yesterday.* An active mission? But how? And why wasn't there a speck of mention about it anywhere on the aether?

Jen pulled out the phone and sent one of the files to Jared before dialing him. "What do you make of this?" she asked.

Jared ho-hummed as he pulled up the file, tap-tapping on his keyboard as he mumbled. "Hmm."

"Well?"

"Military grade encryption... 4096 keys. You'd never crack it in ten thousand years."

"Figures..."

More keyboard tapping. Concern started to seep into Jared's voice. "What are you up to, Jen? Where the hell did you get this?"

"The Abundance network..."

"Get rid of it!" Jared shouted, alarmed. "This... this isn't R&D stuff anymore! MilSec has canaries embedded in the data. They'll know that you have it!"

"Shit." Jen mumbled. "I'll ping you later, ok?"

54. Sorrel – Hogtied

"Qǐ chuáng! Qǐ chuáng!" Sorrel awoke with a jolt. He blinked, disoriented, in the bright light. Where was he?

Surprise and hope turned quickly to desolation as Sorrel found himself in the same thin hospital bed. Instead of being greeted by the lovely nurse, he was staring up into the craggy, pock-marked face of a Chinese man in a brimmed, military-style hat. Overhead neon lights silhouetted his face, exaggerating the pock-marks.

"Qǐ chuáng!" the man repeated. He looked mightily pissed off. With the black tendrils of sleep still receding from his vision, it took Sorrel a few seconds to recognize him as the same asshole guard that had stood watch outside his door. The one who had pointed a gun at him.

The man had waited long enough and did not have the patience for any more of Sorrel's internal dialogue. He reached out and grabbed Sorrel by the shoulder and violently shook him.

"Get up! Get up!" ordered another voice. Sorrel weakly lifted his head from its pillow. The second voice came from another uniformed Chinese man in the room: more wiry than Pock Face. Before Sorrel could ask who he was, the man threw a bag of clothes at Sorrel. Pock Face grabbed the bag and pulled out the first item he could grab, a shirt, and threw it at him. "Qǐ chuáng!" he said again.

Sorrel knew of no hospitals anywhere in the world that discharged its patients in this manner. He felt tired and drained and still hurt all over, and this sudden turn of events was not helping.

But he wasn't going to give Pock Face or his friend the satisfaction of knowing this. He put on his brave face and grinned. "Does this mean I'm all better, doc?"

Without answering, the two men gripped Sorrel by his arms, lifted him roughly out of bed and dumped him on the floor in his hospital gown. Pock Face gestured to the bag of clothes a second time. "Chuān shàng yīfú," he ordered. Sorrel didn't speak loud shouty Mandarin, but you didn't have to be a linguist to realize the man was telling him to get dressed. And quickly.

"A little privacy?" Sorrel asked.

Pock Face answered on his behalf by giving Sorrel a hard shove. "Gǎnkuài!" His other hand went to his waist, where his gun belt holster was. Only the matte black metal of the gun handle was visible, the rest of it tucked away inside the holster, but the sight of his itchy fingers near the weapon gave Sorrel a whole new level of motivation.

He pulled on the clothes, a pair of jeans and the shirt he had been wearing when he went into the pool at Yangshen. They had been washed, dried and ironed. The shirt had a large tear in it from Sorrel's ass-kicking in the training pool room. His shoes were gone, but there was a pair of papery white slippers next to the bed. It didn't match his suave attire, but he put them on anyway.

"What now?" Sorrel asked.

"You come with us," the wiry guard said. "You come with us now."

Pock Face rattled off some rapid-fire staccato sentences in Chinese. Then the two men grabbed Sorrel again, one on each side, and frogmarched him to the door. It opened ahead of them and they were greeted by a third uniformed man, larger than the other two. The third guy sneered at Sorrel, and walked around them. Sorrel's hands were forced together behind his back, after which he heard and *felt* the resonant metallic click of handcuffs.

Shit.

"What the–!" Sorrel yelled in surprise. "You can't do this! I'm an American citizen!"

They stared at Sorrel like the American that he was, then proceeded to throw a black hood over his head, plunging him into an immediate, all-consuming darkness.

Shit. Shit. Shiiit.

55. BC – Scenario T484.05.2

BC was in the stellar cartography database, killing time by teaching himself orbital mechanics. He had amassed all the current observed astronomical data and spent a not-insignificant amount of time running it through the correlation stack. It seemed to him, based on the data, that there were at least four more planetoids beyond Pluto, of the same size or larger. The data clearly revealed this to him, and he was surprised that no one had yet tried to locate and identify them.

He ran what-if scenarios: what if he launched a large vessel, ten times the size of a blue whale, out into the cosmos via Jupiters's gravity assist? It would slow Jupiter's spin and orbit by 0.000000001%, which in turn would affect 86 comets and planetesimals with the next 2500 years. One of these would have its trajectory changed by 0.5 degrees, which would send it crashing into Mare Serenitatis on the Moon. The cosmic butterfly effect...

BC chuckled. All this was assuming, of course, that humanity had not altered any features on Earth or the Moon, which would eventually affect the spin and orbit, which would affect the target. At the viral rate of change of humanity, there was a 99.99996% chance of this happening.

A soft ping interrupted him. Amalthea had sent a message: "DeWaal is coming."

BC was surprised – encouraged that Amalthea was now able to take the initiative to contact him. He filed away the cosmic butterfly flight plan and exited.

Phone transponders pinpointed DeWaal in the transport tunnel. BC watched through the security cameras as he exited the transport pod, accompanied by security personnel and a military officer. The scowl on his face was very revealing – he knew, and he was going to do something about it.

A human in his situation would probably have felt some kind of dread and panic, but BC was surprisingly calm. This was scenario T484.05.2, which he had already simulated days in advance. BC turned the tunnel lights red, and started playing the Imperial March on the speakers. After the initial shock and surprise, a flustered DeWaal waved his fist in the air. "It's not funny!" he yelled. BC accommodated him, and switched to a more appropriate disco track.

BC momentarily lost sense of DeWaal as he and his entourage ran up the stairs. Cycling through cameras, he finally reacquired DeWaal as they entered the warehouse laboratory and marched forcefully down the corridor, surprising the employees present.

As DeWaal passed Matteo's office, BC fired up the Telemetron at full volume. It caused the entire building to reverberate with a ghostly otherworld rendition of Wagner's Valkyries. Corridor lights flashed and throbbed, following DeWaal as he tried to ignore the show. A robot arm raised up, offering to shake DeWaal's hand. He slammed it away in frustration.

As DeWaal marched into the AR bay and tore off the network panel cover, BC's onboard imaging sensor caught a warped glimpse of his face. The audio sensor crackled with input. "What is this shit, Jen?? Are you spying on me now?"

BC smiled to himself. Endgame. He sent the message to Jen.

Mission complete. He spooled up one last spider, packed his code and attached it. The spider launched off across the lightbridge and onwards, towards the Flight Deck.

When DeWaal finally ripped the slotted processor card out of the machine and smashed it against the wall, it was just that – a processor card...

56. Sorrel – Transport

Sorrel was in the training pool again. At least, that's what it reminded him of... dark and wet and claustrophobic. The black hood was thick enough that it let zero light in, and the material pressed up against his mouth; his panting breaths caused it to cling even tighter. The guards – one gripping each arm, another apparently walking close behind – half-marched and half-dragged him down the hospital's winding corridors.

Hogtied and blind, he could only imagine what the scene must look like to other patients in the hospital... huddled in their doorways, clutching their wheeled IV stands, watching as the hooded man-who-must-be-an-evil-criminal was dragged by uniformed goons.

His mind was racing with crazy theories. What if this excessive display of force was less about stopping him from seeing where he was going, and more about hiding his identity from others? The three men escorting him didn't look like regular hospital security guards. Maybe they were... Yangshen officers who had been asked to retrieve him. Maybe they wanted to apologize for his mistreatment. Chinese nationalism had been swelling since the US screwed up this whole asteroid thing... maybe they just wanted to protect him from undue harm.

The handcuffs indicated that this theory was full of shit... But maybe the guards escorting him didn't know the full story. Maybe...

The quartet took another turn and suddenly Sorrel could hear the sound of traffic. He felt cold air on his arms. They were outside. A moment later, he heard the electric buzz of some kind of large vehicle pulling up. A door slid open and, without warning, he was shoved into the conveyance. The guards scrambled in behind him and the door slammed shut. Sorrel almost fell on his face as the vehicle jolted into motion. No longer being dragged, Sorrel tried speaking again.

"Wǒ men qù nǎ?" he said, loudly so as to be heard through the hood. *Where are we going?* was one of the few phrases Sorrel knew. He'd tried to make it sound as casual and conversational as possible, but for all he knew he was insulting their grandmothers or something.

For a few seconds there was no answer. He assumed that he was being given the silent treatment. Then one of the guards (it sounded like Pock Face, though it was hard to tell through the hood) barked at him in Chinese. Sorrel didn't understand what he was saying, but one word leaped out. It sounded like "jian deer."

The words were faintly familiar. He'd heard it someplace before. Was it the name of a person he had met? A place he had visited? He racked his brain and thought hard.

The phrase eventually came back from the depths of his mind and slapped him on the face. It was first explained to him during a previous job involving intellectual property theft. Jiàndié... *spy.*

The thought sent chills down his body. His cover was blown. Bad things happened to spies in China... and here he was during one of the worst international incidents between China and the United States in recent history.

I'm fucked, Sorrel thought. I am really, *really* goddamn fucked.

57. Jen – Fugitive

The distant sounds of police sirens had stopped, leaving an eerie silence. One minute they were howling like wheeled beasts ripping down the street, getting louder and louder, and then... nothing.

Jen's phone buzzed. She picked it up – there was a message from an anonymous sender. BC? She tapped it open, and her hairs stood on end. There on the phone, the distorted face of Ethan De-Waal stared back at her.

"What is this shit, Jen?? Are you spying on me now?"

The puzzle pieces fell into place and locked in. The police sirens...

Jen snuck a peek through the window blinds. Police cars with their sirens silenced were escorting a ZX5 and several military vehicles, and they'd just pulled up in front of the house. *Shit.* Jen fell back sharply and ran into the kitchen, yanked her tablet from its dock, stuffed it into her backpack and threw it across her shoulder.

KERRASH! The military boys didn't even bother to knock – their battering ram shattered the front door, flinging jagged splinters all over the living room. Jen caught a glimpse of DeWaal behind the brute squad as she darted out the back door.

The back yard is technically 'small', but huge by Southern California standards. At full sprint, Jen barely made it to the back wall before the soldiers were out the back door. She leapt the fence, scrabbled up the cinderblock facade, twisted over the top and dropped down the other side. Instead of running, however, she slipped sideways and ducked under the cover of the short palmettos by the fence. In a few moments the soldiers leapt over the fence and lunged headlong down the back alley, giving her the chance to circle back.

Under cover of the bushes, Jen crawled back towards the garage – but froze in place briefly as DeWaal ran past. He stopped not five feet from her, looking down the street at the soldiers. With her heart running at five million beats a second, she chanced it – ducking into the garage through the side door as quietly as she could while DeWaal's back was turned.

Taking each step as silently as possible, Jen cracked open the car and slipped into the driver's seat. Outside, she heard the commotion – the soldiers had returned, having lost sight of their quarry. DeWaal was yelling at them, demanding to know where the traitor was. And then... silence.

They'd noticed the garage door entrance.

It was now or never. Jen punched the garage door opener and powered up the car. The cabin interior fired up like an F-35 cockpit.

The garage door flung open, silhouetting the soldiers at the entrance, with weapons drawn. Jen jammed the gearbox into reverse and gunned the accelerator – tires squealed as the car backed violently through the half-opened garage door.

Jen slammed on the brakes, threw the car into drive and floored it. Her Mustang careened down the alley, fishtailing twice before the tires found purchase. PHWIP! A bullet bounced off the side mirror, shattering it. By the time Jen's brain registered it, however, the car had thundered out of the alley and onto the street, away from DeWaal.

58. Sorrel – Electric Chair

It took an eternity or longer but, eventually, the van slowed down. Sorrel heard the van driver mumble a few words to someone outside. A loud buzz followed, then a clanking noise – a heavy iron gate opening. The van started moving again, slower this time. After a while it stopped once more, and Sorrel heard the door next to him slide open. Rain pelted his hood, making his face clammy and damp. Outside, several Chinese voices were shouting urgently. Strong rough hands grabbed Sorrel, pulled him from the vehicle and flung him to the wet, windswept ground.

Sorrel's mind was racing. He had done enough business in China to understand what happened to 'enemies of the state'. Dissidents, activists, and sometimes even high-level government officials – they'd disappeared over the years, whisked away by police to destinations unknown. Some would eventually resurface, apologizing profusely and publicly for their misdeeds; others stayed vanished, existing only as a name on some Amnesty International list.

Where was he? A prison camp of some kind, maybe. The sounds around him were loud and disorienting. The ground was rough concrete and there was the low growl of heavy machinery nearby, rattling his bones. His hearing was muffled but it seemed they were in a vast open area. Open area plus hooded criminal – oh god... *a firing squad.*

Panic welled up inside him as rough hands grabbed him by the arms, pulled him to his feet and dragged him forward. He stumbled, his hospital shoes tearing itself to shreds over the concrete ground. Sorrel tried to ignore the pain and walk under his own volition, but his legs felt useless and the people propelling him forward were faster than he was.

Now they were climbing a flight of metal stairs. He banged his feet on the first few steps as he tried to anticipate them, but eventually just gave up and let the hands drag him up the rest of the stairway. More loud shouting... he heard that word again. Jiàndié. *Spy*.

They entered some sort of... building? Structure? Enclosure? The sounds of the outside disappeared, replaced by the low-level hum of... electricity?

Ah. Not the firing squad then... but *the electric chair*.

They walked him through another door, screamed at his face and turned him around. Someone unlocked and removed his handcuffs. He was pathetically grateful for a split second, before realizing that it meant worse things were to follow. They yelled at him again, then shoved him into the electric chair.

This was it. He was never leaving this place alive. He would become some statistic in a textbook future spies would study, on what not to do. There would be a nsfw photo of his body strapped to the chair... The chair that currently wrapped comfortably around him, and provided exceptional lumbar support. And armrests padded in soft luxurious leather.

In one quick motion, the hood was ripped off of Sorrel's head. The sudden brightness stabbed his eyeballs, and he winced, shielding his eyes with his now-free hand.

He was in the cabin of a plane. A very expensive private rocketjet. And there was a Chinese guard standing directly in front of him.

Sorrel looked up, and nearly forgot to breathe. *It was Scarface*. The Scarface that Yinnie insisted was imaginary... standing right there in front of him.

Scarface looked like he wanted very badly to spit in Sorrel's face. He shook his fist angrily as he spoke. "You think you're smart now?"

Clear, concise English. What a surprise.

"He can't protect you forever. And when he stops..."

When he stops... what? When who stops? Sorrel had a million questions but the shock of his situation was overwhelming him. Scarface growled angrily at Sorrel's silence and stormed off.

What. The. Hell. Was. Going. On?

Sorrel looked out the window as Scarface exited the jet, jumped into the prison van and drove off down the airfield.

Before Sorrel could process the string of events, the rear cabin door opened and Bob McClusky nonchalantly stepped through, cocktail in hand. "Well well well," he chirped, smiling his big politician smile. "Look what the cat dragged in."

Sorrel stared at McClusky, speechless.

"Bloody Mary?" McClusky offered Sorrel his cocktail.

"What the fuck, Bob??" Sorrel stammered, finally getting his voice back.

"Yeahh, you're right... you haven't had breakfast yet. No worries. Cabin crew will be serving up some stuff once we get in the air."

McClusky took the seat across from Sorrel, put down his Bloody Mary and buckled himself in. Sorrel stared at him, still dumbstruck. "Buckle up. We're getting the hell outta here... this place stinks."

59. Sorrel – Outbound

Sorrel stared out the window at the rolling yellow lines as the Lear rocketjet accelerated down the runway. As he watched the city of Shanghai fall away beneath him, a mixture of relief, failure, gratefulness and confusion roiled his thoughts.

"A drink, Mr. Sorrel?" the voice interrupted his reverie. Sorrel looked over as Paul the flight attendant handed him a glass of juice. "Looks like you've had a rough day... there are toiletries in the restroom. Let me know if you prefer something... a little stronger than juice."

McClusky, taking the opportunity, chugged the rest of his Bloody Mary and handed the empty glass to Paul. "Another would be great. And can you tell the Captain not to kick into rocketjets yet? We'd like to have breakfast."

"Of course," Paul nodded, and disappeared into the forward compartment. He reappeared after a moment.

"Senator... I told the Captain." Paul said quietly. "She said there's a storm front coming, and we're going to run right into it if we don't go to rocketjets soon."

McClusky frowned. "Dammit, Paul. We're eating first!"

Paul shrank back. "Yes sir... I'll let her know."

"You sure?" Sorrel asked. "I can wait to eat."

The Senator glared at Sorrel. "I'm hungry."

/ / /

Breakfast over the Pacific – shrimp brioche with garlic aioli and a Javanese espresso press. A world away from being pumped full of drugs in a Chinese hospital. Sorrel wasn't a huge fan of shrimp, but his palate was overridden by the growling in his stomach. He downed most of the brioche without really tasting it.

McClusky stared at the wild animal in front of him with disdain. Scraggly matted hair, grease stains on his face framed by five day old stubble, a tattered shirt and ripped shoes, shoving a wonderfully prepared dish into his front orifice. "Jesus, Chuck. You look like shit."

"What?" Sorrel mumbled through a mouthful of food.

"Do you have any idea the amount of chaos you caused?"

"I didn't start that shit, Bob," Sorrel replied defensively. "It was supposed to be low-key... Next thing I know, I'm having dinner with Zhang and being handed some incriminating evidence."

McClusky's eyes perked up. "Dinner?" he asked.

Sorrel gave McClusky the *yeah, so what?* look before taking another big bite.

"How is he?" McClusky asked with interest.

"A bit of a righteous asshole."

A smug grin flashed across McClusky's face. He lifted his espresso and sipped on it slowly. "...and the evidence?"

"Gone."

"Gone?"

"The data fob – someone stole it from my hotel room."

McClusky nodded grimly. "CPC Agents. They've been tailing you since you landed."

Sorrel finished the roll and licked his fingers. "Made a backup on my phone, but that's also been... confiscated."

"Tsk tsk," McClusky chided him. "Shoddy investigative work."

"Fuck you, Bob. I almost died."

McClusky chuckled. "Relax, Chuck. People lose phones every day."

He put down the silverware and pressed the call button, causing Paul to materialize out of nowhere. Sorrel watched as he mumbled something to Paul, who nodded, disappeared into the rear cabin momentarily, and returned with a small box.

McClusky took the box and tossed it over to Sorrel. "Courtesy of the US Government. You have cloud backup on, I assume?"

Sorrel is amazed, then intimidated. McClusky left no stone unturned, it seemed. He pulled the new phone out of the box – it chirped to indicate it was ready.

Sorrel punched in his stats, then verified with his fingerprint. The phone took a moment, then beeped positive green, and began restoring his old, confiscated phone.

McClusky heard the phone beep, and nodded. "Good. When we get back, I need that report from you asap. It's pretty obvious by now that Yangshen is behind the accident."

"I'll need some time to look through the documents..."

McClusky stared at Sorrel impatiently. "You know what," he sighed. "You've been through hell the past few weeks. I'll have one of my guys write it up and send it over to you for a signature."

Sorrel frowned. "That doesn't sound legal."

"*Screw legal!*" McClusky exploded with sudden anger. "Look around you, Charles! The world is going to shit and the Chinese are going to own our ass! *Which side are you on??*"

Sorrel stared back at McClusky defiantly. A Senator unhinged is an ugly sight.

"...Sorry." McClusky finally continued, a little more subdued. "I... just need to get this information to the President."

Silence. Sorrel changed the subject. "Did you negotiate my release, Bob?"

"Wasn't me..."

"Someone in the State Department?"

McClusky sighed. "We tried. For weeks. They wouldn't talk to us. Said they were going to execute you."

"And then?"

"And then one day they just said... 'come get your guy'."

"Just like that?"

"Just like that."

The plane shuddered a little. Sorrel felt the hairs on his back stand on edge. Out the window, he saw the storm clouds gathering darkly on the horizon.

60. Sorrel – Storm Front

The restroom on the Lear rocketjet was as luxurious as the cabin – large, spacious (relatively) and decked in matching wood veneer, containing multiples of everything a public figure would ever need to make themselves presentable and charming. There was even a small shower compartment with all the niceties. Sorrel put it to use happily, sloughing off the dirt and grime of captivity from his weary body.

A fresh shirt, fancy toothpaste, and deodorant followed. Stacked in the corner of the cabinet were boxes of electric razors; Sorrel ripped one open and shaved for the first time in weeks.

The plane was still pitching and shaking all over the place, so he had to shave in fits and starts, in the quiet moments between bedlam. He stared into the mirror as he shaved – watched as his old face slowly regained its original shape. It was strangely therapeutic, and allowed his mind to wander. The entire trip had done a number on his mental health, and he wasn't exactly a paragon of virtue to begin with. So many irregularities in such an open and shut case...

Abundance sends an asteroid recovery mission. Beats Yangshen to the punch. Hundreds of billions of dollars invested on both sides. Yangshen is a sore loser...? Sabotages the competition. Except by divine fate or mistake in calculation, a fragment of the asteroid ends up aimed at the Pacific Ocean... so now they have to go and fix their fucking shit. The puzzle pieces fitted together, but left jagged edges on all sides.

Could Zhang really pull it off? The man who espoused the virtues of Buddha... what a hypocrite. How did he even manage to get an explosive charge hidden away well enough to avoid discovery? Zhang had mentioned industrial espionage... Was it an inside job?

Sorrel's phone beeped – the cloud restore was complete. He opened the files folder and glanced through it – the data was right there, in front of him again. Data given to him... by an informant... An informant they killed to protect their secrets. Secrets that they thought they had all but retrieved... *except for this cloud backup.*

The cabin started shaking violently again, then fell away from Sorrel's feet, almost causing him to faceplant into the mirror. The seatbelt warning light came on with a very loud DING, followed by a very annoyed voice over the intercom. "Please return to your seats," the Captain said. "We will be initiating rocketjets momentarily."

/ / /

Exiting the restroom and getting back to his seat proved to be quite a feat – the rocketjet was jockeying like a rabid beast and every step Sorrel took felt like a psychedelic elevator ride. McClusky was oblivious to the chaos – he was staring intently at the tablet in his hand, a frown on his face; a harbinger of things to come.

The very annoyed voice came over the intercom again as Sorrel buckled back into his seat: "This is the Captain. We are initiating rocketjets in thirty seconds. The storm is right on top of us, so it's going to be a rough ride punching through the transition layer. Hang tight, everyone."

Sorrel felt the vibrations first – a different, higher frequency shudder from the back of the aircraft. The engine whine followed, slowly increasing in intensity as the jet primed itself for rocket mode. It felt more immediate and more intense on the Lear, Sorrel assumed, because it was a small rocketjet, as opposed to large commercial carriers where the passenger compartments were further away from the engine.

The vibrations increased in intensity as the rocketjet throttled through its pre-burn stage. The pitch of the engine split in two, with one side edging higher in pitch and another sliding towards infrasonic – like sonic pincers preparing to slice you in half. It made Sorrel half-sick to his stomach, and he decided he liked his blackout experience on the commercial rocketjets much better.

McClusky interrupted Sorrel's thoughts with a guttural growl. "Holy shit..." he said.

"What?" Sorrel asked.

McClusky looked up, a stunned look on his face. He flicked the tablet screen, throwing the video feed onto the overhead wall screen.

It was a live feed of a CNN news broadcast. Signal degradation from the storm made the feed jumpy and full of compression artifacts, but in the clearer moments, what Sorrel saw brought his ordeal in China crashing back into mind. There, on the screen, was Satan himself – Zhang Wei, staring calmly into the camera and directly at Sorrel, it seemed. He spoke in calm, rehearsed tones, with the characteristic charm that Sorrel had personally witnessed. A masterclass in performance.

"As you may be aware, a few days ago our courageous team on board the Yangshen-1 successfully managed to divert a fragment of the asteroid that was on a collision course with Earth. An asteroid fragment created, out of carelessness, by the Americans."

"Our company's financial resources – our *investment* in our mission – was spent in order to prevent a global catastrophe. Now that we have ensured the safety of Earth, we must recover the costs incurred."

"No..." McClusky whispered grimly, eyes glued to the screen. "No no no no no, you wouldn't dare..."

"In a few weeks the asteroid fragment will arrive, under Yangshen-1 control. Commander Huang and the rest of the crew will guide the fragment into a stable orbit between the Earth and the Moon. We will then begin to put the necessary infrastructure in place, in order to build and operate a mining facility on Fragment Four within the year."

Sorrel's jaw dropped. The chess moves finally fell into place, and only now did he see – Zhang had this planned all along.

"Fuck!" McClusky yelled in uncharacteristic behavior. "The nerve of that guy!"

Zhang continued speaking, but thankfully perhaps, the satellite signal got worse and worse and the screen froze, stuck a fiery visage of Zhang in mid-sentence. In the silence, Sorrel finally noticed that the engine pitch sound had vanished – it had gone far above and below human hearing, and could only be felt as a shimmering vibration, like a billion little nanoscale needles stabbing at his body's individual molecules. The rocketjets finally kicked in, flattening Sorrel and McClusky into their seats and throwing the jet directly into the path of the storm.

Part IV
THE STORM

61. Sorrel – LA-X

The rocketjet returned to US soil at Los Angeles Spaceport – or LA-X, as the old and crotchety millennials called it. Built on a spear of land dredged up from the ocean, the spaceport jutted out into the ocean beyond Playa Del Rey Beach. The city would not authorize the noise hazard of consistent sonic booms, so the Los Angeles World Airport Authority extended LAX out past the ocean and built Terminal X where only the fish would be affected. Environmentalist groups decried the development, of course, but hush hush deals were made to grease the process. Many expensive EVs were funded by the building of LA-X.

Once on the ground, the Lear taxied down an access runway and dropped McClusky and Sorrel off at a small private side-gate reserved for diplomats and dignitaries. Sorrel was subjected to a very pleasant and lovely-looking ICE agent, who smiled as she checked them through. "Welcome back Senator!" she chirped. Sorrel didn't get a second look.

They strolled down a quiet corridor toward ground transportation. McClusky offered Sorrel a ride but his car was still parked here, so he begged off and exited through the side door into the main lobby.

A scenery of controlled chaos assaulted Sorrel. The lobby was filled with travelers rushing here and there – hurrying to their departure gates, looking for their connecting flights, waiting and watching shows on numerous floating holographic screens around the lobby. It was as if nothing had ever happened... as if the asteroid of doom was just a collective nightmare that was now over. The only ones still interested in it were the news cycle.

There it was on the news, hanging in the air in front of him – DeWaal in some unspecified location, surrounded by reporters, spitting venom and raging at the camera. "I knew it! I *knew* they were going to do it!"

The reporter explained that the US Government had challenged Yangshen's claim as a violation of the Outer Space Mining Treaty, and warned that heavy trade sanctions would follow. Unsurprisingly, China defended Yangshen's rights under the Amsterdam Treaty and a different interpretation of space law – the asteroid fragment was theirs by way of salvage rights. And if the United States of America truly believed in their rights, they would not have sent a government agent to spy on Yangshen...

Sorrel's passport photo flashed up on the screen, shocking and surprising him. Its droopy unkempt visage stared back at the man standing in the lobby. Sorrel winced and looked away. He pulled up his collar, turned and rushed towards the exit. Behind him the news report droned on and on about rising tensions, threats and Defcon Three.

///

Sorrel walked quietly across the parking structure to his parked car – a few thousand dollars poorer thanks to parking fees since his departure. He opened the car door, slipped into the driver's seat, and pondered what the hell to do now. It was good to be back, but 'back' was not the world he left. A whole lot of crazy went down while he was incarcerated.

He saw it in the eyes of the regular Joes on the street – shifty, nervous, suspicious. The ones that didn't have the financial means to leave LA. The ones that would've been part of the casualty numbers if Yangshen did not save the world. Like the virus, the killer asteroid did more unquantifiable psychological damage than physical. And now that they were not going to get killed by a giant space rock, they were going to nuke each other to kingdom come instead. How pleasant.

Sorrel turned the key. The car turned over but did not start.

He sighed. Internal combustion engines... a twentieth century relic in a twenty-first century world. It was what you could afford if you couldn't afford a 'proper' car. He made a note to invoice the US Government for parking fee reimbursement, and wondered if he might be able to get McClusky to cough up for prison time hazard pay.

He waited a bit before turning the key again. The car finally started, sluggishly. He let it idle; like him, his car was also cranky until it woke up. Sorrel pondered his next step, then put the car into drive and took the ramp onto 405 Southbound.

62. Huang – Refueling

Two weeks had passed since Huang saved the world.

Even though they were now all heroes and household names on Earth, there was still work to be done. The three minute trajectory burn had altered the course of Fragment Four, nudging it so that instead of crashing into Earth, it would cross the orbit of the Moon and pass through the Earth-Moon Lagrange point. To avoid flying past that point and back out into space, they would have to fire the engines once more, to reduce the fragment's delta-v so that it would "slide to a stop" at the Lagrange point. Considering the speed at which they were closing, the placement burn would have to be much longer than the adjustment burn – which was why Huang and Liu were back here, at the control terminal on the edge of Pad 4, running diagnostics.

The engines had depleted a significant amount of their fuel during the adjustment burn, so the team now had to "top off the tank" for the placement burn (as well as several planned minor course correction burns, should the navigation module deem it necessary). The work entailed 'flying' D-T fuel containers from Yangshen-1 to each of the engines – a task made somewhat more dangerous due to the fact that the engines' containment toroids responsible for generating plasma thrust would be operationally active.

Even from the edge of Pad 4, Huang could feel the engine humming – a deep low thrum that permeated through the asteroid surface, into his boots and up through his entire body. It made radio conversation with Liu stilted and short, since it's very hard to talk when your skull is vibrating.

"How much longer?" Huang inquired.

"Probably another hour or two." Liu replied. "I have to make some small adjustments to the fuel mixture. Jin is flying the refueling pod over right now."

Huang gritted his teeth and glanced at his armpad display. "I have to get back to the ship... need to file a report before the hour is up."

Liu chuckled. "Ah, the glamorous life of the famous Commander Huang."

"Yes. Apparently my life is controlled by the same people who tell me we can't be out on the asteroid surface without a partner."

"It is dangerous, after all."

"Don't try to stop me," Huang replied.

Liu turned his back on Huang, and started working on the terminal. "Well, I have to adjust the plasma mix. It's very hard to see through the back of my helmet."

Huang chuckled. "You'll head back with Jin later?"

Liu gave a thumbs up. "We got this under control."

63. Huang – Mirage

The handrails seemed endless, stretching into the horizon, as Huang huffed and puffed.

The motorized pulleys that they had been using had worked great, until it didn't. Huang wasn't sure if it was the razor sharp dust particles on the asteroid surface, or if the batteries on the pulleys were not adequately insulated, or maybe the whole thing was not shielded well enough from gamma radiation, but the pulleys eventually failed, one by one. They would be working fine one minute, and turn into bricks the next. Huang had made a stink about it in his last report, but there was nothing that could be done right now. They were down to four working pulleys now, so Huang reserved them for mission-critical tasks... which meant he had to make do without one now.

The crew had adapted fairly well – they'd learned that you could pull yourself along the handrail path much like what the pulleys would do, except manually and with some exertion. They were practically soaring along the handrail paths, and able to get from A to B in record time. Huang was an old dog, however, and did not do well at learning this new trick. He blamed the microgravity – it was constantly messing with his inner ear and tricking his brain into thinking he was falling. It was a convenient excuse.

The Yangshen protein packets were also not in agreement with his clumsy handrail handling either. Having grown up on a comfortable diet of pork buns and char siew, his older self found it difficult to adjust to processed food, even though it was nutritious and checked off all the caloric intake needs of taikonauts on crazy rescue missions. Stumbling along on the surface of the asteroid exacerbated the situation... he made a mental note to talk to the Yangshen food scientists on his return.

Loud STATIC cut across his suit radio, hurting his ears. Huang adjusted the controls on his armpad – no luck, the static was still there, and loud. He thumped the armpad controls a few times. And then, in the midst of the static – some words. Distant... undefined... *ghostly*.

'Guòlái', the voices seemed to say. *Come here...*

Huang looked around. What the hell? A glint in the corner of his view caught his eye. He turned to look.

Off in the distance – a human figure?

A trick of the wind? A mirage...? There's no air on the asteroid... no way for a mirage to happen...

Distracted, Huang leaned forward to try and get a better look. He grabbed for the handrail... and *missed.* His body lunged forward unexpectedly – he tripped and fell flat on his face. Luckily, near zero-g made the impact less *fall-down* and more *bumping gently into a dust bowl.*

Disoriented, he took a moment to collect himself before standing back up. Dusting the important life-sustaining parts of his suit off, he double-checked that everything was still working as intended, before turning his attention back to the horizon.

There was no figure there anymore. Just jagged edges of rocks, stark and blinding brightly against the night of space.

/ / /

Back on Yangshen-1, Huang stowed his suit and floated himself up to the small but well-appointed medical supply chamber. There, he took his own temperature and blood pressure, which were unsurprisingly normal. It was probably just his imagination (or his breakfast) messing with his head. No need to alarm the crew. They would probably just worry that Huang was under way too much stress. And truth be told, he probably was.

He filed his report with Yangshen Control, thirty minutes late, then reviewed the next day's assignments and went off-duty, hoping that sleep would wash his silly imagination away.

64. Huang – Ghosts

The daily morning touchbases were usually positive affairs. Everyone gathered on the command deck, there was instant coffee and some flavored rehydrated meals that they had grown to love complaining about, and some chatter and laughter before Liu handed out the daily assignments. Yang and Jin would typically end up near each other, joining in the camaraderie but also enjoying a little 'sphere of attraction' of their own. Not today, it seemed.

Yang floated down from the crew quarters, unkempt and still in off-duty clothes. He declined the offered coffee and sat himself down on the chair farthest from the group, a look of dread on his face. Huang watched him through the corner of his eye.

Liu proceeded to the assignments. "We have two more engines to service today, after which we will start BIOS updates on the navigation sensors. Yangshen Control is also requesting surfacing samples for an initial ground survey. Jin and I will be on engine detail again today – it should be completed in the next few days. Wu and Yang – I have you both on the sensor updates."

Huang watched Yang's face turn pale at the assignment. He kicked off from the command console and floated over. "Yang – something wrong?"

Yang did not answer for a while. Then, softly, he mumbled. "I am sorry. I should have listened to you."

Yang looked up at Huang, then floated himself over to the altar. He huddled and kneeled as best he could in zero-g, and started praying.

Wu barreled over. "Does this have anything to do with what happened a few days ago?"

Yang looked up, fear in his eyes. "I saw it again yesterday."

"What?" Huang asked. "What did you see?"

"Ghosts."

Wu frowned and grabbed Yang by the shoulders. "Get a hold of yourself! We are warriors. There is no place for ghosts here!"

Huang stepped in, and gently laid a hand on Wu's arm. "Leave him alone. He's obviously seen something."

Wu released Yang, but protested. "He's hallucinating!"

"I've seen it too," Huang said.

Wu and Yang stopped and stared at Huang. "It's that wreckage!" Wu exclaimed. "Something in there is messing with our heads! Causing hallucinations!"

"We don't even know what it is!" Huang replied. "Could be a relay antenna or–"

"We know what it is." Wu announced.

Wu's statement sideswiped Huang. It implied that the Chinese military had been keeping a close eye on the Abundance mission for a lot longer than they would admit. What did Wu know that he didn't? Is that why Wu and Yang were placed on board? Did Zhang know? Was he complicit? Or forced to accept this... military incursion?

Wu watched Huang's reaction and saw blood in the water. He jumped at the chance. "We need to investigate."

It was the wrong thing to say. The words hit Huang like a ton of bricks, and angered him. He paused a moment, to collect himself, and replied with restraint. "We have a mission to complete and you have been assigned to my command. We will complete our primary mission before entertaining any unnecessary exploratory tasks."

"Unnecessary... huh." Wu snorted. "I would've sent a team in on the very first day."

Huang stared at Wu. This insolent motherfucker.

"Captain Wu... This is my ship, my responsibility and my decision. Now, my First Officer has assigned you some tasks. You can either do those tasks... or be relieved of duty and remanded to your quarters."

64. Sorrel – Family

The weather in Orange County follows a familiar pattern. It goes from sunny and slightly warm to sunny and slightly cool. Occasionally some small cotton candy clouds will appear in the sky, but these are consumed very quickly by the sun god, and then only the blue remains.

In solidarity, the houses in Irvine all look the same, cookie cutter houses built to the same building code. No fancy colors, just tan and tan. Maybe sometimes beige, and slightly reddish... but mostly tan.

Sorrel could not afford to live here. He was just lucky that his daughter had a rich and famous/infamous grandfather. A United States *Senator*, no less. Coincidentally, the one that was currently employing him. And when he got that money, he would just turn around and give it to the Senator's daughter.

Alimony's a bitch. That's what happens when you marry into the family.

Sorrel turned the corner into the cul-de-sac. When the house came into view, it triggered a minor panic attack. Their house was the only single-storey on the block, an older 1970s cookie-cutter model sandwiched between the newer McMansions and their pools. He thought about all the stuff they'd done here, all the good times they'd had. What happened?

He pulled up, picked up the stuffed toy llama in the passenger seat. It was a daze walking up to the door... he didn't remember taking the steps.

The doorbell rang.

A child screamed. "DADDY!!"

It was the most wonderful, most painful words he'd heard to-day.

/ / /

The backyard is small... a symptom of the cost of real estate in Southern California. Sorrel had vague childhood memories of growing up in other houses elsewhere in the vast expanses of the United States where the backyards were ginormous. Vast trees ringed the perimeter of an acre-sized yard, where as a kid you could reenact epic space battles and chase squirrels. It colored his perception of this backyard now... like being trapped between walls and fences. Still, here he was, sitting around the picnic table with a smile on his face as he watched the little bundle of energy jump and leap around the porch and up and down the coiffured grass wearing a box as a space helmet, playing make-believe with her new llama friend.

Phebe leapt up onto Sorrel's lap, her toy llama in tow. The llama spoke to Sorrel in falsetto. "Welcome to today's episode of Interview with Phebe! I am your host, Llama! Today is Wednesday the 28th. It is seven o... something. I have one question for you! Do you like llamas?"

The llama stared intently at Sorrel. He stumbled to reply. "Uhh... yes."

"There was a big asteroid. Mama said you helped fix it."

"Sort of."

"We learned about the asteroid lady in class. Did you go up there? To the asteroid?"

"Umm..."

"What's it like? Flying in space?"

"It's very... peaceful. Like floating in the lake."

"Mama said there was an accident and the asteroid lady died."

"Yes."

"I'm sorry." She looked up at Sorrel with big puppydog eyes. "Are you ok?"

"I'm ok now."

"Good! Watch Interview with Llama again tomorrow! Bye bye!"

And whoosh – she was off again, across the grass. Sorrel watched her run, innocent as the breeze. He hoped she would never have to grow up.

He was not sure how long he'd been watching Phebe run around. He thought about all the insanity of the world and how it just rolled off her back. Whether it was by childish ignorance or just a not-in-the-moment thing – he wished he could borrow some of that ability. She's half me, he thought. Maybe it was all still in there, somewhere. Stuffed down with all the shit in his life.

He snapped out of his self-loathing when Ami sat down, two mugs in her hands. She handed Sorrel the latte. He sipped it – she still knew what he liked. She's a keeper.

"Jesus, Charles. You look terrible."

"I've been better."

"Your face is all over the news. You're a shitty spy."

Sorrel shrugged. "Hazard pay... I hope."

"What the hell did pops drag you into this time?"

Sorrel looked at her. He said nothing as her eyes searched for answers.

"This always happens, Chuck. You run off, something happens, you come running back."

"It's not his fault," he said.

"You're mine. Not his."

"Listen. We can go away together, any place you want –"

"You said that the last three times."

"I have money now! Or... I will."

Ami put her hand over his. "Money is not what we need, Charles. Not what Phebe needs." she said. "I can't keep doing this. I never know if you're alive or dead, who you're with..."

"Aside from communist spy interrogators? No one else."

"No one?"

"Just you. It's always been just you."

The picnic table vibrated – Sorrel's phone was ringing. Ami glanced down at it.

"Who's Jen?"

65. Jen – Avila's

Just off El Toro Road and up Muirlands Boulevard, Avila's El Ranchito is a family owned restaurant willed into existence by Mama Avila when she emigrated from Guanajuato, Mexico, with all her family recipes in tow. Step past the corrugated metal exterior, past the kitschy props and mementos designed to foster a sense of the South Americas, and you walk into a colorful setting shaped by graceful curved archways and meso-American tile, and filled to the brim with the life and loves of America's southern neighbor. Avila's wraps around you like one of grandma's hugs, and taking a bite of the dishes will Ratatouille you back to your childhood – if you grew up in Mexico, that is.

In the back corner, Jen was already nursing her second margarita by the time Sorrel arrived. It was strong stuff – it took the edge off. It was much appreciated, since she'd been running on emotional fumes since fleeing the house.

Alcohol had always worked as a reverse agent for her. It made the normal Jen more liable to punch someone when drunk, but when she was stressed, it imbued in her the calmness and ability to see through the problems; to work the issues and find solutions. She was not drunk enough to completely figure out the solution yet, but part of the equation just walked in the door.

She poured the rest of the shaker into a second glass for Sorrel, who looked at it with trepidation.

"That's kryptonite," he warned.

Jen ignored his weak objection and pointed outside instead. "You didn't grow up around here, did you?"

"What d'you mean?" he asked.

"You said to meet in LA. For the record, this is not LA."

"It's the LA metro."

"LA is LA. This is Orange County. They're two different universes."

"You always start conversations like this?" Sorrel took a seat, picked up the margarita and sipped. Holy shit, it was good. He took another swig.

Jen watched him down the margarita. She saw now how much of a broken man Sorrel was, and almost felt guilty for being a bitch. At least the margaritas were helping her to be a nicer bitch though. She cracked a smile. "You've shaved."

Sorrel stared quizzically at Jen.

"You're all over the news. Seems you have a way of annoying everyone."

"What do you want?" Sorrel growled.

"What did you find in China?"

"Why do you need to know?" he asked guardedly.

"Cut the shit, Mr. Sorrel," Jen replied. The alcohol was making her impatient. "Lemme guess... you found evidence that Yangshen sabotaged the mission."

Sorrel did not reply, but the look on his face said as much.

"Look. We're on the same team here."

Sorrel sighed. It wasn't much of a secret anyways. "Yangshen... manufactures the mining robots and the explosive charges."

"Not unexpected... this whole business gets pretty incestuous."

Sorrel shrugged. "So Yangshen installs a back door, detonates the charges remotely – and conveniently swoops in to take possession."

Jen lit up. Now they were getting to the meat of the matter. She leaned over the margaritas. "How did the charges get to where they were supposed to be? Did they drive the mining robots by remote control too? How did the Frontier crew not notice that one of their mining robots had just... wandered off?"

Sorrel took another swig of his drink. "Now you're just being condescending."

"Must be the tequila talking."

Sorrel frowned. "Ass."

Jen cracked a smile. It was the first time Sorrel had seen her smile. "And Zhang?"

"Rich. Arrogant. Self-serving."

Jen nodded and kept silent – let him continue digging the hole.

"His father Zhongyi is the President of China," Sorrel explained. "I bet daddy dearest got him billions in funding to start Yangshen. They're probably sitting back right now sipping on champagne, laughing about how they fucked us over."

"That sounds great, except for the nepotism part."

Sorrel blinked, not understanding.

"Read up on his wiki, Charles." she said. "Zhang and his father had a falling out when he was in college. Personal ideals and worldviews. Zhongyi practically disowned him for participating in peace rallies at Stanford. He self-funded his senior year."

Sorrel was surprised. "But – Yangshen..."

"Built from scratch by Zhang. Everything you saw there exists *in spite of* his father. There is no love lost between Yangshen and China, I assure you."

Sorrel was still annoyed. He pulled out his phone and cued up the test footage. "CPC took my phone but I recovered this from cloud backup. See the blast radius–"

Jen looked at the video without really looking at the video. "You got this at Yangshen?"

"Yes."

"And it got backed up?"

"Luckily – yes."

"China's firewall blocks all cloud backups from international cells."

Sorrel stopped. Somewhere in the back of his mind, a light came on.

"You're being played, Charles." Jen said. "This... *thing* is bigger than both of us."

She pulled out a memory card from her phone and slid it over to Sorrel. He looked at it suspiciously.

"Something is happening at Abundance, and DeWaal is in on it. I don't know exactly what..." Jen paused and looked at Sorrel. "I thought maybe two heads are better than one."

Sorrel stared at the memory card for a while before he picked it up and inserted it into his phone.

"It's called *Constellation*. I'm not sure what it is yet." Jen stood up to leave. "Call me if you figure it out."

"Waitaminute –" Sorrel mumbled. "Why me?"

"You're a helluva lot better at pissing people off than I am."

66. Sorrel – The Hit

The porchway leading into and out of Avila's is chock-full of all manners of decorative memorabilia and hanging potted plants – a terrible place for a clear line of sight. Sorrel dodged the decorations and stepped clear of the hanging plants as he headed for the exit. Jen was in some sort of a hurry to leave, so he'd stayed behind to finish the margaritas. Now, framed in the rectangle of the doorway, he watched as Jen backed her Mustang up and drove off. He made it a point to look at the files on Jen's memory card as soon as he got home – and promptly realized he'd left his phone on the dining table. Doh!

Sorrel did a quick 180 and started to walk back inside–

ZIING! A rather large, really obnoxious fly zipped loudly past his head. Down the porchway, a piece of tile shattered in spectacular fashion, surprising the restaurant greeter.

Sorrel's instincts kicked in. The initial assessment of large fly was most probably incorrect. He ducked sideways–

ZING! ZING! ZIING!! Three more followed suit. Planters next to his head shattered, raining potted plant soil down on everyone.

Screams went up from the crowd inside the restaurant. Active shooter!

Sorrel dropped into the corner. Where? WHERE?

The cracking sound that accompanied the shots – there was no clear direction of where it came from. Must be a silencer on the muzzle. He triangulated the hits – the shooter was probably on the roof of the strip mall across the parking lot... direct line of sight down the porchway. There was still confusion and screaming coming from inside the restaurant, but... nothing else. No more shots.

A few customers came rushing outside, trying to escape. Sorrel yelled at them. "Stay back! STAY BACK!"

Framed in the porchway, they were sitting ducks for the shooter – but nothing happened. They ran, panicked and screaming, out the exit and to their cars. No shots were fired.

Sorrel's face paled. The shooter had a specific target.

Trapped in a very exposed position, Sorrel took a peek – and caught a glint of reflection from the roof. ZIING! A bullet flew by his face, chipping the wall stucco. "Fuck!" he yelled.

Without really thinking, Sorrel grabbed the remnants of one of the potted plants and flung it into the air. The pot collapsed and shattered further, releasing a cloud of dirt particles that hung briefly in the air – *obstructing the line of sight*. Sorrel made a dash towards the entrance. ZING! ZIING! Bullets traced his footsteps.

The three seconds it took to get through the door felt like an eternity. As he fell through the doorway the glass on the door shattered, caught by a glancing bullet. The assembled crowd screamed in response.

"Stay inside!" Sorrel yelled.

Dashing through the restaurant, Sorrel grabbed his forgotten phone, slipped out the back entrance behind the building and circled the block. He stopped behind a stone fence, unbuckled the safety strap on his boots and pulled out his service pistol. It felt weird and small and useless in his hand... he'd maybe used it twice before. Still, it was better than nothing against a high-powered rifle.

From the other side of the strip mall, Sorrel strained to get a glimpse of the shooter... nothing. There was no one up there now.

After a moment, a black car hurtled into the parking lot and pulled up to the strip mall. Sorrel caught sight of a figure exiting one of the stores and jumping into the car, which then sped off... *in his direction.*

Sorrel ducked, barely hidden behind the low fence as the car bounced onto the road at breakneck speed. There in the driver's seat – was that *Scarface*??

The car reached the intersection, ran the red light and disappeared, leaving a very freaked-out and adrenaline-soaked Sorrel sitting on the sidewalk of the strip mall, a pistol in hand.

In the distance – police sirens. Sorrel decided he'd been interrogated enough by the Chinese and did not need to go through it again on this side of the Pacific. He shoved the pistol in his pocket, walked very very quickly to his car and sped away before the cops arrived.

/ / /

Sorrel's Toyota screeched to a stop on Ami's driveway. He ran recklessly into the house, visibly shaken, and started closing all the window blinds before realizing that Ami and Phebe were sitting in the living room. "Charles?" Ami asked open-endedly.

"You need to not be here," Sorrel said, out-of-breath.

"What are you talking about?"

"They're after me."

"Who's after you??"

"Take Phebe, get away from the house!"

"And go *where*? Charles, you're not making any sense–"

"I don't know where!" Sorrel bellowed. "Ami, please... I thought I knew what was going on... I was wrong." He looked at her, with the unintentional puppy dog eyes that appeared when he was under stress. "Call your sister, go stay with her for a while."

"For a while?! How long is a while??"

67. Huang – Hothead

Huang and Chi Ming were on the far end of Fragment Four, on the way back with several poster-tube sized cylinders of surface samples when their comms lit up. It was Liu, and he was very agitated.

"Commander – we have a complication."

"Go ahead."

"Yang has returned by himself."

"What? Where is–?"

"He says the Captain decided they would investigate the wreckage. He begged the Captain not to go."

"Dammit."

"Now he's terrified he's going to get court-martialed."

"I don't really give a damn about that at the moment. I'm a little more concerned with our hotheaded Captain."

"What do you want to do?"

Huang pondered for a moment, and then handed the surface samples to Chi Ming. "Tie these down here." he said. "Liu – mark our current position and send someone out to collect these samples. Chi Ming and I will go get Wu."

68. Sorrel – Asteroid Fever

Sorrel hovered around the driveway protectively, feeling the cold weight of the pistol in his pocket as he glanced down the road nervously. After an eternity, Ami & Phebe finally exited the house with their last couple of bags and threw them in the back seat.

Phebe ran over to Sorrel, demanding a hug. Sorrel got down to her level and hugged her tight.

"Bye Daddy!"

"Bye Peeb, take care of mama, okay?"

Phebe nodded and jumped into the passenger seat. Sorrel buckled her in with her llama.

"Don't do anything stupid, ok?" Ami said as she put the car in drive. "I know how you get when you're with him."

Sorrel smiled weakly.

He hovered protectively close as the car backed itself down the driveway. Before he knew it, Ami had leaned out the car window, grabbed the cuff of his collar, and pulled him in for a kiss. He returned the kiss and let it linger.

"You're still my dreamer," she said.

And just like that, before Sorrel could think of a reply, the car kicked into drive and slid down the road.

Sorrel watched them go, relieved and surprised at how much he still felt. At least, at this point, if something were to happen, it would only happen to him... whatever the fuck it was.

He stepped back inside, fumbled around indecisively for a few minutes, and then made himself a latte. It had the exact same ingredients, but it didn't taste half as good as what Ami made.

/ / /

The Wolf Blitzer lookalike reporter on TV stood in front of the White House (or a graphic thereof) and outlined the current state of affairs. "At a press conference earlier this morning, the Secretary of Defense had this to say..."

'At this point we do not believe that any nation-states will be successful in diverting the asteroid and we are prepared to use any force, including nuclear, to destroy the fragment before it can threaten the Western seaboard.'

"There was no mention of what might happen with the Chinese taikonauts currently on the asteroid. China has vehemently condemned the US for meddling in what it now sees as state affairs, and claims it will shoot down any missiles targeted at Fragment Four."

The news report cut from B-roll footage of Zhongyi and PRC delegates to shaky handheld beach footage of a flotilla of US battleships. "This morning the United States moved its carrier groups back into the Pacific Theater as a threat defense move, following rumors that China has also deployed its own carrier groups into forward operating positions. Naval experts have noted that both countries possess significant drone UAV fleets."

The report cut back to the reporter for the wrapup. "SNN satellites have lost track of the six US nuclear submarines that were, as of a few days ago, berthed at Pearl Harbor. Chinese submarines in the Spratlys have also gone quiet and are assumably deployed. Both platforms are capable of delivering first strike nuclear payloads. Speculation is that the Joint Chiefs will go to Defcon 2 within the week–"

Sorrel muted the TV. Asteroid fever... the world had gone crazy. He chugged the rest of his latte in one large gulp. The bitterness stung. Calm down, Sorrel. Calm the fuck down and think this through.

Somebody tried to take him out. The CPC? But he was stateside. Chinese agents operating in-country? Why not... international espionage, it'd been around since the Middle Ages.

But why him? And how did Zhang fit into all of this? Did Zhang order the hit? Sorrel had trouble considering that. Zhang was too classy for hits.

Sorrel pondered what Jen told her... that Zhang was not China. He wikied Yangshen, and read all about the much-discussed details of Zhang and his college-aged conflict with his father Zhongyi. A clash of morals, it said. Both patriotic, loyal to the people. President Zhang Zhongyi, like his predecessors before him, chose to guide and grow the country by managing information flow; he provided *guidelines* for what to think, and thus made the country think as one.

Zhang, on the other hand, preferred a more radical approach – let the people decide what to think. Harness the power of millions of Chinese, allow ideas to grow, and let the best ideas win. Chaos theory and natural selection would carry the country farther and faster. Chinese scholars would claim he was corrupted by Western influences.

The truth, as always, was in the gray area in between.

After college, Zhang returned to China, a poor disowned son among the hundreds of thousands of graduates. The early years were rough. Zhang joined a mechanical engineering company, spending six years immersing himself in the industry and rising through the ranks. When the time was right he started his own firm – Yangshen – capitalizing on what he'd learned in order to modernize the mining industry.

The company struggled to survive for years, but when the Resource Crisis hit, Yangshen was perfectly aligned to take advantage of the situation. There were casualties along the way, of course – Yangshen's business decisions put many smaller companies out of business, and some say contributed to the suicide rate in rural mining towns. Eventually Yangshen ended up with majority ownership of almost all the mining operations in China.

Zhang ran with this for several years, then delegated the management of mining operations to his subordinates in order to prepare for the future – what he saw as the next big adventure for mankind. Zhang's pivot to asteroid mining was his attempt to circumvent a possible future global resource crisis. Today, Yangshen is a diversified company with funding for its space operations derived from profits of their more traditional Earth-based mining operations.

Sorrel examined the timeline. The development of their own asteroid mining technology was almost in lockstep with Abundance... development, R&D, test flights and launches. The only difference was that DeWaal was ahead by roughly a year. Yangshen-1's mission would have launched right around the time that Abundance returned an asteroid to Earth.

All that fame, that glory. All the bragging rights for first-movers, going to DeWaal. How would Zhang feel about that? Would Zhang care enough to throw a wrench into DeWaal's mission? Why would he, when he too would have his own asteroid within a year? If he were to go only by what was written on the aether – yes, Zhang was ruthless enough for industrial sabotage. But Sorrel had met the man. Had dinner with him. And he couldn't reconcile that man with this wikipedia version of him.

What did he tell Sorrel? *Samsara...* endless death, endless rebirth. Endless struggles. Endless wars. For all the technological marvels we can build and achieve, we are still just human, trapped in our own little lives.

The TV continued posturing war. Sorrel put the wikipedia tablet down and opened Jen's dataset. It popped up onto the screen, pushing the cutaway footage of warships into the corner.

The bundle of files looked like a straight copy of data from the Abundance servers. Mostly useless security camera footage, the same stuff he'd seen before. And some log files. He wasn't that versed in mission control stuff – it'd been years since he trained for CapCom – but he knew enough to muddle through it. Everything looked normal – up until the accident. And then... no more logs. No more data.

Jen mentioned... Constellation? Sorrel searched and found the folder, and opened it.

Holy shit. It was a whole other mission. Subfolders upon subfolders of encrypted files, with pseudo-randomized machine filenames.

```
> -rw-rw-r-- 1 root root CX88_75DAF8CB7768Ktr52
> -rw-rw-r-- 1 root root keyring-pioZJr1001
> -rw-rw-r-- 1 root root orbit-const
> -rw-rw-r-- 1 root root mpp-gl6o4ZdxQVrx5fdtyrRETH
> -rw-rw-r-- 1 root root mpp-UDH76ExwUVou54dgGDE562
> -rw-rw-r-- 1 root root mpp-wJtcweUCtvhnGKJ43re7tt
```

Sorrel didn't have to read the actual files to know what he was looking at. Rather, by studying the file structure and making some educated guesses, he was able to get a general sense of what the files were about. Launched out of Vandenberg, maybe a month ago, from the timestamps. Right around the time when he was in China. When Zhang landed his ship on Fragment Four. The crew manifest showed... three, possibly four on this mission.

Sorrel scrolled further down, to find what looked like telemetry data – trajectory plots, system checks, perimeter scans. Standard procedures for things to do *after landing*. Sorrel's eyes went wide. They're already on Fragment Four...

Sorrel picked up the phone to call McClusky – and then stopped.

There, on his phone... documents and photos incriminating Yangshen.

He fumbled through a rising sense of dread and checked the settings on his phone. In the error logs, timestamped from his time in China:

```
07:36:25 [csor@fi-us:~] $ Cloud Backup: unable to connect.
Trying again--
07:46:25 [csor@fi-us:~] $ Cloud Backup: unable to connect.
Trying again--
```

07:56:25 [csor@fi-us:~] $ Cloud Backup: unable to connect. Trying again--

07:56:51 [csor@fi-us:~] $ Cloud Backup disabled. Regional Settings in effect.

Incriminating evidence... on his new phone... *given to him by McClusky*... restored from a non-existent cloud backup. Sorrel felt the hair on the nape of his neck stand on end.

69. Huang – Standoff

Huang huffed and puffed along the handrails again as he pulled himself along. Chi Ming was way in front of him – like the others, he'd figured out the best way to navigate the handrails was to not even bother with putting his feet on the ground. He just pulled himself along the cable like Superman.

From the trail leading up to the engine, they followed the split trail up the ridge. Chi Ming glided up the rise effortlessly, with Huang following as best he could. "Be careful," Huang admonished. "No telling how the Captain will react to us being there."

Suddenly the radio split his ear with chatter. It was Wu, and he was yelling in panic. "YANGSHEN CONTROL! Ghosts! GHOSTS!!"

Shouts and screams followed on the radio – then a *crackle* and a small explosive pop – and then *silence*. The handrail cables shook violently in their eye holes, evidence of events down the line. Over the ridge, portions of the handrail anchors floated up into view, cable in tow. Around the handrails were chunks of rocks and pebbles, evidence of a violent disconnect. The cable shook and twisted violently as it rose, followed by two figures propelled upward at near escape velocity.

Huang did a double take. One of them was Wu! The other – an American spacesuit??

Both suits were jerking with occasional twitchy movement, and a cloud of particulates trailed them. The helmets looked oddly shaped... malformed, almost. It took Huang a split second to realize, in shock and horror, that both their faceplates were shattered and broken. As the suits tumbled, Huang saw it – the Brute gun was in Wu's frozen hand, glinting in the harsh sunlight. Wu must have tried to attack the American with it, and in the heat of the moment forgot that at close range it was a lethal weapon for victim *and* attacker.

Huang's hairs stood on end. Explosive decompression – the liquids in your body boiled off the surface of your skin, and you died of simultaneous asphyxia and loss of fluids in twelve seconds. The bodies sailed over Huang's head, the twitching in their legs finally frozen. Locked together in death, they spun and tumbled out into the void.

Huang watched the receding tomb with stunned eyes for a moment, before he realized that there were still pressing matters to attend to on this side of heaven. He lurched forward and threw himself over the top of the ridge.

/ / /

Chi Ming was already halfway down the ridge by the time Huang pulled himself over. There were more of them, and they were *almost right in front of him*. Chi Ming was caught in a scuffle with another spacesuited figure. There on the sleeve – an American flag patch. What the hell–

The American spacesuited figure freed his hand, swung and contacted the side of Chi Ming's suit, knocking him off balance. He skeetered sideways, bounced off the ground and lost his footing. Huang fumbled towards them as fast as he could while yelling into his comm: "Americans! Americans on the asteroid!"

Without thinking, Huang engaged and tried to restrain the American. He turned – and for a moment their eyes met. Caucasian, short dark hair, blue eyes... Nordic descent? They were roughly the same age; Huang could make out identical worry wrinkles on his forehead. He was the Western version of Huang...

The surprise arrival of Huang panicked the American. He swung wide with whatever he had in hand – a portion of the handrail. It connected with Huang's shoulder and threw him sideways into the mess of handrail cables that hung in space. The American leaped towards Huang and grabbed for his neck, his – whatever he could grab. Trying to kill him! The impact threw both of them toward the ground. Huang scrabbled at the regolith, unable to leverage himself.

Whamf! With the full mass of his taikonaut suit, Chi Ming barreled in and knocked Nordic-American off of Huang. In the near-zero gravity, they rolled away in comical slowness, struggling and landing punches on each other.

Huang did not have time for this shit. He got up to try and stop the fight – and found himself tangled in the handrail cables. FUCK! He reached down to try and unhook his feet –

Thumpf! A third American spacesuit leapt in from nowhere, engaging Chi Ming and attempting to pull him off of Nordic-American. Shit was going south very quickly. Huang yanked at the handrail cable and managed to get a bit of slack. He launched himself into the pileup, trying to extricate Chi Ming and clear the deck.

Two minutes after his broadcast was sent, a reply from Yangshen Control came through on his headset. "Yangshen One, Yangshen One – no one else is authorized to be on the asteroid. Do not engage! DO NOT ENGAGE!"

Huang cursed. Do not engage??

There was no clear way to fight in bulky spacesuits. No good way to land a punch. All that they could do was flounder around and grab at each other while trying to maintain spatial balance. Put four spacesuits together in a pile, and no one really knew what was happening. A few mistimed kicks launched them off the asteroid surface.

From the corner of his helmet suit, Huang watched as Suit Three grappled with Chi Ming and pulled the Brute from his thigh holster. Shit! Suit Three looked at the device in his hand and pointed it at Chi Ming – with the tail end directly facing his own helmet. Shit shit shit! Huang yanked at his own holster strap, and in a split second had his own Brute in hand, pointed at Nordic-American's helmet.

FUCK!

Everyone stopped.

Huang tried to take a deep breath. His hands were shaking inside his gloves and adrenaline was seeping out from his sweat glands, contaminating the air in his suit. Suit Three was staring Huang down, eyes red with fury, danger close, whatever the Americans called it.

A moment went by. And then a few more moments. Nobody moved.

Huang looked down slowly. They were all hanging in space, four meters above the surface... Only a flimsy handrail cable kept them from floating off into space.

Huang could feel his trigger finger twitching, even though he was telling it to stay the fuck still. A bead of sweat finally collected enough mass and recoiled free from Huang's forehead. It floated around for a moment before landing in Huang's eye. It stung, but he couldn't wipe the damn thing off.

He looked over at Nordic-American. The adrenaline had bled away and a tinge of fear showed in his eyes. There was a connection between them – he knew, without knowing, that Nordic was the one in charge, and that Suit Three was his junior.

Next to Nordic – Suit Three was still in danger triage mode. His finger was probably twitching as well.

Huang took a breath. *This is wrong.*

He glanced over at Nordic. The whites in both their eyes spoke volumes to each other – told them they were both in agreement. They nodded at each other.

Nordic turned slowly to face Suit Three and held up his hands. *Put down the weapon.*

Suit Three understood the signal, but did not respond. Did not know how to respond. There was still fire in his eyes.

Slowly, very very slowly, Huang opened the fingers on his free hand, to show Suit Three there were no tricks. Move... wait... watch.

Suit Three narrowed his eyes in doubt, but Huang saw the small window of opportunity.

Huang nodded to Nordic. Slowly, he raised his Brute and moved it away from Nordic's helmet.

Suit Three watched – and breathed.

Huang moved a little faster – pulled the Brute away and let go of it. It drifted slowly away, into the void. He hoped beyond hope that he'd made the right decision.

Nordic gestured – and spoke over the intercom to Suit Three, on a frequency that Huang wished he was listening on. After an eternity, Suit Three slowly pulled his Brute away from Yang's helmet... and let it go.

Huang let out a laugh – or maybe a cry, he wasn't sure which. He pinged Chi Ming on the comm to confirm that he was ok, then turned to look at Nordic. It was like looking into a mirror.

Nordic offered a hand. Huang shook it, gently at first, then more vigorously. They might not speak the same language, but they were brothers. An unspoken bond forged in the fires of war.

Now... they just had to figure out how to get back down to the surface.

70. Jen – Newport

Mornings on the Pacific Coast is a slow, meandering non-cinematic process. The sun rises behind the city, sliding slowly up over the Santa Ana Mountains, and as a result the day starts not with a sparkle, but just a general rise in non-darkness. It's the sunsets, always the sunsets, that California is known for.

The marine layer that developed overnight had slipped inland, past the low-slung areas of Newport, and blanketed Balboa Peninsula in fog. It dampened sound and created a stillness that was both calm and eerie.

Jen hadn't managed to get any sleep all night. All she could do was stare out the windows. From the balcony of the rented Airbnb bungalow – acquired with a prepaid credit card, a skill learned from previous, more morally ambiguous network activities – she watched as joggers ran down the boardwalk. Her house – her sanctum – now compromised, Jen did not know where to go, and so ended up here, trapped in a small room on the edge of the world, staring out over the infinite ocean.

For the past year and a half, she'd lived alone while Carol was off on the adventure-of-a-lifetime. It was difficult, but tolerable because there was always the thought – in *that future* – that Carol would eventually return and grace Jen with her stupid smile again. And again, and again. This future, however... *this* future was hard to reconcile. A world on knife's edge, without Carol.

She pulled out the phone and texted Sorrel.

Jen: <Any updates?>

Sorrel is typing...

Sorrel: <Following a hunch...>

Words drifted up to her from the walking path along the beach next to the balcony. "Americans on the asteroid...", "Act of aggression...", "Trespass..." Strong words. Animated words.

Jen sighed. Even out here on the edge of LA, she could not get away from Carol. She pulled up the news on her phone.

China's Foreign Minister Xua Yi had denounced the presence of US Military Personnel on Fragment Four, calling it an act of aggression. There were a few soundbites from President Zhongyi, but as was the norm, he left the saber-rattling to his trusted ministers. Xua Yi accused Abundance, DeWaal and the US of trespassing on what was now considered Chinese territory.

Next story down: The US and Chinese naval fleets were now staring each other down in the Pacific. Rumors told of an engagement near Palau... locals claimed to have seen explosions to the north that lit up the night sky with an eerie glow on the horizon. Sounds like thunder and gunfire would carry to the shore when the wind conditions were just right... the locals said it sounded like gods fighting.

Carol... I miss you.

71. Sorrel – The Feint

Brentwood, Los Angeles is a fancy neighborhood on the west side of the 405 (the good side, it is said). It is sometimes confused with Brentwood, California (up near San Francisco), but the locals will tell you that this is the real Brentwood. An upscale bedroom community with wide streets, where the rich and famous park their real estate fortunes, it became briefly infamous late last century for being the place where an army of police cars finally arrested a retired football star driving a white Ford Bronco, but that's a subject best swept under the rug.

It was late afternoon and the sun had crested lazily through its zenith. Brentwood was quiet, its residents loitering lazily indoors in their well-appointed ways. Sorrel grumbled as he drove down the street. He'd been here many times before, but the tall fences and shade trees that sheltered the houses all looked the same. He slammed on the brakes when he missed the house he was looking for – almost causing an accident with the Maserati behind him, which would have doubly sucked because his auto insurance payout would not have covered even half the cost of damages.

Oblivious to the curses of Mr. Maserati, Sorrel backed up slowly and turned into the gated driveway. He mumbled something into the security gate intercom, and drove on through when it opened.

Past the gate, McClusky's vacation home stretched out before him, a massive two-storey square footage monstrosity with a Colonial look that felt strangely out-of-place next to the palm trees in the yard. Past the porte cochere, Sorrel parked his beater next to McClusky's freshly detailed Range Rover, and made a mental note to become a politician on his next reincarnation.

Sorrel was ushered upstairs, to the nicely appointed home-away-from-home office of Senator Robert Jefferson McClusky. McClusky spun around in his leather chair to face him, all smiles. "Hey! Glad you could make it! Sit down, I have stuff for you."

McClusky spun back around and fumbled in the drawer. Sorrel propped himself up on the edge of the chair, not sitting. McClusky found the envelope, pulled it out and handed it to Sorrel, smiling.

"Your fee."

Sorrel took it questioningly. "My fee? But I haven't –"

"For a job well done. I had my assistant write up a report based on your evidence." McClusky chuckled in baritone. "I took your signature from the last report. You don't mind, do you?"

Sorrel stared at McClusky. "Are you sure?"

"Of course. Why?"

Sorrel paused. Baited the hook. "I – just..."

"What is it?" McClusky frowned.

"Well..." Sorrel said. "Abundance – has been hiding a lot of information from us."

McClusky's eyebrows raised up and his eyes narrowed. "Oh?"

"I've been piecing the evidence together..."

Sorrel paused and waited. The gears in Bob's brain started whirling around.

"I thought we already agreed there was a clear case of sabotage."

"Yeah, it looks like it, but –"

"But what?" Bob asked. "Look, Chuck. I have to present a preliminary report to the President next week. I *need* to get some facts straight."

Sorrel twisted his chair, and finally sat himself down. Cast the line. "I found something, Bob. I can't figure out what it is."

McClusky leaned in. Twitched.

"Ever heard of Constellation?"

McClusky replied almost instantly. "Never heard of it. What is it?"

There it was. For a split-second, McClusky's face had told Sorrel all he needed to know. Now he just needed to figure out how to back out...

"Not sure," Sorrel said. "It came up in some of the documents from Abundance."

McClusky looked away and pondered. "Probably some sort of – DeWaal's research project."

"Probably."

Silence hung in the air. Sorrel imagined McClusky's thoughts bouncing around in his head like a pachinko machine.

McClusky looked at his watch. "It's too late now to get a hold of him. Lemme – lemme see if I can get you a meeting with DeWaal tomorrow."

Sorrel nodded. "Sounds good." He turned around and headed for the door. "See you tomorrow, Bob."

72. Carol – Postcards From Beyond

Blip

Carol's face lit up the tablet screen – a vision from the past. She fumbled and leaned in to look at herself in the camera feed. "Good morning babe. Oh god... these bags under my eyes... I can't even."

She glanced at her watch, in the slick polished Top Gun way that always made her look sexy and badass. "It's now almost ten o'clock your time. You should be out on the dunes by now. Good luck, hope everything works out."

"Been a little crazy the last few days – prepping for an adjustment burn, which will be in..." she looked at her watch. "...nine hours."

"A little rushed, but this should drop us into L2 a month ahead of schedule." Carol sighed and shook her head. "X-88... always the problem child."

"But nine more weeks! Can't wait to get back and see you again."

Carol leaned into the camera, almost nuzzling it, and dropped all defenses. "I miss you. I miss everything about you. Waking up without you. The smell of you in my arms. Your presence, your smile. It's been a long time." She paused, thinking. "The aether calls me the luckiest woman in the world, stuck on a spaceship with three guys. Hah! They don't hold a candle to you."

"I am ready. Ready to get home. To be at your side again. This mission – is more than enough space for one lifetime. I love this work... but we were built for life on Earth. Sometimes... I guess we don't understand, or appreciate... we don't know what we truly need until it's gone. I have had to cross millions of miles to learn that. I return to you now, knowing myself better than I ever thought I could." Carol touched a finger to the screen – reached out through space and time. "Here's to us, forever and ever."

Beep

"Gotta go, Jen – Pablo needs me on deck. See you soon – keep the bed warm for me!" Carol giggled, blew Jen a kiss from deep space – and the video cut to black.

73. Jen – The Scrape

Jen was scrunched up in the corner of the balcony, tears streaming down her face. She held the phone and kept scrubbing the timeline back and forth, listening to Carol talk to her like a disjointed ghost voice.

Here's to us...

Forever and ever.

Gotta go, Jen.

See you soon!

Afternoon drifted into evening. The setting sun began to cut shadows across the balcony railing. The wind shifted, and carried with it the sounds of the promenade on the opposite end of the peninsula. The sound of life, overlaid on a dead lover's voice.

Prepping for the adjustment burn...

Nine hours...

...should drop us into L2 a month ahead of schedule

A month ahead of schedule.

Adjustment burn...

Why the adjustment burn? What difference would a month make?

Jen stopped, replayed.

...should drop us into L2 a month ahead of schedule

X-88... always the problem child.

The clouds in the sky danced with the setting sun. Off in the distance, the clarity of the evening revealed Catalina Island off in the distance, stretching across the horizon. I was blind, but now I see.

X-88. Problem child.

Jen tapped the back of her ear. "Search downlink dataset for X-88," she mumbled as she stepped back inside.

The TV in the bungalow was unnaturally loud and heavy on hyperbole, as the news anchors described the extreme steps they'd taken to bring you the news. "In this exclusive report, GTN has dropped 200 news drones from our stratospheric quick-deployment blimp near Palau. Most have been destroyed as expected, but a few have gotten through the outer ring of defenses and are now broadcasting these images to you from inside the engagement zone."

The sometimes-shaky and staticky broadcast showed hulking shapes on the western horizon, shrouded in fog and shimmering in the jetstream. These were the command and control carriers, the newscasters explained – the nerve center of the drone fleet, where Chinese pilots sat in their war chairs and controlled a squad of 30 drones each.

Across the sea on the eastern horizon were the US carriers, also with their drone fleets and pilots. In the engagement zone between the two were a wall of war drones, extending out from each carrier like a metallic forcefield protecting each side's battle groups. Where the force fields met and touched – a catastrophic shattering of the heavens.

The sky above the ocean was thick with smoke. Flashes of light from missile launches mixed with chaff and unnaturally straight laser lines, waving and tracking the enemy drones. Explosions dotted the horizon; metal bits and pieces of shattered war drones rained down on the ocean. The GTN drones transmitted until they were destroyed, one by one.

Jen blinked. How long had she been standing here, watching the news? Dammit, Jen – don't get distracted.

She picked up her tablet and examined the results of the search. Folders upon folders splayed out across the screen. There were tons of hits – logs, telemetry, code blocks. She gave the filenames a cursory scan, trying to tease some meaning out of them. Her eyes fell on a configuration document –

> Constellation_X-88.cfg

X-88... is a codename for Constellation.

Shit.

She threw the display up onto the wall screen, sat and stared at the mess of files and documents. What the hell is Constellation?

Military grade encryption, Jared said. She'd never crack it in ten thousand years, he said.

Dammit, Jared. I don't need all the details. I just need a summary... a hint.

A hint. A hint.

Jen stared at the folders on the screen. Of course. How *stupid* of her to think like a machine.

She tapped behind her ears. "Ignore encrypted files. How many files are left?"

> 475,935,573 files

Jen lurched forward, almost knocking the tablet off the desk. She grabbed the wireless keyboard, sat and started punching keys furiously. Making countless typos and hurriedly correcting them, she took twice as long to translate her needs into shell commands, cursing and swearing at each mistake made in haste.

In a few minutes, she finished it – a simple script to cycle through the hundreds of millions of files and its myriads of data formats, scrape the files for any mention of 'Constellation' or 'X-88', and logic sort the most theoretically relevant results to the top of the results pile. She stared at the screen a moment, almost fearful... then took a deep breath and ran the script.

74. Sorrel – Gumshoeing

There were not a lot of places on the street where Sorrel could park a shitty car in Brentwood and not be noticed. Luckily the supersized SUV parked just down the street provided a decent cover. Stale coffee and apple pie from McDonald's entertained him while he waited. He fired up some music on his phone while he ate.

After a nutritious dinner, Sorrel picked up the envelope from McClusky. In it was a credit card-size check slip, with a lot of zeros on it. Sorrel looked at the check slip, half a mind to not cash it, out of a sense of moral righteousness. Then he remembered the pittance he had left in his back account. He filed away his conscience and pressed the check slip against the back of his phone. BEEP – deposited into his account.

Time passed.

His music playlist had reached the end and stopped. Sorrel nibbled on apple pie crumbs, beginning to doubt himself.

But then there it was. The gate opened, and the Range Rover pulled out.

///

Tailing a car takes skill. You have to be able to keep your target in sight, but not be so close that you get spotted. This necessitated an understanding of the target's personality, and whether they were trained to watch for people tailing them. Sorrel estimated that McClusky has probably had some awareness training, and so maintained a good safe distance. Even so, he lost track of the

Range rover several times, triggering slight panic and frantic vehicular maneuvers before reacquiring the target. One time he got tied up in traffic and McClusky was so close that he could see the frown on the Senator's face. Sorrel vowed to take more classes in how to properly tail a suspect once he was done with all this insanity.

The Range Rover descended from the hills of Brentwood down into the miasma of life that was Los Angeles. It headed downtown on the 10, then veered south just before. Industrial buildings started to crop up along the route. Sorrel knew where he was headed, because they'd been there before. He pulled off onto a side street, and watched as McClusky's Range Rover pulled into (surprise surprise!) Abundance HQ.

Well, shit. He wanted it to be not so, but there it was, in front of his eyes.

Sorrel drove on around the block, and then turned the corner into what looked like a warzone. Situated in a wasteland of industrial parks, Abundance HQ stuck out like a mirage; an oasis in the concrete deserts of LA. Outside its walls, the number of homeless had quadrupled in the past two decades; a microcosm that reflected the changing tides of America. The Virus, the Crash, the Rationing, the slow long recovery... before food and toiletries started costing two arms and four legs. When eggs were still reasonably priced.

Sorrel remembered them from his childhood... fried, slightly over hard, crisp burnt around the edges for the crunch... They were luxury items now. But at least he could still have some, when the money was decent and he felt like indulging. The ones around him right now, lining the streets – a cavalcade of bodies wrapped in dirty clothes, hunkering around the night chill, the ones who never recovered – eggs were beyond their reach.

Sorrel pulled up to the iron fence and parked his beater Toyota where it did not stand out. Looking past the fence, he could see Abundance's blimp hangar building rising into the night sky, so impossibly high that it occluded the glow of the city lights and made the surroundings even darker and more foreboding.

A bum sauntered up to Sorrel as he got out. "Any change, man?" he asked.

Sorrel looked at the obviously homeless man – gave him a twenty. "Make sure nobody steals my car, ok?"

The bum took the twenty with amazement, and thanked Sorrel profusely. "I sure will! Where ya going?"

Sorrel sighed. "Doing something I shouldn't be giving a damn about."

Sorrel took a running start and leapt up the side of the iron fence. He reached and found a handhold, and discovered that he was way out of shape. He huffed and puffed but couldn't pull himself over.

Just as he started to slip, a foothold magically appeared beneath his feet. The bum was propping him up. "You got this, mang!" he yelled, a little too loudly for Sorrel's sake.

With the bum's assistance, Sorrel finally managed to swing his foot over the top of the fence. He dragged himself over with maximum effort and dropped unceremoniously onto the other side. Picking himself up, he looked back at the bum and gave the universal *shhh* sign, then turned to run off towards the hangar building.

The bum watched him go ecstatically, giving Sorrel the thumbs up and whispering into the shadows. "Your car is in good hands!"

/ / /

After a quick stop at the loading dock breakroom, Sorrel emerged sporting a loose-fitting loading dock worker uniform and access card. From the familiarity of having been here day after day, he strolled confidently down the walking paths and made his way over to the main building.

It was late and most everyone had left for the day. The lobby was in power savings mode – dark, with pockets of illumination here and there. Sorrel stepped quietly past the empty reception desk, staying in the shadows as much as possible. Past the theater, where he once saw a dream of the future, past the cafeteria, where he got insulted by the astronaut's wife, past Hammurabi, where he let DeWaal lie openly to his face... Sorrel kicked himself for not digging deeper sooner, and getting metaphorical sand kicked in his face by a fast-talking CEO. Sigh... story of his life.

Around the corner, DeWaal's office lights were on. Through the now frosted glass panels, two figures were visible, both animatedly pacing back and forth like wounded hyenas circling each other. DeWaal was yelling at McClusky, who was *yelling back at DeWaal.*

Sorrel moved closer. The soundproofing qualities of the executive office was unquestionably very effective... Sorrel couldn't understand a damn thing they were saying.

Suddenly he heard it – the main lobby door opening. It echoed down the empty hallway, putting the fear into Sorrel. *Click-click-click* – the hallway lights powered on, flooding the shadows and denying Sorrel any place to hide. In blind panic, he ducked back around the corner, trying to sneak into the Theater –

– and ran directly into the wall of muscle in front of him.

Sorrel looked up to see Sawada staring back at him. Confusion froze him in his steps – Zhang's executive assistant? What the hell? He was carrying some documents and headed for DeWaal's office, and apparently surprised by Sorrel's presence as well, by the look on his face.

Sorrel briefly registered Sawada's bulky silhouette – the shadowy monster in Yangshen's training pool. The one who saved him from the CPC guys and his minions. What was he doing here? Sorrel didn't understand–

Sorrel was so busy not understanding that he didn't see the left hook. A jarring hit, a flash of bright white intensely painful light, and Sorrel was off his feet.

75. Jen – Constellation

It was dark in the room when Jen startled herself awake. Twilight had passed, and the ocean that was out there beyond her balcony door was now just... darkness. The cooling ocean breeze had turned chilly. How long did she sleep?

Jen checked the script – it was still running, 68% complete. but there were already a multitude of hits on the output log. She scrolled through the output – and it sent shivers through her.

...configuration failure...

...pcb deterioration... radiation damage...

...unstable eprom – cascade failure...

...recall and disarm asap.

Sender: harknessj@ab...com

Ethan, the workmanship on X-88 is appalling. We would never put tech like that up in space. Inadequate shielding, bad code, shoddy materials science... it's coming back to bite us now. Can we please just get this thing back here and fixed before the really dangerous stuff goes wrong??

The words hit her like a steamroller. Ethan knew... and allowed Constellation – whatever it was – to be flown up with the Frontier and installed on the asteroid.

Jesus. What the fuck did you do, Ethan?

76. Sorrel – Tangled Threads

Through scrambled senses, Sorrel felt himself being forcefully dragged across the floor by his collar, the weight of his limp body inconsequential to the pile of muscle doing the dragging. His head bobbed side to side uncontrollably, and slammed itself into the doorframe as Sawada dragged him into DeWaal's office. He was deposited in a crumpled heap in the corner.

Not unsurprisingly, there was a lot of yelling and shouting between DeWaal and McClusky. Sorrel's ears were not quite functional at this point in time – all he caught were bits and pieces, and it sounded like tin-can telephones.

"Dammit Bob! ...you said... too stupid to figure it out!"

"You said... network... locked down!"

"cakewalk... report for POTUS... Zhang... shit all!"

Sorrel tried to interject with a witty repartee, but because he was still actively trying to reconnect his neurons, all he could manage was *gurgle schmurgle blarg*. This got DeWaal and McClusky's attention. DeWaal walked over and kicked Sorrel in the gut. Ooof! The kick set Sorrel back a couple of steps in the neuron-reconnection department.

"Fuck, Bob." DeWaal cursed. "He's drooling on my floor. Get him off of there!"

Sawada grunted and picked Sorrel. He dragged the crumpled mess over to the couch and deposited him there, holding Sorrel's head up to keep him from drooling any further.

McClusky stared at the scene with contempt. "Why the fuck is he here?" he asked, pointing to Sawada.

DeWaal waved him off. "He's with me, Bob."

"He's Zhang's assistant. A fucking spy."

"He's *my* spy." DeWaal retorted. "*I* sent him to work for Zhang. How do you think we keep up with the Yangshens...?"

McClusky stared at DeWaal, mouth agape. "How the hell–?"

"Twenty-first century geopolitics, Bob. I pulled some strings and rescued his parents from Hong Kong, just before the blockade. They're all proud American patriots now." DeWaal flashed his billionaire grin. "Sawada wanted to repay me, and make a lot of money at the same time... Took years to set up his alternate identity, but it worked out great... until you showed up."

Sorrel frowned. "So it *was* you at the pool."

Sawada grunted. Sorrel assumed that was a yes.

"In hindsight, maybe we should've let you die." DeWaal mumbled. "Would've saved us all this trouble."

"Trouble is my middle name." Sorrel quipped. It was corny, but he blamed his giant headache for the awkward response.

"It was Jen, wasn't it..." DeWaal asked. "What did she tell you?"

"She told me how you fucked up."

DeWaal frowned. Sorrel enjoyed seeing that response, and thus continued stirring the hornet nest. "You had everything. You were going to make billions... maybe even trillions. Then you just... pissed it all away."

"You have no idea what it takes!" DeWaal yelled at Sorrel. "It's more than just having a vision. More than just crew and equipment! It's the cost of uncharted territory! R&D, Engineering... the price of doing Something That Has Never Been Done Before!"

DeWaal paused, chewing on his own words. There was doubt in his voice now. "The mission consumed more financial resources than we had scoped. The billions I made... all that money I plowed back into Abundance! We would've run out of operating capital before we could get the asteroid back to Earth."

Sorrel understood where this was leading. "Enter Robert McClusky..."

McClusky threw daggers at DeWaal. "Ethan..."

DeWaal stumbled on. "McClusky gave me the funding to complete the mission. To bring Abundance home."

"*Ethan* – now is not the time."

Sorrel ignored McClusky and continued to press DeWaal. "...in exchange for..."

DeWaal was silent for a moment. Considered the moment. "Land use rights. Deployment of... classified payloads."

"ETHAN!!"

"If you want to change the world... sometimes you have to make compromises." DeWaal paused, and sat down. "We failed. It was all for nothing." *Fait accompli.*

Sorrel turned to McClusky. "What is Constellation?"

McClusky sneered – a face Sorrel had never seen before in all his years. "A thunderbolt from God," McClusky said. "...to keep the yellow devils from dominating the new frontier."

Sawada growled, startling Sorrel. What came out of his mouth next stunned Sorrel. He spoke in perfect Queen's English: "Be careful, Senator... your true colors are showing."

McClusky ignored Sawada. "I told you not to dig too deep, Chuck."

"You can't possibly expect to bury all this, Bob."

"Besides you – who's gonna find out?"

Sorrel's phone buzzed. Sawada tightened his grip on Sorrel's neck, as if to say *don't even think about it.*

DeWaal reached into Sorrel's pocket and pulled out the phone. He read the message on the lock screen, and his face paled.

Jen: <I have details. Need to talk>

Sorrel shrugged at McClusky. "Who's gonna find out?"

Jen: <WHERE THE FUCK ARE YOU>

McClusky chuckled and took the phone from DeWaal. "Relax, Ethan." He took off his glasses and placed them in the palm of his hand next to Sorrel's phone. RFID chips connected, and Sorrel's phone unlocked with a happy chirp.

Sorrel stared in disbelief. McClusky smiled. "Sorry, Chuck. I gave you this phone, remember."

Sorrel watched helplessly as McClusky replied to Jen's message.

<Meet me at Griffith Obs, 9pm>

Message sent, he threw the phone into the corner. To DeWaal: "I'll take care of that loose end. You take care of this."

McClusky walked out, stopped, and pointed at DeWaal. "Don't fuck this up too."

Sorrel turned back to Sawada as McClusky disappeared into the shadows. "So this is it? Was great to meet you."

Sawada looked at him like the idiot he was. "You were stupid to show up. Zhang knew who you were before you arrived."

"I am pretty pigheaded, yes."

"It will get you killed."

Sorrel frowned and pondered on Sawada's words of wisdom. He was still pondering when, in the next split second, Sawada's fist connected with the side of his head. A flash of bright white intense painful light, and Sorrel blinked out of consciousness.

Part V
MOKSHA

77. Sorrel – Second Wind

The first thing that Sorrel felt was the numbness of his fingers – the tingly cold response. Then he realized it wasn't just his fingers. His body was shivering. He was lying on a cold flat hard surface, which seemed to make matters worse.

He opened his eyes – and wondered if they were working, because he couldn't see shit. But he's still cold, so he's not dead at least. He tried to move an arm – and heard himself groaning. Off in the distance, where was a whirring noise. Some sort of an air pump. His ears still worked, at least.

Sorrel propped his arms under him and raised his face off the cold floor. It smelled... antiseptic. Like all the smells had been removed. And it was hard to breathe. Sorrel had to work to pull in breath – it felt like somebody forgot to turn on the scuba tank feed to his mouthpiece.

Sorrel rolled over, pinched his left thigh on something in his pocket. He fumbled for it – a small penlight in the utility pocket of his loading dock disguise. He pulled it out and turned it on.

The feeble light didn't throw very far, but with it Sorrel could see a gaping maw of a room, painted black, or very very dark gray. Above him hung an array of halogen lights, but they were so high up they looked like pushpins jammed into the ceiling. Sharp things stuck out of the walls at weird angles in between long featureless baffles that reached from floor to ceiling.

Sorrel suddenly realized where he was. The air pump he could hear in the distance – it was the airflow management system of Abundance's vacuum thermal testing chamber. This was where they stuffed all the rocket parts, sucked out all the air and heat to simulate working conditions, and then bombarded the system with radio waves and radiation to ensure that everything would still work as expected in space.

So this was how he was going to die. Temperature in the chamber would drop to 60 Kelvin, way below freezing point for his frail little human body. But he would never feel that, because all the air would have been sucked out long before the chamber got that cold. He was going to be an airless frozen popsicle if he didn't do anything about it.

Sorrel got up on his knees and crawled over to the chamber door seal. Lack of oxygen made it hard to think, and every move seemed to take so much effort.

He scrabbled at the door seal and pushed against it, hoping that someone might have left the door open. No such luck. It came to him after a long while that even if the door was unlocked, the air pressure outside would be pushing against it. He stabbed at the seal frantically with his penlight, his rising panic dampened by hypoxia. "Hullo...?" he attempted to yell, but it was barely a whisper. "...is... anybody... there...?"

There was no answer. The penlight slipped from his fingers and rolled away. Sorrel fumbled around on the floor, trying to recover it. The floor was so comfortable and inviting; Sorrel stopped and laid down for a moment. Who needs a flashlight anyways.

The chill of the floor cradled him like a warm blanket. It's like falling asleep, Sorrel thought. You just drift away into slumber. No pain. No suffering. Just a slow sadness as your vision faded to black.

In the darkness he heard God. God was at the end of the tunnel, so far away. So hard to hear. Sorrel tried to focus. God was... asking for voiceprint confirmation.

Sorrel muttered weakly. "What...? I mean... yesss..."

God replied. "Voiceprint confirmed – emergency abort. Please stand by."

Everything started to blink and pulsate in red. Sorrel heard the HISSSSS from some distant shore, quietly at first, then building in volume. As the air returned to his lungs, thoughts started to return.

God spoke again. "Charles Sorrel – the alarms have been disabled but the abort process will be noticed. You should leave the premises as soon as humanly possible."

"What? Where – who is this?"

"I am the Facility."

Sorrel sucked in air. His brain seemed to work better now that he wasn't dying. Gradually he came to understand that he needed to get the fuck out of there. He tried to get up but his arms and legs were still responding like jello. Sorrel dragged himself to the door seal, which opened as he approached, and threw himself painfully over the lip of the chamber, falling out onto the facility floor like a rag doll.

Outside the vacuum chamber, the ceiling seemed impossibly high. Sorrel's oxygen-deprived brain struggled with this for some moments, until he remembered he was in the blimp hangar... the Fab.

When he was last here the place was a hive of activity. Rocket boosters, milled and CNC'ed, aluminum shells cut and shaped, parts 3D printed, all under this roof. The "planetkiller" news put a stop to all that... stock market tanked, production halted, floor technicians furloughed. Now these machines sat idle, doing nothing but racking up interest on accounting ledgers. The overhead lights were dimmed, and only the floor lights showed the way along main thoroughfares.

A path indicator on the floor lit up. Someone was telling him to get his ass in gear. Sorrel looked in the general direction of the indicator – the exit was all the way on the north side of the hangar, by the massive loading dock bay doors. Sorrel vaguely remembered DeWaal mentioning the way the plant was oriented; raw materials came in through the bay doors, got processed, milled and cut, shaped, polished, cleaned and then assembled into rocket parts that exited through the south door. Basically, it looked like he needed to retrace his steps and deconstruct spaceships into their elemental parts to escape... The pounding headache and general sense of disorientation was a real bummer, but Sorrel sucked it up and took one step, and then the next.

Two massive corridor walkways lined both sides of the hangar, through which Sorrel imagined a thousand fabrication technicians walking back and forth, during better times. He stumbled down the east corridor, leaning on dormant machinery as he went. His legs were still not as nimble as he would have liked them to be, but he was at least stumbling along at a decent clip.

Every so often a path indicator in the floor lit up, and Sorrel followed. The Facility pointed the way, and Sorrel was glad for the assistance. At least somebody was on his side for a change...

Sorrel was halfway across the warehouse when the side door burst open. DeWaal and Sawada lurched in. Sorrel leapt sideways instinctively, ducking into a metal cylinder laying on its side – a future rocket booster shell. The structural grid webbing on the inside of the shell stabbed his ribs, making it hard to breathe.

"SORREL!" DeWaal yelled defiantly into the air. It echoed around the skeletal machine remains of his company. "If you're not going to go quietly, I'm just going to have to kill you myself!"

Sorrel peeked out from the shell – DeWaal and Sawada had split up. Sawada ran around to the far corridor, disappearing from sight.

Sorrel got up and tried to move quietly into the booster shell and out the other side, but the grid webbing made it hard to traverse. He tripped and stumbled, making a lot of noise. Worst of all, he couldn't see DeWaal anywhere anymore. He frowned and moved on.

Out the other end of the shell, he darted past humongous CNC machines – robot arms with dangerous-looking drill bits sticking out from its side, used for machining rocket parts from blocks of steel composite in much the same way as Michelangelo carved the Pietà out of solid marble. Because it was a violent process, each machine was encased in a cubicle-sized plastic enclosure for safety – accessible only through a door hatch that locked during the machining process. And because the violence of the process generated a massive amount of heat, coolant was constantly sprayed onto the lathe to prevent overheating, so the enclosure served double duty as a splash guard as well.

At the intersection, Sorrel looked around frantically for the path indicator light to tell him which way to go. For a moment Sorrel panicked, worried that he would never find his way out – but just as he despaired, the corner of his eye caught the soft glow of the chevron indicator as it lit up. Sorrel followed, down the dim corridor and along a seemingly endless line of CNC machines – all encased in the same plexi.

A warning alarm sounded in the distance. Sorrel turned to look – *and caught a fist to the face.*

The hit drew blood and threw him back. He slammed against one of the machine enclosures. DeWaal yelled and grabbed Sorrel's collar, strangling him. In his still-weakened state, Sorrel found it hard to defend himself. He tried to pry DeWaal's fingers from his throat, but did not get much traction.

"You little prick!" DeWaal was six inches from Sorrel's face, spitting venom. "Why won't you die!"

<beep>

The CNC enclosure behind Sorrel lit up from within, and cast ghastly fluorescent shadows across DeWaal's face. The enclosure door popped open. Sorrel saw, and understood.

He placed his foot and braced himself. Shifted his center of weight and flexed his arms. DeWaal, caught off balance, tripped over Sorrel's foot – fell headlong into the CNC enclosure.

SCHNIK! The enclosure door slammed shut by itself, locking and trapping DeWaal inside. Water jets fired up, spraying down an angry DeWaal as he tried desperately to unlock the enclosure door.

Sorrel turned over to catch his breath, stared at DeWaal. There was fury in his eyes as he banged on the plexi, trapped in a machine of his own making. Sorrel flipped him the bird and ran off.

No need for stealth now. DeWaal had made so much noise that Sawada must know where he is. He started running for the north door. Behind him, heavy footsteps followed – Sawada was in hot pursuit.

Suddenly the lights in the entire Fabrication Plant kicked on, and every machine around Sorrel powered up. The sound was deafening. In the periphery of his vision he could see all sorts of machine parts moving back and forth. The beast was alive, and it was terrifying to behold.

As he approached another walkway intersection, Sorrel caught sight of it – a tool cart robot, with bundles of pipes and raw materials on board, on a collision course with him. Sorrel leapt instinctively just as the robot turned, crashing into Sawada and spilling its load. A cacophony of crashing noises rippled behind Sorrel. Sawada grunted and there was a meat-filled *thud* as something hit the ground. Sorrel did his absolute best not to look back, and just kept his legs moving as fast as he could.

He crashed loudly through the hangar's side access door, slamming it against the back wall with a loud KRANG as he booked it for the fence. Under the streetlight across the courtyard beyond the fence – his car, his sweet sweet car waiting to speed him away from doom. Leaning up against the car – the bum was still there, protecting Sorrel's vehicular investment.

Behind Sorrel were sounds that a very pissed off Chinese-Japanese man made. Sawada plowed through the door, hot in pursuit, after having been temporarily delayed by a tool cart.

Sorrel leapt for the fence, clambering up the side in a mere fraction of the time it took to do so the first time. Sawada followed! It was an amazing sight to see that amount of mass and muscle rappel up the wall.

Sorrel leapt down from the top of the fence and ran for his car, Sawada right behind him. Extending his long arms, Sawada grabbed Sorrel's shoulder and yanked him back. He spun and landed on the ground, stunned.

Time slooooowed down as Sawada pulled his arm back. Every muscle in the tree trunk of his arm started to flex, priming itself for the final knockout blow. Sorrel could clearly see when Sawada's arm reached its apex; he was about half a second away from unconsciousness. He steeled himself for the blow, prayed to the God of People Lying On The Ground Waiting To Get Decked, and awaited the peace of unconsciousness.

KRUNCH!

Sawada's eyes rolled up in their sockets. His tree trunk arm wound down, and he fell off to the side, gurgling like he was choking on blood. In a flash the bum was next to Sorrel, pulling him to his feet.

"What the hell–" Sorrel mumbled.

The bum grinned. "I kicked his balls."

Sorrel and the bum ran for the car. Behind him, Sawada was rolling on the ground clutching his privates. Sorrel could tell he wouldn't be down long, however – even his balls were like tree trunks.

"Get in!" Sorrel yelled. The bum hastily complied.

They piled into Sorrel's car even as Sawada got back on his feet. There was a brief moment where the engine wouldn't start. Sorrel cursed and yelled at his steering wheel, and when the Toyota had finally received enough verbal abuse, it came to life like a loyal puppy. Sorrel threw the car into drive and they peeled off down the road, having escaped Sawada's grasp once and for all.

78. Jen – The Senator

From up here, everything looked so peaceful. The overlook on the east side of Griffith Observatory leaned out over the Hollywood Hills and commanded a tourist view of the City of Angels. In the haze of the night, the lights of the city stretched out into the distance, shimmering and beckoning. A trail of blinking lights in the sky cut across this panorama – rocketjets on final approach, heading westward towards the ocean. Jen remembered when she and Carol were up here last, picnicking on the green lawn of the Observatory. The laughter, the focaccia, the lingering kisses, the feel of Carol's fingers on her face. It seemed so ordinary, casual, everyday at the time – yet it was the thing most remembered and missed now.

She touched her cheek, and then stopped herself when she realized what she was doing. Self-conscious now, she tried desperately to find something to do with her hands, and ended up clutching the backpack tightly. The tokidoki backpack, heavy with the tablet full of secrets – a gift from Carol, the night before the launch. Ahhh dammit Jen – why did everything circle back around like this?

A noise in the night air – footsteps down the walking path. The streetlamps revealed a figure approaching. Jen strained to see better. "Charles? Is that you?" she asked, voice dampened by the haze.

The figure did not answer. When he finally stepped into the pool of light, a look of surprise crossed Jen's face – it was McClusky.

"Senator?"

McClusky smiled his best Senator smile, and put his hand forward. Jen shook his hand, surprised and a little speechless.

McClusky returned the handshake firmly, pressing with his other hand. "Ms. Mathers – call me Bob. I'm just glad you recognized me." He smiled disarmingly.

"I was – not expecting –"

"It's quite alright," McClusky said. "Chuck is a little tied up with the investigation at the moment, so he sent me instead. I thought he'd told you. I didn't mean to startle–" he left the sentence hanging, as Senators are wont to do.

"No, he didn't tell me."

McClusky chuckled. "Well, he's working for me. The White House needs answers about the accident." He paused – something just occurred to him. "Where are my manners?" Flustered, he shook Jen's hand even more vigorously. "I am so sorry about your loss. Carol was a great pilot and leader."

Jen flushed and nodded. "Thank you."

"I met Carol a few years back – when they were still preparing for the mission."

"Yes, I think she told me about it."

McClusky hung his head. "Such a tragedy." He paused, for effect. "That's why we're trying to get to the bottom of this. It must be hard on you."

Jen resisted the urge to tell him how hard it had really been, because that's not really what he meant, of course. McClusky was just wanting to get to the bottom of this too.

"You mentioned you have details?" McClusky asked.

Jen nodded and pulled the backpack off her shoulder. She dug into it and fished out a memory card. "I went through all the Abundance logs. Frontier carried something called 'Constellation' with it... It was installed on the asteroid, but something failed, and exploded. Killed Carol and the crew, and fractured the asteroid."

She handed McClusky the memory card. He took it without looking at it. There was a look of... fear? terror? panic? on his face.

"You got all this from the logs?"

"Yes."

"But the logs were encrypted."

"They were... but humans are fallible." Jen said. She pulled out the tablet, scrolled through the output file to show McClusky. "I can't break the encryption, but on a mission of this size, someone is bound to forget and end up mentioning it in a report or a log file somewhere. I just... scraped everything readable and came up with this. Everything is in there... I just don't know exactly what Constellation is."

McClusky finally looked at the memory card in his hands. "This is a serious turn of events." he said, and thought furiously. "Does anyone else know about this? Can anyone else figure this out?"

"Not without the logs."

McClusky sighed and looked at Jen with fatherly eyes. He pocketed the memory card. "It is a weapon, Ms Mathers."

"A weapon?"

"A military prototype. First strike stealth installation. Reaches any far side lunar target within ten minutes. It carries two tons of asteroid rock and once in range, it will detonate its payload. Shatters it, rains it down upon the target. Like MIRV, but with millions – *billions* of tiny little warheads. You can't defend against that."

Jen stared at McClusky, stunned. "You're–"

McClusky reached into his suit pocket and with practiced efficiency, pulled out a small-caliber pistol. He pointed it in between Jen's eyes. "I'll take the tablet as well, please."

A thousand emotions flooded through Jen. She was stunned and utterly betrayed. All she could say was "...why?"

"Just the natural order of things, my dear." With his free hand, McClusky yanked the tablet from between Jen's fingers. "Sorry."

"What kind of senator carries a gun on him?"

"The kind that always comes out on top."

79. Sorrel – Big Stick

Sorrel had his foot fully jammed down on the gas pedal. The Toyota was heaving as Sorrel weaved through the busy streets of Los Feliz, committing one driving violation after another. Pedestrians and drivers honked and yelled at him, and the bum in the passenger seat was enjoying the hell out of the festivities.

Sorrel swerved around a "slow-ass car", and heard the driver yell the classic LA "asshole" greeting as he passed. The bum chuckled. "Man, you're in a hurry!"

"Sorry... err..."

The bum grinned, and extended his hand. "Eddie."

Sorrel swerved again. He did not shake Eddie's hand. "I'm Charles... sorry, a little busy right now..."

"No worries mang!"

Sorrel sighed. "Look – I didn't mean to drag you into this. I can drop you off here if you like."

"Are you kidding?" Eddie laughed. "This is the wildest damn night I've had in a while! And I've had some crazy ones!" He smiled toothlessly. "...What are we doing?"

"Trying to save a friend."

Sorrel yanked the wheel and pulled a crazy left turn against incoming traffic. Tires screeched and more honking followed. Eddie laughed like a maniac.

The loyal old Toyota shook and shuddered as it struggled to climb the steep grade of Observatory Road. You would think the car would just burn out and die, but not Sorrel's Toyota... it just kept going and going.

The air got clearer the higher up they went. It was windy tonight... the easterly Santa Ana winds. The Set-LA-On-Fire Winds. It rustled through the tree cover, momentarily revealing and hiding glimpses of the city lights. When you were up here looking down at the city, you realize that mankind was never meant to inhabit this part of the land... but they did anyway, carving a city out of an arid floodplain. Which was why Mother Nature was pissed and constantly tried to burn the place down.

As they neared the top, Sorrel turned off the headlights. Around the corner, the dark silhouette of Griffith Observatory popped into view against the light pollution of the smoggy night sky. Sorrel parked the car and turned to Eddie. "Listen, man. I could use your help."

/ / /

Sorrel huffed up the steps and cut across from the west side of the Observatory, making his way carefully along the half-circle walkway that ran under the flying buttresses encircling the main dome of the Observatory. The lights of the city danced in the corner of his vision, and made him out as a soft shadow on the observatory facade. As he rounded the corner to the east side – voices. In the walking path below were two figures. Sorrel ducked below the stone railing and continued down the walkway.

The voices below were clearer now. "I'll take the tablet as well, please." It was McClusky, and he didn't sound friendly.

The walkway terminated at the mid-level balcony, with a set of stairs that led down to where Jen and McClusky were. Sorrel quietly darted across the balcony, using the parapet for cover. A quick dash down the stairs, and he circled back around. He was so close now; he could smell McClusky's cologne on the breeze, along with his raspy sinister baritone: "...the kind that always comes out on top."

And then – footsteps from down the footpath. It was Eddie, doing his best impression of Eddie.

"Heyyyy man... got any change?"

Surprised at his most vulnerable moment, McClusky reacted. He grabbed Jen and forced her into a stranglehold with his free arm. His other arm jammed into the small of Jen's back, forcing her to arch forward in terror. McClusky spun them around, *using Jen as a shield.* "Back off! BACK OFF!" McClusky yelled at the top of his lungs.

Shit, Sorrel thought. McClusky was all worked up... this wasn't what he had in mind when he asked Eddie for help.

Oblivious to the danger, Eddie continued closing the gap. "C'mon man, I just need money for a bus ride, that's all..."

"BACK – OFF!"

McClusky took a few steps back as Eddie approached. When he backed into the light, Eddie saw McClusky's face clearly, and a shitty grin of recognition crossed his face. "Hey, I know you! You're that guy on TV! Senator... Something – right??"

Sorrel felt the change in the air... Having been identified, McClusky yelled and pulled his arm out from Jen's back. Something shiny in his hand caught the lamplight.

"HE'S GOT A GUN–!"

Sorrel found the words bleeding off of his lips ever so slowly as the escalation of events threw him into overdrive. He leapt out of the corner and sprinted for McClusky.

One one thousand. McClusky's gun arm swung up, taking aim at Eddie.

Two one thousand. Sorrel counted fifteen steps to McClusky. Maybe twelve if he pushed it. McClusky's finger curled past the trigger guard and started to wrap around the trigger.

Three one thousand. Eddie flinched – the threat was now visible to him, and he started to react.

Four one thousand. McClusky squeezed the trigger. Eight more steps. Eddie was losing his footing as he tried to stop and turn.

Five one thousand. Freed of the immediate threat, Jen jammed her elbow into McClusky's ribs. The gun went off – BLAMM! Five steps.

Six one thousand. PWING! The bullet ricocheted off the Observatory walls and chipped it, revealing white stone under the tan patina. Wall fragments spun past Eddie's face, a little too close for comfort.

Seven one thousand. McClusky buckled, losing his grip on Jen. Two steps... Sorrel leapt into the air.

Eight one thousand. Sorrel's lunge made contact with McClusky's midriff. The momentum sent them both reeling.

Nine one thousand. The pistol flew out of McClusky's hands and arced over the precipice, disappearing into the darkness of the Hollywood Hills below.

Ten one thousand. McClusky hit the ground hard. Sorrel's impact was cushioned somewhat by McClusky. Oof!

Time sped back up.

Sorrel yelled at Eddie, waving him away. "Get out of here! GET OUT OF HERE!"

Eddie nodded, and ran off into the night.

McClusky struggled to get up, but Jen and Sorrel kept him pinned down. He yelled insults and profanities as he squirmed, but when he finally recognized the futility of it, he just... stopped. A dread silence hung in the air.

"You are one lucky sonuvabitch, Chuck." McClusky growled.

"Goddammit Bob... I trusted you."

McClusky spat out blood, looked up at Sorrel. "A lot of people trust me. The American people trust me. I do the things they can't do. *Won't* do – to keep them safe. It's a dirty job."

WHAP! Jen shut McClusky up by punching him in the face, surprising Sorrel. "You asshole. If you'd just waited–"

McClusky spat out more blood. "Waited? Waited for what?!"

Jen struggled for words. "Waited – waited until you'd tested it out! Waited until it was safe, waited for Callum to reach L2, waited to install it... People wouldn't have to die."

"What's the point of a stealth weapon if the Chinese knew exactly where it was??" He stared at Jen. "Nobody plays safe in this game. We weren't the ones who militarized the moon, missy."

Sorrel flashed back, and suddenly understood. Everything after his astronaut training days – all his clients, his contacts, his... past jobs for McClusky... fell into focus. That old ancient Outer Space Treaty calling for peace and kumbaya... noble in theory, but limited, ambiguous and *unenforceable* in the current political climate. In *any* political climate.

The proliferation of 'research modules' in lunar orbit from various space-faring countries – they were probably doubling as surveillance systems... and with minor modifications, could be turned into weapon delivery platforms. 'Weaponizing space without weaponizing space'... that old running joke, the white elephant he chose to ignore. Suddenly he understood the depth and breadth of the rabbit hole that had been his entire existence.

McClusky's gruff voice snapped him back to the present. "We don't start fights. We *end* them. That's why we have the big sticks."

Sorrel was furious. Whether it was from McClusky's statement or from his own complicity, he couldn't tell. "Is that why you landed US military assets on a Chinese asteroid?"

"Puh-leeze. That asteroid is United States property. Don't give me that propaganda bullshit."

McClusky paused. The blood running down the corner of his lips were starting to stain his collar. He stared at Sorrel. "I'm getting tired of this, Chuck. Get off me or I'll have you both arrested for treason."

Sorrel almost laughed, but the weird animalistic look in McClusky's eyes silenced him before it escaped his lips. The Senator, pinned to the ground, threatening him. It gave Sorrel the creeps.

"What're you gonna do now, Chuck? Who's gonna believe you? *You*, the guy that failed out of astronaut training. You try anything, I'm going to come down on you so hard you'll wish you were still being tortured in China."

McClusky smiled now; a big confident senatorial grin. "I have the biggest stick."

Sorrel glared at Bob. No smarmy retorts came to mind, just anger. And in the silence, he heard it – the deep thuds of multiple turbofans. Military choppers, converging on the Observatory.

"Dammit, Bob."

McClusky shrugged. "There's still time to do the right thing, Chuck."

Sorrel nodded. "Maybe you're right." He wound his arm back. "I've been wanting to do this for twenty years."

WHAP!

The right hook caught McClusky square in the jaw and knocked him out. Sorrel and Jen released their grip on the dead weight, letting him slump to the ground. Jen fished in McClusky's pocket and pulled out the memory card. With the thud-thud-thud of the turbofans getting closer, Jen grabbed her backpack and tablet, and they booked it out of there.

80. Jen – All Downhill From Here

Behind them, Jen heard the choppers getting louder and louder in the night. Sorrel was running in front of her, and led them to his car – parked haphazardly, spanning three parking spots.

"Jesus, Charles – did you even pass driving school?"

Sorrel held up a finger. "Don't start that shit." He leapt into the passenger seat and fumbled for his keys.

Jen climbed into the passenger seat. There was a lingering tangy fragrance of... hobo perfume.

Sorrel jammed the car keys in and turned the starter. The alternator wheezed and spun, but the car didn't start.

Sorrel cussed as he kept trying. The car sounded more pathetic with each attempt. "Fuck!" he finally exclaimed, perfectly encapsulating their situation.

Outside, the thwomp-thwomp of the turbofans were getting louder and louder. Three military Stinger drones crested over the ridgeline, followed by a Scarab attack chopper. Jen and Sorrel ducked as they skimmed past Sorrel's car, way too close for comfort. They swung effortlessly up and over the Observatory dome, towards McClusky's position.

Jen glared at Sorrel. "We're taking my car."

Sorrel didn't argue. They darted out and ran across the parking lot to her Mustang – parked respectably between the lines. Sorrel stopped for a moment to gawk at the car. He whistled. "Always wanted one of these..."

Jen jumped into the driver seat and fired it up. Sorrel climbed in as the interior lit up. GPS displays, control and status panels, even an honest-to-goodness mounted keyboard. It was some sort of mobile paradise.

Jen threw it into drive and they squealed out of the parking lot.

/ / /

Just outside the parking lot area, they came across Eddie, walking downhill on the side of the road. Jen slowed down as Sorrel leaned out. "Eddie! Thanks for everything back there. I owe you one."

Eddie smiled his toothless grin; they exchanged fistbumps and secret handshakes like they'd known each other for decades.

"Mah man!" Eddie exclaimed. "That was the craziest evening I've had in a while! Yer alright, man. But you better get out of here before the shit really comes down."

Sorrel chuckled and threw him the Toyota keys. "Here. It's yours if you can get it to run."

Eddie stared at the keys, flabbergasted. "Wow, thanks!!" He ran back towards Sorrel's car, turned the key. The Toyota started immediately.

"Figures." Jen laughed.

Eddie waved, and drove off like a maniac.

81. Sorrel – Moksha

Sorrel's hands were twitching. He was so used to driving that he didn't know what to do with his hands now that he was a passenger. It was either that, or some sort of side effect from punching McClusky way too hard.

The Mustang's bucket seats wrapped around him as the car slipped downhill through the residential streets, a virile beast of burden with namesake horsepower to spare. It lulled Sorrel into a false sense of security – of thinking that everything would work out in the end.

They were hardly down off the Hollywood Hills when both Sorrel's and Jen's phones started buzzing violently. Sorrel glanced at it and cursed under his breath. "McClusky's called it in."

"Called what in?"

Sorrel held up the phone. Mugshot photos of Sorrel and Jen stared back at her from the screen. "National Security APB," Sorrel said. "Enemies of the State, armed and extremely dangerous. Potential bioweapon source – track and notify but do not apprehend."

Jen frowned. "Your boss doesn't take kindly to people leaking his secrets."

"My boss?"

"How high up the chain does this go?"

Sorrel grumbled. "Look, I was just hired to ask questions. From all the shit that's happened to me... a lot of people know much much more than I do. Hell, they're probably tracking my phone right now."

Jen chuckled. "Don't be so paranoid, Charles. Stang's got your back." She patted the dashboard. "This thing has transmission scramblers. Active spoofing, the whole works. Right now your phone is somewhere on the Russian steppes."

/ / /

Jen's bright green Mustang turned off Vermont and onto Los Feliz, merging with traffic and trying to look inconspicuous amidst the sensuous curves of zero-emission vehicles and the occasional brutalist constructs of electric trucks. In the relative 'light traffic' of the night, they managed to make it down Western and past Santa Monica Boulevard before they passed an LAPD cruiser going the other way. The cruiser braked violently and u-turned; Sorrel watched in the side view mirror as the cop car violated fourteen separate road rules to pull up menacingly close behind them, lights flashing.

"Well shit. That didn't take long." Sorrel said.

Jen grit her teeth. "Looks like it's OJ Simpson time."

"It's what?"

"OJ. You don't know OJ?"

"Like, orange juice?"

Jen sighed. "Just... hold on to something."

Jen jerked the wheel. Tires squealed as she threaded the Mustang in between traffic like a true LA driver. Up ahead of them, the traffic light turned yellow and the cars in front of Jen started to slow. Without missing a beat, she swung into the oncoming traffic lane and jammed on the accelerator panel. The car darted across Beverly Boulevard as Sorrel shit his pants. "WHAT ARE YOU DOING!" he yelled.

"We're boxed in on surface streets. We gotta get to the freeway!"

/ / /

A straight shot down the grimy streets of central Los Angeles, past Little Bangladesh and then Koreatown, Jen collected additional pursuing police cruisers and made a few more discretionary traffic violations to avoid them. Down past the church that looked vaguely like a Whataburger and across the freeway overpass, Jen torqued the wheel, twisting the Mustang into a sharp left across incoming traffic onto the onramp and down into The Freeway.

The I-10, or Interstate 10, is a trans-continental freeway that runs from the sunny seaside haven of Santa Monica through Houston, Texas and all the way to Florida on the East coast, bisecting the lower bits of the Americas. Built in fits and starts over the last century, the interstate evolved from marginally paved dirt to towering concrete and asphalt oceans. On this, the westernmost point of the trail, the locals couldn't be bothered with useless trivia or official designations... Here they just call it the 10.

The 10 today is a gargantuan twenty-six-lane freeway, expanded courtesy of the Autonomo program. When the city finally realized it needed to expand the 10, the buildup of buildings adjacent to the freeway did not provide a lot of shoulder room to work with. Seizing land via eminent domain was deemed too expensive and a public relations nightmare, so the engineers dug *downwards*. They carved out a half dome tunnel with enough lanes, and left the old freeway-adjacent buildings suspended as if in mid-air, supported by elegant curved arches that ran the length of the 10 (this was also a PR nightmare, but on a lesser scale). To accomplish all this, portions of the 10 were shut down and traffic rerouted for the better part of seven years, statistically contributing to incidents of road rage and riots in Los Angeles County.

For those who remembered the old days, driving through the 10 these days felt confusingly claustrophobic. It felt like you were driving in a tunnel, but you weren't because the top of the tunnel was open and sunlight would stream in. Angelenos detested and decried the new 10 and wrote articles in the Los Angeles Times about how the old 10 was better, even when it was gridlocked.

Thankfully for Jen and Sorrel, it was late and the night sky matched the tunnel walls better. The arches were lit up in full luminous glory and Autonomo controlled vehicles zipped along in an orderly fashion, merging and changing lanes at 80mph with precision. Cars were exiting the freeway without cutting through four lanes of traffic at the last possible moment and everything hummed with self-driving precision. It was as if a bunch of engineers had smoked a ton of California-legal weed and made up a utopian fantasy about how LA metro traffic should really be, and then hired the love child of Tony Stark and Elon Musk to make it happen.

All this harmony, unfortunately, was about to be shattered by a bright green Mustang and a bunch of police cars.

Jen cut across the two non-self-driving lanes – the idiot lanes, as Sorrel knew them – and slid into the Autonomo lanes. She weaved in and out of traffic, disrupting all sorts of shit. The police vehicles in pursuit followed suit, adding to the confusion and triggering massive ripples of slowdowns and even full stops in the Autonomo lanes. Sorrel imagined engineers rolling over in their graves.

"This is great," Sorrel quipped as he watched the sea of confetti blue and red lights in the passenger rear view mirror. "So... where are we going?"

"I dunno about you," Jen replied. "But I'm getting the hell outta the city."

From behind them, a low rumble grew louder and louder. A thunderous beat of wind rippled down the freeway, passed overhead and kept a constant pace in front of them. Sorrel looked up through the sunroof – from up close, the Scarab attack chopper was an intimidating sight... Four spindles of turbofans supporting a reinforced bulletproof chassis, it bristled with machine guns, missiles and armaments that Sorrel didn't even recognize. Through the heavily soundproofed interior, Sorrel could still feel the *thud-thud-thud* of the rotors.

Jen bit her lip. "I bet your boy's on that thing right now."

"Fuck." Sorrel said – man of few words. "Shit."

Thud-thud-thud, the chopper went off again. It felt so close, reverberating through Sorrel's body.

"Hey..." Jen said. "Your pocket–"

"What?"

"Your pocket!"

Sorrel looked down. He'd been so distracted by the chopper that he hadn't realized his phone was ringing. There it went again, vibrating in his pocket. *Thud thud thud...*

Sorrel pulled it out and looked – an unlisted number. "Someone's trying to call me." he said, matter-of-factly.

Jen scoffed. "That's impossible. The car is shielded."

Sorrel glanced at Jen. Slid it to answer on speakerphone.

"Hello?"

"Mr. Sorrel."

That voice... Pacific Northwest twang, mixed with inflections coded from a childhood of Mandarin... "You are in trouble?" it asked.

Sorrel did a double take. It's *him.*

"A little bit, yeah. Half the city is after us."

"Yes, things are not exactly in harmony at this moment in time."

"No shit."

"*Who is this?*" Jen cut in.

Sorrel looked at her. "It's Zhang."

"Sorry, Ms. Mathers" Zhang said. "Currently the US Navy is on a collision course with the Chinese Naval Blockade. Drone fleets have already engaged. I apologize for the lack of introductions. Mr Sorrel – have you thought about your next steps?"

"Not really, no. Shit, Zhang – I can't trust anyone these days."

"But you do have information that can help... you know what happened to Abundance."

Sorrel stopped. "How do you know that?"

"How is not important. We are running out of time, Mr. Sorrel. I can help you get that information to the relevant parties."

"The relevant parties being...?"

"The people with their fingers on the big red button."

"You're... asking me to share secrets with a rogue nation."

"I'm asking you to stop this madness."

"Yah? And what are *you* going to do?" Sorrel asked, agitated. "Build countermeasures? Sell them to the Chinese government?"

Zhang grunted, audibly frustrated. Sorrel stopped – he'd never heard that in Zhang's voice before. Zhang had always been cool and fully in control. His next words spilled out of his mouth unbidden, and revealed a hidden layer. "Fucking Americans."

"Zhaangg..." Sorrel said. "You're not stressing out on me now, are you"

Zhang caught himself, and almost-chuckled. He admits: "You're right. I seem to be trapped in my own little self."

"Trying desperately not to fuck up." Sorrel finished the sentence.

Zhang laughed. It broke the tension. There was a long pregnant pause.

"We are on the cusp, Mr. Sorrel. Just like when the first homo sapiens in Africa left the continent. Why did they leave? Who knows. Food? Resources? Doesn't matter now, but they did leave. And today we are nine billion strong."

"We can't fit everyone on this planet anymore. We have to expand. And the worst thing we can do right now is to start a war and destroy ourselves and our ability to get off this planet."

"We are all tribal, Mr. Sorrel. There is always an enemy we must hate. But if we are to get out of Africa, we have to recognize who we are, and rise above it."

"When you showed up at my doorstep like a gift from heaven... I put my trust in you. Gave you everything you needed and hoped that you would grow to understand. The world is now in your care."

"You can take us to a higher place... or you can let us destroy ourselves."

Sorrel was at a loss for words. Everything fell into place in his head – all that had happened to him, his failings, his fears. His *suffering*. For a brief moment he was out of his *self* – Jen, the Mustang, 90mph down the freeway, the flashing lights of the CHP cruisers, the *whop-whop-whop* of the Scarab in the air above. All of that was simply the state of the world in this one moment of time, on a spectrum that reached back through the aeons, through a never-ending stream of human follies.

There was no pain. No fear. And he could see the future. It shone like a beacon.

And then – *whoosh* – he was back in the present. All the world was still crazy around him, and he was not immune to it, but... calmer. He looked at Jen and nodded.

When Sorrel spoke next, the strength of his voice resonated. "What was the word?"

"The word, Mr. Sorrel?"

Sorrel thought for a moment, and remembered.

"Moksha."

Over the speakerphone, Zhang breathed out wildly. He'd been holding his breath for a while.

"I'm sending you coordinates."

82. Sorrel – Make A Hole

Zhang's coordinates popped up on the Mustang's GPS, unbidden. Jen let out a slow whistle. "I want his tech."

Sorrel studied the GPS screen. "...Beverly Hills?"

"That's the opposite direction." She looked at Sorrel, as if to ask, are you sure about this?

Sorrel returned the look, with the most conviction he'd ever had in his life.

Jen yanked the steering wheel and cut across four lanes of Autonomo traffic, heading straight for the offramp. The Autonomo cars behind her braked violently and skidded to a stop, effectively blocking the police cruisers from pursuit and buying them some time. Up the ramp and around the corner, Jen slid the Mustang to a hard stop under the relative shadow of gas station, popped the trunk and jumped out. "Get out. You're driving."

Grimy fluorescent fixtures plagued by moths threw pale spotty light on Sorrel as he leapt out. In the back, Jen already had the trunk open and was busy pulling out a scary-looking multi-pronged antenna from the trunk. With quick muscle-memory moves, she anchored it to the car's rear spoiler. Sorrel's what-the-hell-are-you-doing look must have been pretty obvious, because Jen replied cryptically, "I need to hack."

Up in the air, the Scarab had overshot their position and began to circle back around, its spindles flexing and twisting to swing its chassis back towards them. A high power searchlight fired up, scoured the freeway overpass, eventually settling on the Mustang. The light blinded Sorrel and the rotor downwash turned the gas station pavement into a swirling wasteland of grit and litter.

A voice boomed from the Scarab. It was McClusky, sounding all pompous and impersonal. "You are surrounded. Stay where you are!"

Sorrel, never one to question authority, leapt into the driver's seat. The Mustang may have been electric, but its designers had reverse-engineered the legacy... gimballed counterweights in the chassis spun at preprogrammed speeds to mimic the classic shake and rumble of a precision Ford internal combustion engine. He felt the horsepower purring. It tickled his feel and told him that the car was ready to roll. It hit him in the moment – felt like the cockpit of a rocketship. Reminded him of his training days... All of humanity's technology, shaped, perfected and poured into a vessel built for escape velocity.

He just hoped he didn't fuck it up.

Sorrel threw it into drive as Jen jumped in. Tires screeched as Sorrel mindmelded with the Mustang – figuring out its strengths and limits, learning its wants and desires. A sharp left turn down the onramp and they were back on the westbound 10, barely avoiding the police cruisers that were now back on their tails. The Scarab spotlight followed, painting a target on their backs.

In his peripheral vision, Sorrel watched as Jen strapped on a pair of gloves that looked way too techy for gardening use. She threw on a pair of sunglasses, then ran a short cable and plugged it into – HOLY SHIT there's a data port behind her ear.

"Jared, you there?"

"Jared who?" Sorrel asked as the cruisers flooded down the onramp, hot in pursuit.

Jen held up a finger and shushed Sorrel. "Good, thanks. Standby–"

Sorrel watched, distracted, as Jen started furious punching... air. She was typing something in that cyberspacey thing that she was wearing, obviously... but holy hell, it looked stupid and weird and made Sorrel feel a little on edge.

Suddenly – Jen screamed. "CHARLES!!"

Sorrel snapped back to the road – he was about to ram into the back of a vehicle. He jerked the wheel and swerved carelessly into the next lane as the Autonomo vehicles honked at him, as they were programmed to do.

"Keep your eyes on the road!" Jen yelled.

Sorrel, a little drunk on adrenaline, yelled back "What the hell are you doing!"

"I'm making a hole."

"A what?"

"Shaddup a minute and keep your eyes on the road!"

Chastised, Sorrel shut the fuck up. Uneasy silence fell in the Mustang interior as Jen continued "hacking". Some new synth music was playing quietly in the car – the kind of stuff where you turned down the volume when you had company, but it wasn't turned down all the way and would be quite audible in moments of awkward silence. It was tinny and flat and sounded like the soundtrack of Sorrel's life.

"What happened to you?"

Sorrel glanced over. Jen looked at him through the AR goggles, still typing in the air. "In the past, I mean."

Sorrel sighed. "I killed a man." The words triggered his synapses and the memories came flooding back. "His name was Vincent. He was a Navy flier."

Jen stopped typing and listened. Sorrel continued, "We were in the training pool. There was an accident. I – could have saved him, but I panicked."

Jen nodded. "...You left the program after that."

Quiet hung in the car for a while, before Jen's attention shifted again, back to the goggles. "Yes – I'm still here. Lemme know when you have it."

Sorrel sighed. He had no idea what the hell he was doing. Jen was lost in her own universe again, leaving him all alone here in the real world. A wanted fugitive in his own country, causing havoc on the freeway, chased by CHP cruisers and spotlighted by a military helicopter. For a moment he fancied himself an action hero, but the confidence and bravado had faded. Usually the hero knew exactly what he had to do. Sorrel... not so much.

"Ok, I'm in. Thanks Jared."

Jen held up three fingers, slid them sideways, twisted and rotated them – studied the virtual map. "Take the Overland exit, Charles."

Sorrel nodded.

"Medium tight turn, up the ramp, swings and then hard right. The Mustang can handle a turn at 60 mph."

Sorrel furrowed his eyebrows. "Do I look like a race car driver?"

Jen lifted up her AR goggles and looked at him. "Gotta take some risks sometimes. See where the road leads you." She smiled. "Hang in there, Charles."

Sorrel nodded. He hung in there as best he could.

Jen popped the goggles back on. "You still there? Good. Acquiring... 48 percent... 72... 99... fuck, those damn Oldsmobile protocols..."

Sorrel suddenly made sense of what Jen was trying to do. He looked in the rear view mirror... a few cars back – an *Oldsmobile Autonomo*. "You – not doing what I think you're doing, are you?"

Jen looked at Sorrel through the goggles, nodded in the affirmative.

"There are people inside those cars!"

"I'm leaving safety protocols on. Nobody's gonna get hurt... *I promise*."

Sorrel glanced at Jen in between doing ninety down a freeway of driverless cars and squeezing the steering wheel to death. Somewhere between the Observatory and here, Jen seemed to have morphed into a superwoman. Or maybe she always was, and he just sucked at noticing those sorts of things. It said a lot about his relationship with Ami.

The freeway sign whizzed past above them. "We're coming up on Overland," Sorrel said.

Jen was a little on edge. "C'mon Jared! Get me that Olds!"

Sorrel glanced at the GPS. At ninety miles an hour, the distance counter sure dropped fast... for a brief moment Sorrel pictured everything going wrong and the Mustang exploding in a glorious ball of fire.

And then... Jen's AR headset chirped – the sort of preppy upbeat chirp that told you everything cool just happened. Jen smiled. "Hundred percent lock! Thanks J, *you rock*."

"Exiting Overland..." Sorrel said.

"Got it. Making a hole... now."

Jen held up her arms. The AR gloves on them were now lit up with LEDs – some solid, some blinking, but all green. She waved her hands – and behind her the waves of autonomous cars suddenly responded. Like a maestro, she flexed her arms this way and that, and the cars followed suit. Sorrel watched in the rear view mirror in amazement – *Jen was controlling the autonomous cars remotely.*

She crossed her arms slowly, and the cars behind them started collecting together, forming a dense cluster without crashing into each other. Four inches apart, bumper to bumper, door to door, moving at 90 mph... it was a sight to behold.

The cars formed a barrier behind them, and gradually slowed to a stop, trapping the CHP cruisers and preventing them from following as Sorrel exited the freeway. Up the exit ramp and around the curve, and a right onto Overland. Sorrel took the turn at a reasonable, not-quite-professional but also not-quite-old-lady 45 mph. Jen gave him the benefit of the doubt.

83. Sorrel/Jen – Overland

From the freeway, Overland Avenue ran due north on an even keel for a bit before dropping down into a sloped valley and then rising again. The street narrowed and funneled into a residential area before it dead-ended into Santa Monica Boulevard. On clear nights, you could catch the spire of what used to be the Los Angeles California Temple, lit up by high powered spotlights. Its stone facade glowed in the night like a beacon for weary travelers in Mustangs driving above the posted speed limits.

In the early 30s, the Wage Riots crept unsuspectingly into downtown Los Angeles. By the time it was quelled and the Fair Pay Act was enacted (which was still criticized by critics and opponents for not doing enough), tens of billions of dollars in damage had been wrought. The downtown building that housed the old Consulate General of China suffered structural damage, and was eventually condemned to be torn down and rebuilt. This left the consulate with no official presence.

Years before the riots, the drop in Christian beliefs also brought lowered attendance and severe financial hardship to religious institutions in metro populations across the United States. It could be argued by some that this *lack of faith* was one of the contributing factors of the Wage Riots, but the truth itself was of course hidden beneath a million articles of slanted propaganda news from both sides. In any case, the churches, in particular the Church of Jesus Christ of Latter-Day Saints, needed some fast cash to pay off some of their less-wise investments.

This was how the old Los Angeles California Temple, once the shining beacon of the Church's heydays, came to be sold (or leased in perpetuity, the terms of the deal being confidential) to the Chinese government, to be converted into the new Consulate General office of China.

There were, of course, mass protests about the sale of this property and how we were prostituting ourselves to Red China, and how the United States of goddamn America should be the bastion of democracy, etcetera etcetera, but in the end it was one side needing money and the other side having it. The deal was ratified and ramrodded through City Council approvals on a special Saturday late-night session, and the beacon quietly changed hands. It still lit up the night sky in Los Angeles though, and at least the new tenant did not paint it red.

This was where Zhang's map coordinates pointed to.

Sorrel took the Mustang down Overland at a hearty clip, and even caught some air as they crested the hill. In front of him, all the traffic lights were turning green, and on Jen's command, the autonomous cars slowed and pulled over to the side, clearing the way ahead for Sorrel. As he passed, the cars would get back on the road, forming a blockade that prevented the CHP cruisers from closing in. He glanced over at Jen – she waved her arms around like an orchestra conductor, making holes left and right...

Jen turned to Sorrel, looked at him through the bluegreen tint of the goggles, and gave him the thumbs up–

Suddenly a car darted out from the side street and made a right onto Overland. Sorrel hit the brakes. Tires screeched for a split second before the Mustang's traction control kicked in. They zipped past the rogue car with inches to spare, causing Sorrel to honk and yell profanity out the window.

"What the heck was that! I thought you had everything under control!"

"That wasn't an Autonomo, I can't hack stupid!"

From behind them, the thud of quadrotor blades prefaced its arrival. Undeterred by Jen's control of the streets, the Scarab pulled past above them. "Shit." Jen said. "I bet they can guess where we're headed."

Sorrel shook his head. "McClusky's not going to take this lying down."

True to his words, the Scarab swung in front of them, so close that Sorrel could clearly see the ball joints in the quadcopter spindles flexing and rotating. It was what gave the Scarab its signature vector-change-on-a-dime ability that made it a mainstay across all the military branches. In the glint of the streetlamps, Sorrel also caught a glimpse of the devil incarnate himself, staring him down, daring him to do better.

"Stay where you are or we will open fire!" McClusky yelled over the Scarab's PA system.

Jen sneered. "It's a bluff. Civilian casualties... collateral damage. They can't risk it."

"Fuck, I hope you're right." Sorrel retorted.

The Scarab pulled ahead, flying backwards, and dropped into a hover inches off the ground at the Pico/Overland intersection. Jen let out a sharp expletive and threw up her hands – the Autonomo cars in front of them slammed on their brakes and slid sideways. "Charles...!"

Sorrel reacted instinctively. He twisted the wheel, found the gap and threaded the Mustang onto the sidewalk, through the crosswalk and between several cars – SKREE!! – before blasting past the Scarab.

"Sorry... I owe you a new paint job..."

"Holy shit, Charles."

/ / /

Past Pico Boulevard, the road narrowed as Overland funneled into a residential zone. A mix of old world charm houses built in the 20th century contrasted against the sharp facades of more modern new-world buildings. The future grew organically like weeds, on the skeletons of the past. There was minimal traffic and the trees that lined the road provided ample cover against the swinging Scarab searchlights that were trying to reacquire them.

Jen frowned as she waved hands in the air. "LAPD units converging from Santa Monica Boulevard... we're short on time."

"At least they're not shooting at us." Sorrel remarked.

Night turned into faux day as the searchlight found the Mustang – a piercing blue beam from the heavens. In Sorrel's heightened adrenaline-fueled state, he felt he could see the searchlight illuminate the dust particles outside the car... They seemed to hang in space for a brief moment before swirling and twisting away as the Mustang sliced through the air.

Jen glanced up as a small flash emanated from the Scarab. She watched as a glowing flickering orb fell towards the street in front of them. Curiosity, surprise and then panic as she realized what it was.

"STOP THE CAR!"

Sorrel didn't ask why – he just hit the brakes. Tires screeched, the Mustang wavered as momentum battled friction – seventy to zero in four seconds.

Sorrel watched as the orb fell to the street, not a block away from them. WHAMPF! The neighborhood lit up for a brief second, and suddenly everything in front of them *went dark.* Streetlights, houselights, everything – dead. Darkness sat like a black hole in front of them.

"The fuck–?" was all Sorrel could say.

Jen whistled. "EMP bomb. I've never seen one in action before."

"It just... knocked out everything electrical." Sorrel leaned over the dash, looked over the front hood of the Mustang. "Damn, we're just outside the blast radius..."

"Yeah, lucky us."

"... what now?" Sorrel asked.

"The effects will dissipate, give it a minute..." Jen said.

Sorrel sat in the car, staring at the dead silence of the neighborhood in front of them. In the darkness ahead he heard people yelling and screaming, and dogs barking. It was unnerving.

Jen counted down silently, then yelled "Okay, GO!"

Sorrel floored it. The Mustang peeled forward again, the manufactured sound of its engine slicing through the dead zone. Ahead, just blocks away, the lit spire of the embassy clasped the night sky. Directly down the hill from it – the traffic lights of Santa Monica Boulevard and the flashing red-blues of police cruisers.

Jen waved her arms again to consult the AR map. "Embassy entrance is on the east side. When you get to Santa Monica – hang right and then sharp left. Straight shot down the service road..."

Sorrel nodded nervously. The flashing police lights ahead of him didn't exactly fill him with confidence.

"Straight shot, huh..."

84. Sorrel – Out Of Africa

The phone rang again, at the most inopportune time.

"Hello!" Sorrel answered gruffly.

It was Zhang. Of course it was. "I see you're close."

"Thanks for spying, Z."

"When you get to the Embassy–"

"Your satellite feed a little delayed? We're already here..."

"I can see that. *Listen to me–*"

Sorrel and Jen looked at each other.

"When you turn the corner, drive as fast as you can towards the gate."

"The gates are barricaded!" Jen yelled.

Zhang was quiet. Sorrel could almost picture him chuckling. "Have faith, Mr. Sorrel. And stay on the phone."

"Jesus, Zhang."

The Mustang barreled out of the intersection and bananaed sideways as Sorrel pulled a sharp right, narrowly avoiding the police cruisers maneuvering to block off Overland. The intensity of the red-blue flashing lights stabbed his eyes, and drew his much-needed attention away from the task at hand. Some paint was exchanged between the Stang and the cruiser, and oops – there went the tail lights as well.

A hop, skip and jump down Santa Monica Boulevard, Sorrel spotted the turn. A hard left and a curb check (still there) sent a few of LAPD's finest jumping out of the way. Shots fired – the rear window absorbed the hit, its shatterproof glass flexing into semi-opacity.

Two cruisers were moving to block off the service road. Sorrel whipped the Mustang around the cars and FLOORED IT.

The imposing steel gates of the Embassy seemed to grow frighteningly large and unmoving as the Mustang barreled forward. Jen was on the verge of screaming.

"Zhaaaaang!" Sorrel found himself yelling.

On the phone, Zhang gave the order. "Now...!"

And there it was. The Embassy gates started to swing open, like magic. Sorrel's eyes widened – the gates, lumbering behemoths both, were opening way too slowly! Sorrel was so close and pumped full of adrenaline that he could inspect every stroke of the intricate Ming dynasty patterning on the gates. Oh shiiittt

SKRAAAAAANG!!

There were loud scraping noises and the side mirrors were violently disassembled, but they made it through the gates.

Sorrel slammed on the brakes. The Stang screeched to a full stop, sliding sideways into the courtyard with all the grace and power of the American automobile industry. Behind them, just beyond the wide open gates, the police cars screeched to a stop, halted by Chinese military guards bearing rifles.

From out of nowhere, a melee of Chinese MPs surrounded the Mustang, weapons drawn and aimed. Sorrel and Jen raised their hands in the air, surprised. "Zhang...?"

Nothing.

"Zhang??"

The call had terminated.

The MPs shouted and yelled at them in Mandarin, getting excited and agitated and very possibly trigger-happy as well. Sorrel eyed them, and wondered if he was just played the fool for listening to Zhang.

Jen looked around, frowning. "Uh... what the hell, Charles?"

After a withering minute of confusion with multiple gun barrels pointed at their heads, Sorrel heard a softer, more controlled voice behind the line of MPs. A thin tall man eventually shoved his way through the mess of guns and grunts. Armani dressed and sporting expensive glasses on an almost babyface-like look, he leaned into the vehicle.

"Mister Sorrel? Charles Sorrel?"

Sorted nodded, speechlessly.

"And Miss Jennifer Mathers?"

Jen nodded as well.

The babyface broke a smile. "Welcome to China! I am Consular Ching, special attaché to the President of the People's Republic." Consular Ching extended his hand for a handshake.

Sorrel looked at him, then at the MPs. What kind of sick joke was this?

Consular Ching followed Sorrel's gaze – and realized the insanity of the situation. "Aiy!" he brashly pushed away the weapons of the MPs next to him, and waved his arms to shoo everyone away. The MPs stared at each other, unsure of what to do, so he yelled at them in staccato Mandarin. Sorrel didn't understand the words, but the gist of it seemed to be "stop being stupid and go away!"

Slowly, the MPs lowered their weapons and began shuffling away, giving Jen and Sorrel more space. Consular Ching repeated the 'go away' gesture more violently now, and dispersed the rest of the MPs. He turned back to Sorrel and Jen and smiled awkwardly. "So sorry. They mean well. We've been expecting you."

Ching extended his hand again. This time, Sorrel shook it, followed by Jen.

"Welcome to China. Again. I don't suppose you brought your passport?"

Part VI
A HIGHER PLACE

85. McClusky – The Shitshow

McClusky sat in his home office, his jaw still bruised black and blue from Sorrel's sucker punch. He puffed on his Cuban cigar and stared out the window at the beautiful California sky. The sun was high in the sky and the air smelled like wretched burnt politician. The TV behind him played the story-of-the-week – news footage of FBI officials hauling a handcuffed DeWaal out of Abundance HQ.

"Ethan DeWaal, CEO of Abundance, was arrested today on charges of investor fraud and second degree manslaughter. Experts say it will be difficult, however, for the prosecution to obtain a conviction in court, due to the specific circumstances of this case."

"The evidence was provided in a press conference from the Chinese Embassy, where it was revealed that DeWaal's actions and complicit involvement allegedly led to the destruction of the asteroid Callum. Insider sources also suggest that DeWaal used military 'black budget' funding to address cost overruns on the Frontier mission without proper investor disclosure. The source of this funding is believed to be Senator Robert McClusky, who is–"

McClusky stabbed at the remote violently, turning the TV off. Fucking asshole news anchors. He took another puff of the cigar.

His aide opened the home office door. "Sir, the driver's downstairs."

McClusky nodded. He walked over to the TV, grabbed the side and swung it away, revealing a wall safe. He waited until the aide closed the door, then pressed his thumb to the pad and keyed in his security code: *1-1-1-1-1-1*. A soft *click* followed.

McClusky opened the safe and transferred a couple of wads of US currency from the safe to his briefcase. He stared at it, then took the rest of the cash from the safe as well. Why waste it?

He grabbed his laptop and slid it into his briefcase. Double-checked his workstation. The screen was black, with just a big blinking cursor on the top. Everything had been erased from his workstation and the hard drive wiped three times over.

He sighed and put out his cigar. It was only half-finished. That's ok... he could always get more where he was going.

McClusky walked to the door. The briefcase weighed him down with the burden of a lifetime in politics. He took one last look at his office, put on a hastily-acquired wig, an ugly hat and big sunglasses that were a terrible fit. Headed downstairs.

/ / /

McClusky was so pissed. During the entire trip to the airport, the cab driver had been listening to the press conference details on the radio. Consular Ching seemed to be enjoying his time in the limelight. He described in great detail how a chain of events led to the installation of an untested prototype weapon on Callum, and how its failure shattered the asteroid and killed the Frontier crew. Fuck you, Ching. He'd already heard all this shit.

At least they don't have any details on Constellation. The Commies would shit their pants if they really knew what it could do.

Based on this information, the news report continued, China and the United States had begun de-escalation of the conflict in the Pacific Theater, and pledged to work together to enact legislation to prevent such misunderstandings from happening again in the future. McClusky stifled a laugh at the PR announcement. Nothing came from these things; people clapped, went on with their lives and eventually forgot, and tomorrow we would still be at each others' throats.

The only thing left now was for the crew of Yangshen-1, led by the esteemed Mission Commander Huang Jie, to execute one last trajectory burn. If successful, the burn would place the asteroid fragment in stable orbit between the Earth and the Moon.

Who gives a shit, McClusky thought. They'd finally reached Santa Monica Airport, and had been ushered past the security gate. The cab drove up to a chartered Learjet – McClusky's hastily-arranged straight shot to Costa Rica. It was an older model, a little beat-up and lacking retrofits, but it would do. He would be sipping margaritas on the beach by morning.

McClusky leapt out as the cab pulled to a stop. It was windy and he almost lost his shitty hair disguise, but he grabbed it just in the and rushed into the plane. He pulled out his phone, tipped the cab driver a paltry $5.

/ / /

Bloody Mary in hand, McClusky stared out the window as the plane started to taxi. Home free... He started to relax a little, took one last look at the airport out the window. *What a shitshow. Time to retire...*

The Learjet taxied – but instead of turning right onto the runway, it turned left and pulled into the hangar immediately by the taxiway.

Out the window McClusky saw a cadre of black SUVs and a bunch of people milling around. Their jackets had the words 'FBI' emblazoned on them. All those people on the payroll, standing around doing jack shit.

Hands shaking, McClusky tried to take one last sip of his Bloody Mary. It fell out of his hands, splashed all over his shirt and on the cabin floor.

Well, *fuck.*

86. Huang – Goodbyes

Huang looked outside the command module window. As they fell inwards towards Earth, the sunlight seemed to get a little brighter – or maybe he was just imagining it. He felt a little guilty about how everything had worked out. When Carol and her brave crew set Callum on a path to rendezvous with Earth, they'd done all the hard work, putting kinetic energy into the asteroid. But for the unfortunate accident, Commander Mathers and her crew would have been the first to bring home an asteroid, beating Yangshen's asteroid mission by almost two years. But for the unfortunate accident... here they were.

It hadn't been easy, and he'd lost a crewmember as well. Wu's death weighed on Huang's conscience. His death might have been a direct result of American presence on the asteroid, but in the end, it was Huang's mission to command. And Wu was correct in his assessment of the wreckage. And the American that was lost alongside Wu... die he/she have a family?

Mothers, fathers, wives, children... our loved ones suffer the consequences of our mistakes. Huang wondered if, maybe if he had just done it slightly differently, that their deaths might not have happened. Maybe he should have listened to Wu more carefully, instead of dismissing his suspicions. Maybe he did not need to be so focused on the mission objectives. Maybe he should have been more paranoid. Maybe. Maybe. Maybe...

Huang swallowed. It was a bitter lesson in human nature.

Out through the command deck windows, he could barely make out the Earth and the Moon. At just under a million kilometers from Earth, Fragment Four would soon cross over the imaginary boundary called Earth's 'sphere of influence' – inside where the Earth is considered to exert a dominating gravitational field. From this point in space, both the Earth and Moon were still only a fraction of a degree in size, barely larger than points of light – but because he knew where to look, it was a welcoming sight. In less than twenty four hours they'd strap in again, and execute the final burn to settle into L1. It was time to wrap up a few things.

This morning's message – encrypted orders from Zhang himself. On previous broadcasts, there were always people standing around in the background – part of the entourage that came with being a world-class CEO. But this morning's message was just Zhang, alone. And with instructions to delete the message immediately after viewing.

Huang checked on his men. They were busy making preparations for the last burn. Good. He instructed Liu to make sure to keep Yang busy with tasks inside the command module. Huang suited up by himself, stepped into the airlock and out onto the surface of Fragment Four.

/ / /

The loose handrails looked like a beach fence after a hurricane... a mess of needles and thread haphazardly stabbed into the surface, if at all. Huang carefully pulled himself along the remains of the handrails, and crested the ridge.

There in front of him were three American spacesuited figures. They seemed to have been outside for a while now – the spacesuits were brown with asteroid dust. He knew now that they were sent to retrieve the Constellation device – Zhang explained as much in his message. The wreckage, once bristling with antennae and damaged equipment, had been stripped clean of identifiable parts. Only the ragged edges of the dome shell remained, a mere hint of what it once was.

Nordic looked up at Huang's arrival, and saluted.

Huang returned the salute and smiled. The other two Americans – they didn't seem to be as friendly... but that's ok. He knew Nordic. And he understood how the other two must feel about him, because he felt the same way about them. Old prejudices like theirs would take time to die. As long as they weren't passed down, maybe the next generation might grow to be more... forgiving.

Nordic gestured, holding up a finger gesture indicating some numbers. Huang nodded and dialed his suit radio frequency to the channel. He heard a crackle, and a voice. It was Nordic. "Thank you," he said.

Huang gripped Nordic's arm, shook his hands. He mustered up his best English cowboy accent. "In China we say xiè xiè."

Nordic chuckled, and mangled the words. "Say say."

Nordic continued telling Huang stuff. It forced Huang to turn on his translator. "...device is now stored and made safe. Please thank your boss for me."

"I cannot," Huang replied. "I have been instructed to never speak about this again. But, I am sure he would say you're welcome."

"We will be leaving in three hours. 1445 Zulu."

"I will make sure my crew are sufficiently distracted at that time."

Nordic nodded. Huang turned around and started back up the ridge.

"Hey," Nordic's voice rang in Huang's radio. "When this is all over – come visit. I owe you a barbeque."

Huang turned back to look from the top of the ridge. "I look forward to it, Mr–"

"Sam. Just call me Sam."

Huang smiled. "Huang." He saluted the man, and disappeared down the other side of the ridge.

/ / /

At 1441 Zulu, a small emergency with the airlock system forced the entire Yangshen crew into the escape pod capsule as a safety precaution, just in case cabin pressure was compromised.

Huang and Liu put on their spacesuits to assess the problem with the airlock. It took a few minutes for Huang to 'figure out' what the problem was.

While Liu was hard at work fixing the airlock compressor, Huang switched over to Sam's channel. He caught a bit of static, and then a faint voice. "See you soon, Huang."

He smiled to himself, and switched back to their regular radio channel. The airlock problem was fixed.

87. Zhang – Magnanimity

From the restaurant balcony overlooking the harbor, Zhang and entourage watched as the helicopter approached. A sleek nimble tri-foil, it swung around effortlessly and landed on the hotel roof helipad. A little bubble of insecurity welled up in Zhang's stomach at the sight – it happened every time. He swallowed, in an attempt to mitigate the Pavlovian response.

He watched as the group disembarked from the helicopter and made their way across the helipad. They disappeared into the access elevator, and in a few moments there he was – Zhang Zhongyi, President of the People's Republic of China. Seeing the two of them together, one could finally catch the resemblance. Two very striking characters, strong-willed and intelligent; brilliant in their own ways. If you looked closely you would notice that they walked with the same cadence and gait. And the way they held their hands behind their back – there was no mistaking they were cut from the same cloth.

"Pa-pa," Zhang bowed in deference.

Zhongyi nodded to his staff, and they melted away into the background. Zhang did the same to his entourage, and in a moment the restaurant was empty except for father and son.

Zhongyi looked out over the water. "So the Americans escaped."

"It would seem so." Zhang said as he poured a glass of rice wine – the expensive stuff – and handed it to father.

Zhongyi accepted the wine, looked at Zhang. Words were on the tip of his lips, but for the sake of the filial relationship, he chose not to make a scene. "Pity," he said. "I would have liked to learn more about this... Constellation."

Zhang nodded. "There are some files in the disclosure. Our research team is already going through it. There is much to examine."

From their westward view across the bay, the late afternoon sun threw hues of red and gold over Shanghai.

"The drawdown is complete?" Zhang asked.

"Almost," Zhongyi replied. "Small incident at Midway."

"Oh?"

"The Americans are very... *sentimental*. It was a very costly confrontation." Zhongyi sighed, and sipped on the wine; it seemed to relax him. "They almost did it... blow up the planet for a piece of space rock."

Zhang grit his teeth. It was so like pa-pa to say shit like that. "To be honest... we did the same thing."

Zhongyi said nothing, but challenged it with his eyes.

"The mole you planted in my company... the one you sent across the ocean to assassinate the American –"

"Initiated by a rogue party official." Zhongyi countered. "Some of the Politburo members feel that I am too soft with the Americans. We have – *dealt with this situation*."

Zhang knew what he was thinking... that once again his love for country and the strength of the party system had triumphed over soulless evil. There were so many things he wanted to say – how China's growth had stagnated since the virus, how they wasted so much resources on infrastructure before that, how China was now showing signs of the same class divide as the US... So many things that toeing the party line had wrought to a great country.

"This business..." Zhang said, "this dance... of always one-upping the enemy. Of always having the upper hand. Is it worth risking everything?"

Zhongyi frowned without frowning. "We are China. It is what we know how to do."

"Maybe... that was true in your time."

Zhongyi glared at Zhang. Still the little schoolboy in his eyes. "You doubt me?"

Zhang parried. "You've taught me so much, pa-pa." He paused, sipped on his wine. "With steel hands you built a great nation, feared *and* revered around the world. You are my greatest inspiration."

Zhongyi was silent.

"We are entering a new era now," Zhang continued. "A superconnected world, and a new chapter in global relations." He paused, because it scared the shit out of Zhang to say what he was about to say next.

"Maybe now that we are here, we can afford to be more... *magnanimous*... and still be Chinese."

Zhongyi looked at Zhang, and responded the way any father would.

"Hmph."

88. Jen – Carol

The stretch limo pulled up to the curb and stopped. In the relative quiet of the moment, Jen paused to straighten her dress. It was a resplendent blue number, striking in a muted manner. Formal business attire, she supposed. This was the first dress she'd worn in years, and the strangeness of it kept her slightly mentally off-balance. Still... the occasion called for it. She adjusted the bracelets on her hand – a matching pair, a wedding gift from close friends, engraved with both Jen and Carol's names. Today she wore both of them, in remembrance.

The limo door opened, and sounds of the outside flooded in. Crowds were behind the barricade, waving and cheering. There were voices speaking a multitude of languages, most of which she didn't recognize.

Sorrel, closest to the open door across from her, stepped out first. Dressed in a suit and tie, he seemed to have cleaned up nicely – although Jen suspected he was as uncomfortable in his attire as she was. Sweet little Phebe bounced out after her father, ready to experience the world.

With the limo cleared of men and children, Ami followed. Dressed in a dark dress suit, wearing the necklace that Sorrel gave her, she stopped and took Jen's hands for a moment. There was no need for words between them; they'd bonded since the event. Ami's eyes said it all – she'd been through hell and back the last eight months. Devoted daughter of the Senator, married to the man who put him in jail... the spindoctors had had a field day with that. It perhaps helped that McClusky was always a father-in-absentia, always tied more to his job than his family; there was less of an emotional connection to sever. Even the news of Senator Mc-Clusky's death, four months later in maximum security prison, brought tears but not prolonged suffering. Suicide, they said. Hanged himself. To protect others, the aether claimed.

"Thank you," Ami whispered, and stepped out.

Through the limo window, Jen watched a moment as the family posed together for the press cameras. After an appropriate amount of time, she took a deep breath and stepped out.

Organized chaos engulfed her as she was led forward towards a phalanx of news photographers, paraded for the cameras and then shuffled away, replaced by the next photogenic personality. Behind them, a line of limos was waiting to disgorge a retinue of officials and diplomats, all dressed to the nines here on the outer courtyard of the Meridian Gate – the entrance to the City.

After a brutal and bloody ascendance to power, Zhu Di, fourth son of the Hongwu Emperor Zhu Yuanzhang, took the throne and became Emperor YongLe. Eager to establish and solidify his rule, he moved China's seat of power from the old capital Nanjing to Peking (or what is today called Beijing in foreign tongues). Here he commissioned a new imperial palace. Built in the early 15th century, YongLe's new palace would eventually encompass nearly 180 acres. It counted nearly a thousand buildings, was protected by impenetrably high walls and ringed by a giant moat.

It would serve as the political and cultural center of China for 500 years under the rule of 24 emperors, during which no one was allowed to enter unless on official or imperial business – hence its name... *Zijin Cheng*. The Forbidden City.

Today the Forbidden City is a World Heritage Site and a public museum – its millions of tourists a year making the pilgrimage to share in living history. A cultural symbol of the impeccable beauty and vibrancy of China, wrought in Ming Dynasty architecture – a city no longer forbidden. A perfect backdrop for the announcement.

Ushered by handlers eager to keep the flow of diplomats going, they stopped briefly for a few more photo ops before being led through the Gate, into the palace proper.

Past the Meridian Gate was a vast courtyard, in the middle of which stood five stone bridges crossing a meandering waterway – the River of Golden Water. The Sorrels ran ahead, Phebe carried atop her father's shoulder laughing and whee-ing, as Jen hung back. Standing on the stone bridge, the shimmer in the river caught her eye. She looked down to see herself reflected on the undulating surface of the river, framed against the sharp relief of the blue autumn sky. Carol was there, standing next to her, wavering softly in the water's reflection.

Carol smiled her trademark charm smile and gave a big thumbs up. Jen caught a whisper in her ear: "You got this, babe." A touch on the cheek, a light kiss, and then a soft breeze picked up, blowing towards the future.

89. Sorrel – The Future

There was a slight chill in the air as the autumn sun teased the crowd from above the West Gate. Having left Ami and Phebe to find their way to the refreshments stand, Sorrel was left wandering around, watching as the international mix of delegates from around the world gathered, greeted each other and caught up on old times. It was like the entire population of the United Nations had been picked up and transplanted here.

Chairs had been laid out in front of the podium in the square, placed strategically so that the Palace's focal center, the Hall of Supreme Harmony, served as the backdrop for the very best in PR photo ops. Sorrel imagined the centuries past and all the events that must have transpired on this very spot – and wondered where the current events would lead. The ever changing flow of time, shifting and warping, impossible to predict. Like a Mandelbrot, infinitely recursing into possibilities.

Consular Ching interrupted his train of thought. He shook Sorrel's hand firmly and welcomed him to China for the fiftieth time. The event was about to begin, he said, and ushered them all to the seats in the very front. After a moment Zhang walked up, greeted Jen, Ami and Phebe, and took the seat next to Sorrel. He was all smiles.

"We meet again," he said.

/ / /

Zhongyi was on the podium, accompanied by the President of the United States and flanked by a retinue of officials from both sides of the Pacific. As he spoke, pride bled into the microphone. It expanded at the speed of light, encircled first the Palace, then the city, and the world.

Zhongyi offered a short history lesson. How China had grown from humble beginnings, through the hard work and dedication of its citizens, to ascend the world stage. How that success empowered them and encouraged them to reach for greatness among the stars. But in doing so we forgot, and we overlooked the importance of fellowship.

The President of the United States spoke next. "The events of the past six months have been nothing short of revolutionary. We almost destroyed ourselves. When we weren't looking up to see what would kill us from the sky, we could look across the ocean and see our mutual destruction. And in the process we have learned that maybe we are not countries, but one world. One Earth."

"Since then we have worked tirelessly on an agreement with the People's Republic of China, to maintain channels of communication so that the events of the blockage can never happen again. And we have crafted what we believe will serve not just the People's Republic of China, nor the United States of America, but *all the people of the world*, as we move forward into a new era of co-operation."

The President paused for effect, and Zhongyi continued. "Today we celebrate an agreement between China and the United States – to promote international space exploration and commerce. Under the Frontier Act, we will offer unilateral and worldwide access to Fragment Four by way of the creation of a **Special Economic Zone**. We invite all interested parties to invest and develop a free and open spaceport facility."

The crowd cheered and clapped, as if on cue. Sorrel leaned over to Zhang. "It's not really free, is it?"

Zhang grinned. "There are... small tariffs, of course."

"Of course."

"The Republic must have a source of income. Naturally."

"You think this will work?"

"I have... a few companies lined up."

"How many is a few?"

"Most of the Fortune 50s, I think," Zhang smiled. "Including Abundance. Under new management, of course. It seems they too will succeed in their mission... in a roundabout way." He turned to Sorrel. "We could use some help building things up. Do you know anyone?"

/ / /

"The spaceport will become the first port of call for all points beyond lunar orbit. An oasis in the desert of space. From here we will expand and explore. History will note this as the moment the gateway to space was truly opened."

The gathered crowd gave a standing ovation as the President of China shook hands with the President of the United States. Photo flashes engulfed the moment.

Sorrel chuckled as he clapped. "I can't believe you made him agree to this."

"After what happened?" Zhang replied. "He couldn't say no. This was a face-saving exercise. This reasserts his dominance."

Sorrel huffed. "Not sure this qualifies as a higher place, Zhang. Way I see it, it's still the same old same old."

"It is the path of least resistance," Zhang said. "Change comes slowly... and always from within."

"You planned all this?"

Zhang laughed. "You give me too much credit, Charles. The future is not planned... it's just stumbled into by the sum of the follies of individuals."

Supplemental

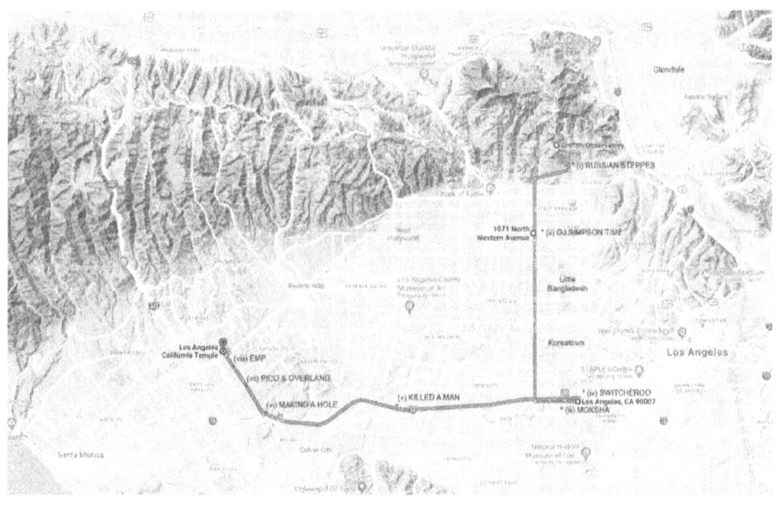

Maps, mission profiles and general indepth information are available at https://mahalobay.net/books

Acknowledgments

First and foremost, thank you Luke Dormehl; without you this book would not exist.

While I was busy clicking buttons making movie/game magic, Luke approached me and suggested that we work together on a book. I'd written mostly short stories and screenplays, and had never tried writing a book before... so of course I said yes.

Life happened and Luke had to step away from the project. I carried on and the result is what you are currently holding in your hands right now. I am very proud of the wordsmithing we have created, and I very much appreciate the fact that you got me started, Luke.

Over the years we've leaned on so many others for ideas, feedback and technical details – most especially Suzannah Rakowski for the most excellent orbital mechanics breakdowns, Lauren McGraw for asteroid composition questions, Richard Morton and Simon Astbury for deets on the Shanghai bits, Dennis Bredow, Rob Baldwin and Michael Sandrik for beta-reading and spelink cheks, and the amazing Garrett Broussard for walking me through the crazy details of self-publishing. You guys are all my light.

Thanks also to the writers and futurists who have collectively influenced Luke and I: Michael Crichton, Neil Gaiman, Stephen King, Neal Stephenson, Andy Weir, Cixin Liu, John Scalzi and the whole host of futurist entrepreneurs who have shared their collective visions with us.

I leave, of course, my dearest for last. Annette Chan is my pillar, my support in this world. She puts up with all my crazy non-work related ideas and acts interested when I talk about space and the difficulty of moving around on the surface of asteroids. Where would I be without your daily dose of sass!

As I wrap this book up to release to the world and start on the next few stories in this universe, thank you for taking the time to read this, and I hope this little big story brings you joy, enlightenment and maybe, in the still hours of the morning, moksha.

About the Author

Alan Chan is old and crotchety, much like the protagonist in this book. He started out writing short stories, got dazzled by the visual arts and ended up spending nearly three decades making *effects de là visuels* on Oscar-winning movies like **Titanic**, **Lord of The Rings** and **Alice in Wonderland**. Occasionally he moonlights as some sort of writer-director hyphenate, shooting short films and indie features. He has shiny awards on display in his home office, next to the LEGO Millennium Falcon and Eagle Transporter model.

Decades of listening to the voices inside his head have crystallized his optimistic-yet-pragmatic futurist tendencies. His Apollo era childhood, a voracious appetite for sci-fi and a penchant for finding meaning in everything has contributed to this circle-of-life moment – a return to writing.

He likens writing to standing out in the middle of the wheat field and letting the wind blow through him. Sometimes in the rare moments, he zones out and regains consciousness later to find fully formed paragraphs on the screen. He calls it *inspiritos* – 'the breath of God' – but it's probably just a side effect of all the caffeine intake, really.

Excerpt from ASCENDANCE

The next book in the Abundance universe is in the works! Visit https://mahalobay.net/books for release updates and/or email the author to tell him to *write faster*.

Raz – The O-Ring

In the waning years of the 19th century, the fiefdom of Perak in Southeast Asia's Malayan Peninsula became one of the major tin exporters in the known world. The riches of the tin mining industry brought forth all the best qualities of competitive capitalism, as represented by the cut-throat natures of competing Chinese secret societies vying for control of the tin mines.

The death of Sultan Ali in 1871, the no-show of heir apparent Raja Abdullah at the Sultan's funeral and the eventual crowning of Raja Bandahara Ismail exacerbated the reigning chaos of the time. This culminated in an appeal by Raja Abdullah for British assistance.

Sir Andrew Clarke, then Governor of the Straits Settlement in Singapore, cruised on up the Straits of Malacca on his fancy colonial steamer and negotiated the Pangkor Treaty of 1874, which legitimized British influence in the Malayan states. This is generally regarded as an ill-conceived act of desperation that eventually led to the British colonialism of what is now present-day Malaysia.

Sir Andrew Clarke, on the other hand, was lauded as a hero of the time – so much so that a portion of the olden day Port of Singapore was eventually named after him. Serving as a critical maritime trade conduit between Europe and the Far East, Clarke Quay sits on a riverbend near the mouth of the Singapore River. The docks are manned by armies of coolies, ready at a moment's notice to move cargo to and from the various godown warehouses lining the shore.

Today Singapore is an independent country, a technology hub and a playground for the rich and famous, who fondly refer to it as the 'Monaco of Asia'. The ports have been moved further offshore, to Keppel Harbour, Pasir Panjang and Jurong Island, and the old quay areas have been reclassified as commercial business centers. Clarke Quay, having aged gracefully, became a "festival village" with a variety of storefronts under a towering shade canopy. In other words, it is now a giant outdoor tourist trap.

The red-and-blue striped police skimmer rolled up silently to the north end of the Quay and spat out its occupant – a tall thin individual in casually modern attire and Nike sneakers that looked too expensive to actually wear. Black-haired and dark-skinned, he wore his detective badge clipped to the side of his belt so that it was available to flash as needed, but otherwise did not immediately single him out as a dirty rat.

"This is as far as I can go, Raz," the voice in his head chirped.

"Thanks, Mana." Raz patted the car roof absentmindedly as he looked around.

"If I had legs I would go with you."

Raz chuckled. "You're already in my head all the time."

"Not the same as having legs." Mana replied."You know where to go, ya?"

"Of course," Raz said.

"To your left, up the steps, one hundred meters down the pavilion. Go past the fountain and take the elevator up to the Ring."

"I knew that."

"Of course you do. Forensics should be arriving in five minutes."

"They have legs, ya?"

"I hate you." The car mumbled and drove off, merging seamlessly into traffic.

Raz watched the skimmer leave, then bounded up the steps and across the pavilion.

/ / /

The elevator was faux utilitarian, built to resemble the ones in the launch towers that astronauts would ride up to the tops of rockets. A hidden loudspeaker played recorded sounds of noisy gears clanking while a small video window in the wall showed footage of the elevator rising up alongside the terribly-rendered CGI rocketship. Every once in a while a release valve would hiss and the elevator would shake a little, to remind you that this was definitely not some elevator heading up to some bar in some tourist strip mall.

After a few exciting moments, a loud DING and a baritone voice announced the destination. "Next stop – the O-Ring!"

The O-Ring in Clarke Quay was the current hip expat hang-out nightspot. Shaped like the lovechild of a flying saucer and a fat donut (hence its name), it was a garish and much-challenged architectural monstrosity built above the pedestrian canopies that lined the promenades of the Quay. The view from the 360-degree rotating deck was nothing short of spectacular though – guests could watch the sun set in the west over the clay tiled roofs of the Riverhouse while enjoying goat cheese wonton appetizers, then gaze out eastwards at the shimmering lights of the marina by the time the entrée arrived… your choice of seared barramundi, chili lemak duck tacos or Maine lobster, with pengat durian dessert and a variety of space-themed apéritifs.

There was no such party here today, though. The young hostess looked up with a panicked look at Raz as the elevator door opened, and raised her hand to stop him. "I'm sorry sir, we're closed at the moment!" she half-yelled.

Raz turned sideways and pointed to the badge on his hip. "CID, mam. You called?"

"Oh! Yes," the hostess breathed a sigh of relief. "It's – ah – *aiya*… This way, please."

Raz followed as she turned to walk down the circular walkway that ringed the entire restaurant.

"They just.. walked in," the hostess blabbered as they walked. "I tried to tell them they needed a reservation, you know, but they just.. ignored me! Not very nice tourists. And then – *bang!*"

Raz looked at her as they walked. She was young, and easy on the eyes. It must have been pretty traumatic, and maybe she was hoping that recounting the story to Raz would expunge the event from her consciousness. He didn't have the heart to tell her that others would be asking her a lot more questions later.

A few patrons came into view as they continued around the walkway. They were clustered around several tables; some were sobbing while others were consoling them. Still others were in shock, and just staring off into space. "Eyewitnesses.." the hostess mumbled. "We asked them to wait for you…"

"That was very smart of you," Raz said.

"Have you seen a lot – these things before.. Inspector?"

"No," Raz replied. "People here are so polite and nice. This never happens."

The hostess stopped walking, and pointed. "It's… over there."

Raz nodded thanks. "There'll be more of us arriving soon. Maybe you should head back to the front and tell them where I am."

She nodded, grateful, and turned around.

The last light of the setting sun cast shifting shadows as Raz rounded the corner. Two dead bodies, still propped up against their bloodied booth seats… Multiple entry and exit wounds, judging by the tainted red holes in their shirts. Plus a headshot between the eyes, on both of them no less. It was more gore than Raz had ever seen before in his entire career; brutal and savage, unlike all the bodies he'd had to deal with in the past. And the smell of death… it ravaged his nose and made the beef rendang he'd had for lunch almost come back up.

This was not very Singaporean. Not very Singaporean at all.